LIGHT
FUNNEL

KA Barron

This edition published by Kevin Barron in 2016

ISBN 978-0-473-37969-8 (Softcover)
ISBN 978-0-473-37970-4 (ePub)
ISBN 978-0-473-37971-1 (Kindle)
ISBN 978-0-473-37972-8 (eBook)

Map of Unama, Metsakant and Outreterre

PART 1

Prologue

I REMEMBER THE morning my friend came with all his men. The priest was riding beside him. The sun was low above the trees across the valley and a mist was smoking up around their bare branches. It was going to be a beautiful day, the kind I loved in that place. We never had days quite like those at home.

There was still time for the light keepers to witness the early sun as it mingled with the mist and glowed on the trees and the brittle skeletons of frosted grass. Before the funnel started collecting that wonderful light, there was still time to see the river steaming to join the sky.

It was after I had called the keepers up to the walls that we saw my friend and his men coming down the track. They rode horses and their pennants drooped in the still morning air. My friend's armour was newly polished and shone in the low rays of the winter sun. He and his men were wearing a new livery: sable surcoats bearing a silver sword like a cross.

He paused for a moment at the gate and saluted me.

"You said you would take us to Faerie," he said. "So we have come."

He always called it that no matter how many times I said it was not its real name. Looking back, I know I saw in his face that his heart was not his own. It was the snake's beside him. When the priest looked up at me, there was no friendship in his face, only those cold, dark eyes. I had always brushed off his hate before, but that day my heart knew something was wrong. Even as he came through the gates.

I went down from the walls to greet my friend. He shook my hand, but did not look me in the eye.

And then there was a cry from Tapani who was still on the walls. He said there were more men coming and I looked and saw them. There were hundreds. They came with wagons and horses and lances and armour. They all wore the black livery. I wondered why my friend had brought so many with him. He had never seemed a proud man to have so large an entourage. I went to ask him, but he turned away.

Then the priest shouted an order. Iron men gripped my arms and held me. I called out to my friend. I saw men on the walls where Tapani stood. They stabbed him; the first delf blood. I do not know how much more they spilled. I was not there to see that part. I could not stop them. And the dreams came.

1

THE SMELL OF the damp soil filled Nicholas Berwick's nose. He could feel his heart beating and he took deep regular breaths, trying to stay calm. Somewhere around him, but out of sight, there were others crawling through the long grass with him. He stopped for a moment and listened. He dared not stop long. They were relying on him just as he was on them. No one must be alone up front; that was certain death. A breeze rustled the grass stalks, borne down from the mountains behind to the sea somewhere ahead. The only sound was his own breathing and the gentle hiss of the grass.

He peered straight ahead. It was unmistakable. The devils' tower stood menacing and tall against the unnatural gloom of the sky. It tapered a little as it went higher, then its top blossomed into the mouth of the funnel, now uselessly open to the sky. There was no sign of life amongst the lower buildings clustered at its base, but he knew the devils were there, waiting for them in the deep shadows of the sunless land. He had seen them before, hurling livid death from their battlements, standing at windows, conjuring up the spirits of Hell as burning furies to kill his friends and comrades in a screaming death. That death could be his soon if he was not watchful, if he did not retreat at the right time.

Surely they were close enough? When would the captain blow his whistle? Their orders were to keep crawling until they heard it. They knew how fast to move to keep close together, worming forward on arms, toes and belly. They had practised.

He kept moving, elbows digging in, pulling himself along. Then the whistle went. It was the two short blasts to be ready. He slipped the long-arm from his shoulder and licked his dry lips. The long-arm was loaded and ready. Then came the single, longer blast. He raised himself onto one knee, lifting the gun and cocking it in one motion. Other troopers rose out of the grass around him.

He picked a window in the tower, squinted along the barrel and fired. As he did so, his comrades' long-arms went off too. Then they were on their feet and running towards the tower, his fingers winding open the breech on the long-arm to drop in another ball as he went.

He paused to tip in the powder and scanned the walls, waiting for the demons to appear, but the night remained darker than night should be under that turgid, unnatural cloud. There was a call from down the line. It passed from man to man until it reached him.

"Don't fire, keep moving!"

Keep moving. How far would they move forward? They had never been so close to the Light Tower as they were now. This was suicidal; the devils were surely luring them in. Then another thought occurred to him. Perhaps they had gone, retreated. Maybe there were no more demons.

There was a single blow on the whistle and the lines of men halted. All of them knelt, ready to turn and run. He looked over to where he knew the captain was. It was so dark he could not see any arm movements. Then came a long dipping note on the whistle which ended on a short upward blast. The men around him moved. It was the command to outflank. He was on the right wing and the troopers around him were running again, trying to keep apart from each other to provide smaller targets as they looped to the side of the tower. He knew the left flank would be doing the same thing. He wished he was in the centre. They would be staying where they were, directly in front, with a slightly shorter run to their lines and cover. But even a little shorter could make all the difference if you needed to outrun a demon.

They were looking for the gate, the single way into the tower. One of the troopers next to him was carrying a bomb over his shoulder. He would never have expected to have a chance to use it. Berwick was relieved he did not have that extra weight. He searched each of the windows nervously.

Suddenly there were flashes and gunshots from the walls. So the devils were there after all, but it was dark and Berwick and his comrades were running targets and hard to hit.

"Look!" came a shout. Then he saw the glow from a mid-level window in the tower. He felt a sudden chill, then saw almost with relief, that it was a fiery bolt. The crossbow bolt fell harmlessly into the grass. Two more followed. There was a cry to his right. Someone was hit. For a moment, he was in two minds. Should he help his fallen comrade? The fire had caught on his clothing. The man was calling now, frantic.

Berwick realised he could see better. The still burning bolts had provided some substance to the night. The attacking men had more shape now, which meant they were much easier to see. The gunfire and crossbow bolts began again from the walls. Now was the time to return fire. They might not hit anything, but they hoped it would keep the devils back until they were at the gate. There was a fusillade of shots from the first rank. They had become mixed up as they ran, but they knew their role. As they reloaded, the second rank fired, then the third. Meanwhile the bombardier kept running for the gate.

The rolling volleys were doing their work, their closer range made them more effective. The fire from the devils' tower had reduced. It is hard to stand at an open window when men are shooting at it. Even the devils feared that.

There was another glow, this time from the funnel tower.

"Demon! Fall back!"

The soldiers did not need to be told. They were already scattering. The demons were coming. Berwick did not look back. He neither needed nor wanted to see it swooping down at him. The hairs on the back of his neck were up and he was running for his life.

There was light now, like the golden light of a setting sun as it dropped below the last of the cloud. The seed heads in the grass glowed red. He had two shadows. There were two demons.

One of the shadows tipped around to his left, but the other stayed in direct alignment with him and the tower. He did not turn, but he could tell there must be a demon going for each of the flanking parties.

His second shadow went suddenly long. The demon had dived. There was a scream, but it was instantly cut short by an explosion. For a few seconds a new light was added to the night. That was one of the bombs. A bombardier was dead. Both shadows wavered, but the one he cared about most stayed long. The demon was still coming, unscathed by the explosion. It was hunting down more prey.

There was another scream and it blended with another. The light behind him felt brighter now. There must have been two men too close together. Others were around him. There were more gunshots, this time from the ground. Someone was not yet running. The first shadow stopped moving. The centre must have stayed to shoot at the sorcerer. They knew that those who raised a demon had to be able to see it to control it. That was the devils' weakness and that was what some of the troopers were bravely trying to exploit.

The angle on the second shadow changed abruptly. The demon pursuing them had changed direction. It was heading for the centre. This was their chance. At that moment he did not think that this chance came at the expense of other men, of some of his friends. That would come later. He just knew he had a reprieve; for how long he did not know. He found new energy and ran on.

He heard the screaming begin behind, while around him, he was aware of men running. They all felt the same. There was no shame in running from a demon. You could not fight a demon, only kill the sorcerer.

He could see the earth rampart of his own lines now, the wall they had dug out of range of weapons to provide cover from a sorcerer's guiding eyes. The first shadow simply moved with him, but the second was shifting again. It had finished its feast, there was no more time now, he simply had to race it to the rampart.

He had made this run before, but it had never been so long. They had never been as close to the tower as they were that night. He could see the brightness growing as the demon gained on them. They were so fast. How much further now, he wondered, perhaps a hundred yards. It was so far. Then the light began to fade. Eighty yards. It *was* dimming. Sixty yards. The demon was fading, he knew it. He risked a look over his shoulder in time to see the last light of the demons wink out.

Forty yards. Surely he was safe now. The rampart came up to him and hurled himself through the canvas gate. Arms grabbed him, slapped his back. There was not the usual joking. They were counting the men in. They were waiting for the captain and the men from the centre. None returned.

Berwick was still catching his breath sprawled on the ground when the scarred face of Lord Lyell's constable leaned over him. He put out a calloused hand and hauled the trooper to his feet.

"Which wing were you, trooper?"

"The right, constable."

The constable straightened and called out. "Someone from the left wing, report to me."

A few minutes later, Berwick was standing in Lord Lyell's tent with another trooper called Clune. He had expected there to be more inside it than there was. In front of them, the Lords Lyell and Walter and their constables sat on simple folding chairs. There was a map unrolled on a small table behind them and a low cot in each corner. With the captain of the attack presumed dead, the two soldiers had recounted what had happened in front of the light tower. As the four commanders turned to each other to confer, the light of a torch on either side of the tent cast shifting shadows on the canvas stirring in the night breeze.

"It was only a matter of time before the devils realised what we were doing," said Lord Walter, his lean, aged face frowning under still thick grey hair.

"Aye, they be conserving their light. It sounds as though they only used it when they thought we were too close to the gate," said his constable. The two men were similar in age and Berwick guessed they had fought together for years.

Lord Lyell was resting his square head on one of his large fists, leaning forward in his chair. He nodded, but said nothing.

"We still need to make them use up their light," Walter's constable continued. "But if they wait until we be as close as we were tonight, we won't be able to bear the loss of men. We should try again to push between the towers. Maybe they won't risk using the demons at great range if we go for the furthest point between this and the next tower."

"It be time for a change of tactics, Charles. But your suggestion puts more of our men at risk." Lyell looked up at the two troopers who were still standing patiently in front of them. "You said one of the demons stopped moving and hung in the air."

"It did," said Clune. "It had been coming for us."

"When did it happen?"

"It was behind me, my lord," Berwick replied. "But I was watching their shadows and I did notice one stop." He cast his mind back, trying to order events in his mind. "I think there was a volley of shot before it happened. From the captain and the men in the centre."

"They killed one of the sorcerers!" Lord Walter exclaimed.

"Or wounded it," said Lyell's constable. He was a stocky man with a scar down one side of his face from forehead to chin.

"Then that be news for celebration," Lyell said, showing his teeth in a grim smile. "Their stock of light be lowering enough that they conserve it and now one of their sorcerers be out of combat. Perhaps that will make outflanking the tower easier. Their morale will already be weak after days and days of darkness and waiting. This will sink it lower still."

He turned again to the soldiers.

"Thank you, troopers. You did well tonight. God was with you."

As Berwick and Clune turned to leave, their leaders continued the conversation behind them.

"I have an idea," Lyell's constable said. "But I think we might need to assay with the Archbishop about whether it be canonical or not."

Then they were out of the tent and amongst the sounds of the camp once more. Berwick looked at Clune who merely shrugged.

"They can have their talk and planning," he said. "My belly's forgot when I last ate."

Berwick took a deep breath and realised he too had a great desire to eat and perhaps the quartermaster would let them have some rum too.

More than a week went by. The soldiers had tried some further probing raids, but only managed to raise a demon on one occasion. Berwick and Clune were standing on the beaten earth firestep, resting their chins on the top of the rampart and looking across into the land of their enemy.

Behind them, a raiding party was waiting quietly for the order to advance. Berwick could not help but look at them. He felt it must be like looking at himself, he had been in that position so many times. Today was not his turn. Today was his turn to watch others. Most of the faces were blank. Some muttered jokes to each other and only a few looked afraid. He wondered what he looked like when he was waiting to fight.

"They must have good eyes, Nick," said Clune. He was looking away to the right.

"The eyes of the devil, if they can see in this gloom. But that be how they built them, someone told me. Spaced them out across the land so they could watch the whole border between them. Can you see anything that way? I can't see anything this."

"Who told you something was going on today anyway?"

"Ragga. He said Smithy overheard the constable talking to the sergeants-at-arms. It could have happened already. I can't see anything."

"Smithy be as reliable as his donkey. If you'd've told me it was him, I wouldn't even have bothered sitting up here to watch."

There was a call from behind. The waiting soldiers stiffened then began to file out through the canvas gate in the earth wall. As more and more men came from behind the nearest tents, Berwick realised there were at least twice as many men as in a usual raiding party.

"Hey. Look down this way. It be Lord Lyell and Lord Walter. If they be up at the rampart, maybe there will soon be something to see."

They turned their heads to the left. Eastwards, the land rose gradually. Somewhere out of sight was another light tower. The raiders went out bent and when they reached the agreed point, all began to crawl. Others were at the wall now. Most were watching their comrades crawling towards the light tower. Berwick and Clune were looking up and down the line.

"I thought I saw something then," said Berwick.

"Where? Your eyes be better than mine."

"There, follow the line of my arm."

It was miles away, but there was a darker patch on the land. If they watched it long enough, it appeared to be moving.

"It be going into Metsakant. Be they ours?" Berwick asked. Clune shrugged and kept looking.

"I think they be trying to break through between the towers," Berwick added.

"But if we can see them, so can the devils," said Clune.

Even as he spoke, they caught the brightness out of the corner of their eyes and turned towards the light tower across the dead ground. It was too far away to see clearly, but a demon was rising from the tower closest to them. For a moment it hung in the air, then it shot off toward the eastward horizon. They watched it go, heading towards the darker patch in the distance.

"Poor bastards. Be they turning back?"

"I can't tell any more than you can!"

The demon became nothing more than a speck, a distant star fallen to the grey earth. As it did, there was a burst of gunfire from in front of them as the raiding party opened up. With still no demon flying at them, the raiding party kept moving forward, firing as it went. After a few minutes, another demon emerged from the light tower. The gunfire seemed to falter, but the second demon followed the first and the volleys continued.

"It be an attack across the whole front!" said Berwick with excitement.

"Look, their lordships be looking the other way now," said Clune.

They looked back at the tower and once more a fiery light formed in the air outside the tower, hovered for a moment, then sped towards the west. Another appeared in the distance before it arrived.

"This be not going well," said Clune.

"Then there be something we don't understand," said Berwick frowning at the Lords. Walter and Lyell appeared to be congratulating each other.

2

SOLIMO AWOKE AND lay still, trying to continue his dream. He wanted to know how it would end, but it was already beginning to fade. He rolled over and looked out the window. The broad leaves of the sunflock on the sill were a pale green in the dim light. Dawn was not far away. He pulled himself out of bed, felt the cool wooden floor on his feet. A well-worn path led across the rough timber to a tall, narrow cupboard and from there to the door.

He ate a breakfast of fruit from the garden hall, closing his eyes to savour the taste as he chewed slowly, then washed it down with a beaker of water from a wooden bucket on the end of the bench.

By the door he removed a long, blue coat from a hook and put it on, freeing his long black hair from the collar. He opened the door, stepped out and closed the door behind him.

The small birthing house and the well next to it were the only features in the broad triangular courtyard. It stood at the centre with the three sides made up of the funnel hall, garden room and cottages. He crunched across the gravel to the gateway.

From outside the walls of the light tower he had a view from the top of their hill. Solimo could see other hills covered in open grassland. In places there were woods visible in the bottoms. In the dim distance to the north, he could just make out the border range.

He enjoyed this time of day with only the birds for company. The last stars were fading from a clear sky. The air was clear and clean in anticipation of the sun. The light tower stood on the highest hill between the border range and Kyntilla away to the south. Not only did this afford a watchful view over the lands around, but it kept the funnel tower above the morning mists which sometimes settled into the valleys.

The tall funnel tower contained a single room. Above its grey slate ridgeline, rose the light funnel itself. Widest at the top, it was almost as wide as the building beneath it. It stood above the funnel hall like a huge flower, its polished brass lining showing where it curled over the lip.

Solimo went back into the courtyard, walked over to the single green door in the side of the funnel hall and went in. The top third of the wall was made up of windows of interlocking triangles, alternately inverted to provide a continuous view of the sky.

The room was tall and vaulted, plastered in plain white. The first rays of the sun were visible on the western wall and lit the long grey funnel which dominated the room as it descended from above the roof. It ended in the centre of three shiny brass cylinders with rounded ends lying on the floor. At the outer end of each cylinder was a seat and a set of pedals attached to a chain.

It was still Star Shift and Esella was cycling the pedals at her seat, waiting for Solimo to take over. Her long black hair fell over the neckline of her dress of a deep blue. She was singing a slow song of the fading stars quietly to herself. Lost in the music, her face appeared stern, but when she saw Solimo, she smiled at him, and a light showed in her dark eyes.

"Bright day, Solimo."

"And a bright day to you, Esella."

He took off his coat and hung it next to Esella's on a stand by the door. He took his place on one of the other seats and began to pedal. They pedalled together for the short time it took for the last and brightest stars to be washed from the sky by the rising sun. Then Esella dismounted from her seat, smiled and nodded to him and went out. Sun Shift had begun.

He enjoyed turning the pedals. As he did so, he would fall into a kind of dream where he was lost in the sky and in the heart of the funnel. He could feel the texture of the light and was alive to its depth and colours. As it grew and deepened and lengthened, he would match his pedalling to its strength, skipping lightly in bright sunshine and pushing firmly in cloud until, if the cloud were heavy, dark and thick, he would barely pedal at all. That light could not be used.

He began to hum without any conscious thought. It came naturally with the pedalling and the brightening glow of the sun as it crept down the wall. Its volume increased with the brightness. Words came of the leaves and flowers turning to face the sun and being caressed by the warmth of the new day.

Early in the afternoon, a door at the far end of the room opened. A short woman trotted in. Her grey hair framed a gentle face made wiser rather than older by the lines in it.

"Bright day, Doctor," Solimo said.

"And to you. Clear skies, eh?"

She bent and opened a flap in the side of the machine and removed a pile of sheets of sponge. She replaced them with thinner sheets, closed the flap and left with the thicker sheets of sponge, nodding at Solimo as she went.

The brightest of the afternoon was gone when the outside door opened. A tall delf with broad shoulders and a mane of wiry hair entered. He had a beard on his chin, but shaven cheeks. Solimo always envied the calm strength in Mondo's face. He looked up to him and would have been intimidated by him were it not for the wrinkles in the corners of his eyes and his frequent smiles. His older skin was more the colour of burgundy leather than the copper of Solimo's.

"Bright night, Solimo. The moon is up already."

"Bright night to you, Mondo. Where have you been?"

"I went to see Lofi."

Solimo's brows furrowed, puzzled.

"From the tower at Atorni," Mondo said in explanation. "He had been to Kyntilla, so we met on the road. I have only just come back."

They pedalled together for an hour and more.

"Have you seen the Light Doctor today?" Mondo asked.

"Yes, this afternoon. She must have been out on calls this morning."

"She told me yesterday that she was going away for a while, perhaps a week. I did not know if she had left yet."

"She must be going north. I was hoping she would take me."

Mondo laughed. "But who would mind the vegetables?"

"You and Esella," Solimo said.

"Only if you want them wizened and the harvest small," said Mondo with a smile.

At intervals, they sang together. Solimo enjoyed the contrast of Mondo's baritone with his own tenor. His own words seemed to skip over the deeper surface of Mondo's music.

Once the sun had set and the bright glow above the horizon had gone, Solimo took up his coat and wished Mondo a bright night. Outside he looked around him and stretched his limbs. He liked to survey the full circle of the horizon. The distant range was purple in the dusk and the smudge of forest below them a dark greygreen. It was a clear evening and the glow of daylight loitered a while after the sun had set. The moon hung low, open and blue in the deepening sky.

Away in the distance he could see a few lights from some of the scattered farmsteads that occupied the hill country. Summer was ending and, as if in reminder, a cool breeze brushed past him, a gift of the sun's passing.

As his eye followed the line of mountains from west to east, he noticed something. He squinted in the failing light, trying to work out what it could be. It was beyond the mountains to the north east. There seemed to be a long patch of dark cloud in the sky.

3

THE LAND WAS open and a light breeze was blowing across the hills. Thick cloud had hung around for several days and the ground was sodden with a series of showers which had ploughed across the land. The Light Doctor had been spared them, following in their wake as they broke against the mountains which were closer here than back at the Kunnaslaki.

The Light Doctor stood by her horse and rapped on the farm gate set into the surrounding walls. The sky was beginning to clear. She was relieved. This was her last visit and she wanted a dry ride home.

There were footsteps from the other side of the gate.

"Who is it?"

"The Light Doctor."

A young efficient-looking delf in an apron opened the gate and smiled at her. She took a brief look around at the low hills then led the Light Doctor into the farmyard which was enclosed on its three sides by the farmhouse and two barns.

"I am Mena. Come in, please. Ma and Pa are in the upstairs room at the back."

The Light Doctor took two cloth bags from her saddle and followed the young delf into the house, past the rack of long-arms on the wall, their barrels gleaming briefly as the door opened and closed. Eso and Kaia were sat on chairs on either side of a darkened room.

"The first thing you should do is open the curtains," said the Light Doctor. "You ask me to bring some light, yet you will not let them have any."

"They like it like that," said Mena. "I have not even heard them sing in weeks."

"Despair breeds more despair," said the Light Doctor. "You need to break the circle."

She pulled open the curtains. The couple looked uncomfortable. The room was filled with plants which sat in pots on the furniture and on the windowsill was a long plant tray from which more plants twined up around the curtain rail.

"What a lovely room," said the Light Doctor.

"We did not ask you to come," said Kaia glumly.

"Mena should never have asked you. I do not know why I agreed to this," Eso added.

"Tell me what is wrong," said the Light Doctor.

No one spoke.

The daughter looked impatient.

"I am sick of the two of them arguing. They never apologise when they should and the arguments are silly. It is like they have forgotten why they were married."

"I need to get out and mend the wall," muttered Eso looking out the window.

"I can help you remember," said the Light Doctor.

From her bag she took a glass bowl and a cloth envelope. She removed a number of small packets wrapped in oilskin and selected three. Unwrapping them, she stood holding three small sponges over the bowl.

Eso and Kaia watched her with interest despite themselves.

"Shall I do this?"

"Load of nonsense," Eso muttered.

"If you must," Kaia said, looking at the floor.

"That means yes," said Mena crossly.

"I will need to provide a careful mixture of all three I think for this one. Moon with a drop of Star and a final dash of Sun."

The Light Doctor pulled up her hood so it fell over her eyes and her face could not be seen.

"Do not worry about the hood," said the Light Doctor. "I am making this light for you, not for me."

She turned to the daughter. "You will need to leave too. You do not need this."

The Light Doctor squeezed the first sponge. Drops fell with slow quietness. The room was filled with a silver light that took all the colour out of it. It was all black and grey and silver. It was as if they were in a new room. Kaia and Eso stared at it and as they did so, it moved to envelop them. They became lost in the still ghostliness of the room. It seemed to have faded away to leave only the two of them there. Their eyes drifted and caught on the eyes of the other. There were no thoughts in their minds, they simply held each other's eyes in the lonely moonlight. Their breathing slowed. They had forgotten about the Light Doctor, forgotten about their daughter.

Eso felt as if he should say something, but he did not know what to say. So he gazed at Kaia's face and the creases in the skin around her eyes, her red cheeks from years of wind and cold and sun, working in all weathers alongside him. He lifted his big hand without thinking and touched her cheek. The room felt cold, but he realised he had a warm glow inside him. She felt his hand on her face, felt his calluses, yet the touch was gentle. His shoulders had always been broad, she remembered. That was what she had first noticed about him.

The light began to fade, but the two delf did not move. They did not see and were not aware that the Light Doctor took out a second sponge. The light seeped out in thin lines, secret and magical. It was a light that gave no shadows, but left an awareness of shapes in the room.

Something opened inside the couple. Each of them felt it, but could never have described it. It was like spending all morning in the byre breathing dust, heat and dung and then walking out into the cool breeze across the hills. It was like finally sitting down after a long day in the fields.

Thoughts surfaced, things they had not had time to think of, had put down somewhere during a busy day and never gone back to, thoughts which had become covered in dust at the back of a cupboard, left undisturbed for too long.

The Light Doctor squeezed the third sponge. There was a sudden cascade of light. It was bright, white and yellow. It lit up the room like sunshine and all the plants shifted, raising themselves towards the light. Kaia and Eso felt a sudden surge of joy. As the light faded away and the room returned to them, the surge was gone, but its echoes remained, like a dream after waking.

The Light Doctor removed her hood. Eso and Kaia were sitting quietly hand in hand. One of Eso's eyes appeared to be watery.

The Light Doctor stood quietly and crept out. The daughter was waiting, looking expectant.

"Give them some time alone," she said.

"Has it worked?"

"It has helped to reawaken something," the Light Doctor replied.

"Stay tonight," the daughter said. "It is too late to go back now."

It was a quiet evening, but there was a warmth about the house which had been missing before the Light Doctor's arrival. Over dinner, she caught the daughter staring at her parents once or twice. Had her mother become shy? Was her father talking a little more than usual? He hummed absently after the plates were cleared, but did his eyes flick up with an unusual brightness when Kaia came back into the room?

As she was leaving the next morning, Eso pressed a wrapped cheese into the Light Doctor's hand and patted her awkwardly on the back.

The Light Doctor smiled and pulled herself up on her horse. She rode out of the shadow of the farmhouse and into the sun which shone through scattered cloud.

As she rode around the side of the house, the mountains came into view and she stopped and stared. Behind them, it still appeared to be night. Dark cloud was showing behind their summits. Even as she looked, she fancied she could see it grow wider. She frowned and turned the horse for home.

Solimo was finishing his shift when the Light Doctor rode up. He was standing in the doorway looking at the distant black mark in the sky. It had grown over the last few days and was clearly visible.

"What is it, Doctor?" he asked, forgetting even to greet her.

"I am not sure," she said, shaking her head thoughtfully.

They watched it for a few moments before she dismounted and led the horse through the gate.

4

CHARLIE KICKED THE ball to his Dad who trapped it, kicked it up in the air and bounced it on his knees. The big black dog Charlie's Gran used to own trotted into the garden and started to bark at his Dad. His Dad kicked the ball. It hit the dog, flattening it completely so that it lay in the grass like a greasy puddle. Charlie went to look for a new dog. He started to walk towards craggy tree-covered mountains. Suddenly the dog leapt out from behind a rock, its lips curled back in a snarl. Charlie turned to run.

He woke kicking at the bedclothes. He stifled a shout and lay back with relief, the morning light leaking under his curtains. The memory of the snarl haunted him, although he could already no longer remember it clearly. Then he realised it was Saturday. That cheered him up immediately and he leaped out of bed.

It was early and no one else was up, but he prided himself on not being like teenagers he knew who wanted to lie in bed all morning. He was eleven and could think of better things to do with his time. By breakfast he had already routed an army which had besieged the castle his Dad had made him three years before. The garrison had been saved by a ragtag mixture of musketeers and cowboys who had come out of a range of hills made from his duvet.

"Is Dad up yet?" he asked his mother.

"No," she said, trying to sound neither cross nor sad.

After his breakfast, Charlie trotted quietly back upstairs and stood outside his parents' bedroom door listening for a minute. He could hear nothing, not even the radio.

He went outside and kicked the football around. He kicked it against the wall of the garage. He dribbled it around a couple of garden forks he stuck in the lawn and kicked it through a goal made of two upturned flowerpots. That was too easy, so he made the rule that he had to kick in the same movement as the last dribble as if a defender was coming at him. And he put the wheelbarrow in the middle of the goal for good measure.

Feeling thirsty, he went to the backdoor and started to take off his boots. He could hear his mother's voice raised.

"Well why don't you at least *look* in the paper?"

"There'll be nothing there I can do," his father replied.

"You never know until you look."

"They wouldn't want me anyway."

Charlie crept inside. His father was up, but not dressed. He was sitting in the living room with three days' stubble and the same sullen face he seemed to have been wearing for the previous two months.

"Everyone's been losing their jobs. I wish you'd stop taking it so personally!" said his mother and turned and walked out. She suddenly saw Charlie. From the look on her face he realised he was not supposed to have heard that conversation. He looked past her into the living room.

"Dad?" he said.

There was no response.

"Dad, will you come out and play football with me?"

"I'm busy, Charlie," he replied, picking up the paper.

Charlie watched him turn to the job pages, look at them for a few moments then mutter something under his breath. He avoided looking at Charlie again and turned to the sports section.

"Cricket season starts soon. Could we go to a game?" Charlie asked.

"We can't afford it Charlie."

"Mum's working."

"A call centre is not the road to riches."

Charlie felt like he had been told off. He didn't like it. He hadn't done anything wrong. He stomped out, grabbed his bike and cycled off down the road.

Fraser's house was a ten minute ride away on the edge of town. They built some spaceships out of Lego. Charlie's had a digger arm to scoop up raw minerals from the surface of asteroids as it flew past them. Fraser's had huge laser cannons mounted on its wings.

Charlie went and looked out the window at the open fields and the hills beyond them, criss-crossed by dry stone walls.

"Would your Dad take us up to the crags again?" Fraser asked. "That was dead good last time we went."

"I doubt it," muttered Charlie.

"But he's not working, he's got loads of time to take us."

"He doesn't do anything anymore. He just sits in his chair and gets cross with me."

"Then let's go to the wood."

They skirted the edge of town on their bikes and were soon following a track between hedgerows of hawthorn and hazel. They passed a couple of people walking their dogs. Where the fields started up the first slope of the hills, they locked their bikes, put them behind a bush, climbed over a stile and started walking up the public footpath. At one point, the track went along the top of a shallow sloping field beside a wall. The other side was steeper and wooded. They checked that no one was looking, climbed over and skidded down, using the trees to slow their progress. At the bottom they followed a stream, crossing it at a point they knew and walking along the opposite bank. There was a thick hedge of hawthorn, but they knew a place where they could get through.

Once on the other side, they were in the quiet of a wood. No roads came near there. They had never even seen anyone else there. It was a secret place that only they went to.

They gathered fallen branches and leaned them against a gnarled oak to make a den. Then they were Robin Hood and Little John trying to evade the Sheriff's men. They formed an ambush, fired a fusillade of arrows at their imaginary foes, then came out swords swinging.

By the time Charlie returned home, his mother was putting on some dinner.

"Hi Mum."

She saw him flick a look into the living room. His father was dressed now and watching television.

"You need to give him some time, love," she said. "He'd had that job for years. Now he doesn't feel like he's looking after us."

"Why do you get angry with him then?" he asked.

She hesitated.

"I'm not getting angry. I'm just trying to encourage him."

"Sounds like angry to me."

"Charlie!" snapped his mother without conviction.

"What's for dinner?" asked Charlie, thinking a change of subject might be useful.

"Shepherd's pie. Go tell your Dad it's nearly ready."

Charlie went and told him. His father grunted.

5

SOLIMO WAS SINGING. He liked to sing. All of them sang sometimes in the funnel hall, but him most of all. He would wake from his half dreams and find himself singing. The tunes would come and go. Some stayed in his head, some returned to him unasked and others were lost to his memory. Often there were no words, only sounds or humming. They could be languid or bright, melancholy or soft. They would creep out of the day, out of the light, out of the cloud, out of the wind.

He became aware of the Light Doctor. She must have come through the corridor to the garden hall. She was standing in the doorway, not wanting to close it lest she disturb him.

He dropped his voice and the song faded.

"Do not stop for me," she smiled.

"I am sorry. I did not see you there."

"I did not want to disturb you. You sing beautifully. The sun is inside you today."

Solimo smiled and looked down. Singing was such a small thing to be able to do.

"There is a quality in you neither Mondo nor Esella have," she said. "They take the light and shape it. You let it shape itself for you."

"I have much to learn. Esella is so confident and Mondo...I will never be like Mondo."

"No. You will never be like either of them. And they will never be like you. And that is as it should be."

She stopped and smiled at him. She always had something encouraging to say.

"I was thinking of asking you to come with me tonight and now I am decided. You will come with me. I am going to see Lempi."

"Is she better?" Solimo asked.

"Lempi will never be well again. She has asked for me. For us."

"She would not ask for me."

"You give yourself no credit. No, she did not ask for you by name because you hide your light and only shine it secretly on the paths of others. But you will come with me all the same."

Lempi was dying, that was certain. Solimo and the Light Doctor stood quietly by the bedside. A single candle flickered on a small cabinet across from the bed. The light reached out and caressed her wrinkled face. It was an unnatural grey and her cheeks were hollows, carved deeper by the shadows. Her grey hair was spread over the pillow like a fan. She watched them.

"I am glad you are here," she said, her voice a whisper. She coughed and gave a quick frown from the pain of it.

"I do not think there is much the light can do for you, Lempi. You need the physician."

"No, no. I have wasted enough of her time. She cannot help me. I know it is almost time to leave…" She paused, wrestling with a cough that she knew would hurt her. She mastered it and her eyes focused on them again.

"I have a favour to ask. Many years ago, I wronged someone." She seemed to be rushing out the words before she coughed again, or before she lost her nerve.

"I was sorry. Terribly sorry. But he died. I never told him. I have always remembered it and though my years have been happy, it has always been a dark cloud on my sun. Now I cannot rest and it haunts me. You can help me."

The Light Doctor took her hand and placed her other hand on it.

"I understand you, Lempi. You are right, we can help. Can you wait just a moment while I talk to Solimo."

The corners of Lempi's mouth twitched into a fleeting smile and then she closed her eyes a moment, to rest.

The Light Doctor let go of Lempi's hand and beckoned Solimo over to the doorway.

"Solimo, she needs the moon."

"But it won't be him."

"How do you know what it is? Even now we do not understand our light lore. But it is what she needs if it eases her passing."

He nodded.

"And I think you would do it better than I."

His eyes widened.

"I am not ready."

"Of course you are. And you are softer. This is your chance to show yourself that you are near to becoming a Light Doctor."

He looked as though he were about to raise another objection, but she put her hand on his wrist, looked into his dark eyes and simply raised her eyebrows a little. She trusted him, he could see that. He felt as though he would be letting her down if he did not do as she asked.

"Then I will," he said simply.

He took a sponge from the canvas bag that was sitting on a chair over by the wall.

"Would you take the candle to the doorway?" he asked the Light Doctor. When she took it, their shadows swung across the room. Lempi's face became smoother without the candle so close. The Light Doctor moved outside with the candle and set it somewhere in the hallway.

Solimo knelt on the floor and pulled his hood up over his head so that it covered his eyes. Then he took the sponge in his hands, enclosing it. He shut his eyes and linked his fingers, closing them around the sponge so that it was squeezed inside them. As he did so, he relaxed into himself, his breathing became deep and regular.

He felt nothing on his skin and yet he felt something. A shiver washed over him as his hairs stood on end. He could imagine his hands around, but not touching, a ball of ice, yet they were not cold.

He was not asleep, but in his dream there was a lanky delf with a pick axe walking up a moonlit lane to a bed where a young delf lay. As he came, she sat up and he saw she was not young at all, but grey haired. It was Lempi.

A pale silver glow came through his fingers, then he slowly opened his hands. They contained a silver mist which began drifting out of its ball shape. The room was bathed in a ghostly light which created dim shadows on the walls.

The mist began to drift upwards and started to form the shape of a person. It was not a clear shape, but like a beam of moonlight through fog. It floated up from Solimo's hands and hung at the foot of the bed.

Lempi opened her eyes and saw the shape.

"Onni," she said. "Onni, it is you...I need to tell you...I am sorry. You knew that did you not? You have always known it. Do you forgive me?"

Slowly, she raised an arm off the bed cover. The form still hovered at the end of the bed. There was no movement apart from the drifting of the light which made it.

There was silence in the room. Lempi continued to gaze ahead of her. She gazed until the glow began to fade and the shadows with them, until the room was in darkness.

Solimo breathed himself to wakefulness, raised his head and pushed back the hood. He saw from the yellow light ahead of him and growth of his own shadow that the Light Doctor had returned with the candle.

He raised his head and looked at Lempi. Her hands were resting on the covers together. Her eyes were closed and her mouth was drawn back in a small smile. He felt the Light Doctor's hand on his shoulder. He looked up at her and she nodded at him with a gentle smile.

"Well done," she said.

6

IT WAS A gradual change, but it occurred to Charlie that they had not heard his father speak for several days. It had taken a while to notice simply because his Dad had not come into contact with him. He would sit in the lounge, go out for walks or sit in the computer room. Charlie had gone in to use the computer before lunch. His father had been sitting there already, the computer on and his head tilted half onto his shoulder. At first he had thought he was asleep, but then Charlie had seen him blink. He seemed to be simply staring at the floor.

"Dad," said Charlie. "Dad, could I play on the computer..."

His voice faltered as he realised his father had not moved a muscle at either his entrance or his question. He felt suddenly uncomfortable. He thought maybe he should not be seeing this. It felt wrong. He backed out of the room quietly and stood in the hallway, listening for a sound of movement, some recognition that he had been in the room at all, but there was a dead silence behind him.

His mother was in the living room reading the paper.

"Mum?" he said.

He wanted to tell her. Ask her if his Dad was – what did he want to ask her?

"Mmm?" she asked, without looking away from the paper.

"Nothing," he said.

She looked up briefly, not really seeing him, her mind still focused on the article she had been reading, then returned to the paper. He turned and walked out again. She had looked tired. He did not need to bother her. She was already upset by his Dad, although he had not heard them argue for a few days now. And that was good.

But why would his Dad not play with him anymore?

Charlie wondered if he was too old to play with his Dad now, or perhaps his Dad was bored playing kids' games. Did Charlie pester him too much? Or maybe it was that time when he had told his Dad he did not want to go to watch the football. Had his father been disappointed? The idea of getting the train to Nottingham and joining the crowds on the way into the ground had not appealed to him that day. He had just built a fantastic castle and was about to besiege it. Was his Dad upset with him for not going with him?

He tried to think of times they had played together since then. They had gone to the park to play football. They had watched that James Bond film together. His Mum had come in and rolled her eyes at them and said "You boys."

He had grinned at his Dad and his Dad had grinned back. When was that? That was weeks ago. He tried to think of any times since then. He could not. Charlie must have annoyed him or bored him.

He sat in his room looking out of the window. Big white clouds were sliding noiselessly through the air, colliding with each other, trailing smoking edges. Blue sky with high vapour trails would appear between them, then disappear as one of the clouds closed over the gap. He watched the light on the roof opposite change from bright to dull as the sun sprang out for a few moments, then was covered again. A bigger cloud was edging in from the side of the window, dragging its bulk, bloated and grim, behind what now looked like very small clouds.

There was a dark cloud in his head too. He went downstairs again and reached the living room door. He hovered there, his glance going back to the computer room, so silent he could hear the hum of the computer. He looked at the living room door again. He heard the rustle of turned pages and pushed the door.

His mother looked up, saw him and put the paper down on her lap.

"What's the matter with you?" she said. Then, more gently, "Charlie, is something the matter?"

He went in quietly and pushed the door behind him so that it swung closed. He did not want his Dad to hear anything they said.

"Mum," he began. He felt foolish asking it. "Is Dad upset with me?"

"No of course not," she said immediately. "What made you think he is?"

"He just ignores me..."

"Oh Charlie." She took off her glasses and held out her hand to him. He went and stood by her. He felt like a baby. He could not bring himself to take her hand although he wanted to. She let it drop onto the arm of the chair.

"Your Dad's just...not himself at the moment. You know he's taken losing his job badly. He'll get over it, but he just needs some... I don't know, some thinking time."

She searched his face and Charlie could feel he was not being helpful in giving her any clues about how to continue, although he wanted her to.

"It's nothing you've done. It's nothing I've done come to that, so don't go thinking that either. It's just that job. I'd never realised he was so attached to the damn thing."

That last comment was to herself he realised.

"How long's he going to be like this? It's weird."

"Yes it is, love. I can't pretend it's not. But you've just got to be patient with him. Now go on. Don't worry about it. Having one of you miserable about the place is bad enough. I couldn't stand it if you had a long face as well."

"Okay," he said. He did not feel better, but he wanted to believe her. Maybe it *was* the job, but he found that hard to understand. Surely not having a job was just like being on holiday. He went back upstairs. took out a book and tried to read, but he kept looking out the window. He heard the living room door open and his mother cross the hallway.

"Richard," he heard her say. "Richard, look at me."

There was a pause.

"You're worrying Charlie. He thinks this is his fault."

No, Mum, don't tell him. Charlie squirmed.

"He doesn't know why you're like this."

Stop Mum. Despite himself he went to the door and opened it a little to hear better.

"Richard, he misses you."

He did. She was right. How could he miss him when he was just downstairs? He was at home all the time and yet Charlie missed him like he had not seen him for weeks.

"*I miss you.*"

It was so soft he had almost not heard it.

He listened for a response. Was there a movement or was that just his Mum coming out? He pulled back from the door, not wanting her to know he had been listening.

He quietly closed the door and knelt on his bed, his elbows on the windowsill. All trace of the sun was gone now and big gouts of rain were starting to blob onto the glass. Within a few minutes it was pouring.

The rain fell on the window of the computer room too, but Richard did not notice.

7

THE BLACKNESS HAD grown larger. It covered the mountains in shadow. Every day Solimo would look at it. One morning, when he was pedalling, there was a loud knocking at the gate outside. He stopped pedalling and wondered if any of the others would have heard it. The knocking came again. He climbed out of his seat, left the funnel hall and walked across the courtyard to the gate.

"Who's there?" he called before opening up.

"My name is Raul Hunter. I need to talk to the Light Doctor urgently."

Solimo opened the gate cautiously. Raul Hunter wore a long leather coat and a battered felt hat with the brims turned up. He was older than Solimo, perhaps in his early thirties, but shorter and broader. There was sweat on his grim face and he was half looking away, frowning distractedly. His hair was tied back and lay over his collar. Behind him was a horse with a long-arm in its saddle holster.

"I need to see the Light Doctor," he said.

As he said it, he cast a nervous look at the blackness.

"I am here, Raul, talk to me," came a voice from behind Solimo. He had not heard her come out. "I have not seen you for a few years. You should come inside. You look tired out."

She sounded surprised and curious, but pleased.

"That I am. I have ridden hard, my horse is blown."

"I will see to him," Solimo offered.

"Thank you," said Raul. Solimo stood back to let him inside. The Light Doctor reached out a hand to his arm, guiding him towards the funnel room.

"Now. What brings you to Kunnaslaki, or indeed Unama?" she asked. "Has the hunting grown so poor in Metsakant?"

"Metsakant is under attack," said Raul. "Unama will be next."

As he brought the horse through the gate, Solimo saw the Light Doctor usher Raul into the funnel hall and sit him on a bench, then she perched on the edge of one of the unused pedal stations. He felt a chill of fear. What did he mean Unama could be under attack?

When he had finished seeing to Raul's horse, he walked to the gate and looked towards the distant border range and that ominous dark mass above them. Then he looked across the hills that rose in waves between Kunnaslaki and the mountains. The grass rippled in the wind. Shadows from the clouds slid across as if dragging a dark train behind them, the light on the hills coming and going as the shadow passed over. One moment, trees on a hillside stood out brightly against the dark green of the grass behind; the next, they were dull shapes against an almost luminous green.

The Light Doctor came to the door of the funnel room.

"Solimo!" she called. "Fetch the others. We need to have a conference."

When the three Light Keepers arrived in the funnel hall, they found the Light Doctor had set out a table with five chairs. Raul was already seated at the table. He had had a chance to wash and was no longer red faced and sweating.

"Please, sit down," she said.

Raul gave a quick, familiar nod to Solimo. He simply looked at Esella and then away from her to Mondo. Mondo walked over to Raul who stood as he approached. Mondo clasped his shoulders briefly.

"Raul Hunter. It is good to see you. You should visit us more often."

Raul nodded. Solimo looked between Mondo and Raul and wondered how they knew him. He was older than they, but younger than either the Light Doctor or Mondo. Esella seemed equally puzzled.

"Raul is from Metsakant," said the Light Doctor. "I want you to hear what he has to say. But first, I want to ask you all something. What do you think about the blackness in the north?"

They exchanged looks.

"I had thought perhaps it was a storm," said Solimo, "although it looks like no storm I have ever seen."

"It worries me," added Esella. She looked at Raul and pushed her hair over her shoulder. "It looks unnatural. It is not meant to be there. Every morning when I leave the funnel hall my heart sinks when I see it is still there."

Raul looked grim, but said nothing.

"And what about you, Mondo? What do you think?" said the Light Doctor, turning to the older man on her right. He was looking down at the table top, his fingers folded together.

"I think it is the Order. They are responsible for it."

The Light Doctor turned to Raul.

"Raul, tell them."

"The Order is attacking Metsakant. The darkness came and then the Order followed it. Because of the darkness, we are starved of light, sunlight, moonlight, anything. They have spent weeks probing at our light towers."

"Are you saying the darkness and the Order are connected?" asked Mondo.

"If they are not, they are certainly taking advantage of it."

"But surely the darkness is cloud and it will pass over."

"I do not know what it is, but it is not cloud," Raul said. "It clings to the air. And when it is overhead, it brings a feeling with it. It is not the usual feeling of the dark we can drive away with a candle. There is something more to it, a feeling of dread. We find it hard to sleep. We have nightmares." He suddenly rubbed his hand across his face. "We are all so tired."

"It stinks of the Order," said Esella vehemently. Raul looked at her. The Light Doctor's voice was calm in response.

"The timing is suspicious, but perhaps they were just quick to see the advantage." She turned to Mondo again. "What do you think?"

"I have a feeling..." he stopped, looked at the others, shook his head and continued. "Have they somehow perverted light lore? I wonder about Etuvara."

The Light Doctor nodded thoughtfully.

"You have touched on something that I have long wondered about."

Solimo and Esella looked from one to the other.

"What could they do? Light lore is about *light*. This is darkness!" said Esella fiercely.

"I do not know what they could do. We lost so much light lore with the last of the Mages. We know we have a fraction of the knowledge that they had. But there is something more pressing which Raul has come here to ask us."

"We need more light," said Raul. "It took us a while to realise what they were doing. They kept attacking us, but they were feints to make us use up our light. They worked and now our supplies are running perilously low. The light keepers thought this was just an upsurge of the usual border raids and were extravagant in their initial defence. The Ironheads have long been afraid of the wraiths and they thought that a bold display would see them off. But the raids continued; their soldiers fall back at the first sign of the wraiths. So we started to hold back on them, using them only when the light towers were truly threatened. We relied on long-arms and bows, but most of our people are not warriors. There were some of us who harried their flanks. That certainly caused some trouble, but we also brought back information that showed this was more than raiding. It was the precursor to invasion. What we need is light. Without that, we have no hope of holding back a professional army. The Ironheads are attacking with only men from two manors."

"Raul has asked me if we could help them with their supply of light," said the Light Doctor. "I have told him I will take some, but I wanted you to know about it. After all, if, as Raul believes, Unama could also be attacked, we may need all the light we have to defend ourselves."

"Surely, they would not attack both at the same time. Unama is much larger than Metsakant," said Mondo. "And if what you say is true, then Metsakant's defence is also ours."

"I agree," said Esella.

"I know nothing about war," said Solimo. "I trust your judgement in this."

Raul nodded his thanks.

"Good. Then there is no time to be lost," said the Light Doctor. "Raul and I will leave in the morning."

"I will go," said Mondo. "It will be dangerous."

"There is no need," the Light Doctor replied.

Mondo looked at her with concern.

"Are you sure this is not about Etuvara?"

"Etuvara? You said that before," Esella asked, frowning.

The Light Doctor turned to Raul.

"May I tell them?"

Raul shrugged. She took that as assent.

"It was a village in the Tanglewoods, north of Metsakant, and just over the mountains from Outreterre. Mondo and I were young keepers back then. We were learning herb lore in the Tanglewoods." She paused and looked at Raul. "Under Raul's father, Keido Keeper."

"Your father was a Light Keeper?" Esella asked Raul. He nodded, but did not look at her.

"The Order crossed the mountains and raided Etuvara. Raul was the only survivor. No, he was the only one we found alive, the only one who escaped. We found him when we returned to the village."

"Where had you been?" Esella asked.

"Keido would send us out into the woods for days at a time to live off what we could find," said Mondo. "We were away when the attack came."

"We returned too late," the Light Doctor said. "By the time we arrived, the Order had swept through. We were in shock. We looked for survivors and found only Raul. The Order had been quiet for years, apart from their raids. We thought war was coming and we had to get home, to warn people."

"But war did not come," said Solimo, puzzled.

"No. And we always wondered why not," said the Light Doctor. "The raid seemed like a sudden squall that rises out of nowhere and passes quickly. Metsakant and the northlands were on alarm, but after a few months, they settled down again. Now, I wonder, as it seems do you too Mondo, if there was a reason for that raid that we are only now beginning to understand. If this is what I think it is, I fear it will spread across Unama and maybe the whole world. It will reach here and the light funnel will no longer work. There will be no unpolluted light left to collect. All will be darkness. And we could not bear that for long."

"Even so, I can go instead of you," Mondo said quietly.

"We need to know the truth. I know the most light lore. I need to take a look at this darkness myself and consult with the Light Doctor of Metsakant. I do not know what I might find there, but I may need to interpret what I see. It should be me that goes."

The next morning, Raul was in the stables saddling his horse when Esella came in. She held out a packet wrapped in cloth.

"I put together some food for you to take. I have already given one to the Light Doctor."

"Thank you," Raul said awkwardly.

There was an uncomfortable pause.

"Shall I put it in your saddle? It might come unwrapped if I pass it to you. I do not think the cloth is quite big enough."

She said it quickly and her words fell away at the end, wishing she had not said them. They were unnecessary.

"Please. This pouch," he said and pointed, but did not look her in the eye. She went to lift the flap and brushed his hand. He pulled it away and continued to fit the bridle.

"Thank you," he said again. An uncertain smile flitted across Esella's face.

"We will see you when you come back," she said. "Safe travels."

Less than an hour later, the three keepers were standing at the gateway to the Light Tower. Facing them were the Light Doctor and Raul, sat astride horses. The Light Doctor smiled at them all.

"You all look so serious. Farewell," she said. "Walk in the light."

Then she and Raul clicked their tongues and the horses began to trot down the hill. The keepers watched them for a few minutes, then Mondo turned to the other two.

"Well," he said. "We have light to gather. Solimo, I believe it is your shift."

8

CHARLIE'S FATHER WANDERED long corridors. There were many open doors into offices and he would look into each room. There were people in each, but few noticed him, or if they did, they would shut the door in his face. He walked and walked and the corridor became blacker. There were cold, dank steps with narrow empty windows through which a dark wind blew.

"We're closing down your division, Richard," said the man in the suit who was walking beside him suddenly.

"Why isn't there anything for me?" Richard asked.

He awoke shivering and lay staring into the darkened room. He could hear Helen breathing beside him, but he felt alone. He could not sleep. He kept thinking of the closing doors, of doors slamming in his face. What was the point in morning? It was just another day to live through before going to bed. He lay thinking hopeless thoughts, longing for morning, yet dreading it at the same time.

Raul reined in his horse and waited for the Light Doctor to catch up. Her horse was smaller than his stallion and could not keep up with it.

"Does your horse need a rest, Doctor?" Raul asked.

"We will rest at the farm in the next valley," she replied. "I know them and need to ask them a favour."

"Heimo?"

"You know it?"

"Everyone in the north knows Heimo. And I have traded game with them."

They started again, climbing up the hill until they were able to look down to where a triangular complex of buildings squatted on a small, rocky hill in the middle of the valley. Its buildings were two storied and turf-roofed. They were set around a yard with a gated archway. It was the only entrance. A low, roofed tower sat at each corner. The windows looking outward were short, horizontal slits. Washing hung from the walls airing in the afternoon sun. A ditch ran around the outside, parts of it filled with water. Outside it were gardens, some filled with the last vegetables of the season. Another lower wall ran around these.

"It never looks like a farm to me," said Raul.

"No, but it has never been successfully raided either."

They trotted down the slope and up the track to the gate which stood open. The yard was deserted but for a young delf chopping wood in the yard. She looked up as they approached. Her hair was cropped short, accentuating her fine chin and high cheekbones, but her eyes were bold and dark. Her blouse sleeves were rolled up to the elbows and she wore patched trousers.

"Bright afternoon, Olla," said the Doctor

"Bright afternoon, Doctor. I saw you on the hill, but did not realise it was you." She looked at Raul with recognition. "No tussock bantams for us today?"

"Not today," Raul said.

"How is your mother?" the Light Doctor asked.

"Hale and hearty and out in the far paddocks. She should be back in an hour. Come in for a bowl. I will make up a couple of beds too."

The kitchen was large and square. A workbench with cupboards beneath ran along three walls with shelves and more cupboards hanging above. In the middle of the room was a long, heavy table that could comfortably seat twelve. Herbs, pots and vegetables hung from the ceiling. A smell of sweet baking was coming from an oven and a large stock pot was bubbling on the range.

"Sit down and tell me what you are doing here and why you need an armed escort these days."

"Raul came to ask me about the blackness."

"We wondered if you knew anything about it. Is that why you are here?"

"It is and I need to ask you and your mother for help."

"Well you will not want to tell your tale twice I suppose, so have some of this soup and by the time you have done, the cake will be ready."

It was an hour later. The sun was setting and an orange light was gleaming on the wall of the kitchen through the window to the courtyard. They heard horses in the yard and the kitchen door was opened. Two delf entered. Margreta was tall and broad. Her dark hair showed thick strands of grey and was pulled back into a ponytail. She wore a heavy woollen jacket, breeches and boots. Kurk was tall with an outdoor face under an unkempt greying mat of hair. He wore a leather waistcoat over a pale blue worsted shirt. He was carrying a brown felt hat, stained with sweat and rain.

"Doctor! I thought I recognised your horse. And Raul Hunter of all people. We have not seen you for a while down here. Kurk has been missing his game pie!"

"Have you been busy?" asked the Doctor.

"It is always busy, you know that," said Margreta. "The stock roams for miles. Kurk says we should be bringing them in soon. He thinks it is going to be a bad winter. I just do as he tells me. After all, I am the muscle, he is the brains."

Margreta laughed. Then her face became serious. "Are you here about the blackness? What do you think of it? I have had Olla and some of the boys clearing the ditches again. It started over the Vuori and I would bet my best bull it has something to do with the Order."

"We think so," said the Light Doctor. "We are going to Metsakant. The Order has invaded and is wearing down the light towers. They are using the darkness to blot out the light."

Margreta's face lost any remnants of jollity.

"But what is it?"

"I am hoping there might be answers there."

"You might get more answers than you want from the Order. Are you sure you should be going?" Suddenly she frowned at the Light Doctor and pulled her to one side of the room, away from the others. "I thought you had put that all behind you. It was not your fault."

"I was afraid then, but I will act now. Someone needs to go and see. We never went back after the sack. We should have done that too. Perhaps Raul was not the only survivor."

Margreta frowned.

"You told me you searched everywhere! You said you could have looked no more unless you had taken the stones apart."

"We were late and we never followed the Order back into Outreterre or even to the border. It still haunts me. Maybe we could have saved some of them. It was as if we betrayed them twice."

"And maybe you could have got yourself killed," Margreta said crossly. "You did not betray them. Must we have this argument every year? Metsakant is a long way from us and we just did not get there in time. Let us not argue any more. Have you eaten? Good. We will take a ride around the valley before supper."

9

RICHARD WAS COUNTING his job applications. He had done fifty. Thirty-eight had never replied. Eleven had sent him a brief email telling him his application was unsuccessful. One had sent a letter telling him the same thing.

He had begun so well, sitting down each morning to search job seeker sites on the internet and read the daily paper. He had tried to treat it like a job in itself.

He was not sure at what point the job descriptions had seemed to be beyond his capabilities. He lowered his sights and went for jobs requiring fewer and fewer skills. Still he got nowhere.

He felt cut off from the world. When he went into town, he bought nothing. He avoided friends if he saw them, hating the friendly interest of the question "How's the job hunting coming along?"

He had friends, former colleagues, who were also job hunting, but he avoided them too. They might have found something. He began to feel as though he had no right to be in town: people in town had a purpose. His alternative was to sit at home and clog up the house. He knew he was making Helen's life miserable. And Charlie's. Charlie was too young to understand. He would one day, though, when he had a family to provide for. He hoped this never happened to Charlie, not cheerful Charlie.

There he was, coming home from school now. Richard saw him walk up to the house, heard the front door open and close, then the sound of Charlie's schoolbag hitting the floor as he relieved himself of the weight of the day in one, swift easy action.

"Don't come in here," he whispered to himself. He could not bear the look Charlie gave him sometimes. There was concern in his face, but he did not want his own son's pity. And there was fear. That he certainly could not bear. He used to be Charlie's rock, but now he was an old rowing boat, holed, faded and washed up on the beach. Full of rubbish.

He only relaxed when he heard Charlie thunder up the stairs.

Helen came home at six o'clock. She had some shopping with her, a bag of vegetables.

"How about a stir fry?" she asked cheerily. She had learned not to ask about his day. Every time she did not ask, he regretted his furious outburst at her that last time she had asked. He wanted to apologise for it, but it was a long time ago. He should have apologised then. It was too late now.

"I'm not hungry. I'm going out for a walk."

He could have said that more kindly too. He could have bought some vegetables, prepared dinner. Why hadn't he even done that? He felt ashamed of his inaction. He couldn't even be helpful while he was at home. He put on his overcoat and left the house. He resented their return, their purpose. Alone at home, he was in a limbo. He could pretend they did not exist. But once they came home, they brought the world with them. Their days, their needs.

The sun was still shining. It had been a glorious summer. But he could not enjoy it. It was a waste of summer. *He* was a waste of summer. He walked to walk off his mood, but the more he walked, the more he brooded and the deeper he went into his mood. He sat on a bench in the park, watching the people become fewer until there was just him and the setting sun. All brightness was leaving him. The sun was choked in clouds before it reached the horizon, lost in the blackness that was reaching out to him too. The clouds had leaked down into the trees and the darkness was spreading across the grass towards him like slow, reaching hands. It was crawling towards him from all sides. He should go home.

He stood up, hunched his head into his jacket and walked quickly. Sometimes he would speed up almost into a run, but he felt conspicuous, the darkness would see him, notice him. He had to reach home before it found him.

Helen and Charlie were in the living room, laughing at something on television. He hesitated in the doorway, looked out behind him. The streetlamps blinked on up the road, all except the one outside their house. That remained unlit. The dark had found him. It was closing in. He shut the door quietly, ran up the stairs and collapsed on the bed, fully dressed. He hugged himself, curled up. Darkness was coming up the stairs. He could feel it coming. He did not know where to hide.

Suddenly he felt tears welling up in his eyes, then he was crying. He felt his chest heaving with sobs. He put his hands to his face to try to stop himself. He buried his face in the pillow to stifle the sounds. There was nowhere to run any more. There was nowhere to go. He shut his eyes tight. He tried to calm his breath. If he was very quiet, perhaps it would miss his room. His breathing became slower. He tried to think only of his breathing. In, out. The sound of the exhalation through this nose. In, out. The sound of the sea on the shore, rolling in, wave after wave…

He could see the sea, a grey churning sea off a rocky shore on which he stood. He was not alone. There was a crowd around him. They were like giant birds, each one perched on a rock. They were birds with grey human faces and long curved beaks. Their shoulders were bare and grey and merged into ragged wings or a cloak. They stood silent and forlorn and watched him. A chill went through him.

He backed away from them and as he did so, it became darker on either side. He turned to see why and he was again in that long corridor. He walked and the further he walked, the darker it became. There was a heaviness on him. The darkness had found him. It was all around him. It had swallowed him. He could only walk. It was oppressive. It felt like he was walking through rock. He could see only dimly, but he became aware of space in front of him. He put his foot out and there was nothing there, just an immense blackness. He tried to pull his weight back but it was too late, he could not stop his forward motion. He fell.

10

MARGRETA INSISTED ON giving them extra provisions before they set off again the next morning. As they were about to leave, she grabbed the Light Doctor's reins and gave her a stern look.

"Be careful," she said.

The Light Doctor did not reply, she simply clicked her tongue at her horse and they rode out of the gate and up the hill.

Raul and the Light Doctor rode without speaking for a while. It was Raul who broke the silence.

"How long have you known Margreta?"

"Since we were children. I always stop by when I am in this part of the country. Heimo is always welcoming and she keeps a good kitchen."

"Yes, the glow of its lights across the empty land is a beautiful sight when you come on it in the evening," said Raul.

They rode all of that day, seeing no one and talking little. They went up and down the hills, or wound amongst them if they were too steep. The further north they went, the lower the hills became. It was dusk when they reached the top of a long ridge. It was the last of the hills. In front of them the land was largely flat and beyond the plain, another day's ride away, were the Vuori mountains. Their craggy peaks stood high above a cloak of trees which spread down beyond their feet.

"No delf lives beyond this point," said the Light Doctor. "How often do you come over this way?"

"A few times a year. The forests of the Vuori are full of game and few delf go there."

The Light Doctor nodded grimly and raised an eyebrow.

"Have you crossed the mountains?"

"Sometimes," Raul replied without looking at her.

"Hunting more than game."

His eyes flicked up at her.

"If they cross my path."

"Do you come across the Order much?"

"From time to time. I do not think they expect to see a lone delf."

They made camp in a hollow on the lee of the ridge where they were sheltered from the cool evening breeze.

After they had eaten, they sat in a silence for a time, staring into the fire. The logs popped and wheezed. Caves showed through the waving flames. Feeling the heat on his face, Raul was aware of the cooler darkness, pressing on his back and all around beyond the reach of the flickering light.

"What happens if the light fails?" he said.

"The Order fear what we can do with the light. They know we rely it," she said. "We need to find out the source of the blackness. If it comes from the Order, we need to know what it is. We need to know their strength so we can organise our defence. Delf were never a match for the Order. It took the Mages to show us how to weave the sun wraiths. Now we may have the wraiths, but the Mages are gone. We need the sun wraiths. The Order fears them and they are wise to do so. But we need light to weave the wraiths."

She sighed and pulled her coat around her.

"The delf are much changed since we last fought back the Order. The plague they brought with them destroyed our towns and now we are scattered. Simply spreading the word would be difficult. And there are fewer light weavers. Not all light towers in Unama are the same as Kunnaslaki. Some have only one keeper now."

Raul nodded. "It is the same in Metsakant. Being a keeper is lonely even for a delf."

"You never thought to follow your father?"

Raul thought about his father and how little he would see him. He was always at the light tower. He discouraged visits. That was how Raul had come to spend time on his own, taking his horse and his long-arm and going hunting. He learned how to hunt from a young age, teaching himself and listening to the old delf of Etuvara as they talked, freely sharing their wisdom and knowledge of the forests and the animals that lived there.

Raul thought about the people of Metsakant. It was a triangular peninsula jutting south east into the sea. Its southern coast was mountainous, its northern coast dotted with fishing villages and tall mountains formed the land border with Outreterre, as the Order called the land they had conquered. As a child in Etuvara, they had felt secure beneath the mountains, thinking the Order could never climb them. It must have only taken a few. They had brought cobs too. Cobs were climber. He could remember the fear he had felt as he huddled in a barn, hiding behind barrels of strong smelling pitch and hearing the cobs sniffing unseen so close to him.

Raul realised he had not answered the Light Doctor's question.

"No," he said in the end. "I did not follow my father. Maybe I would have done later." He shrugged. "There was no later."

That must not happen again, he thought. Unama would not be caught unawares like Metsakant.

"Most would have seen the blackness in the north," he said. "All we need is a rallying point."

She sighed and pulled her coat around her.

"But how many would answer? Kyntilla and the south have not felt the threat of the Order for centuries. Here in the north, we know them and their raiders, yet how many would answer a call? Where the plague the Order brought destroyed our towns, now we are scattered, pasturing our herds and looking out for raids. And we know little of the Order in the last few hundred years. Maybe there will be answers in Metsakant."

They were on their way again early the next morning. They rode down the ridge to where the land dropped away steeply to a wide, flat moor. They spurred their horses into a gallop, wanting to cross the moor as quickly as possible. They both felt very exposed, but there was no one in sight, just the blackness ahead, spreading across the sky, reaching across the mountains.

They travelled east across waves of low bleak ridges which rolled under them from a horizon that faded into a grey haze. The silence sank onto them, wet and cold. The hooves of the horses flicked through the damp grass which smelt old and sour as it bowed its head to coming autumn.

They came upon the old road that ran from Metsakant to Kunnaslaki. It saw little traffic and less maintenance and much of it was covered in thick tufts of grass.

The landscape was monotonous and their steady pace lulled them into their own thoughts. The Light Doctor had been rolling a question around her head for some time, imagining the responses. Finally, she broke the silence.

"When was the last time you were at Etuvara?"

It was as if Raul had been thinking the same thing. His answer came quickly as though it were part of an existing conversation.

"I have not been for years. I was fourteen when I first went back. I used to go each year. I felt I needed to discover where I was from."

"What was it like?"

"The visits have blurred together. But the place was always a stranger to me. It was not my home. Home was not a ruin."

They rode in silence once more.

"What made you stop going?" the Light Doctor asked, ready to retrieve the question if she sensed her curiosity had overstepped Raul's willingness to talk.

"Ah..." he said.

She waited, looked at him. He was thinking.

"When I was eighteen, the Ironheads' raids started again. We would hear horsemen just before dawn. We would fire a few volleys at them. We lost a good few cattle that year, until my brothers – my foster brothers – and I went out and herded them all in close. Then we started keeping watch. They stopped coming to us. Went looking for easier targets I suppose. But I did not feel as if I could go away after that."

"Too dangerous," agreed the Light Doctor.

"Danger never occurred to me. No, I just knew the family needed me at the farm. The more people there were, the less likely it was the Order would come. They are cowards really. I do not think I believe those old stories of their charges on horseback, the men and horses in bright steel."

"But you left the farm."

Raul kept looking straight ahead.

"Yes. I did. Lena had died a few years before and then old Kilta died too and Kilto took on the farm. It was not the same. I knew I ought to get out. So I packed a bag, took my horse and long-arm and was gone."

"To the forests."

"Not at first. No. I went back to Etuvara. I think I went to say goodbye."

He went silent again. He was remembering, but it was a memory he did not share with the Light Doctor. It was of walking his horse down one of the empty, overgrown streets and coming upon two Ironheads sat outside one of the ugly shells of building. They were eating and their presence seemed to mock the meal times that would once have happened in that house. The grass on the lane had masked the sound of his approach. He had shot one of the men before he even had time to stand up. The other he had grappled with and had turned the man's knife on him. He had never killed before. He had looked at the bodies lying in the dead town and it had felt just and appropriate. He had taken their weapons and supplies and turned around and ridden straight back out of the village. He determined he would never go back after that. He had closed off that part of this life. The Order had taken it, but he would no longer relive the pain of it for them. They would not have that satisfaction.

The Light Doctor watched him lost in his thoughts. She decided she would not interrupt them. She knew now he would share them if he wanted to. She waited a while, and then started a new subject.

"You must know many people here in the north."

"Mmm. Some I suppose. They like the game I bring them. Not much of it on the grasslands where they have to compete with the livestock. But there is plenty in the forests and most delf do not go there. It seems that being this far north is all they are prepared to go. But going closer to those iron bastards is better than waiting for them to come to you in the night and steal your livelihood."

"You are the only delf who fights back, you know."

"No. All the farmers up here fight back."

"That is not what I mean. They defend themselves. You go looking for them. Do you not?"

He turned his head and squinted at her, trying to see what was going on inside her head. A faint smile crossed his lips.

"Light Doctor, are you trying to shine the sun into my head?"

"I am sorry. This land is empty and I need to occupy my head or I will start imagining all the worst things about Metsakant and the blackness. I need some distraction and your appearance has reawakened so many memories of that time. It feels like only yesterday that we found you through the smoke and left you with Kilta and Lena."

By now the eastern forest had emerged out of the mist and sat like a dark green smudge which became ever larger. It began to rain properly and both riders pulled up the hoods of their coats.

Sooner than they expected, they had reached the forest and the road into the trees disappeared around a bend in front of them. Trees and undergrowth grew out on either side, making use of the long light well the road provided. Only there was no light: the darkness had begun to spread over the mountains.

The Light Doctor looked up at it.

"It has reached us. Should we use the road?"

Raul nodded.

"The forest is too thick to ride through. Chances are, if there is anyone else in here, they would have to be on the road too. So we will see them coming, unless they are on the other side of a bend. But it must wait. This is far enough for one day, especially with that in the sky. We will cross into Metsakant tomorrow."

They found a campsite surrounded by large boulders which had tumbled from the mountains above long ago. The Light Doctor did not enjoy her first night under the darkness. She dreamed of smouldering cottages and lay awake for hours thinking the same thoughts over and over again, remembering how she and Mondo had stumbled around the ruins until they found Raul.

The next morning they awoke from habit rather than from the light. The darkness had carried itself a little further into Unama. They went into the trees, riding side by side. It was still raining and they could hear the steady patter of it amongst the trees. Heavier drops were gathering and falling from the leaves, so they tried to stay in the middle of the track, but often the foliage leaned so far over, they were riding through a dim, green-roofed tunnel.

They rode in silence. The Light Doctor looked into the wood on either side. Ferns and spindly plants with long leaves filled the spaces between the trunks. Above, the canopy was dense and let in little light.

After a couple of hours of riding, the road began to rise. The horses' pace slowed. An hour later, the Light Doctor looked to see if she could see the mountains above the trees, but the sky was a ruffled grey. The rain continued, but it was lighter and the only sound was the horses' hooves on the road. They fell in a regular rhythm except when they hesitated to go around a fallen tree trunk or bush sprouting amongst the stones.

She started to doze and caught herself slipping forward. She sat up straight. The trees were shorter now and their branches twisted. They were knotted and gnarled, moss covering every branch. There were boulders too, also swathed in the thick green blanket.

Raul did not seem to tire. He would look forward most of the time, but then sometimes he would turn to left or right and stare.

"It is very disconcerting when you do that," said the Light Doctor.

"Do what?"

"You suddenly look off into the trees. I keep thinking there is someone there."

"I am sorry, I am not aware of it. I am just watching, listening. There does not seem to be anything unusual going on in there. Look!" he said suddenly and pointed up to his left above the Light Doctor's head. There was a tear in the cloud and through it was the bare rocky side of the mountain and a rounded summit. The grey of the rock contrasted with the strange darkness behind. She gazed up through the gap in the cloud before it closed.

"We are near the pass now," Raul said.

The road began to level out, and they could see that there were trees climbing away from them on either side. The highest were ghostly shapes in the drifting cloud. Soon they road began to go downhill. They had crossed the pass and the cloud above them began to thin. They twisted around in their saddles and could see two peaks, almost standing clear of the cloud now and bent trees tucked into crevices. Looking back to the west between them, they could see the end of the darkness, but the sun had moved to the west and shone on Unama and gave light through the mountain pass towards Metsakant.

They continued down and saw ahead of them that the road ran right along the top of a steep drop. They stopped and gazed out.

The mountains ran on to the north east, cutting off the head of the peninsula of Metsakant as it pointed south east into the sea. The forest was thick upon the mountains' flanks which marched into the dim distance where it would finally spread into the Tanglewoods which covered the northern part of the peninsula between the mountains and the coast.

Below them, where the cliff stopped and met the mountainside, trees crowded down to meet a rolling green plain, dotted with copses. The road on which they stood emerged from the forest at the foot of the mountains ran into a town. It had streets of grey stone buildings, backed by a hill a few hundred feet high containing a walled enclosure and a single tower. On the far side of the town it led towards the eastern coast.

Even from that height and in the dim light of the darkness, they could see the panicked crowds in the streets. The reason lay to the northeast where another road led towards the light towers and the mountains. They could tell where the light towers were because each one of them was in flames. On the road that ran between the towers and the town was more flame, but this was the torches carried by the army of the Order.

Raul and the Light Doctor watched all this in silence. There seemed to be nothing to say. The Light Doctor was uncertain what to do. She felt it should be Raul's decision what happened next.

"I do not see any sun wraiths," he said at last. "We are too late."

"We have sponges with us," said the Light Doctor. "We could hold them back."

There was little hope in her voice. Raul shook his head slowly.

"You would only slow them down and then they would kill you. Then if I survived, Mondo would kill me. We are too late to help Metsakant."

His voice was calm, matter-of-fact, but the Light Doctor could see his knuckles were white on his reins belying the emotions he was keeping from his face.

A force was emerging from the town now, skirmishers on horseback riding out to slow the advance of the Order.

This was worse than Etuvara, thought the Light Doctor. As terrible as it had been, it had been on a much smaller scale and she did not have to witness it.

"We cannot sit here doing nothing!" she said. "I could weave a wraith now and send it down. I can see their positions from their torches."

"From up here?"

"I could try!"

They watched the populace milling about. Some were heading for the citadel on the hill, others were already leaving town, on foot or horseback or on wagons.

"Go on then," said Raul. His voice was flat. "At least it will buy them a little time."

The Light Doctor reached into her coat and pulled out a small bowl, then she dug into one of the bags loaded across her horse's flanks and pulled out a small package wrapped in waxy paper.

The Order was forming up on a wider front. He cursed their military precision. Then a bright glow erupted beside him. He did not look at it, but he saw the flaming object shoot away from him, down across the treetops. It showed brightly in the dark of the afternoon and the trees lit up briefly as it flew over them. People in the town paused as it passed overhead. Raul could imagine their thoughts, a moment of hope when they thought that all was lost and he cursed himself for giving them this false hope. They should never have done it.

The Order must have seen it too, although from the look of their burning torches, their ranks were holding steady. They were forming the best possible target to the wraith, standing, waiting for it to attack. They were going to sacrifice their front ranks to it.

Then the wraith was upon them. He imagined the burning flesh and the screams, for the battle was too far away for them to see clearly. He had heard it before.

Then the wraith faded. They watched for a few minutes. The torches were moving again. That was when Raul realised what had happened.

"It did nothing," he said bitterly. The Light Doctor looked at him puzzled. "They just dropped their torches and moved away. You were fighting fire, not men. The Ironheads are using the darkness against us. It is hopeless. Metsakant has as good as fallen."

He turned his horse.

"Let us go back. There is nothing more we can do here."

The Light Doctor's eyes were wide with incredulous horror. She looked at Raul's back as he started to ride away, then back to the fated town, then at Raul again. Was leaving really their only option? Surely she could ride down, use the sponges she had while she still had life in her?

In Metsakant, a few of the skirmishers were galloping back into the town. There were so few of them and they kept going through the streets, following the desperate populace. The torches of the Order were closer than ever.

Raul had stopped. He was looking down at the ground to his side.

"There is no standing army in Metsakant," he said. "If the light towers have been destroyed then there is nothing to stop the Ironheads. They are too close and we are too late. If we go now, we live to fight another day."

He raised his head and looked at her. She could tell his eyes were filled with tears. He turned away again, looking down the road which led back into Unama.

"There will be other days on which to kill them. We must go now," he said, quietly, urgently. "Before I change my mind."

The Light Doctor wondered what it was costing him to turn his back on his people. She screwed up her eyes and tried to see through her own confusion. A voice inside her was telling her not to go down, but to follow Raul. Was this her fear of death? Or was it the voice of reason? It was a Light Doctor's duty to help and to heal. Metsakant needed her help.

Raul tapped his horse's flanks with his heels and it started off again. He was going. Raul would not follow the voice of fear, she knew that much about him. She took a last look at the doom of Metsakant, then followed him down the road.

When you go back on a path you have just travelled, the way seems much longer than it does on the outward journey. The horses trotted along the track down, finding the way much easier and sensing the end of the day. The light was stormy with the setting sun casting a yellow light under the oily darkness above them. The Light Doctor found the bends in the road interminable, expecting each in turn to be the last: the place where the road finally straightened and left the forest behind. Of course it happened only when she had stopped expecting it.

The sun was gone and a chill wind was blowing. They made a camp in the same place as the previous night, amongst the boulders in the trees. They lit a fire and prepared a simple meal, then they buttoned up their coats, wrapped themselves in their blankets and slept.

"Wake up!"

It was Raul. His hand was over the Light Doctor's mouth. She awoke immediately.

"Something's out there," he whispered. "More than one."

He took his hand away from her mouth, crept over to the rocks and pressed his back against them. He beckoned her over and she joined him.

He laid his long-arm next to him and handed her his long hunting knife. Then he took up a pistol in each hand, the twin barrels of each were darker than the night. Together they listened, their eyes rolled upwards as if it would help them see through the rocks behind them.

Something hurtled out of the air above them, leaping from the rocks into their small space.

In the last glow of the firelight, they could just make out the dark shining skin thinly covered in hair and wide ears of two cobs standing just in front of where they had been sleeping. Their arms hung by their sides, adding to their ape-like appearance and their two pairs of eyes glowed a dim green.

The cobs launched themselves forward and even as they did so, there were two explosions. The Light Doctor let out a stifled cry as one of the cobs fell onto her. Raul picked up his long-arm and kicked the creature which lay on the Doctor. The other had fallen short. Its leg twitched.

"Wait here," Raul said and climbed up onto the rocks. He listened and heard something running through the bushes away from them. The Light Doctor pushed the dead cob away from her and stood up.

"There is another," was all Raul managed to say, then he was after it, leaping through the undergrowth. The beast seemed at home in the trees, but was not used to being the quarry. It kept turning to look at him and in doing so would blunder into trees. Raul was gaining on it. The plants around them were growing thicker. The animal had to stop and push itself through a gap between two tight growing trees. It changed its mind and came back to try the thorny bush to the left of the trees. Raul took his chance. He whirled the long-arm in his hand so that the butt was upwards like a club. The cob heard him and half turned. It dodged and leaped. At the same moment, Raul swung. Long-arm and cob's head met in mid-air with an audible crack. The creature was thrown backwards by the force of the impact. Raul stood over it. Its head was at an unnatural angle.

When he returned to their camp, the Light Doctor was inspecting the cobs. Both had neat holes in the chest with a large exit wound in the back.

"Short range," said Raul.

He dropped the third from over his back.

"There is little point burying them," Raul said. "Other cob would soon find them. We need to put some distance between us and this place. And quickly. They must have come with the Order. There will be Ironheads as well come morning, if not now. We do not know who else was close enough to hear my pistols or who this one was running to."

They had nothing to pack but their blankets and were on their way a few minutes later. Dawn was close.

"Cob will not follow us in full daylight. And surely not into Unama."

"I am no longer certain of anything," replied the Light Doctor and gestured with her head towards the blackness. "Who knows what is possible with that above us."

11

THE FALL WAS a short one, but Richard had landed on something hard. It felt like rock. He lay there for a few moments. The physical bruises were bad enough, but far worse was the feeling that swamped him, a powerful force, bringing sadness and despair, so big it was not just in him, but outside, and all around him. It was the darkness from the trees in the park. It had found him.

He rolled over and pressed his face against the hard ground. Its coldness broke into his mental flight. A primeval part of his brain cut through his other emotions and he felt a jolt of a different emotion. Fear. He raised his head. And realised he could see nothing.

He stood, slowly, carefully, thrown by the lack of anything on which to fix his senses except one thing. It was the smell. It was strong, unpleasant, animal. It was the odour of excreta and bodies. It was thick, pungent. He wrinkled his nose and tried to sense something else in the dark.

There was a feeling of space on either side, but the darkness seemed alive. He could hear breathing, he was sure he could. He turned. He could not tell how far he was turning, could not see his hand in front of his face. He heard another sound from the other direction and swung about.

He could hear his own footsteps. There was a faint echo. It was an enclosed space and the floor was rough. Maybe he was in a cave. He bumped something. It gave against his leg and he jumped back. He froze. He could feel his heart beating now. He listened and peered desperately into the dark. He tried to move again, more slowly this time. Nothing. Had he imagined it? He stopped moving and listened once more. The hairs on his neck rose and he could feel his heartbeat increase. There was nothing.

He moved forward. Something was there! He lost his balance, put out his hands. They touched something and he fell sprawling. There was a groaning sound. The noise made the space around him feel large, like a cavern or a big empty hall. Except it was not empty. He scrabbled to stand up. His arm hit something else. A groan came from right next to him. Sounds were coming from all around him now. He was up. Fear gripped him. What was in the darkness?

Suddenly there was some light. He saw a figure carrying a small, orange, flickering light over against the far side of what seemed to be a cave. The light did not illuminate more than the wall behind it.

Someone was there. He had to reach them, to reach that light. He set off towards it, running. He did not know what was in the darkness. He bumped into other things. They were all around him. Something grabbed at him. He heard cries of pain. He stumbled a couple of times more. He had to reach that light and whoever was carrying it. It was all there was. The figure was moving. It reached a doorway and disappeared. The torch left a faint glow as it receded.

Suddenly he tripped on something right in front of him. He tumbled over, his arms going out instinctively to protect himself. He crashed onto the hard ground, bruising his forearms and right elbow. It was then that Richard realised all the sounds had ceased. Lying there on the ground, he froze. From out of the silence came a sound like a sniff. Then two more, together this time. He could bear it no longer. He was on his feet again and running for where he thought he had seen the door.

As he ran, he knew there was something behind him, something following him. He ran faster.

He was sweating when he reached the door. He stopped briefly to look back, but could see nothing. He grabbed at the door handle and the door swung open. In the gloom, he could make out a flight of stone steps faintly lit from higher up. There was no sign of the figure he had seen. With one last backward glance, he started up, running again.

At the top of the steps, he heard a howl from behind him. He almost slipped, caught himself and looked back. There was something at the bottom of the steps. Then he was running again, his shoes pattering loudly on the stone. He reached a kind of landing. It was dimly lit by another torch. He heard shuffling on the stone floor behind him. He looked about frantically. Things were moving in the gloom.

There were more steps ahead. This time, they led down. He could see no more than that.

He had never felt fear like this before in his dreams. He ran. He reached the torch and tugged at it. It moved in its socket but stayed put. He wrenched at it and it came out, then he was away across the hallway. He ran for the steps.

Now he could hear feet on stones behind him. They were gaining on him. He knew they could see him although they seemed to have had no trouble in following him in total darkness.

He ran down the steps. It was hard to keep his footing. He was out of breath and his legs were beginning to feel rubbery. He did not know where he was going, he was just following the steps and hoping it led him somewhere. There was another torch below him. Sounds behind him were closer now.

When he reached the next torch, he found he was in a small room with more steps, but this time they led upwards. He pulled the second torch from its socket. He was breathing hard. He heard panting behind him. He swung around, holding the torches out on either side and two figures appeared and stopped on the edge of the light. They were ape-like with large, hairless ears and long, wiry arms. They stared at him with wide, green, cat-like eyes. He began to back up the steps. One step. The creatures moved forwards into the light. They were dark with glistening hair. Although shorter than him, they looked powerful. Their mouths were open and he could see sharp teeth.

He went up another step. They moved to follow, but seemed confused. He tried the next step, but in his fear he did not put his foot flat om the step and he slipped. And they were on him.

He swung wildly with the torch in his right hand. The nearest creature reared back and the other hesitated. He struggled to his feet and backed up two more steps. The apes made another rush at him, this time chattering and snarling. He lunged, whirling first one torch, then the other, shouting incoherently.

They backed away. He regained his feet. He could see green eyes in the darkness further down the stairs. There were more of them. He pulled himself up to his full height, flailed the torches and roared. The two closest to him took a step back. Keeping his eyes on them, he shifted a foot up the step behind him. Then another. The apes did not move. They rocked on their heels as if about to jump.

Then he heard sounds from above him on the steps. More of them must be on their way down. There was no escape. The creatures looked towards the sounds. They seemed calmer now. Shadows and light flickered around him. Then a voice called out.

"Enough! Stand fast!"

Richard turned.

A man was standing behind him, five steps up, breathing hard. He had small eyes in a round face with a thin beard. He was carrying a torch in one hand and a cudgel in the other. He raised the cudgel as if to strike Richard, then stopped. The man came down the steps and stared at Richard's face.

"You be a man!" he said.

Richard said nothing.

"What be you doing here?"

Richard was unsure what to answer.

"I ken you not. Who be you?"

Richard simply looked at the man. He was confused, frightened, tired. The man had a strange accent, neither Swedish nor Scottish, but a little like both.

"Come up here. Be you dumb?"

The man surveyed him.

"Put down the brands and come with me."

The man slipped the stick into his belt which was tied around a thick cloth coat, then from behind him, he pulled out something made of dull metal. A gun.

"Drop the brands. Now!" he said. "Who be you? What be you doing here?"

Richard dropped the torches, but said nothing. It was not that he was refusing to answer, but that no words came to him.

The man in the coat turned to the creatures.

"Pick him up and bring him to the courtyard."

The creatures sprang forward. Each grabbed an arm. Richard resisted, but they had him tightly.

"Struggle not and no scathe'll come to you," said the man.

He was walked up the steps. They climbed far, on and on up more flights, the man walking in front and turning from time to time to look at him.

As they climbed, it grew brighter as the torches became more frequent. They arrived at double wooden doors. The man rapped on them with his fist. They were opened from the outside into a courtyard. It was night and Richard could feel the fresh, coolness of the air and there were dim shapes of buildings.

"Loose him. Go back down!" said the man in the coat and the two apes let go of Richard's arms and loped away. A young man who must have been the one to open the door stepped forward. He was also wearing a coat and carried a long barrelled gun over his shoulder.

The first man frowned at the younger.

"You let any man in there today?" the first man asked.

"No," said the younger defensively.

"Then how came this man down there? Was he was down there for days with the devils then?"

"I let no man in. I never seen him before!"

The man gave him a disbelieving glance. "I'll see to you later. Close that door and keep your eyes open." Then he prodded Richard in the back.

"Move," he said.

They walked across the courtyard. Richard glanced quickly to his right and saw grey walls in the light of a quarter moon as it emerged from behind a cloud. There was a building with a window in an upper floor glowing with yellow light and throwing an oblong pool of light onto the cobbles. Then they were at the door and the man was opening it.

The room smelled of damp. There was a low bed with disheveled blankets, a rough wooden table and four chairs. The floor was covered in rushes.

"Sit," said the man. Richard sat.

"You understand my words," he continued. "Can you speak?"

The man looked Richard up and down. He peered closely at his ears and his face. Then he picked up his hands and inspected them.

"You be a man. How came you down there?"

The man looked him in the eyes.

"How came you to be in the Pits?"

Richard said nothing. He would coast through this dream like he had the others. It would happen to him just as all the others did, without any help from him.

He looked at the man, then looked away. He noticed the fraying threads of one of the blankets. He saw through an open doorway that there was another bed heaped with blankets. He knew the man was still watching him, but did not want to look at him again. The man had an unpredictable feel about him. He tried not to look at the gun. It was an unusual pistol with a long barrel. He wondered if he should try to make a run at the man and take it; turn the tables. But he did not know where he was or how many others there were in this place.

The door opened and another man entered. His dark hair and beard were neatly trimmed and he wore a well-used black leather waistcoat which reached half way down his thighs. Richard felt intimidated by him. He exuded a quiet, dangerous confidence. His dark eyes took in both of them.

"I heard there were a comer in the Pits, Silver" he said.

"Mr Rodon, there was no need to trouble yourself. I can see to this."

"You know the Archbishop will know aught that passes here."

His eyes shifted to Richard.

"Who be this?"

"I wot not. The cobs found him in the Pits. He speaks not."

"Found him in the Pits?" He looked at Richard with interest. "He be not one of your men?"

"He be not. I ken 'em all."

"Then who be you?" he asked Richard.

"Richard," he replied, finding a voice at last.

"You see. It be Richard," Rodon said without any trace of a smile. "And what be you doing in the Pits?"

"I don't know."

"What say you?"

This was worse than being awake, Richard thought.

Rodon frowned at him then stood back. His eyes travelled over him, looking at his clothes.

"He be a sullen wight," said Silver who had lost some of his self-assurance with the arrival of this new man. Rodon nodded, then addressed Richard again.

"Your cloths be well made. From what manor be you?"

Richard simply looked at him. Rodon raised his eyebrows questioningly.

Richard wondered if he was being asked where he was from. He did not think there could be any harm in it.

"Hadbury?" Richard said.

Rodon looked thoughtful. "I know no Hadbury. Be it a new village?"

"No, it's very old."

"How old?" He looked at Richard again. "How old?"

"I don't know. It was in Domesday," Richard said, frustrated by the strange questions despite his situation.

"The Domesday Book?" said Rodon slowly. He asked his next question very carefully. "Where be Hadbury?"

"It's near Derby," Richard said.

The man called Silver looked between them. The conversation had clearly gone beyond him. The mention of Derby seemed quite incongruous. Derby was a market town which became the city in the heart of Derbyshire. It was not hard to be biggest place in Derbyshire, a largely rural county in the English Midlands. Rodon did not indicate whether the name meant anything to him.

"Betell me how you came here," said Rodon.

"I don't know. I'm dreaming."

Rodon raised an eyebrow again.

"You be awake. "

"If you say so," said Richard. He could remember no conversation like this in any of his dreams. It was almost comic.

Rodon's eyes never left him.

"You trow in sooth you be asleep?" said Rodon.

"Yes," said Richard. He found the way Rodon stared at him most off-putting.

"He speaks strangely," suggested Silver.

Rodon turned away from Richard suddenly and looked at Silver.

"Have my things packed now. I will take Richard to Collenium. I ween the Archbishop will see him."

He turned to Richard. "We will travel anon. Silver, bring him something to eat."

Silver had called out for someone from the door. The man who brought food was older than the others with a grey beard and showed no interest in him at all. The food consisted of bread, a hunk of cheese and a couple of apples. He nibbled at the bread, which was dry and almost stale and tried the cheese, which was strong. There was a flagon of something which tasted like weak beer.

Within about an hour, the man called Rodon returned and led him outside to a coach. Four horses stood in front of it, their harnesses jingling as one shifted a foot or nodded its head. Richard looked up. It was a dark night and there were many stars in the sky, but half the sky was dark.

Rodon opened the door of the carriage for him and he climbed inside, The cabin was small, wood panelled and contained upholstered seats with little padding. Rodon sat opposite him, carefully arranging himself into the corner. He reached under the seat, pulled out a coarse woollen blanket and tossed it onto Richard's lap.

"Sleep," he said. "We will not be there til tomorrow afternoon."

12

CHARLIE'S MOTHER CAME into his room before he was even up. She was still in her nightie and looked puzzled.

"Charlie, have you seen your Dad?"

"No. Not since yesterday morning."

"Oh."

"What's wrong?"

"Nothing, nothing, don't worry about it."

But Charlie did worry about it. He heard her on the telephone later. His father had gone out for a walk and not come back. He had been out all night.

The next day, when he returned from school, there was a police car parked on the road and his mother was in the living room talking to a policewoman. The policewoman wanted to talk to Charlie too. She asked about what his Dad was like, where he used to like to go. Charlie was afraid. He felt his eyes welling up, but he managed to answer all her questions. His mum sat opposite. She had been crying. She watched him intently as he answered the questions, as if his answers would contain the clue to his father's disappearance.

It took him a long time to fall asleep that night. Where was his Dad? Where would he have gone for a walk? He tried to remember what time it had been. He tried to remember when they had last spoken, if there had been anything he had said which might have indicated that he was going somewhere. The thoughts and questions circled in his head, but moved no further forward.

His door was always kept ajar at night. He saw his mother going to bed, heard her use the bathroom. He saw the silhouette of her head peer in at the door. Then she came in. He closed his eyes, pretended he was asleep. She straightened his duvet, but she did not leave. He knew she was looking at him. It was maybe a minute before he heard her leave the room and her bedroom door close.

The light from the lamp on the landing shone in through his partly open door. It broadened and dimmed as it stretched across his room creating shadows on the ceiling. One looked like a dragon or a horse. Another looked like a face in profile, with a large nose.

There was a longer shadow across the courtyard. Its source was a man standing in a lit doorway. He stood there for a few moments, then walked across the courtyard towards Charlie. He could see he had long hair, but could not see his face. He was still walking towards him when he spoke.

"Hello," he said.

Charlie woke.

For a few seconds he rode the confusion of dream and reality, but he was at home in his room. The man saying "Hello" seemed to echo in his head. He could still remember the way the man said it; surprised, yet pleased.

He slept again and by the morning, he could remember he had had a dream, but what it was had faded from his memory.

Stretched across the horizon like an unspeakable threat, the darkness was clearly closer when Raul and the Light Doctor reached Heimo. The farm was busier than it had been on their previous visit. They rode under the watchful eye of a man on the wall above the gate and past freshly dug ditches which circled the low outer wall. The yard was full of horses and half a dozen wagons. Children were playing chase around them and sombre faced men were unloading boxes and bundles of food. Olla was directing them and looked over as they entered the gate. Margreta came out to greet them.

"I am glad to see you. I have been worrying ever since you went."

"Where have all these people come from?"

"Come inside and I will tell you."

Margreta cut hunks of bread and cheese and she was passing them out when Olla came in and leaned up against one of the long counters.

"Mam, I have put Varis and Taisto of Long Hill and their families in the new barn. We have space now, but it will soon become very crowded."

Margreta nodded and turned to her guests to explain.

"People started to arrive the day after you left. They are running from the blackness. They fear it and what it may bring."

"How many have come?"

"Nine families so far. That is over sixty people including children. They have harvested what they can, but they are already talking of

66

famine, how the crops will fail in the spring if the sun does not come back. They talk of a feeling of dread."

"We do not know that it is here to stay," said the Light Doctor.

"That is true. But it *looks* like it is here to stay. At first you think it is cloud and it will blow away somewhere else when the wind gets to it. But the wind does not affect it."

"We have had a strong easterly breeze for the last week and it has not done a thing," added Olla. "It still comes on southwards."

"So they have come here for shelter?" asked the Light Doctor.

"That is right. They do not know where else to go with no towns up here. Everyone knows we are the strongest house in the north."

"Well more hands here could be a good thing."

"What have you seen?" asked Margreta, tilting her head down questioningly as if already bowing to bad news.

The Light Doctor sighed. The heaviness that had lifted at the sight of Heimo returned.

"We were too late. The light funnels were in flames and the Order was already advancing into Metsakant."

Margreta and Olla looked at her aghast.

"I failed them again," the Light Doctor said. "Then we were attacked by cobs."

"Cobs? At the pass? Already."

"Worse. It was this side of the pass on the edge of the forest. In Unama. But there were only three of them. Maybe they saw our fire."

The Light Doctor had been wrestling with whether to tell the rest of the story, whether to admit to her further failure. She needed to tell it. It was part of her shame. "And our wraith."

"Your wraith?"

"I tried to help after we had reached the pass. I sent a wraith down at the Order, but it was in vain. They probably saw where it came from and sent the cobs to look. Raul killed them."

Margreta looked at Raul approvingly.

"This is hard to believe. That the Order could have taken Metsakant. Surely there is something we can do? We should muster a force and go over."

"By the time that happens, it will be too late. The people will be dead or captive. I do not know which is worse. And the Order will have reinforced. I believe they mean to take Unama next. We need to learn from the defence of Metsakant. We will not have another chance."

"Then Heimo will be our first line of defence," said Margreta.

"Yes, but you will need light. They are sure to come here as the stronghold of the north. I can leave you the sponges I was taking to Metsakant. I will have Mondo come up too. Can you store it?"

"That will not be a problem. This house has stood for centuries and we will stand for more. It will be safe here. We have deep cellars."

"If they are making this darkness, how are they doing it?" asked Olla.

"I am not sure, although I have some thoughts. We must tell the rest of Unama. Margreta, could you come to Kunnaslaki with us? We need to summon delf from all over Unama to a council. And we need to make sure we have all the light we can. If it keeps coming, the darkness will cover our light towers too."

"You really believe the Order is finally coming again? After all these years?"

"Yes," said the Light Doctor simply. "I believe they are."

"How long before we lose the light above the towers?"

"A few weeks?"

"So little time. Very well. I can leave Kurk in charge here."

"Send out riders to the settlements east and west? Tell them to prepare as best they can, come here or go further south. We will need every delf who can hold a weapon."

13

THE CARRIAGE WAS rocking and swaying. Richard could not tell whether he had slept or just dozed. His head banged on the side of the cabin and he pulled up some of the blanket. He tried to peer outside through gaps in the shutters, but could see nothing. Opposite him, Rodon appeared to be sleeping.

Later still. They were not moving. Richard felt as if he had woken again. He heard men's voices and the sound of horses. He was alone in the carriage. He peered through a crack in the shutters. Horses were being led about in the light of lanterns. Someone called out something and laughed. He wondered what was going on. Then the door opened and Rodon entered, cast a glance at him and said "Changing the horses."

Then they were off again.

When he next awoke, a dim light was filtering through the shutters. Rodon's eyes were still closed and his head was resting on the seat behind, his collar length hair brushing the turned up collar of the heavy coat he wore. His arms were crossed and his legs were stretched out in front of him, reaching Richard's seat.

"What do you see?" Rodon said suddenly, opening his eyes and looking at Richard.

Richard looked away, embarrassed.

"Look I strange to you? You look strange to me. Who be you in sooth?"

Richard stuttered.

"I am Richard Denham, that's all." He looked away again. Rodon seemed to be more comfortable with the silence than he was. "Where am I?" he asked, as much to fill the space as to know the answer.

Rodon inhaled deeply through his nose.

"You be in the Christian kingdom of Outreterre. In Faerie."

" Ootra...?"

"Outreterre." Rodon rolled the R in the second syllable. "Do you not know it?"

"Never heard of it."

"But you ken Faerie."

Richard shook his head, slowly.

"The land of the elves, the fairies, the fair folk. Or as it turned out to be, devils."

"Right," said Richard. What was the man talking about?

"You believe it not. Yet you've been amongst those devils yourself. You were found there, running from the Pits full of devils."

Richard remembered the fear and despair which had gripped him when he had found himself in that cave, but which had been pushed away for a time by the animal urge to flee. The despair had decreased as he climbed that staircase. The fear had stayed while he was pursued. Now he simply felt bewildered.

Rodon pushed open the shutters in the window on his side and looked out. Richard gently pushed at his, wondering if Rodon would say something, but he remained silent. Richard looked outside.

It was the dull, flat light of morning under a featureless, overcast sky. There was scattered woodland and rough fields. Every now and then they would pass a wooden cabin or a rough stone house near the roadway, a collection of smaller buildings next to it. Smoke was rising up from the chimneys. It felt early. Richard looked at his watch. It had stopped.

"What be that on your wrist?" asked Rodon.

This man appeared to be able to watch him without looking at him.

"My watch," Richard replied.

"May I see it?"

Richard paused then unbuckled it and held it out to him. Helen had given it to him. Rodon studied it.

"Passing fine workmanship. But a strange design."

He turned it over and paused. Richard knew he was reading the inscription on the back. "To R. Love always. H."

"A love token?" asked Rodon.

"Our tenth anniversary."

This was a strange dream. He had known he was dreaming on other occasions, but he had never been so aware of dreaming as he was now.

"Where be your wife?"

"At home, I expect."

"Of course." He turned the watch around and looked at its clock face.

"These numbers. They remind me of a sundial."

"It tells the time."

"In sooth? And how can it do that without the sun?"

"It has a battery." He realised the time had not changed. The battery appeared to be flat.

Rodon looked at him strangely.

"One day, you can areckon me of that," he said. Then he leaned over and returned the watch. He took out a thick book from a satchel on the bench seat beside him.

"Be we that different?"

"From what?"

"I take that for yes." He pulled up a short folding table from the door, opened the book and rested it on the table, then took out a pen and some ink. "Your pardon, but I have some notes to write before I see the Archbishop."

Richard watched the countryside trundle by. There were sheep and cattle in some of the fields. At one point they went through a village. Two old men in patched old clothes stopped talking to stare at them as the coach went by. They were being pulled by six horses and they made a good, steady speed. The road was rutted but otherwise in good condition in most places, but there seemed to be little in the way of suspension and he felt his bones might rattle apart. In the end, he closed his eyes and tried to think of nothing.

14

RAUL AND THE Light Doctor saw the spires of Kyntilla an hour or two before they reached them. Raul rarely visited the city, but when he did, it always filled him with a mixed sense of sadness and wonder. It was so unlike the rest of the north country, indeed it sat on a river which was seen as the boundary the north and the south even though it was at least two thirds of the way up Unama.

It sat on three hills and was surrounded by a wood of tall trees. Three roads cut through the trees and between the hills. Raul and the Light Doctor rode down the northern road. There were unmended pot holes and in places the undergrowth was encroaching on the edge of roadway. The northern streets were largely derelict and the woods were beginning to reclaim them. Ivy turned walls into hedges, gardens were overgrown and shrubs were sprouting from the thick moss on rooftops. They passed a small, sleepy inn with a smithy attached to it.

Ahead on either side were Star Hill and Sun Hill. On their left was Star Hill bearing the Campanile, the ancient bell tower. The bells shone as the sun caught them. Sun Hill, the highest of the three hills, was on their right. It bore a large light tower.

As they rode between the hills, more of the buildings looked inhabited and gardens were tended. People nodded at them as they passed. Gardens spread behind occupied houses and onto the land around the unoccupied ones.

Ahead of them was Moon Hill. It was crowned by the high stone walls of the Citadel which dated from the coming of the Order. It had tall, turreted watch towers. There was scaffolding on several.

They reached the city square. A small market occupied one corner while a green with a pond and trees stood in the centre. They rode through and up the road to the citadel. A single warden sat on a stool at the main gates. He wore a coat of deep green with gold facings. He stood up as Raul and the Light Doctor approached.

"I am the Light Doctor of Kunnaslaki and I have a message about the north for the Councillors," said the Light Doctor.

The warden eyed them both blankly then he stepped backwards through the gateway and rang a bell with two sharp rings.

"You will have to wait a few minutes. The secretary is a little slow on his feet these days," the warden said.

The secretary was indeed a little slow, but he arrived. He was an old delf with a slight stoop, a long coat and a small square black hat.

"Here are messengers from Kunnaslaki," said the warden. "They say they have a message for the Councillors. About the north." He looked at them with interest for the first time. "I would have asked," he smiled. "But you don't look like the types to gossip your message."

"No, no of course," said the secretary. "Thank you, warden. I will take them from here. You may leave your horses tethered in the courtyard. There is a rail."

He led them across a wide paved courtyard. Grass was growing up between the cracks on the edges. On the far side was a wooden door studded with iron. The secretary turned the handle with a clank of the latch and they entered.

The sun slanted in through high windows at the end of a long chamber. Three delf were sitting on a raised platform at one end of a long table beneath the window. There were piles of paper in front of each of them. They turned to look as the secretary entered. The room was cool and all were still wearing coats. One was tall and her long grey hair was tied behind her head into a bun. The second was thickset with dark, tightly curled hair and a paunch. He wore a suit of velvet burgundy trimmed with black. The third was thin with a patchy beard. He blinked a lot and looked as though he were about to sneeze.

"Excuse the interruption, your honours, but I bring messengers from Kunnaslaki."

"Indeed," said the delf with her hair in a bun. "Then you must sit and talk to us."

"Yes, sit, sit," said the thin delf unnecessarily, flapping a hand at the unused chairs to the side of the table.

Raul nodded, unsure of any etiquette he should be following. The Light Doctor guided him to a chair. The secretary sat at his side with a little fussing and stumbling. Then he stood up again.

"I must introduce you." He held out a hand to the delf with the grey hair. "Her honour Pava Councillor, his honour Kye Councillor," he said indicating the thickset delf and finally turned to the thin delf with the beard, "and his honour Cornelio Councillor."

"I am the Light Doctor at Kunnaslaki," she began.

"Yes, yes, we know that," said Cornelio. "How are you? We have not seen you in the city for years."

"We are concerned about the blackness from the north."

"Ah," said Pava.

"The blackness, we are worried too, yes, concerned. Wondered what it was. Do you know?" asked Cornelio.

"Let them give us the message and you can ask any questions afterwards, Cornelio," said Kye.

"Of course, yes," said Cornelio.

"Raul Hunter here is from Metsakant. He came to me for help because the Order was attacking their borders under the cover of the darkness."

She paused. Cornelio's mouth opened, then closed as he blinked at the man in velvet.

"We reached Metsakant too late. The light towers had been overrun. We were even attacked by cobs in the forest on the Unama side of the pass."

"Oh dear!" said Cornelio, his watery eyes wide.

"I believe the blackness is the work of the Order," said the Light Doctor. "It is already spreading into Unama and I believe the Order will follow it before too long. The north is already preparing for war. I believe Kyntilla and the south should arm itself and be ready."

Cornelio looked disturbed. His mouth opened and closed again, but he said nothing and only looked at his fellow councillors in perplexity.

The other two shifted in their seats.

"This sounds very serious," said Pava. "Do you have any more grounds for this claim?"

"You have seen the blackness from the north. It is still distant from here, but it reaches across your horizon and it comes closer every day. Ever since the sack of Etuvara we have seen a change in the Order's behaviour, a new aggression in the border raids. At Kunnaslaki and in the downlands, we saw the darkness earlier. We could see that it began over Metsakant and that it grew. Raul Hunter here lived under its darkness for weeks and I have felt it too. Raul, please tell their honours."

"Of course," said Raul. He felt nervous talking in front of the councillors, but took heart from the Light Doctor's business-like tone.

"It filled us with fear and foreboding. We found it hard to sleep and when we did, we had nightmares. It confused our thinking and tested our spirit."

"What evidence have you that it comes from the Order?" Pava asked.

"It blocks out the light,"said the Light Doctor. "And without light we will not be able to weave wraiths. The Order kept attacking the light towers until there was no light left. We will be reliant on mere force of arms against them. That is far from certain. They are all soldiers. We are farmers and traders."

"But they have been penned up there between the rivers and the mountains for a long time. We know some sailed away many years ago. But these ones here, they are not driven by that desire to wander. They stay where they are."

"That is right, but they look across the rivers at our land and they want it. The land is richer here."

"Does it matter why they are coming? If they are, we need to decide what to do about it," said Kye. "So I suggest we return to how we will respond to any attacks."

"How will they attack? Why have they held off this long?" asked Cornelio, twitching his fingers together.

"We have heard stories for hundreds of years about how they fight amongst themselves. And I imagine they have been satisfied with their border raids. And then they have always been in dread of the sun wraiths."

"So what has changed?"

"Much. If they have learned how to control darkness, then they can overcome the one thing which has held them in check all these years since the Mages came to bolster our defences. We do not know how large an army they can muster. There are few now who can weave a wraith. The north has remained as watchful as it can, but the downland towers are not even at full strength. while the south has become indolent."

"I object!" exclaimed Pava.

"The truth is on the Sun Hill," said the Light Doctor. "Kyntilla's light tower is all but a ruin. It would need relining before it could be used and we do not have the time. And Beretska looks always to the sea. Merchant ships will founder without its light. And the darkness could reach them both anyway. Where are there others in the south?"

"I think they will just cross the river and come at us," said Kye. "They have never been the subtlest of people. If we believe they will outnumber any force we could put in the field, I do not see why they could not reckon the same."

"Do you have a proposition?" asked Pava, turning her head gravely to look directly at the Light Doctor.

"We need to watch the shallows above the Great Gorge. It is coming onto the drier season when the river levels drop so it could be the blackness will coincide with the low waters. I have already sent Mondo Keeper north to watch. We need the militias prepared and to make sure we have arms and ammunition. And we need to conserve our light. It takes a lot to weave a wraith. We need weavers up near the river and able to ride to support the militia."

"You have given this some thought it seems," said Pava.

"Heimo in the far north is already preparing itself for attack. It is two days ride from the border, but it is the safest place up there."

"I must also add, if I may," said Cornelio. "It will be hard to use the militia. If they are waiting for the low water, that happens during harvest. Everyone will be in the fields."

"He is right," said Pava. "You will not have a militia."

"The south needs to wake up to what happens in the north," Raul growled, but the Light Doctor put her hand on his arm to quieten him.

Raul slapped his hand down on the table suddenly. "The whole of Unama must be ready. All the communes must be alerted. They should arm everyone and do it quickly. We must arm as many as we can. Everyone in the north is armed. The south must be too!"

"Maybe we are imagining the threat," said Cornelio, his hands flapping up in front of him. "Maybe the blackness is something else and the Order mean no harm by it."

"I have seen that blackness up close," said Raul. "There *is* harm in it."

Kye nodded.

"I agree with Raul Hunter. We must arm ourselves. I can see to the manufactories in Asekau myself. We can warn the communes to prepare as soon as the harvest is in. We should send who we can to the north to help keep a watch."

Pava closed her eyes and bowed her head.

"Yes. I admit I am trying to pretend this cannot be happening, but the signs are not good. We will do as you say. Secretary, please prepare messages to send."

"Of course," the secretary replied.

"I have a request," said the Light Doctor. "I would like access to the Mage libraries."

"Why would you want that?" said Cornelio looking startled.

"I need to read about the creation of sun wraiths and see if there is anything that we have missed. We do not learn our lore from the books any more, but it is handed down from keeper to keeper. Perhaps there is something in them that can help us."

"The words of the Mages cannot be trusted!" Cornelio stood up, his arms outspread. "It was a Mage who brought the Order here and the others were late to our aid. If those books were not trouble, we would not lock them away."

"There are no more Mages, yet why have we kept the books all these years?" said Kye, looking pointedly at Cornelio. "I think we can trust the Light Doctor. I believe it is an excellent idea."

"Very well," said Pava. "Secretary, please could you arrange for the Light Doctor to see the Library."

"Thank you," said the Light Doctor.

The secretary stood, went to the door and waited for Raul and the Light Doctor to follow. The two stood, bowed to the councillors and followed the secretary out.

15

RICHARD WAS WOKEN by a light kick on his shin. He opened his eyes to find Rodon's arm outstretched and offering him a hunk of bread and cheese.

"It be not much, but it will keep you til we can eat something better."

Richard took it and chewed at the dry bread, more as something to do than because he was hungry.

"The road be better here," Rodon said. "We be at Collenium anon. All the manor roads be better nigh the city."

Richard must have looked puzzled because Rodon went on.

"They are the highways between the manor towns and to the city."

Richard nodded, although he was little wiser.

"The manor towns be the seats of the manor lords. The descendants of each knight of the Order."

As he said it, Rodon seemed to be studying Richard's face. Each answer was preceded by a pause. Richard felt as though he were being treated like a child.

The weather had not improved and cloud still lay over the land. Many of the fields were full of crops, others were rough pasture containing sheep and cattle. There were also tangled patches of woodland which the road often went around rather than passing through.

Towards the late afternoon, Richard saw a tower in the distance. As they came closer, it became twin towers. Soon after, a long roof behind them became clearer.

"The cathedral of St Collen," said Rodon.

They were approaching a walled town. It stood on a hill at the end of a low ridge. At its base was a line of trees which he realised was following the line of a river.

They crossed the river on a stone bridge from which the roadway climbed to the base of the walls. They passed through a gate with heavy wooden doors braced with iron. A man in a black coat and steel helmet stood up as they went by and bowed his head briefly in salute. Then they were in a busy lane of low, meanly built houses of wood, plaster and thatch. A few were more solidly built of stone.

The people caught his attention. They had thin faces, used to work and hard living. The men's hair was above their collars, while the women kept theirs tied up, usually under a bonnet. Their clothes were drab browns and greys; loose trousers, waistcoats or jackets for the men and dresses below the knee and tied at the waist for the women, often with a shorter jacket or a shawl.

They passed more buildings. These were shops with shuttered frontage open to the street. There was a bakery and a greengrocer. One was full of metal pots, another full of jars and several had raw meat hanging from rails. Leather hung in the window of one and another contained what appeared to be rifles and crossbows. Each was busy. People talked loudly and shouted to each other across the roadway, while smells of rotting vegetables and manure, both animal and human, rose from the open gutters on either side of the street.

They crossed a couple of narrow lanes and came out into a cobbled square. It was lined with stone buildings of two or three storeys. Some had tile roofs but many were thatched. A few stalls were set up around the edge of the square, but the few people there were packing up the stalls.

The square was dominated by the twin towers of the cathedral he had seen. The coach went through a narrow archway in one of the large stone buildings and stopped. Rodon threw open the door of the carriage and stepped down, pre-empting a man who had rushed out of the house and then stood back.

"Follow me," said Rodon.

They passed through a door and went down a stone passage, up a wooden staircase and along a corridor. They reached a closed door and Rodon opened it. Another man with the air of a servant, stood inside the door.

"Mr Rodon," the servant said diffidently.

The room was wood panelled with bookshelves on one side. A crucifix hung prominently on the end wall. There were several leather armchairs and two desks. At the desk by the window sat a man with close cut greying hair. He was absorbed in a book which was open on the desk top. At the servant's statement, he looked up in surprise.

"Thomas! I hoped not for you so early."

He was older than Rodon and his eyes were set deep under thick eyebrows. He was clean shaven and both his chin and nose were rather square and prominent as if he had been roughly hewn from stone and never finished. He glanced at Richard as he entered, but looked enquiringly at Rodon.

"What of my funnels?"

"We have capped the eastern funnels which point to Metsakant and uncapped the western," Rodon replied.

The man stood and raised his hands and his eyes to the ceiling.

"Praise be to God!" he exclaimed. " 'Give glory to the Lord your God. While ye look for light, he turns it into the shadow of death, and make it gross darkness.' "

Richard was taken aback by the ejaculation. The man, who appeared to be a clergyman, turned his attention to Richard.

"And who be this?"

"This be the reason for my early return. His name be Richard Denham. He was found in the Pits amongst the devils. He betells he be from Hadbury." He paused a beat before adding with quiet emphasis: "Near Derby."

The older man's eyes opened in surprise, then he frowned at Rodon and still frowning turned back to Richard and stared at him.

"Sit, if it please you."

He gestured at one of the seats and Richard sat. The other two took two of the other seats.

"May I introduce myself," said the man. "I be John Sibbald, Archbishop of Collenium. Thomas Rodon here be my assistant and a scholar in his own right. I hope you mind not, but I would pose some questions."

He smiled kindly.

"You betell you be from...Hadbury near Derby?"

"Yes," said Richard.

"And where be Derby?"

"England," Richard replied suspiciously.

The Archbishop paused thoughtfully before resuming.

"And how came you here in Outreterre?"

There was both puzzlement and deep curiosity in the tone.

Richard said the first thing that came into his head.

"In my dream. I dreamed there was the sea and strange creatures. Like birds, or people. No, birds. Then I was walking down the corridor."

"Bird people? And you walked down a corridor? What corridor?"

"The one in my dream."

"Tell me of this corridor."

He had a gentle tone and a deep, soothing voice. Richard felt this Sibbald was interested in him, concerned about him.

"It was long, full of rooms. No one wanted to talk to me."

"In sooth? Why not?"

"They didn't want me. Didn't want to give me a job."

"A job? What be that?"

"A job...an occupation...employment."

"Ah, I understand now. Pardon, but you use foreign words to me. So you have no employment. Tell us about yourself. Be you a clerk? Your hands and complexion betell you be no labourer."

"I don't *have* a job, I told you." Richard bit back the anger and put his head in his hands.

"Be not upset, Richard. Pardon my questions, but you seem not a vagrant. You be well dressed and well fed, but your speech be strange."

The Archbishop paused for thought.

"Who be king in England?"

"There's a queen. Elizabeth."

"A queen? Be the kingdom safe?"

It was a strange question. "Yes."

"And does England still fight France?"

"Not really."

Richard looked impatient.

"Pardon my questions. But I am trying to divine if you be in sooth from England. What be its cities?"

Richard looked at him.

"London, Manchester, Birmingham... Leeds, Sheffield."

The Archbishop narrowed his eyes. "What of York and Oxford?"

"Big towns." This was irritating. What did this man want?

The Archbishop held up his hand.

"A few more questions, I beg you. What does Crécy mean to you?"

"It was a battle."

"Who be Coeur de Lion?" The questions were being asked with genuine interest, politely, kindly. Richard felt no reason not to reply.

"Richard the Lionheart. Crusader king."

"Who be the kings of England?"

"Starting from when?"

"As early as you will."

He pondered a moment. He had studied these and had read about them since. He enjoyed watching historical documentary series. They passed the time.

"Harold. Alfred the Great. Canute. Edward the Confessor. William the Conqueror. Henry. Eight Henrys. I can't remember which came when. And six Edwards too I think. Or was it eight? Elizabeth the first, James, Charles the first. Oliver Cromwell. Charles the second. George the first and the others. Six of them. William and Mary. Queen Victoria…. I've missed out some."

Throughout this list, the frowns on the faces of both listeners became deeper and deeper. The names came to him as he recited, they reminded him of a time when such knowledge seemed to matter. He spoke without enthusiasm, like a schoolboy who saw no relevance in what he was taught.

The Archbishop turned to Rodon.

"Thomas, be you sure you ken not this man? Has he never studied? Never been a priest?"

"Never, Your Grace."

He looked back at Richard.

"How know you these things?"

"We were taught it in school and I studied history at university."

"God's breath," said the Archbishop in a whisper. Then he stood and walked to the back of the room. For a moment, his gaze rested on the crucifix. Then he turned back to Rodon and Richard.

"I believe you be from England in sooth," he said. There was real wonder in the Archbishop's voice. It puzzled Richard. For the first time he really looked at the Archbishop's face. No one had been interested in him for years, not like this.

"Where am I?" he asked.

"You be in Faerie, Richard of Hadbury. In Outreterre. Our forefathers thought to echo the crusader kingdom of Outremer, although ours has been a much harder history, cut off as we have been. But, your pardon, where be my manners? You must be tired after your journey. I have many questions, but they must wait until after you be refreshed. We shall talk more over dinner."

16

AFTER THE SERVANT had led Richard out of the room, the Archbishop turned to Rodon.

"He be a sign. This man be sent by God to help us. To help *me*."

"But how could he be from England?"

"He talked of dreaming," said the Archbishop.

"Yes, that was what first set me thinking."

"Dreaming be full oft named in the texts, but it be never clear. I wondered if it meant prayer, but I think not."

"We should take him to the king."

"Verily, Thomas. And we must tell His Majesty of the funnels' success. The whole of Outreterre must assemble for the last and greatest part of the campaign. Now the king can lead all the powers of Outreterre. The kingdom will be united at last."

Rodon raised an eyebrow.

"You be determined to involve the king. If the manor lords come, the king must follow. The king should have remained a duke. That title made half the wars since the founding of Outreterre."

"Yes, yes, and idle, wounded feelings made the other half. Eft soon we have a worthy cause. This be not simply the Church's holy war. The whole of Outreterre must march against the devils if we be finally fulfilling God's plan and bringing His name to all heathen lands."

He stood and walked over to the window.

"Richard's arrival must be linked to the victory in Metsakant. The funnels be proven. We will simply tell the king and the other manor lords of it and hasten their preparations for war."

The Archbishop opened the window and leaned out, spreading his hands on the cold stone of the windowsill. Outside was the courtyard. The towers of the cathedral loomed over him. Rodon waited silently for him to speak. The Archbishop turned, his heavy brows furrowed, his eyes rolling slowly around searching for an idea. It was almost autumn. He could smell it on the air, the leaves were beginning to fade. Rodon watched as the Archbishop sniffed and turned to him.

"The weather's changed has it not? We have had little rain. The waters will already be low."

"They be. I've heard it from the freebooters," Rodon replied.

"Good. Send a message to Lord Lyell to ready his men to harry the north as soon as the darkness be formed enough."

"It may be low enough above the Great Gorge to send wagons and infantry too. Using that and the Pass of Metsakant gives us a two-pronged attack."

"Good." The Archbishop smiled without it reaching his eyes. The devils will feel the whole north be alive. It will throw them into confusion."

He moved over to the desk and sat with his chin on his hands staring at the wall for a few moments before speaking.

"What make you of our friend, Richard?"

"He be unusual," Rodon replied.

"Mmm. Tell me how?"

Rodon knew from long years of experience that the Archbishop had already reached his conclusion. He watched the Archbishop's face as he replied.

"He be melancholic. He speaks little. He was hard to engage, although I bethought I saw a spark toward the end."

"I agree. He has just had the most astounding experience, but did not seem to realise it."

"You trow in sooth he comes from England, Your Grace?"

"I do. I do!" Suddenly the Archbishop's eyes were alight. "It be glorious be it not? That he should arrive, at this time. When we be planning the last step in God's plan."

"But how did he come to be here? This means there be a way back to Christendom!"

"Perhaps. Or maybe it be only possible to pass one way. Like the passage to the afterlife. My readings of the devil philosophies be unclear. But for now we must work only on the crusade. Thomas, think on it. The Order came to Outreterre hundreds of years ago. *Hundreds!* And what have we achieved? Our ancestors won a glorious victory, then they fled and hid behind the Styx. They lost their faith, they fought amongst themselves. Their fear in the devils and their demons cowed them."

"Because the demons be powerful. They can kill us, yet cannot be harmed themselves."

"Thomas, you talk like a peasant soldier. Oh the demons be powerful, yes. But *we* know they be merely conjured puppets of light. We have shown they can be overcome if we remove their light. Metsakant is proof that their defences be weak once the demons be excised. God has shown us the way." His eyes were shining and he was pacing up and down. "And now Richard comes to us at the time of our first victory. How did he come? And why?"

The Archbishop paused. His face was fierce with concentration, but one written with the joy of exploration.

"I will solve this."

His fist was clenched and his eyes were looking inward, though they appeared to be looking around the room. Rodon watched the Archbishop thinking. He could not think where those thoughts were, what path they wandered in the older man's mind. Slowly his eyes refocused on Rodon, narrowing in a cunning smile.

"Describe Richard to me. His mood."

"I have said melancholy. He also feels worthless, rejected, without hope."

"And where have you seen this before?"

The Archbishop's finger was raised, ready to pounce.

"No one I know," Rodon replied, knowing it was indeed someone he knew or the Archbishop would not be asking.

"Think again. No *man* you know."

Rodon raised an eyebrow. "The devils?"

The Archbishop's lips turned up in a humourless smile.

"Just so. The devils be in the pit. We have kept them without light and hope for a score of years and more. They are in *utter* despair."

Rodon was frowning, but listening.

"Do you not think they could have attracted him? Like iron to a magnet?" He could see the Archbishop wanting his reaction. "Do you not think their despair could have drawn him here?"

"Your Grace, the idea be fabulous. How could it happen? Why has it not happened before?"

"It has happened before, but not when I was here and could question them. As for how, the devils talk about the worlds being closer at times. Perhaps he dreamed of us. He appeared in the Pits. Be that darkness reaching out? Be it powerful enough to open a way into Christendom?"

"I know not."

"No, but I do. This be our sign, Thomas. This be why Richard came to us. It betokens the Pits be ready. The funnels be ready. It be time to take Unama! We shall leave the western funnels uncapped. They shall become the trumpets of the Seraphim and they will announce the doom of the delf and the final victory of the Order of St Collen!"

Richard had been shown to an upstairs room. There were heavy curtains in front of a draughty window, a firm bed in the middle of the room, a chest at its foot and a wooden chair in the corner. Richard washed his face using a jug of water and a bowl which had been placed ready for him on the chest, then he lay back on the bed and stared at the ceiling. He lay there until the servant knocked on the door and led him into the garden.

A table and chairs had been arranged under a leafy bower. The Archbishop was standing there alone. He held out his arms in welcome.

"I thought it would be pleasant to sit in the garden and talk. You have had something of an ordeal and it cannot be easy now either I trow. Do sit down."

The sun had come out and was gently warming the shrubs and trees which crowded around the bower providing a dense wall of leaves. A man brought out a tray bearing a decanter and two goblets.

"This be a honey drink. I think you will find it most refreshing."

Richard tasted it. It was cool and a little sweet.

"Now then, I know you understand not how you came to be here. I understand it not either. Yet, in the meantime, I should tell you of where you be."

The Archbishop leaned back, ready to expound.

"We know now that you be in the kingdom of Outreterre. Our ancestors came here over five hundred years ago. It was a crusade. They thought they were entering Faerie where of course the inhabitants were not Christian. Perhaps it be Faerie in sooth, but it be now our home. Our ancestors had to fight when they came here and unfortunately, we fight still. The devils be on our borders and until now, we had found no defence against their sorcery and demons. The failings of our ancestors have been compounded down the years as we fought amongst ourselves. Even crusaders bring their petty jealousies with them and it was our punishment for our first failure that the fires of those jealousies were fanned."

The man was talking about failure. These people too had experienced the disappointment he had.

"*I* am a failure," Richard said. "*You* do not look like one."

"And I intend not to be one, Richard. But we failed. As Christians we failed. We allowed ourselves to be defeated by the devils, to hide from them for five hundred years and to be satisfied with this northern clime between the mountains where the winters are bleak and the summers dry, while the devils enjoy the bounty of the south. But I will change that. We be unified once more and we have begun a new crusade. We will complete the conquest that the Lord intended for us. You see we be the descendants of the Knights of the Order of St Collen."

Richard shook his head, his face puzzled.

"Did we disappear from memory so quickly?" the Archbishop said sadly. The door opened again and the servant returned with a tray bearing bowls of stew and vegetables, fresh bread and glasses of wine. The Archbishop paused while it was served.

"Please eat."

The food tasted very good. Richard did not remember eating in a dream before.

"Forgive my eagerness," said the Archbishop. "But I need to talk to you some more. I need to know how you came here."

"It's a dream. Anything's possible," Richard replied.

The Archbishop looked concerned.

"You were very lucky you found us. We be a bastion of Christianity in a heathen world."

"What are the...devils? Were they in the...in the pit as you call it?"

"We call them devils, yes. Or elves. It be close to what they call themselves: delf. They look rather like us, but they be not human. I believe that when Lucifer fell from Heaven, many of the angels that fell with him, fell here. They be the spawn of those devils, if not devils themselves. They worship light, as a memory of what they have lost, but they can summon demons. I see you doubt me. But think for yourself, how felt you when you were in the pit? When they were around you?"

Richard shut his eyes at the memory. A shadow seemed to fall across the garden. He felt again dark hands reaching out to clutch at him. He remembered the feeling that everything was lost.

"I see you remember," said the Archbishop. "Did it not feel evil? Was it not tangible evil filling the air around you? And these be merely ones we have tamed and keep from the light. Though they worship light, they are dull. You will see some soon enough. We make them work here in this garden in the dark when it is safe. They helped to build this city and the roads."

Richard was still looking confused. The Archbishop leaned towards him.

"If you still do not believe, think about where you be now – and where you were only this morning."

The Archbishop sat back to look at Richard. Richard was still riding the dream, watching to see how it would unfold. He kept expecting to wake. Never had he been so aware in a dream. The clergyman leaned forward again.

"I can tell you be a man of learning. You have studied history. That be how I know you speak truly. Few people here have access to the knowledge you showed us, or care about it. I too be a man of learning. I have studied this world of Faerie and I have studied the writings of your world which was once ours. But I do not yet understand where your world be. Our history records that a devil was persuaded to bring our ancestors here. But it be not clear how that happened. They talk about a passage through Limbo which the devil had opened, which led them here. There is nothing there now except a monument where it stood. The passage itself was never found. It be said it closed suddenly."

He leaned forward. "But now you have come here. The first in my lifetime."

Richard looked up.

"Yes. There be stories down the centuries of people from your world. None knew how they came to be here and I do not believe any masters of philosophy were able to question them as I did you."

"Did they go home?"

"I cannot say for sure. Some vanished and were never seen again."

Richard looked at the garden. Was this really a dream? He could see every leaf, every flower. There were cracks and chips in the paving at his feet. Where was this dream coming from in all its detail? What was happening to him? He suddenly put his hands to his skull and pushed, pushed until it began to hurt. The Archbishop looked alarmed.

"What troubles you, my son?"

"This is a dream."

"Richard." The Archbishop put his hand out and rested it on Richard's shoulder. "It be no dream."

Richard looked into the Archbishop's eyes. How could this be real? He stood and walked over to one of the brick pillars which stood at the corners of the bower. He put his hand on it. The brick was cold and rough. It felt real enough, but then, dreams felt real while you were in them. It was only when you awoke that their unreality became apparent. He was aware the Archbishop was watching patiently.

He shook his head. "No," he said. Where was he? What was this? He felt a sweat break out on him. He shivered. This was impossible. Was he mad?

"You be not in your world any more Richard of Hadbury, but if you could come here, surely there be a way back. I have studied our histories and the writings of the devils. I have some theories, but I will need to ask you some questions. And perhaps we will need to go back to the Pits, to where you passed between the worlds."

"Will it mean I can get back?"

The Archbishop spread his hands.

"I know not, but if not, you be welcome to make a life with us. Many years ago, our ancestors did the same."

"I have a family."

The Archbishop thought of his own family. His father had been disappointed when he had entered the clergy. He had never liked his son to show an independent mind. He still remembered how his father's face had turned purple with fury and how he had brandished his fists at him. He had turned his back and walked from that house, not realising he would return only the once to see his widowed mother on her deathbed. His father had ordered him home from the seminary, but in the seminary, John Sibbald had realised, his father could no longer tell him what to do. There he could hear the word of God the Father and obey that.

"Some would be happy to be free of a family."

Richard looked at him sharply. "I love my family. I need to get back to them."

Then he stopped. His eyes clouded.

"What troubles you?" The Archbishop studied Richard's troubled face. "Please, think of me as your friend. I be a man of God as well as a scholar of natural philosophies. Be you certain you want to go back?"

Richard remembered Charlie and Helen as he had last seen them. He had stood outside and looked at them through the window of the living room as they watched television. They had been laughing.

"I was made unemployed. The company was downsizing."

Richard was looking down at the ground. The Archbishop spoke to him gently.

"Richard, I do not understand."

"I was working…" he faltered. "Business around the whole world has been very difficult. Companies were closing down. Ours didn't need so many people. They said I was no longer required. Since then I've looked and looked, but no one wants me."

"What is your craft?"

"Nothing that could be of interest to you."

"Nothing? How can you do nothing? You do not look like a beggar. There be more to you. You are a clerk; you can read and write?"

He nodded.

"You can use a sword? Can you shoot?"

He had shot clay pigeons a couple of times.

"No. A little. No one needs those now."

"How the world has changed."

Richard grunted.

"The world is still full of death and wars," he said.

The sun went behind a cloud low on the horizon and a chill fell across the garden.

"Come, let us go in."

He rang a little bell and a servant appeared.

"The sun has gone for the day," said the Archbishop. "It will be dark soon. Let the gardeners in."

The servant nodded and went away. The Archbishop gestured for Richard to stand and they walked back down the path. As they reached the house, Richard heard the click of a latch. With a rasp, a gate opened in the high wall around the garden and four men entered. They walked with a stoop and their eyes were wide as if with fright or surprise. Their skins were pale brown and they carried garden tools.

The Archbishop was watching him.

"You have seen your first devils."

"Those are devils?"

"Yes. They look harmless enough, but we keep them away from the light because they draw their power from it. They make good enough servants if they know their place. Even a devil has its uses. Ah, I see you are now more confused than you were before. There will be time to show this world to you. You will learn about it in your time with us."

Richard looked again at the devils. They did not look like devils as he had always imagined them. They looked lost.

17

THAT AFTERNOON, THE secretary, accompanied by a warden, led the way up onto the Hill of the Sun and into the courtyard of the light tower of Kyntilla. It was at least twice the size of Kunnaslaki in height and width, but there were small plants growing out of the stonework and the gutters of the buildings.

"Why is this not working?" said Raul to the Light Doctor in a low voice.

"Kyntilla lost interest in the light many years ago. They felt the Mage's betrayal far more than the north. He was from the south."

"We worry less and do more," said Raul.

"Perhaps. But now they prefer physicians and potions to the simplicity of light. A few still come north to become light keepers. They help us keep the chain of light towers working. So knowledge of the lore is rare down here. And as you say, they are too far from the raids on the border to feel insecure." She looked up at the old structure. "Its lining has not been maintained and would take months at the best to make anew."

"Why does it take so long?"

"The lining is made from leaves grown with distilled light. It is better if the light comes from the funnel itself, so it is a long gradual process. Without the lining, the distillation is difficult."

Raul shook his head in disbelief.

"We all have our different ways, even amongst the delf," the Light Doctor said and smiled. "We cannot make them use the light just because we value it still."

The secretary stopped at the central well in the courtyard and tried to lift a stone hatch in the ground next to it. It would not move. He fussed at it a few times and then the warden bent down and lifted it for him. It revealed a stone stairwell which led down around the outside of the well.

"Where does that go?" asked Raul.

"Into the hill," said the secretary. "Not too far. The library is in a cave protected from the light and the damp. Light damages books you know," he added, as if light were a careless youth.

Down the steps they went. The way was lit by windows cut in the walls of the well. Within a minute or two they had reached the entrance door. The secretary removed a key from under his robes and handed it to the Light Doctor.

"Do look after it please," he said. "I will leave the warden on the door to see you are not disturbed. There are candles and lanterns inside," he added. He turned to go, but then stopped. "Everything must stay inside this room, you understand. You can take nothing with you."

With that the secretary departed back up the steps. The warden watched the Light Doctor unlock the door and open it. He peered over her shoulder, but there was nothing to see except darkness. A dry, dusty smell greeted them; a smell of age and leather and wood.

As the secretary had said, just inside the door was a shelf containing lanterns and candles. Raul took two, lit them and held them up. He was surprised. He had expected a much larger room, but twenty paces would have taken him to the other side. Each wall was lined with shelves which reached to the ceiling. Most were full of books. A table with four chairs sat in the middle of the room.

The warden sat down on a chair outside the door and the Light Doctor entered the room. She turned to Raul.

"Would you be so kind as to fetch us some food. We will have to be here all night."

Raul agreed and tuned back to the staircase. As he started up it, the Light Doctor was turning her head to read the title of a book, her arm already extended to take it from the shelf.

When Raul returned with some bread, cheese, fruit and water, the Light Doctor was poring over a couple of open books on the table. A small pile of other books sat at her elbow.

"How is it going?" he asked her.

"Slowly. I keep being reading too much. I am glad you came back, I had become distracted again."

She closed the book, stood and went to find another.

The guard changed before Raul went to sleep and another was on duty when he woke. The Light Doctor did not seem to have moved from her position at the table, but there were different books next to her and a perplexed look on her face.

"Is everything all right?" Raul asked.

"Mmm," she replied unconvincingly.

He sat watching her for a time. There were many books. Some she ignored, some she took down and flicked through only briefly. Others she spent much longer on, sometimes writing a few brief words on a paper beside her. As a hunter, he was used to watching and waiting. Out in the forest he could wait for a long time, tuned in to the sounds of the trees, the birds and small animals in the undergrowth and the branches. He would relax in his nest, motionless until the forest forgot he was there. He would find distraction in the way the wind stroked the treetops, letting them sway, but down on the ground, there would be barely a movement.

He could not find that state in the Mage library. It was the books. When he was hunting, he did not know how long he would have to wait. Any moment could be the time when his prey would come into sight. But here, he could see the books, shelf after shelf. He could see how many the Light Doctor had gone through and how many she still had to look at.

"Can I help?" he asked at last.

The Light Doctor took some moments to acknowledge his question.

"I barely know what to look for myself. I just know I will know it when I find it."

He nodded.

"Then I will fetch some more food."

She nodded again without looking up and Raul went back up the steps to the daylight. He disliked being penned in underground. He needed the open air. Dusk was approaching with cloud coming up from the south. It would be bringing the warm rains which fed the grain of the southlands and kept the coastal forests moist. He preferred the drier forests of the north which had their season of crisp leaf fall.

When he returned, he could see some progress because the gap on the shelf which showed from where the Light Doctor had taken down a book had moved further towards the end of the shelf. Raul served her some soup he had put in his own camp pot. She thanked him, but continued her searching, putting the spoon to her mouth without looking at the food.

Raul had eaten at the street stall where he had bought the food. With nothing left to do again, he laid out his bedroll on the stone floor again and fell asleep.

He assumed it was the middle of the night when he woke again. He was awake long enough to notice the Light Doctor had moved to a whole new side of the room. He assumed she had not slept.

In the morning, he went for more food for their breakfast. When he returned, he found her waiting at the top of the well, the hatch closed and the warden gone.

"We will eat as we ride. We must return to Kunnaslaki as quickly as we can."

18

CHARLIE OFTEN DREAMED of his father. He was watching television with him, then his father stood up and walked into the kitchen. Then Charlie was his Dad, or his Dad was now Charlie. He looked out the kitchen window into the garden and there was a man beckoning to him. He had long straight dark hair and olive skin. Charlie wondered if it was one of the travellers who sometimes arrived on the edge of town. When he went outside, there was no man there, but just a tall, stone building with a strange chimney.

The Light Doctor refused to tell Raul what she had found in the Mage libraries, save that she needed to share it with the other light keepers first. She had been insistent, but he was concerned that she seemed worried.

Raul was used to his own company and did not feel the need to talk, but when they did, it was of other things: the turning seasons, the early harvesters north of Kyntilla in the arable lands before the hills of the north. All the same, he was relieved when they reached Kunnaslaki. The silence between them had been laced with a feeling of doom.

Mondo was absent in the north, having gone to visit Heimo, so only Solimo and Esella were once more summoned to a conference in the funnel hall.

"We had a mixed reception in Kyntilla," she told them once they had seated themselves quietly and expectantly. "But I was able to visit the Mage library."

Solimo's eyes lit up. He had always wanted to visit there.

"I would have liked longer, but the counsellors are suspicious of any one with a desire for deeper knowledge of light lore and I did not want to outstay my welcome."

She paused to look in their eyes. She is worried about telling them, Raul thought.

"What I discovered was fascinating. If we were to act on it, there would be great risks. We would be opening a door and we have little knowledge as to where it might lead. All the same, I have thought about this a great deal and I believe the risks are necessary."

"That is not a promising beginning," said Esella, flicking her eyes questioningly at Raul and back.

"She told me nothing," he muttered.

The Light Doctor paused. She knew what she was about to say was going to sound very strange.

"We must dream the Light Funnel to a place of safety where there is sun."

For a moment, no one spoke.

"Is that really possible?" asked Solimo.

"It is. The books in Kyntilla confirmed it. Besides, the Last Mage must have done it." She paused to watch for the reaction, but the three of them were clearly waiting for more. This of itself, while a thing of wonder, was not enough to make her worry. She took a deep breath. "But it is only possible to dream *between* worlds, not within a single world. So we cannot dream the light funnel to a safe place in our world."

"Then where to dream it to?"

"Into the world of men."

For a moment there was silence around the table. It was as if the three of them were wrestling with which question to ask first. When Solimo spoke, he only managed to repeat her words.

"The world of men?"

He said it slowly.

"Yes," she smiled gently. "The otherworld. I know you dream of it sometimes."

"To save the light from the Order, you propose to take the tower *to* them?" said Esella in disbelief.

"Not to the Order, but to the world from which they came." The Light Doctor's response was measured. "The sun, moon and stars shine in their world too. Our dreams tell us it has changed much since the Order came. Besides, a world is large and the Light Tower is small. It will be hard to find."

The three sat and looked at her.

"My dreams of that world frighten me," said Esella.

"That does not mean there is anything there to frighten us. The unknown will always have its share of terrors."

"Are you saying that I worry unduly?" Esella snapped.

The Light Doctor bowed her head and raised her hand.

"I understand your concerns, but I think it is a risk we need to take. You have to trust me."

She paused, a faint wry smile passing over her face. "And there is one more thing you have to trust me on." She could foresee the reaction to her next announcement. "We will need a human to pull the dream through into their world."

Esella stared at her.

"That is madness." She said it with finality. She could not believe the Light Doctor would even think such a thing.

"I hope not. But there is no other way. The dream must be pulled by someone who is deeply familiar with where it is being taken."

"And where do we find this person who will help us so easily?" Esella said with a sneer.

"In dreams. I have thought about this and I think we need to find a child to do it. They believe in the wonderful and no one will believe *them* should they tell anyone else."

She turned to look at Solimo who was looking at her with wonder.

"And I believe Solimo is the one to find them. Esella, you and I have cluttered dreams. Do not look embarrassed Solimo, there is nothing to be ashamed of – or proud of. It is just the way you are."

"I am not embarrassed," said Solimo. "It is just that..."

"What?"

"...I have already been dreaming of a human child. I have seen him several times. He seems to be searching."

"Does he see you?"

"Yes."

"And how often has this happened?"

"Three. That I remember."

The Light Doctor sat in thought.

"You did not tell me about your dreams," said Esella reproachfully.

"I am sorry. I did mean to, but I was trying to understand them myself," he replied.

"What does it mean?" said Raul.

The Light Doctor turned to him.

"While I was in Kunnaslaki, I read many things. The books talk about the worlds bubbling towards each other. Sometimes parts of the worlds are closer than at other times. They can stretch; they can touch. This child in Solimo's dreams might be the answer. There is already a link. He will be easier to contact." She smiled. "And I was right Solimo. You *are* just the one to do it."

Esella sat back in her chair shaking her head.

"This just seems too dangerous," she said.

"It is dangerous," the Light Doctor agreed. "But I do not believe we have another choice."

"If we must dream between the worlds, can we not dream it back to this world?"

"I have thought of that. We must assume that everywhere here bounded by the sea could be subject to the Order. And we know no one beyond the sea and we cannot reach them in dreams. If the Light Tower is to be safe, it must be not be in this world."

Before they parted for the evening, the Light Doctor called Raul back.

"Raul, did your father talk much to you about light lore?"

"A little."

"Then perhaps you may have heard things I do not know. In my readings at Kyntilla, I found references to the fourth light, the light at the heart, the inner light."

"I have heard of it."

"The references I found were intriguing. I had always thought it was metaphorical, but these talked of funnelling it. I could find no more because those books were missing."

"I always thought it was a metaphor," said Raul. "Or at best the least of the lights, and that is why we do not use it."

The Light Doctor nodded. She continued to ponder after Raul had gone. Then she shook her head, stood up and walked out into the courtyard and back to her cottage for the night.

19

RICHARD WOKE FEELING strangely refreshed. He lay and stared at the wooden beams in the ceiling. For a few moments, he did not remember where he was, but he felt as though he had slept well. He could smell the mustiness of old building. Through the window he could hear voices and shouts, snatches of music, horses' hooves and the occasional rumble of cart or wagon.

He realised he was feeling a sense of relief. Why was that? It came to him that he no longer had responsibilities. Here there was nothing he could do for his family, no reason for the fruitless, soul-destroying search for employment.

What were Helen and Charlie thinking? Were they worried about him? If this were real, surely they would have called him. He sat up, reached out for his trousers which were folded over the back of the chair next to the bed and groped in the pocket for his mobile phone. It was still on with most of its charge, but there was no signal. He thought about it for a moment, then turned it off.

He rubbed his face with this hands. The covers had fallen off him when he had sat up and it was chilly in the bedroom. There was a jug and a bowl on the chest at the foot of the bed. He poured some of the water into the bowl, dipped his hands in and rubbed his face again. Then he lay back again, pulling the blanket back over him. It smelt musty.

A ray of early sunlight reached through the window, catching motes of dust. They drifted across it, winking out of existence as they left the beam.

This was an experiment in starting again, Richard thought. These people seemed interested in him. That was unusual. Helen and Charlie came to mind again. He must have been a disappointment to them. First having no job and then watching all his motivation dribble away as he became useless to them. He had so wanted to be their rock. Suddenly he missed them terribly.

He was summoned to breakfast by a servant.

"How go you this morning?" asked the Archbishop over fruit and fresh bread.

"Hungry." He had had no appetite the night before.

"Good."

"And I want to see my family."

"I be sorry Richard, I have no answer to that now."

"They're probably better off without me."

"How can you be you so sure? But we should study how you came to be here and perhaps there be a way back for you. We should begin our investigation back at the Pits where you arrived."

"If I can go back, then you could too."

"I think not. This be our home. We have been here for generations. I think I would be...foreign in England now." He rubbed his chin thoughtfully. "Although I must admit to some curiosity. I be sorry if I bored you with my questions last night."

"You've been kind."

"It be the very least we can do for a guest who has travelled so far and in such trying circumstances. I only wish we could do more."

The Archbishop wiped his mouth and hands on a napkin and sat back.

"We should show you Outreterre. We will start here in Collenium with our spiritual home, the cathedral of St Collen."

The cathedral adjoined the Archbishop's residence on the next side of the square. After Richard had finished eating, the Archbishop took him there. The autumn sun was shining a yellow light on the grey stonework.

"Have you visited any cathedrals?"

"Some," Richard replied.

"Then I be curious about what you will think of it. Perhaps it be not so grand. Our ancestors came prepared for war, not for the building of monuments, although we have extended it the best we can down the centuries."

The twin towers which faced onto the square did indeed look more like fortifications than cathedral towers and a great wooden door, studded with steel bolts sat in the middle.

They went through and were inside a wide nave flanked by pillars. It was laid out in the cross-shape floorplan which Richard had seen on many cathedrals, but while the nave had the length, it lacked the soaring height of its European contemporaries with a lower, vaulted ceiling. The space was empty and he was surprised by the lack of seating, although it made the space feel larger. The Archbishop apologised for the lack of ornamentation, but Richard found the austere style more to a modern taste. He was shown a later extension in the chancel and here there was finer work and taller windows.

Statues were positioned between each pillar in the nave. The two closest to him were roughly sculpted and seemed to suggest robed figures rather than look like them. Windows of clear glass allowed light to fall into the interior. The weak sun was slanting in through the windows and onto the wooden rood screen which marked the boundary between nave and high altar. There was a wooden pulpit with figures of knights and angels carved around it and in the middle of the aisle was a great stone tomb bearing the statue of an armoured knight.

"What think you?"

"I like it. It's plainer than others I've seen."

"The early members of the Order were soldiers, not artists. They brought the artisans to support an army not build a cathedral. Other craftsmen would have followed if the way had not been closed. It has fallen to later generations to provide the decoration you see, but they have had to learn the crafts anew."

They walked up the aisle until they reached the tomb.

"This be William, Earl of Allingham. He led the crusade into Faerie and founded the Order of Saint Collen."

The Archbishop placed his hand on the knight's sword.

"It falls to me to fulfil what he began but that our ancestors failed to complete." He looked down on the stone knight thoughtfully. "I dream of him," the Archbishop said quietly. "He rises from this tomb to lead us to victory."

He smiled at his foolishness and his voice took on a brighter tone.

"I will be saying Mass this evening."

Richard realised it was an invitation.

"Thank you. I'm not Catholic."

"I do not understand," the clergyman said, frowning.

"I don't go to church."

The Archbishop reached out his hand to hold Richard's upper arm.

"My son, our Lord be forgiving. The door be always open. If not tonight, then Sunday when everyone will be here."

"Everyone? Does everyone go to church?"

"Of course." His frown deepened. "Does this not happen in England?"

"No. Well, some people."

The Archbishop's eyes narrowed.

"Has England grown heathen?"

A wry smile briefly crossed Richard's face, but there was a look of surprise and even hurt in the Archbishop's eyes. If this man had a medieval mindset, what would he make of the Reformation, of Henry VIII and modern churchgoing, not to mention the presence of mosques, temples and synagogues in modern Britain?

"Not heathen, no."

The Archbishop let his arm fall and said nothing more, but Richard could tell that the matter was not at rest. Richard wondered if he had offended his host, he did not want to upset this man who had befriended him.

"I'd like to come in here at quiet times and just sit...if I may," he offered.

The Archbishop's face softened.

"Of course. You be always welcome in the house of God. Come, I will show you the rest of the city."

The Archbishop led him outside into the square. Stall holders were setting up in rows. They threaded their way through piles of cloth, cages of chickens, wooden boxes, metal jewelry and a man lighting a cooking fire, and entered the dim, narrow streets which led off the square. They were muddy and smelly with foul looking puddles around which the Archbishop stepped without altering his pace. Shops lined both sides. Above, two or three further floors jutted into the street, in some places almost touching from one side to the other. Bedding hung out of windows, a child with hair in her eyes watched them pass beneath her.

The first street they walked down was dominated by butchers. There was an overpowering smell of fresh meat, especially in one where a red-faced man was butchering a carcase into joints and hanging them on hooks above him.

They turned into other lanes and Richard saw bakers and grocers, shops full of ironware and another containing a forge. Swords with narrow blades hung on the wall.

There were buildings that were quite clearly ale houses, dimly lit through small, grimy windows and already containing a few customers. Outside one, four men were sitting at a table loaded with tankards.

They were dressed in long black leather waistcoats over red tunics and wore long riding boots. Two were wearing soft black hats rather like a large beret. When they saw the Archbishop walking by with Richard, they stood and raised their cups to him in salute.

"You know them?" Richard asked.

"They be men at arms of the Order."

"You mentioned the Order before. What is it?"

"The Order of Saint Collen was founded to claim Faerie for the Lord. All the retainers of the manor lords have always been a part of the Order, despite their many quarrels."

"Why do you need an army? Who is there to fight?"

"We be in a perpetual state of readiness, shall we say. The devils still resist us just as they resisted the Word of God. For centuries our people have lived in fear of their demons and pray they stayed beyond the rivers. Our soldiers guard our borders and are the heroes of the people."

"And the rivers?"

"Styx and Acheron." The Archbishop laughed. "Our forebears named them after two of the rivers of the underworld. One flows east and the other west. They divide us from the land of the devils. It be a fair and fertile land which they squander. Those rivers, together with the mountains, help to keep our borders safe."

The Archbishop looked at Richard. "We will show you more of our fair country. Tomorrow we must visit His Majesty the King. Later we shall ride out to one of the manors. You do ride?"

"Badly. I learned to ride years ago, but haven't ridden since then."

"Ah well. You will be a little sore I think, but we will go easy and give both you and your horse frequent rests!" He patted Richard on the shoulder and laughed. Richard managed a weak smile.

20

CHARLIE WAS FINDING it harder to concentrate at school. Sometimes his mother took him in the car when he had previously walked.

One lunchtime, Max Thorpe found him. He had heard him making jokes to a couple of his mates over the previous few weeks and he had been dreading the boy taking a closer interest in him.

He had a head which Charlie always thought was oversized. It contained a wide mouth with large teeth which seemed to get in each other's way when he talked. Max was broad and had not lost all his puppy fat. He leered at Charlie.

"What did you do to your Dad? Did you scare him off?"

"Piss off Max," said Charlie.

"Just asking about your Dad. I bet he's enjoying himself now he doesn't have to put up with you."

Max cocked his head on one side and made a face. Charlie turned around and started to walk away.

"I'm talking to you," said Max.

"Interesting. I'm not talking to you."

"Interesting. Interesting," Max mimicked, sticking his nose up in the air. "You should talk to me. I might know where your Dad is."

"You know where my Dad is?" said Charlie, whirling around, knowing even as he said it that there was no way that Max would know.

"No. Duh! Why would I know where your bloody Dad was. As far away from you and your sad lives as he can get I expect!"

And then Charlie hit him. It was not aimed, it was simply lashing out and it caught Max on the jaw and by surprise. For a moment, he just looked at Charlie, then he swung his own fists at him and Charlie was rushed back against the classroom wall, knowing the blows were hitting him, but not feeling them after the first few. It felt like half an hour, but it was probably barely a minute before a teacher dragged Max off him and they were marched off to see the headmaster.

That evening at home, his mother sat him down. She looked worried and distracted. He felt uncomfortable. It was going to be a serious conversation. He did not want one of those.

"I got a phone call from the headmaster," she said. "He said you'd been fighting because of your Dad."

She left that hanging, looking at him to see if he would respond. Charlie could not think how to and did not want to anyway. He avoided her gaze and looked at a pulled thread on the arm of the sofa. It was like a loop. It reminded him of the loop of his shoe lace. His mother had taught him how to tie his laces by calling the loop a rabbit's ear. She gave up waiting.

"I know you're upset," she went on. "This is hard on you. Look, I'm sure your Dad's all right. This isn't like him."

Charlie knew she was struggling without him responding. Her words were coming out in a rush.

"Don't worry, we can be strong for each other, okay?"

Charlie wasn't okay. His mother's speech had not helped at all. She put her head in her hands. He wanted to hug her, but he dared not move. He did not trust himself not to cry.

"I'm sorry Charlie. I'm not being much use to you am I?"

He swallowed. She needed him to say something. He had to say something. Anything.

"Don't worry, Mum. He'll show up."

Even as he said it, he felt as though he believed it, although he did not know where he could be. His mother needed his comfort though. He realised suddenly that this conversation was for her, not him. He would have to be strong for her. "Maybe he's gone to look for a job. In Nottingham or London or somewhere."

They ate a quiet, simple dinner. His mother tried to ask him questions about his day at school, but their hearts were not in it.

The king's palace was in the heart of Collenium. It was ringed with a wall. Black and red uniformed guards, a silver sword embroidered on their tunics, saluted them and let them through. None paid Richard any heed. Being accompanied by Rodon and the Archbishop seemed to be enough.

The palace sat amongst rough lawn and small trees. At its centre was a box-like keep with high windows and a central tower. Around it, other buildings had sprouted in stone, brick, plaster and wood.

They were shown through panelled corridors by a liveried servant and two guards and into a wide hall. In the middle, three men stood poring over some papers on a round table. A man in a long blue gown was writing at a small desk next to them.

"Your Majesty," said the Archbishop as they entered. He and Rodon bowed and Richard awkwardly followed suit.

All four looked up. One of the men at the table strode forward. He was of medium height and looked younger than Richard. He was broad with an open face and ready smile.

"Archbishop, I heard you were wanting to see me and that it could not wait until tomorrow."

"Why wait to relate good news, Your Majesty?" smiled the Archbishop. "I will not take up much of your time."

The two men who had been standing with the king came over to join them. One was tall and slim with a languid air and a long moustache. The other was elderly and limped as he took a couple of steps away from the table to stand behind the king.

"Lord Giles," said the Archbishop with a nod to the tall, slim man. Then he turned to the other with a smile. "Lord Henry, you be looking well. I heard you have been ill."

"It was nothing, merely the curse of age," replied the older of the two. "It be not something I expect to recover from."

The Archbishop smiled before continuing.

"I have some good news regarding my venture in Metsakant. My plans and long years of studying the lore of the devils reaches fruition."

"Archbishop, I had begun to wonder if you loved the devils more than us you spend so long in their books," said Lord Giles with a smile.

The Archbishop returned the smile.

"One must study one's enemy closely to defeat him, Lord Giles."

The king raised his hand to Lord Giles before he could reply.

"Please allow the Archbishop to continue. His work has brought a unity to Outreterre that we have not seen since its founding. He always has my ear."

"Thank you, your Majesty. Thomas be newly returned from the Pits. There he received word from Lord Lyell who was returning to Percival for the harvest. Metsakant has fallen. The next part of the plan has now begun. We have turned the funnels away from Metsakant. Even now they are pouring out darkness. Clouds of despair spread across Unama. We need only wait for it to have its effect and their border defences will be as vulnerable as Metsakant's. The devils will be too weak to resist us long. The border manors have shown the way for the rest of the kingdom."

"Will this at last be the end of the crusade?" asked the king.

"It will. The Lord has sent us a sign. May I introduce Richard Denham of Hadbury. Richard, these are His Majesty King William of Outreterre and two of our esteemed manor lords, Lord Giles and Lord Henry."

All three frowned.

"I ken not this place," said the king, looking puzzled.

"Certes. Richard be from Christendom. He be from the village of Hadbury in England."

The men looked as if they were about to speak. The Archbishop held up a hand.

"I know these alleged visitations be not unheard of, but Richard is the first I have met and I have questioned him closely about his world and the history of it which few ken. He was found wandering in the Pits. The Pits, my lords. This be my sign. He professed a melancholy. I believe the Pits drew him here. Their power be strong. He be a sign from the Lord that He be with us on our venture. Now be the time."

The Archbishop stopped talking and watched his audience who were now staring at Richard. Richard felt embarrassed as the men scrutinised him.

"What be Christendom like?" asked the king eventually.

It was several hours later that they left the palace.

"I hope you were not too exhausted by that experience," said the Archbishop. Richard had felt as if he had been talking to overseas visitors in a foreign language. His answers had sounded trite to him, yet they fascinated his listeners.

"They were bound to ask a lot of questions," the Archbishop continued. "But I had to show you to them, you understand. Your coming be important. Tomorrow, you will leave the city. The rumour of you be enough. I will send you to Lord Lyell at Percival. You will need to be well rested before your ride tomorrow."

21

WHEN RICHARD WALKED out and left them, Helen had been shocked. She had been both saddened and angered. She had always expected or hoped that he would pull himself together. Yet he had retreated ever further into himself. She had compensated for it, explained it, tried to understand it; but it hurt whenever he ignored Charlie. She could cope, but what could Charlie do?

When Richard went for a walk and never came back, she had gone numb. It was a gradual process. Initially she had simply expected him to walk back in, expected him to be there when she woke up in the morning. When he was not, she had searched the house. She was looking for clues, but a part of her foolishly thought that perhaps he was only hiding, playing some game on them. Then she had waited through the day, walking past the telephone, wondering who she should call. She was embarrassed and she was scared. Eventually her fear had become stronger and she had started to call his friends. Each call drew a blank.

When that had produced nothing, she had called her own friends, waiting each time until Charlie was outside, out of earshot. Talking to her own friends, she would find herself sobbing over the telephone. Many friends came over during the next few days. The police came too, but they had produced nothing more than a feeling of hope while she was talking to them which had worn off an hour or two after they had driven away.

Her friends brought dinners. They picked up Charlie from school when she was working late. They came over in the evenings with a bottle of wine and a DVD and she would pretend that Richard had gone to bed early or was out. She kept on working because it gave her something to do, something on which to focus. It was a large chunk of normality. If she had stayed at home, she would only pace. She needed life to be normal, both for herself and for Charlie.

She watched him. He appeared to be taking things in his stride, but he avoided talking about it. She tried not to appear worried. Richard must come back. How could he not? She tried to stop counting the days he had been gone, but his absence was so much louder than his silence.

"Mondo! It has been a while since you were up here," said Kurk, reaching up to take his hand in welcome. It had been a few days since they had seen off Raul and the Light Doctor. Mondo gripped the saddle pommel and slid off.

"And you can tell I do not ride often from how sore I feel," he said.

"What is the packhorse carrying?" Kurk asked

"Light sponges. First consignment."

"You did not waste much time."

Mondo looked up at the sky. The light was yellow and sick from a low afternoon sun that appeared already daunted by the darkness arrayed across the full width of the northern horizon.

"It does not look as though there is much time to waste," he said grimly. "Where are you going to put them? It looks as though the whole of the north is camping at Heimo."

He looked around the teeming courtyard. Wagons were lined up and people were still unloading from them. Delf were outside the walls throwing up earth ramparts bolstered by local stone. Extra tents had been set up in the ground between the earth and the walls.

"Aye, it feels that way, but there are plenty more out there taking their chances or gone somewhere else. We would struggle to take more and we really could not hold them all for long."

Kurk went over to the packhorse.

"I always expect these sponges to be heavy. We can take these ourselves. We will put them in the cellar. It is dry and dark down there. Here, we might as well unload them now."

Together they slipped the packs from the horse and carried them over their shoulders through a wooden door and down some steps. The room was piled up on one side with boxes and sacks. Straw-filled mattresses lay on the floor.

"This will be the hospital, if we need it," said Kurk.

"Can you show me your defences?" Mondo asked.

Kurk chuckled. "I knew there was another reason for you to come up here." They returned up the steps and out into the courtyard.

"I am sure there was someone else you could have sent with the sponges," Kurk continued.

"There was not, but yes, I did feel I should come up and look. It is not that I do not trust you and Margreta..."

"Do not worry. I appreciate your advice. You might see something we do not. Go. Have a look around. We just do not know what might be coming our way. But I admit, I hope it will all blow over and everyone can go home."

They strolled out through the gate. Heimo stood on a rocky rise in the middle of a wide valley. Dull green hills marked its horizon on all sides.

"Let us look at it as they would," said Mondo. "Which side of the valley would you come from?"

"Straight opposite the gate," said Kurk. "The hill is not too steep for horses. And it is the closest."

They walked past the delf outside the walls, Kurk nodding at a few and exchanging a couple of words as they went. He stopped to test the wooden boards and stone being packed in behind the earth.

"Line the earth sacks along the top so you could shoot between them," he said, pointing at a mound of earth filled bags behind them. "But it needs to be higher, high enough to stand up straight behind and to make a rider think twice before jumping it."

They left the outer works and made their way across the grass, brightly lit by the low, yellow sun. Their shadows were stretched out next to them and a breeze was picking up as the light faded, making the grass rustle around them as they walked.

They reached the gentle slope of the side of the valley and started up. At the top, they turned and looked back, surveying the farm on its rocky mound below them.

"It looks so small from here," said Kurk.

"Yes, but it means you can concentrate your defences. I like the outer ring. You can get two lines of fire."

"We had no choice, we had that many people they would not all fit inside the walls.."

They stopped talking and looked about them. Mondo walked up and down the hill crest for a hundred yards in each direction while Kurk watched him thoughtfully. Finally Mondo came back to him, pointing as he spoke.

"I think there is a blind spot. Look, in the corner to the left of the gate. There is a whole v-shaped section where you cannot fire. Someone could get right up to the walls."

Kurk followed the pointing arm and squinted. Then he slowly nodded his head.

"You are right. We will chip some stones out of the corner and make more loop holes. You have earned your dinner tonight. Shall we take a look from across the valley for good measure?"

Mondo did not reply. He was distracted by a horse galloping down the far side of the valley from the north, clearly in a hurry. He exchanged a concerned look with Kurk, then they both broke into a run down the valley back towards the farm.

"If that is news of the Order coming, we are not ready yet."

"You will have to be ready."

The rider had beaten them to the gate and was already talking to Margreta when they entered, breathless. She saw them coming in.

"I am glad you are here, Mondo," said Margreta.

"Are they coming?" he asked.

"No," she replied. "Or not yet. The girl here says it was raiders. Big pack of them. They have burned Topi's place. Took the stock."

"Where is Topi? Where is the family?" Kurk asked, agitated.

The rider turned her face to them. It was blackened by smoke and streaked with tears. She looked at Kurk, then started sobbing. Margreta pulled her towards her and hugged her. Then she looked up at Mondo.

"I hear you have brought sponges. Take them and some of the boys. Go and find those ironheads.

22

CHARLIE LAY IN bed, thinking. Where would his father have gone? Where did he like to go? The man in the high crowned hat was beckoning to him again. He walked over to him. They were outside now.

"We need your help to find him," the strange man said.

"To find Dad?"

"We need your help to find a secret place."

"Is that where Dad is? Is Dad in the wood?"

He was standing in the secret wood. Through the trees he could see a tall, stone building with something strange poking up out of its roof.

Saturday morning was a flat grey day. Charlie's dream had given him an idea of somewhere quiet he could go and not be disturbed.

"Mum, I'm going out. Don't look like that. I'll be back."

"I don't like you going out on your own."

"I just need to think about where Dad might be. But I need to walk and think."

"You're like your Dad. Don't be gone long. Come back by lunchtime."

He assured her he would and went out. He took his bike and rode it to the edge of town, then along the track to the bushes where he locked the bike up. He went over the stile and followed the path to the secret way until he found himself in his and Fraser's wood.

He walked under the trees. This was a difference between him and Fraser. As far as he knew, Fraser never came here on his own. Charlie enjoyed being inside his own head as he walked there and he would meander through the trees dreamily. He loved to hear the swishing of the leaves. He loved this wood in each season. It would not be long now before it was autumn. He could smell it. The green leaves were beginning to look tired from a season of soaking up the light and feeding its energy to the tree.

He found his favourite spot on the edge of a clearing in the heart of the wood, put his hands behind his head and stared up at the leaves.

Where was his Dad? Why would he leave them? His mind wandered down paths until the gently flapping leaves above him were no more than a backdrop to his thought. His eyes were open, but he did not really see what was before them; they were inside his head following the paths and trackways of thought.

"Excuse me."

Charlie sat bolt upright.

"Sorry, I did not mean to startle you." The voice was quiet and polite. It came from a tall man in a long, dark blue coat and a hat with a high rounded crown and a brim.

"I only like to walk here," said Charlie quickly, thinking it must be man who owned the land. "I don't do anything to the wood. I like it to think in."

"It is a very beautiful wood," replied the man. He did not seem to mind Charlie's presence in the wood.

"Do I know you?" asked Charlie. There was something familiar about him. He looked different. He looked like someone he ought to remember. His face was narrow and bony with a long, straight nose. Charlie thought he looked something like a native American in the colour of his skin and his long, straight hair. The resemblance ended there, for there was something else about his face which he could not describe that was unusual. He had a rounded chin, thin, straight eyebrows and large, dark, oval eyes.

"You might have dreamed of me."

"Eh?" But even as he said it, he realised it was true. "Are your ears pointed?" asked Charlie before he could stop himself. It was quite a personal remark, even to a stranger.

"My ears are thin at the top. You have funny round ones," the man replied.

This was bizarre.

But then he was alone. Had he looked away? Where was the man? He looked around. There was no sign of him. He had been dreaming again. It had felt very real. He felt spooked. He shivered, looked at his watch and decided it was time to go home.

That evening, he took a book into the living room where his mother was, but did not read much. The telephone rang and his mother grabbed the handset. It was a friend calling to check up on her and to see if there was any news. There was never any news. They watched television together in the evening and he went to bed wondering what he had just been watching.

He woke with a start. He had just been dreaming again. What had he been dreaming of? He felt nauseous. The room seemed to spin, then come to rest. He got up and went to the bathroom without turning the light on. He washed his hands and drank some water from the tap then looked at himself in the mirror. He gasped. There was a face behind him. He whirled. There was no face, just his mother's shower cap hanging on the peg. He took a deep breath and went back to bed.

He was asleep again within a minute.

He was walking along a gravel path and came to a rock. He stood on it and as he swung his leg to step down onto the other side, he realised there was no path there, only a sheer drop into a quarry or stone bowl. He lost his balance, flailed his arms and fell. But he did not fall. He was outside the stone building with the strange roof again. He was in a courtyard with two other sides, both lined with buildings. The door in the building with the great flower in its roof opened and the man with the hat walked out.

"You made it. That was very quick. We thought it would take longer, perhaps a few weeks. We have never done this before."

"Done what?"

"Made someone like you dream of here."

"Where am I?" asked Charlie.

"This is the Light Tower of Kunnaslaki. My name is Solimo and I am very pleased to meet you."

"What is a light tower?"

"It distils light. It concentrates the essence of it."

"Cool." The man was making no sense.

"You have dreamed of me before and now we meet in a dream. Dreams are the frayed edges of reality. Our worlds are linked by dreams. Every once in a while, someone dreams so vividly that a thread wraps itself around a thread from another reality. And there the worlds join. Some can do this deliberately. Others do it by accident."

Charlie stared at the strange man who waited patiently for a response before continuing.

"Sometimes people can pass between the worlds using their dreams. I know you will think it is magic. I do not understand how it happens myself, but we know that it does. What is important is that you are real and so are we. Your world is only a dream away, and we need you to dream with us. We need you to dream this building back to the clearing in your secret wood."

"Why?" asked Charlie. He was still immensely confused. He knew this was not real, but it felt real.

"We need the light of your sun, moon and stars, in case we cannot see ours. You see the light funnel?" he gestured at the strange shaped chimney. "Light enters it and is distilled. We collect the light so we can use it later."

"Okay."

"Come. I will show you."

Charlie followed the man. They entered the building. He was in a room containing a tall brass funnel which sprouted out of three boxes, each with a saddle and set of pedals.

"Our light funnel," said the man. "We are in danger of losing our light, Charlie," said Solimo, suddenly becoming serious. "There is a blackness in the sky and it is spreading. Look."

He took him to the gate in the courtyard. Charlie gasped. The sky above the mountains was indeed black. Not black like a storm cloud, but black like ink. He felt frightened.

"What is it?"

"We do not know for sure. But we need to do something to safeguard our light. We need to point our light funnel at your sun, moon and stars."

Charlie frowned.

"They are the same ones. Or almost the same. But to do this, we need the light funnel to be in your world."

Charlie tilted his head quizzically.

"I said before that our worlds were linked by dreams. Well, we need to dream it into your world and to do that, we need you, from your world, to guide us there. You just need to go to sleep when we do in your world. You will pull. And we will...push."

"Okay," said Charlie, who couldn't think of anything else to say.

"Wait here and you can meet the others. We will need all of us to dream the funnel into your world."

He went out the front door, leaving Charlie alone in the funnel hall. Charlie went to inspect it more closely. As he approached, his reflection loomed up at him upside down in the polished surface of the curved brass. The outside of it was unremarkable. It ended at the centre of the three cylinders with their saddles and pedals. He bent and peered at them.

He heard people behind him and stood up straight, feeling guilty. It was Solimo and two women. Neither of them looked quite like people either. One woman was older and short. He thought she looked like a school teacher. She smiled warmly and greeted him. The other was young and tall with long black hair that reached down to the middle of her back. Her dark eyes stared at him with curiosity, as if she wanted to ask something. It was unnerving. Charlie felt shy and looked away.

"This is the Light Doctor and Esella," said Solimo. Esella was still looking at him strangely.

"Leave him alone, Esella," said Solimo.

"He could be a spy. If the blackness comes from the Order, then asking help from one of them could be the worst mistake."

Charlie was puzzled.

"What's the Order?"

"They are from your world," the younger woman said, in a voice that indicated that was enough to explain everything.

"Well I've never heard of them."

"It was hundreds of years ago," said Solimo. "They came with swords and said they wanted souls and gold."

"Souls and gold?"

"They wanted death and gold," said Esella grimly. "But we have no gold. We only value light. They killed delf and they stole the land. We brought the light against them and forced them back. They left behind plague which destroyed our people. Now they bring darkness."

She looked bitterly at Charlie as if it were he doing these terrible things. Solimo intervened, talking more gently.

"If the darkness comes, we will have no light. So we need light from your world to give to ours."

Solimo glanced at Esella.

"Let us go back to your world, Charlie," said Solimo.

"We all need to lie down here," said the Light Doctor. "We could lie on the floor. No, I think benches would be better. Shall we move those ones over?" She was like a teacher. "Solimo, would you move the ones in here. Esella, please fetch one from the garden hall."

They did as she asked and the benches were arranged so that they met in the middle in a cross shape. In the centre, she placed a low table on which she placed a small, clear bowl of crystal. Next to it, she put a pile of sponge-like squares.

"We will lie down on these benches and sleep," said the Light Doctor. "We will dream. The light will do the rest. We will follow it. It will not harm you," she added. "It will be just like sleeping and dreaming. Are you prepared to do this?"

Charlie looked at her. She had very kind eyes. He knew he was not supposed to talk to strangers, but he felt nothing but trust for these people. And besides, he was dreaming it all anyway.

"Yes," said Charlie immediately.

They all lay down except the Light Doctor. He could see the blue sky through the high windows. It was a deep blue with the lateness of the afternoon and showed no sign of the darkness that was visible elsewhere in the sky.

The door into the courtyard had been left open and a light breeze drifted through it.

"Think of home, Charlie," said Solimo quietly. "Think of your little wood. Think of the trees, the leaves and trees, the branches and the swaying of the leaves, the whispers of the leaves of the trees, the branches, the branches and leaves..."

It was hypnotic.

He was aware of the Light Doctor taking the sponges from the table and squeezing them into the bowl before she took her place on the last bench.

Yellow light spilled from the first sponge, silver from the second, while a thin, dark light dripped from the third. The lights mixed, the bowl filled and overflowed. Rivulets of light spilled onto the table, ran onto the floor and the ends of the benches. The table was awash with light. The room was bathed in a strange mix of light and the walls swirled with it. The light was so bright, their heads were hardly visible. H closed his eyes.

Then he heard singing. It was a high, clear tenor voice. It was a song that was the breeze through the door. It was the clear blue sky, the light on the wings of a butterfly. It was wind through his hair, scudding clouds and water glittering in the sun. It lifted him through the windows into the blue. A cloud came into view and he sailed through it and above it, into the clear air below the sun.

Charlie was in the sky with the sun behind him. He could feel its light and warmth. The moon was up there with him and the stars were spinning around it. Light flamed all around him. It was bright, but shot through with ghostliness and a sense of mystery which took his breath away. It seemed to pulse and breathe and soothe him. He felt enveloped and wafted on a wave through a world of shimmering light. He felt euphoric. He drifted back through cloud or fog. Then things became brighter again.

He opened his eyes. The sun was shining into them. He blinked and moved his head away.

I'm awake again, he thought. That was some dream.

He felt completely refreshed.

"Good morning, sleepyhead," said Solimo.

Charlie opened his eyes stared at him, wide-eyed. Solimo was standing over him.

"You are awake," he said.

"But..." said Charlie.

He was not lying under the trees. He was still in that room. He sat up and saw the door was still open. But outside it were trees. He stood and ran to the door and out into his wood. He was in the clearing, except now the clearing was filled with the funnel building. None of the other buildings were there, just the three sided structure with the huge flower chimney hanging above it.

Solimo was standing in the doorway and smiling at him broadly, like it was a joke. Then Charlie started to laugh. He laughed out of bewilderment, then he laughed out of wonder. He laughed because he believed and because the world was so much bigger than he had ever thought.

23

THE FREQUENT RESTS the Archbishop had suggested for their journey would indeed have been useful. After a few hours, Richard found his thighs and backside were becoming sore from the unaccustomed exercise. They had set off in the morning. About an hour from the city they came to a round tower surmounted by a cross.

"This be a monument to the first victory," said the Archbishop. "This be the field where the knights of the Order defeated the army of devils which came against them. What remained fled into the city which stood near where Collenium now stands."

He bowed his head for a moment in prayer. Rodon and the three soldiers with them did the same.

"This be a sacred place for us. It was only afterwards that they began to summon demons against us. And mortal men could do little to defend themselves from demons. Few thought to study them as I have. When the city of the devils was burned, it was fortunate that their books were saved. I have made it my life's work to study them."

Richard was reluctant to remount and preferred to walk, but he was shamed into riding again by the gentle cajoling of the Archbishop, Rodon's impassive gaze and the smirks of the four soldiers who rode with them. Unlike the ones he had seen the previous day, these were armed. Each wore a sword and in addition, two had some kind of rifle or shotgun in a holster on the saddle while the other had crossbows slung across their backs.

The second time they stopped, Richard tried to smile at the soldiers as he nursed his aching backside. They nodded at him, but he did not feel as though they shared his joke, such as it was. He decided he would not rest again until they reached the manor.

They rode on a well-made paved road. The Archbishop seemed to be very proud of their system of roads. He said that each of the eight manor towns was linked to Collenium by a paved manor road. They rode through farmland. Fields were divided by dry stone walls and hedgerows, while farmhouses of timber, stone and thatch dotted the land. People would wave as they went by and more than once, someone came out of a house and handed produce to the soldiers. They greeted everyone with a wave and cheered if their benefactor was a young woman. The soldiers appeared to be popular.

Eventually, one of them rode up alongside him. He was a young man, possibly still in his teens. He had dark hair and an open face.

"Excuse me sir," he began. "But we've been talking about you. They say you come from England."

"I do."

"People say it doesn't exist."

"Oh it does."

The soldier looked at him almost shyly.

"But how you can come from another world? I thought they were fairy stories."

"*This* is the fairy story."

"I would like to see England," said the young soldier.

He seemed to be very earnest and polite. Richard wanted to change the subject. These conversations were beginning to weary him. Perhaps he could change the subject away from himself.

"How long have you been a soldier?" he asked.

"These last five years, since I was a boy."

"How old are you?"

"I be almost nineteen. I hope to make corporal anon."

There was a pause. The soldier appeared to want to talk.

"How long did you serve?" he asked Richard.

"I never have."

"Never?"

"No, the army is voluntary now."

"Here, all must serve two years. Then some of us stay; mostly younger brothers who won't get the farm. But it be a good life we keep our loved ones safe."

His name was Nicholas Berwick. They talked a little more about the farm where he had grown up. He had an older brother and sister. His brother would take over the farm when his father died and his sister had married the son of another farmer in the area. There was no place left for him, but to labour for his father and brother.

"That were not for me. So I joined the Order. I want to be a captain. When you leave, they give you land to farm. The longer you serve, the more land you get. It usually be up north, but it would be good to have my own place."

"Berwick," called the leader of the squad of soldiers, an older man with a sour face and long, silvery stubble. "Let the man be and ride to Percival. Tell them we'll be there by late afternoon."

Berwick rolled his eyes at Richard.

"Yes corporal," he said, then spurred his horse and galloped off. Richard had enjoyed the chance to listen and not talk and Nicholas had been an easy companion with his enthusiasm and youthful innocence.

Towards the end of the day, the town of Percival appeared in the distance. It was built around a hill, one side of which was so steep it was mainly rock. On it sat the keep of a castle surrounded by its own wall. A green pennant bearing a golden cup was flying from the highest tower. The town centred on a market square under the castle's watchful gaze. They rode through the town and up to the open gates in the castle's outer wall. The man on the gate saluted as they passed through.

Inside were vegetable beds, neatly laid out, and two men were walking amongst them. One in grimy clothes, appeared to be the gardener. He was talking and pointing at plants. The other man was taking a keen interest. He was tall and powerfully built with cropped silver hair which matched by the beard on his chin. He looked like a man who commanded respect and used every inch of his size to back it up.

At the sound of the horses he looked up, smiled and waved, said something to the gardener and then walked over.

"Archbishop! Welcome to Percival. And this must be your oddity. Welcome to you as well. You be a long way from home and I hope you may consider my house your home while you be with us."

Richard was a little taken aback at being called an oddity. The Archbishop turned with an anxious smile.

"Rest assured I did not call you an oddity. That be entirely Lord Lyell's choice of words. He has a curious sense of humour."

"Certes, it be just my jest and I hope you be not offended."

"Not at all, I suppose I am an oddity here."

Richard climbed off the horse with relief. His inner thighs and backside were sore. Could the imagination make up that discomfort?

"I have just been inspecting my garden," said Lyell. "When I have been away, it be the first thing I do. There be something about a garden. My wife grows her flowers out the back, but here it be business. I was not going to waste some of the best land in the district just because it was inside the walls. Be you a gardener?"

"A little. Although my veg patch is only as big as one of your beds."

"Splendid. Never mind the size, it be the desire that counts, eh?" And he slapped Richard on the back. "Anyway, come in. We will have a drink. Corporal, take the boys round to the kitchen and cook will have something for you."

The keep had been built around a manor house. Lyell's rooms were wood panelled, but the furnishing was austere. There were touches of comfort in tassels around a curtain or a cushion on a bench. They walked past a room that appeared to contain soft furnishings. A voice called out of it.

"Lord Lyell? Be that you?"

Lord Lyell looked put out, winked at his companions then raised a cheery smile.

"Lady Eleanor, what now, my love?"

A woman emerged, seemed about to speak and then saw the Archbishop, Rodon and Richard.

"Your Grace," she curtsied. "I did not realise you had arrived. Forgive my country ways."

"That be right!" said Lord Lyell affectionately. "Fancy making the Archbishop think we shout at each other all the time in the country."

"I will ask you later," she said.

"Pray, do not concern yourselves with our presence," said the Archbishop.

"But what of dinner, be the rooms prepared?"

"It be all done, my love. You were out foraging with the ladies and I took it on myself to talk to the housekeeper."

"I will make something of you yet, my lord," she said with a smile. "But I was just going to tell you that Brownie threw a shoe this morning and Susan fell. I have told her to lie up. The doctor does not think her leg is broken."

"Fell off? Well I hope she took it like a son would have."

"She was a brave girl, my lord."

Lord Lyell grunted. "I will see her later and encourage her to not lie around feeling sorry for herself."

Lady Eleanor curtsied and went back into the room.

They continued down the corridor.

"I apologise for my wife. She believes I can do nothing but fight and begs me always to do other things. Then she complains that my interest in gardening be an intrusion into her running of the household. You cannot please a woman."

"She cannot have been pleased with your news from Metsakant then," said the Archbishop. "And now you be the best to lead a force south of the Styx and cause what trouble you can, sow fear before our main army be assembled."

"The likes of Tilley do that already."

"He be only interested in cattle. After Metsakant, you know best how to tempt the demons until the sorcerers are exhausted. This be the forerunner of greater things. This will be the vanguard of the final crusade."

"I cannot believe we will live to see it! When?"

"The southern funnels are now opened. Give my darkness a little time and then we can unleash you."

They entered a room with barrels set into a wall and rough wooden table worn shiny by frequent use. Lyell gestured to the stools around it and poured something that was unmistakably beer into a jug from one of the barrels. He filled four glasses, toasted their health and drank. The others followed suit. It was cool, bitter and refreshing. Perfect for the end of a long ride. Richard drained his.

"Ah, you like your beer then?"

"First one always goes down quickly."

Lyell laughed and emptied the jug into Richard's glass.

"Plenty more where that came from. Be not shy!"

Richard decided he would be better to slow down, but Lyell had the habit of topping up a half empty glass and soon he was feeling woozy. He was able to answer a few questions about beer at home, gardens and that no soldier used crossbows, but the beer had just made him realise how tired he was after the ride. The Archbishop was as solicitous as ever.

"I think the ride begins to catch up on our guest. Lyell, can you have someone show Richard to his room?"

It was early morning when Richard awoke. He was still stiff from riding. He was aware of dim light outside the curtains. He felt wide awake so eased himself out of bed and went to the window. It overlooked the back of the keep and the flower garden belonging to Lyell's wife. It looked inviting for a walk, so he let himself out of the room. The corridor was empty. He could hear a faint noise as he went down the stairs and it became louder as he looked for a door outside. The source was the kitchen where the cook was loudly instructing a boy how to build up a fire in the oven. She paused long enough to tell him where the back door was before continuing her energetic lesson.

Richard stepped out into the cool freshness of the morning. The air was still, there was damp on the grass, a smell of green that had rested overnight and the first rays of the sun were just touching the treetops. He walked around the garden, looking at the plants. He recognised many, even if he did not know their names. He walked up to the far end of the house where a hedge obscured a pile of pruned branches and some compost heaps.

He did not notice the body at first, then when he did he thought it was a pile of sacks. As he approached, it gave a start and leaped into a crouch. Richard too jumped in surprise and stopped. He recognised the man's features from the Archbishop's garden. This was a delf. He looked old. His lank hair was greying and thinning and narrow ears poked through it. His big dark eyes were wide with fear and he did not move them from Richard's face.

"It's okay. I won't hurt you," said Richard gently. "You just surprised me. I didn't see you."

The delf continued to look at him, but a slight frown came over his face. His mouth moved a little as if rehearsing saying something, but no sound came out.

"Are you alright?" Richard asked. The creature did not move. "Can I help you at all?"

The delf breathed out, then, very quietly, he said: "Help?"

"Yes, help," said Richard. "Are you unwell?"

"Help *me*?"

The question was almost inaudible. The delf's eyes shifted for a moment, then took on a look of horror. He was looking past Richard back into the garden at something. It was only then that Richard heard it. It was the cook's boy with a bucket of vegetable peelings. He walked around the hedge and came upon Richard and the delf facing each other. For a moment, the boy froze, then he dropped the bucket and raced back to the house.

"Devil loose!" he called. "Devil loose!"

The delf suddenly made a break for it. He ran awkwardly around the hedge and down towards the side of the stable block beside the house. On the cobbled stones beside the stable was a low building with a hatchlike door in it. The delf appeared to be trying to get to it. But three of the soldiers were already out of the house with swords and pistols drawn. Richard found himself running down the garden towards them all.

"It's all right," he called.

It was Berwick, the corporal and one of Lyell's household.

"You safe?" asked Berwick.

"Stand back sir," said the corporal. "It's been in the light."

"He's frightened. He didn't hurt me."

The delf was crouching now, looking between the soldiers and Richard, puzzled and fearful.

"Good," said the corporal. "Berwick, see him off."

Berwick raised his pistol towards the delf's head.

"No!" said Richard, running towards them. Berwick looked confused. The corporal looked angry.

"It's been in the light. It could summon a demon to kill us."

"But he looks harmless!"

"That be the evil way of them. Their demons ain't harmless. One of them could kill us all before you could get into the stables for cover."

"Let it be, corporal."

They all turned to see the owner of the new voice. Standing at the back door was the Archbishop, dressed in loose shirt and leggings.

"Richard, come inside. Corporal, take the devil back to its barrack."

The corporal look surprised, but the gardener had come outside too and began to unlatch the door on the low shed.

Richard went inside. He did not see the shake of the head and wave of the hand that the Archbishop gave to the corporal before he followed Richard inside. The corporal turned to Berwick and the other soldier.

"Take it behind the stables. Do it quickly and quietly. He's got light in him. Be careful. Use your sabre." Then he turned to the gardener. "Tom, tell them where to put the body."

The soldiers grabbed the delf who had not moved and dragged him behind the stables.

Inside, the Archbishop turned to Richard, a stern look on his face.

"I must warn you about interfering in things you do not understand, Richard. You be new here. You know not this world. You know not devils. They would kill you."

Richard was taken aback.

"He didn't look like he was going to kill me."

"How know you that? This be the first time you have met one of these creatures, yet you try to judge him as you would a Christian man. They be not Christian and they be not men. They be animals. They be perilous and they hate us all. You too. You be here and they do not like that. But this be our home, our God-given home. And this be your home too now until we find you a way back. Yes, we might find one some day. While you be with us, you must heed our advice, our instruction." His voice took on a gentler tone and he placed a hand on Richard's shoulder. "I be trying to help you."

Richard was staring at the wall now. He was not thinking about the delf. He was thinking about the other message in the Archbishop's words. That he could not go home.

"I don't believe this is real!" he said.

The Archbishop studied Richard's face.

"Then you be wrong, my son," he said quietly. "It be real. I be no figment of your imagination. You be here and you must accept it."

Richard could not look the Archbishop in the face. He felt tears welling up. He walked out of the door. He did not know where he was going. He did not look around, but he went out the front of the house, past the garden, through the gate and out through the town. It was small and in ten minutes he was in open country. He found himself on a low hill bearing a few trees on its crown. He sank down against one of the trees and stared ahead.

He could see hills and fields, woods, the odd cottage. The sun came out and passed across a cottage onto the line of trees behind it and away, leaving them more lifeless than before its visit. It all looked almost familiar. It was like looking at something you knew well, but trying to imagine what had changed. It was a pretty scene and there was a time when it would have given him some pleasure.

He heard someone coming up the hill to his left. It was Berwick. He stopped when Richard looked at him.

"The Archbishop sent me to find you. To make sure you were safe. Be you well?"

Richard started to speak, but his voice was a croak. He breathed and cleared his throat.

"I am well. Thank you. There's no need. Please go back."

"I have orders to watch out for you. And I must say you need it after that carry on with the devil."

He looked down and toyed with the hilt of his sword.

"I'll wait. Be as long as you like. I have nothing else to do today. The corporal would only make me rub down his horse or something."

He turned and went a few yards back down the hill and sat on a rock. Richard tried to imagine Charlie older and dressed like a soldier. He could not do it. Charlie. He put his head in his hands again. At last, he wept.

Berwick looked away, pretending not to notice.

"So what be England like?" he asked eventually. "Be it full of great castles? Be it true there be no devils in England?"

Richard wiped his eyes.

"There are no devils that I know of like yours."

"A world with no devils. Must be a wondrous place!"

"It has troubles enough of its own."

"And what did you do there, sir?"

"I – I was a..." Richard wondered how to explain anything to this bright eyed lad. "I worked for a company who invested people's money so that they could see a return on it."

"Did you sail to other lands?"

"I have travelled."

"I've longed to cross the seas, but we lost the knowledge of ship building we had."

"Why's that?"

"Hundreds of years ago, one of the manor lords became tired of Outreterre and said there must be more to this world. So he built ships and took with him anyone who wanted to see what there was over the sea."

"And what was there?"

"They never came back. They must have all drowned. I don't mind telling you, I be in dread of the sea. It be so big and grey and it doesn't stop. But you've been over the sea?"

"Yes."

"What be it like?"

"Different. I don't know where to start. I hardly know this place to give you a comparison."

"The Archbishop has asked me to look after you. Show you around. Make sure you don't come to harm. If I showed you places, would you tell me stories of England?"

For once, Richard was glad of some company, someone to talk to. In talking about home, he knew he lost Berwick sometimes, but he was rambling to keep his brain busy and to stop himself from thinking too much. They sat under the tree and talked as night fell. Then they walked back to the lights of the manor shining a welcome into the dark.

24

THE LIGHT DOCTOR emerged from the light tower. On her face was a look of wonder.

"We have never done that before. It has been many hundreds of years since anyone did it, Charlie. We are in your world."

Charlie smiled at her.

"We must look at the garden hall," she said.

"But it is not here," said Solimo.

"Follow me," she said.

Esella reached the door inside the funnel hall first and opened it into the corridor. She gasped in surprise. The Light Doctor walked behind her and looked over her shoulder. Her mouth opened and she muttered something.

"I have only read about this," she said.

Esella looked at him.

"Is that a dream?" she asked.

Charlie wanted to see what they were talking about. He walked closer.

"It *is* a dream. The books called it Unlembien," the Light Doctor replied. "The corridor has become a bridge between the worlds."

She turned to the others.

"Be careful. I will go first. Follow me. Do not wander off."

Charlie reached the door at the same time as Solimo and they both stopped. There was no corridor. There was redbrown dust covered in stones and a pink sky. It looked like a picture.

The Light Doctor walked in front of them into what had been the corridor. Esella followed and then Solimo tapped Charlie on the shoulder and gently guided him out in front of him.

Now Charlie could see more. He rubbed his eyes. It felt as though the view would change if you looked away for a moment. His eyes would pick out something, then look back and he was not sure whether something had changed. There was a copse of trees in front of them and over to their left. The trees appeared to be blurred. He stared hard and they came into focus.

The Light Doctor stopped, turning her head as if to listen. Then she licked her finger and held it up. She smiled to herself.

"That is why they say follow the breeze!" she said. "Look at the trees."

The others looked.

"Look – the trees are not moving, but where we are, there is a breeze. Can you feel it on your faces?"

Charlie could feel it. He had thought nothing of it.

"The trees are not moving," said Solimo, nodding in turn. He turned to Charlie. "The wind is blowing between the worlds. There is no wind here in Unlembien."

"But where is the other end of the corridor?"

"It is in front of those trees," said the Light Doctor. "Can you see how there is a path to it? That is the corridor."

Charlie realised he could make out a sense of shape in the air around him. He was still in the corridor. He turned and there was the corridor behind him. He turned back and there was the same view of pink sky and redbrown soil.

"Come on," said the Light Doctor. "Follow the breeze and keep out of the dream. I did not have the time find anything about the dream world. I do not even know if such knowledge exists. This is something no one has done in living memory."

"Is it safe?" asked Charlie.

"I think so," she smiled. "At least here in the corridor. Do not leave it. We may never have done this before, but the Mages did. It is how the last Mage went to your world. And how the Order came here. That is why the knowledge has been kept secret."

The Light Doctor set off and one by one they followed. Charlie felt as though he was not going anywhere, the door ahead of them did not seem to become any larger. He looked back at the door to the funnel hall from which they had come and it was already distant.

"Charlie!" said Solimo quietly.

Charlie realised he had stopped walking. He started again and then they had reached the other door. The Light Doctor opened it.

They were in a room filled with plants and trees which reached up to the ceiling. Charlie could see shrubs and bushes all around him and behind those were smaller trees and behind those larger ones. He could not actually see where the walls were.

"We have done it!" exclaimed Solimo in wonder. "We have travelled between the worlds."

"Indeed," said the Light Doctor. "The books said the corridor was like a thread on a needle. One end is anchored to one piece of cloth. The other end is pulled by the needle through the two pieces of cloth to join them. While the anchor exists, the way between the worlds is short."

The faces around her were blank.

"I do not understand it either. And that is why we must be very careful. No one but us must travel between the worlds. Enough trouble has already come of the Order. And always check the corridor as you enter it. Look around you."

"Why?" asked Charlie.

"You are entering a dream in a different way to how you enter it in your sleep. It is a living dream. It may be all dreams, it may be a particular one. Only the Light Mages understood. Perhaps not even them."

She looked at the three faces around her. They were still puzzled, but she decided she had said enough. They returned down the corridor, into the strange world of dream, and back into the funnel hall.

"We will each perform our shift as we have always done."

Solimo turned to Charlie.

"I have heard that your world is full of magic. Is it true that there are cities that float on the sea and you can fly through the sky higher than the clouds?"

"Eh? You can only fly in a plane," he said.

"What is that?"

"A machine that flies," said Charlie.

"But how can it do that?" asked Solimo.

"It....I don't know. Because it goes fast or something. Or magic!"

He grinned. Esella did not.

"This is too dangerous. We do not know what terrible things are in this world! What good will merely locking a door do? We have just opened the way for millions of these people to come and destroy our world, darkness or no."

"It is not Charlie doing this to us. Be kind to him."

"He is a human like them, from the same world. They are stronger now than the Order were when they came through. I tell you, we are opening our world to an even worse evil."

"But no one even knows this place," said Charlie, eager to explain. "It's where I come to play. No one knows I'm here. Not even Mum and Dad. And my Dad's disappeared."

His face fell as he remembered again.

"What do you mean, your Dad has disappeared?" asked Solimo with concern. "Has something happened to him?"

"No. We don't think so. We don't know. He's been depressed. He went out for a walk and never came back." He paused a moment to take a deep breath. He felt like he was going to cry. He had not cried about his Dad before. "I miss him," he said quietly. He clenched his jaw, desperate not to cry.

"I am sorry Charlie. We should not have brought you here and told you our troubles. You have your own."

"Mum will be wondering where I am. I can't stay here."

"You do not have to stay here," said the Light Doctor. Esella looked at her sharply.

"He knows we are here, " she said. "He could bring anyone back!"

"I won't, I promise. This is my secret place. But if I don't go home, Mum will worry. She's already upset enough that Dad's gone."

"Do not let him!" said Esella.

Charlie looked scared for a moment, but Solimo laid a reassuring hand on his shoulder.

"We are not holding you here," said the Light Doctor. "I trust you Charlie. Will we see you tomorrow?"

"It's school tomorrow. But I could come after school."

"We would like that," she replied. "Even Esella would like it. And I would like to see the surprise in her face when you do not bring soldiers with you."

Charlie laughed. "You think anyone would believe me if I told them? Can you imagine?" He put on a voice as if telling someone. "Hello there, I've been to another world and I made a massive building move from that world to this by going to sleep!"

He giggled at the thought of it. Solimo chuckled. The Light Doctor smiled. Esella remained impassive.

"Anyway, seeya," said Charlie suddenly.

And he was off. He ran across the clearing and into the trees. He had gone only a little way when he stopped and turned. He could still just see the stone of the building through the trunks and foliage. He felt a sudden excitement and smiled to himself. Then he was running off through the trees again and towards home.

Part 2

25

RICHARD WAS LATE coming downstairs after his second night at Lord Lyell's. Berwick greeted him.

"The Archbishop's gone back to Collenium. He wanted to say goodbye, but didn't want to disturb you. He said he'd see you when you were back in the city. Sorry, but it be just me now. And Lord Lyell of course."

Richard missed the Archbishop. He had been fatherly in his concern although perhaps only ten years Richard's senior. Berwick was only a young lad and lacked the experience which would have given weight to his words and sympathy.

A servant brought in some bread, a jar of honey and some apples. Richard stared straight ahead. He ate slowly, not tasting, but eating because it was something to do. Berwick joined him and bit into an apple.

"So what do I do?" Richard asked eventually.

"Why don't we take a look around?" said Berwick, not understanding Richard's question.

"Ah you be up!" said Lyell with enthusiasm as he walked in, his presence filling the room. "Good to see you back with us. Now then, you need activity. You need to get out. Some boys be coming in from trading over the border. Why don't you go over and meet them in a couple of days' time? You'll get to see some of the land."

In the two days before they went, Richard threw himself into activity to occupy his mind. He practised his riding and Berwick suggested some weapons training. They tried a little sword fighting, but Richard preferred shooting. Berwick called it a long-arm. It had a large hammer like a flintlock, but was loaded through the breech, not the barrel. The breech was wound open with the single rotation of a lever in front of the trigger. The first he was shown was short barrelled, like a shotgun. In shape, it was like a crossbow without the bow. He found it was not very accurate. Then Berwick showed him how to screw on a longer barrel. This was rifled.

"That be a bit of devilry," said Berwick. "We found it on one of theirs and took the idea."

With the extended barrel, Richard's aim improved. Shooting at rocks and broken jars gave him something on which to focus. He became used to the kick of the weapon, learning how to compensate for it. He practised until Berwick told them there was no more ammunition, then he put the long-arm over his shoulder and went with Berwick back into the castle.

He was quiet during dinner. As he ate, snatches of the conversation washed around him: farm stock being moved to new pastures, discussion of a newly arrived consignment of long-arms, the size of marrows in the town gardens.

Berwick woke him early and they ate a large breakfast while it was still dark outside. The cook had prepared some bags of provisions which they slung over the saddle of each horse. As they were leaving, Lyell came out of the house holding a long-arm and handed it to Richard.

"I know you've been doing some shooting. Berwick says you'll be better than him anon, so here, take this."

"Thanks, but I won't need it."

"Man, you know not what you might run into out there."

"We could do some hunting," offered Berwick.

Richard looked at Berwick, shrugged and took the long-arm. He nodded at Lyell and slipped the weapon into the holster on his saddle. He had borrowed some clothes and was wearing worn brown woollen trousers and boots with an old black military coat. He felt quite odd as they rode out of the village. He did felt as though he were someone else.

They rode without speaking. Richard smelt the air. It was cool with the first hint of autumn. He felt the horse stepping beneath him and his body rocking with it. He let himself relax, swaying with the movement of the horse. It was a comfortingly regular rhythm. The only sounds were the soft hoof beats, the creak of the saddle and the gentle jingle of the bridle. It helped him to suspend thought.

He came out of his reverie as they crested a hill around the end of the day. It was a ridge line and the slope fell away to a wide valley with mountains on the far side. On their left, was a craggy range covered in forest, gaining height as it led east, their rocky tops bitten and torn. To the west, the forest continued, but the tops of the range were rounded. They led off westwards into the hazy distance.

"We call them the Guardian Ranges," said Berwick. "On the other side is the River Styx. Beyond the river be the land of the devils."

"Have you been there?"

"A few times. On raids."

"What's it like?"

Berwick laughed. "When I was growing up, I always thought it would be like Hell. All ash and volcanoes and the like. In sooth it be rolling green hills. Wonderful country for herds. It be wasted on the devils. There be few of them close to the mountains."

He swung himself quickly off his horse.

"We'll camp here. I always like this view. There be no sign of rain tonight. And I be hungry."

They had thick sandwiches of cold pork in hunks of crusty bread followed by a couple of crisp apples and a few swigs from the water bags. Richard felt he was on some strange holiday.

They unrolled leather lined bedrolls and after riding all day, Richard found stretching out on the ground welcoming. He fell asleep easily.

He woke in the middle of the night. He was stiff and cold. There were a few clouds, but between them, the stars shone brightly. There were hundreds of them twinkling down on him. He forgot the cold and gazed at them. He felt so small.

Striking camp was a matter of stretching themselves and rolling up their beds. Richard jogged around to warm himself up.

"Our path lies down there." Berwick pointed towards the eastern side of the gap in the mountains which was just becoming visible in the dawn light. "We'll spend the night at the Falls Tower. Can you see it? The path there eventually leads to a ford across the Styx. It be only passable sometimes. This time of year be usually good because there's been little rain."

They rode down into the valley. Berwick led them along it for a way before he turned off and started to zig-zag up the slope. An hour or more later and they had left behind all sight of the valley and were in the hills, surrounded by trees. The smell of old leaves was strong amongst the trees and some were beginning to turn. The trees deadened sound leaving only the soft thud of the horses' hooves on the forest floor.

They were following a path that wound through the hills. Occasionally above them, Richard could see steep, bare pale grey rock. There were no streams to cross, but they passed shadowy caves half hidden by trees.

"I'm not used to forest on limestone hills," said Richard, surprised at himself for his need to make conversation. "Ours are covered in grass. And sheep."

"I like not this place. I usually come through here with a bunch of the lads. Begging your pardon Richard, but I don't feel so safe today."

"What's to be afraid of?" asked Richard, looking around.

"Probably nothing. But we be close to the border. I think it be all those caves and dark places even though the devils don't like dark them either. That be why we keep them in the dark. They need the light for their power."

They pressed on. The air was cool and darkness came even before the sun had set in the woody hills. Berwick picked up the pace without saying anything and Richard followed. They were climbing and suddenly they were out of the trees and winding through towers and pinnacles of rock. They rounded a bend and there, on the highest point near them was a small cluster of towers. The flag of St Collen fluttered above the tallest turret, stiffened by the strong breeze which blew over the tops.

"Here we be then," said Berwick. "The Falls Tower. There be a line of guardian towers with beacons along the range. They be a grand place to spend the night."

As they approached the gate, a panel slid open with a rattle and a face looked out at them, studied them closely, then said: "Wait on, I'll open up."

The gate swung open and they entered. They passed through a short tunnel underneath the front tower then they were in a small courtyard with walls and towers rising above them. Richard looked up to the small patch of sky above them, a darkening blue.

The garrison appeared to be small, but they were friendly enough and asked no questions. The trading party was expected in a day or two. They would go out and meet it. Richard was suddenly puzzled, but he kept his thoughts to himself until he and Berwick were alone.

"Nicholas, this might sound like a stupid question, but who are you trading with? You said they're coming from across the border."

"The devils. Yes I know it seems strange because they be our enemy. It be illegal, but it happens. It be done by freebooters. They be outside the law and outside the Church. Nobody says anything, so long as it be the freebooters. The devils have things we need and we have things they don't have. So we trade. It doesn't stop them from hating us."

During the mid-afternoon of the next day, they emerged from a winding path amongst the rocks and reached the River Styx. From its name, Richard had expected it to look hellish, but it ran calmly amongst rocks and was lined with broken rocky bluffs. It was here that the river broadened out. Away down river to the west a mist appeared to rise above the water.

"That be the Falls of Saint George. The river be much shallower here, especially at this time of year. It be the only place to get across in any number. It be only possible at this time of year when the water be lower."

Berwick pointed across the river.

"Over there. That be the land of the devils." He smiled. "See that track? We should find the freebooters up there somewhere. From what the garrison captain reckoned, we should meet them in an hour or so. Come on."

"Shouldn't we wait here? You said that's the land of the devils."

"Don't you want to see it? We'll just cross the river. Not go far."

Richard decided he was in Nicholas's hands. If he said it was safe, then he had to believe it.

Berwick winked. "Keep an eye out!"

Then he lightly touched his horse's flanks and rode into the water. Richard paused to look up at the rocky heights across the river and followed him. The water was only about a foot deep and they were able to cross in a couple of minutes. There was a narrow, gravel beach on the other side. His horse climbed the bank above it in the second attempt. They walked downstream amongst a few low trees growing at the foot of the cliff, then a narrow valley opened up below the heights. Up this they rode, splashing in a stream that ran through the stones.

As they rode up the valley, it widened a little. They began to follow an earth covered ledge above the stream, hugging the rock which leaned in over them, while the other side leaned a little away. The only sounds were of hooves and water amongst stones.

They came upon the freebooters quite suddenly. There were about thirty of them. Richard had not expected so many. They were herding cattle down the valley. The men were a grim bunch; most wore helmets of various kinds and a couple were even in breastplates. They were wearing loose shirts and jackets, wide leather belts or sashes and many were bearded. What surprised Richard most was how heavily armed they were. Almost all of them wore two pistols at his belt, carried a sabre and had one, sometimes even two long-arms in their saddle.

Their leader was wearing a stained and battered broad-brimmed hat. He had curling auburn hair and a beard. The skin on his face was tanned and his nose was broken and bony. He spat when he saw Nicholas and Richard, then pushed his hat up his head.

"Mr Berwick ain't it? Has the Order sent us an escort to the border?" Then he chuckled, but he was eyeing Richard too who, at a distance, must have looked like a soldier in his dark coat.

"We came for a brief scout be all. How be business?"

"Good as you can see. But we must hurry, I don't think the devils were all that keen on the terms of our trade!" He laughed again. Richard decided he did not like this man, but Berwick laughed too.

"They don't understand profit and loss do they?"

"Certes, they do not. We must get on."

The river was in sight when suddenly there was a cry from towards the rear of the column. The leader turned quickly and called to a man closer to him.

"What was that?"

"Up there!" said the man and pointed.

They all looked up. On the eastern heights, at the top of the steep sides of the valley, there were figures. A couple were running, but two had stopped. Men all down the column had suddenly whipped long-arms out of their holsters and raised them to their shoulders. Before Richard could take in what was happening, the firing began. The distant figures pulled back from the edge, but one was still just visible. Then bullets started to fall amongst them too. Nicholas had pulled out his own long-arm.

"Richard, ride back to the river!"

Richard stalled in confusion. One moment they had been on a scenic ride and suddenly they were in a gun battle. The firing increased in intensity. His military trained horse merely shifted uncomfortably, but Richard could feel his heart pumping and he was suddenly sweating and breathing hard. The cattle had begun to jostle one another and bellow. He could not think what to do or where to go, he just dug his heels into his horse and urged it on.

"By Christ, they've raised one!" called one of the freebooters.

He began to turn his horse when he heard another cry above the gunshots.

"They have a sorcerer. Shoot him!"

The gunfire became sporadic. Richard realised there were horses and cattle catching up with him. He risked a look behind and all were riding forward, but many were still twisting and shooting behind. And then he saw it.

Swooping down from the heights was a figure of light. It was like a diver with arms held back along its sides, but it seemed to be made of bright, shimmering, golden fire. A man screamed as it made for him. His horse reared and he fell heavily from its back. The creature was on him briefly then lifted away. The man's body was left burned, smoking and writhing. Then it was flying amongst the horsemen at the rear. They flailed their arms at it and cried with pain.

"Stand fast and fire!" roared the freebooter captain. "Shoot that devil sorcerer down!"

The men at the front fired a fusillade of shots at the figures on the hillside. For a few seconds the light creature ceased its attack and hovered above the men. They rallied and started firing again.

The cattle were in a tumult, they crashed into the river and started to churn across. A couple veered away from the herd, straying into deeper water. They were half swimming and bellowing in fear.

The gunfire from below was so fierce now that there were no answering shots from above. They all entered the river. Richard felt very exposed, but if they could reach the far side, the rocks would hide them from view of the other bank. The freebooters seemed well aware of this, but they could not fire and ride at the same time when they had to control their horses through the river. As soon as they lowered their weapons to try to guide the panicked beasts, the gunfire from above began again. Worse, the fiery creature became animated once more, reared up and made for the front of the group of men. In terror, Richard realised it was heading for him. Berwick realised it too.

"Ride!" he screamed.

Richard tried to goad the horse on, but it would not go fast enough as the waters splashed around him. It did not help that he could not look away from his pursuer. A thought crossed Richard's mind: this is where I wake up.

The apparition was only a couple of yards from him now. He could see its face, or where a face should have been, but there was none. It was reaching out as if to embrace him. He could see through it. He braced for he knew not what, then the phantom simply faded in front of him.

"Ride now! Ride now!"

Berwick was onto him, grabbing the reins and tugging the horse down the track. In seconds they were riding out of the water, the cattle ahead streaming into the rocks. They followed and had soon made cover. Berwick leaped from his horse and ran back. Leaning on the rock he began to give covering fire to the others who were still making the crossing. As freebooters made it past the rock, they too dismounted and joined him. Richard slid off awkwardly, shaking and grabbed at the bridles of the horses to try to hold onto them and keep them out of the way of the herd of cattle.

More horsemen arrived. There were a last few sporadic shots from the freebooters and then silence. The bearded captain stood looking back across the river. A couple of his men looked at him expectantly.

"There be nothing we can do for them," said the captain. "We can't get them out of there or the demon will be on us again. They'll summon another. We leave them. They be dead anyway. Mount up!"

"They have escaped!" called one of the delf.

Mondo stood up, a new light sponge in his hand. He had reached for it when the power of the first one had faded. He looked down on the gorge path and saw that it was empty. Mondo called the other six delf to him.

"There is nothing more we can do here. At least we made them run."

The others nodded and with a last look at the rocks that had hidden the fleeing freebooters, they trudged back to their horses at the foot of the hill.

With a backward glance at where their comrades had fallen, the men remounted and rode off in pursuit of the cattle which had all run ahead. Berwick climbed up on his horse next to Richard and looked hard at him.

"*Now* you see why we don't let them into the light. They use it to summon demons. There be nothing we can do against them. We just have to try to get the sorcerer who's summoned it. Without him, it cannot exist in our world. Five men it took. In how many seconds? Five good men!"

Only now did Richard begin to think about what had happened. He tried to understand the sequence of events. It had all been so fast, he had had no time to be scared, but he was scared now.

"Can they all do that? Raise those things?"

Berwick shrugged. "Their sorcerers can. Who knows how many of the others."

"Can they still get us?"

"They daren't cross the river, but we need to keep going."

"Why did they attack you? Didn't you just trade with them?"

"You can never trust a devil. I would never trade with one!"

They rode quickly, going up into the hills until they reached the guardian tower, then down. By the time they emerged at the foot of the range in open country, the sun had set and there was only its afterlight by which to see. Richard felt very tired, but they went on, stopping only once it was fully dark. Sentinels were posted.

"Lookouts? Will the devils follow us over here?"

"Unlikely," Berwick said. "Don't trouble yourself. They be watching the cattle as much as anything else."

Richard was not convinced. He longed for the solid walls and roof of the guardian tower. Their camp appeared to be a regular stopping point. There was a stone corral in the clearing where the animals were put for the night.

The freebooters seemed to know what to do and went about their business without orders. The captain came over to Berwick and Richard.

"Thanks for your help," he said to Berwick. "And you friend," he said to Richard.

"I did nothing," he stammered back.

The captain laughed. "I reckon that demon was going for the one he thought was the leader. Saw you up front, thought it was you. It could have reached me before it sank back to Hades."

Richard felt that was a generous interpretation of running away, but the man appeared to mean it. He was holding out his hand to him.

"Rufus Tilley," he said.

"Richard," he replied and shook the man's calloused hand. The handshake was firm and fierce. He was touched by the man's acceptance of him. He would not have expected a man like that to have any time for him at all. He looked at Tilley in a new way. Perhaps he was not the ruffian he had taken him for at first.

"We'll have a chance to get back at them," Tilley said, then he looked at Richard quizzically. "There be something odd about you I can't place."

"I'm not from round here," Richard replied.

"I hear that in your voice. Where be you from then?"

Richard paused. "A long way away."

"Ah well, you be welcome anyway. Another arm against the devils be always useful."

"I don't think mine would be," said Richard. And he wondered if he should say any more, whether he would lose Tilley's new found respect. He decided the freebooter would find out sooner or later.

"I can't fight," he explained. "Never have done. We...we don't need to where I come from."

"Can't fight? Don't need to? Where have you been living? Man, that must be a bright shiny place where you be from. Well, we'll just have to teach you!" and he slapped Richard on the back.

"He be no bad shot," said Berwick, "but his sword work be like my old dad at harvest time."

"A long-arm be more useful, but the sword has its place."

The next day when they were out of the hills, they settled down to camp again. The beasts were out in the open and a watch was set once more. While the evening meal was prepared, Tilley rode over and found Richard.

"Come on, man, we will give you a few lessons."

As it turned out, the lesson contained very little teaching. It was more an excuse to take pot-shots at a line of small stones on top of a larger rock. Richard used the long-arm Lyell had given him and was pleased with the results as Tilley looked on with approbation.

That evening around the campfire, Richard sat quietly and listened while the men talked. They were a rough crowd, but they seemed to accept him. He caught Berwick watching him. The young man grinned.

"Never would have thought you'd get on with freebooters, but you be a man of many surprises."

26

RICHARD ENJOYED THE ride back beside the mountains. He was feeling more relaxed on horseback and joined in with herding the cattle. He had always been a little timid around large animals before, but here he was more embarrassed to show his fear than afraid and he found himself shouting "Move over!" or "Get along there!" at the cattle as much as the freebooters.

They were on a wide trail near the base of the range when one of the animals broke away. Tilley saw, but he was on the wrong side of the herd to do anything about it. Richard was closer.

"Richard! Fetch that bitch in here!"

Richard waved and tried to turn his horse towards the escaping beast which was trotting towards the steep river bank. The horse changed course, but once away from the main flow of the cattle, it reverted to a slow walk. Richard tried to urge it on, but this only seemed to increase the horse's reluctance to comply. The steer had reached the bank and was hesitating at the edge.

"Hurry man!" called Tilley.

"I'm trying!" yelled Richard, furiously trying to move his horse faster and breaking into a sweat knowing he was being watched. He saw Tilley start to push his way through the other cattle, but then Berwick came to his aid. Cantering up from behind, he grabbed Richard's reins and pulled his mount after him. The horse followed.

The steer sensed them coming. It snorted and for a moment, Richard thought it was about to leap down the bank. Instead, it jumped to one side and began to trot along the top of it. Berwick let go of Richard's reins and reached the river bank. Startled, the steer ran a few yards back away from it. Berwick speeded up until he was riding alongside, then he began to edge it back towards the rest of the herd. Soon it realised it was safer amongst its companions and ran back to join them.

By this time. Tilley had found his way through the herd. Richard was feeling sorry for himself. Tilley rode up to him, a broad smile on his face.

"Don't tell me they don't ride horses where you come from either!" he roared.

The journey ended at a farmyard of stone buildings.

A group of women came out to greet them. They caught sight of the riderless horses. Fear entered their eyes and they urgently searched the riders' faces to see who was missing. One became more and more anguished. A rider climbed down and started to walk towards her. She saw him coming, saw the serious look in his face and stopped in her tracks. Her head was shaking. He reached her as she collapsed. She broke into loud, wailing sobs. The rider tried to comfort her, but she pushed him away.

"You told him to go!" she cried. "You told him to go! You said it would be an adventure!" Then her legs gave way and she collapsed on the ground, hugging herself and shaking. Tilley watched her for a moment, then turned his horse.

"Let's get these animals away," he said.

A pen made of dry stone wall stood beside the farmyard and the animals were herded into it. When the gate was finally shut, Tilley rode over to Richard.

"Tonight we eat. Tomorrow, you start school."

Tilley taught him sword fighting. Berwick would help, but when they were both there, the lesson would usually degenerate into an argument about technique, with Tilley berating the young soldier for his military precision.

Berwick had first shown him the long-arm, but Tilley taught him to shoot while riding. The riders preferred the shorter barrel for this. It was easier to handle on horseback where accuracy was less important.

The day climaxed with six of Tilley's men joining them as they rode down a slope towards a line of scarecrows. Each of them had to fire as they rode down. One of the freebooters missed, but Richard was able to get his scarecrow with a belly shot. No one was more surprised than he was and even the man who missed shook his hand afterwards.

"That just goes to show what a doughty teacher I be," said Tilley and spat in the dirt.

The evening was another round of drinking and eating. The jokes were ribald and the laughter was loud. Richard felt hopelessly out of practice and paced himself until those around him were so drunk, no one noticed how slowly he was drinking. He was able to remember some jokes which he thought were safe from a cultural context to tell and was rewarded by loud laughter.

The next day, while his head was a little sore, he was up before any of Tilley's men. Berwick did not surface until the afternoon, so he had time to himself. He lit the fire in the main hall, then went and sat on a fence from where he could look back at the still sleeping farm. He felt like an interloper, but these men did not seem to notice. They accepted him despite his difference. He had thought he would be ostracised for his lack of skills, his apparent education, his inability to ride or drink, but these men did not care. He had ridden with them; he had stared death in the face with them. He did not know why they accepted him, but they did.

Perhaps he could stay and become a cattleman with them until he could find a way home. He laughed at himself. What was this cowboy lifestyle? He had always enjoyed walking in the hills and it was something they did as a family, but this was working outside. What had made him into an outdoorsman? The fresh air, the exercise, the activity and the company had all reinvigorated him. And it stopped him from thinking about home.

He had ceased expecting to wake up. He knew it was real, or at least, he knew it felt like reality in a way that no dream had ever felt. He did not understand how he had come to be where he was, but he realised he had accepted it.

He jumped off the fence in search of something to do or someone to talk to so he could stop thinking. If nothing more, he decided, he would lose himself in being with these men and sharing their lives. They would be taking the cattle to market the next day. He was about to learn branding and Tilley had said he would teach him how to tell the value of one animal from another. He thought back to the times he had bought second hand cars and wondered how many of the skills would be transferable.

Tilley was awake and sitting at the long table in the main hall when Richard walked inside.

"I couldn't believe there was hot water when I got up," said Tilley. "Was that you?"

Richard nodded.

"I had porridge and thought you'd all need some too. Get me some pork and eggs and I'll show you something else that's good after a big night."

The women in the kitchen stared at him as he prepared a large breakfast. He grated parsnips and breadcrumbs, added some bacon fat and created a passable hash brown. He tossed mushrooms and a few herbs into a skillet. By the time he had finished, eight of Tilley's men were down and eyed him as he brought in trenchers full of fried pork, scrambled eggs, hash browns and mushrooms. They were soon devouring it and asking for more.

"Shoots, rides and *cooks*!" said Tilley. "How did we ever manage without you?"

Richard watched the men eat, said nothing and allowed the smallest smile to drift across his face.

27

AT THE WEEKENDS, Charlie would go to visit the light funnel. He realised he was probably avoiding being at home where his Mum was trying not to be sad in front of him, but even without that, he would have gone. He simply loved being there.

While he was in the light tower, he would forget about his Dad. It was usually Solimo on duty during the day. Once, Esella had been pedalling when he arrived. He had felt awkward, but did not feel he could leave immediately without it seeming rude. He had made some foolish remarks about the weather. Esella had told him she and Solimo had exchanged shifts that day and he would not be on until the next. Charlie had quietly thanked her and then wandered out, half backwards.

When Solimo was there, Charlie would sit by the wall or walk around the room. They would talk. Charlie found Solimo easy to talk to, more so than any other adult he had known.

"Were you ever bullied at school?" Charlie asked.

"I have never been bullied," Solimo replied.

"There's this boy at our school called Max Thorpe. No one likes him. He was teasing me about my Dad."

"You could make him your friend. Then he would not bully you because you would be his friend."

"Most adults just tell me to ignore him. How do I make him my friend?"

"How do you make other people your friends?"

"I don't know, talk to them and stuff."

Solimo raised his eyebrows and looked at Charlie pointedly.

"I don't know. Maybe I'll try it."

Solimo would ask him about his world. Charlie enjoyed knowing something that someone else did not and educating them about it, but he found it hard to know where to start. He made Solimo pick a topic.

"I had a dream once," said Solimo slowly. "I was in a room. It was very big and bright and lined with shelves which were covered in boxes. They were different sizes and very colourful. I thought I was dreaming of your world. And I had a small cart I could push. It was silver and like a cage..."

Charlie burst out laughing.

"That's a supermarket! You were dreaming of a supermarket!"

"What is a supermarket?"

"It's a shop. A great big shop full of food and things."

"It was very bright."

"Well they have lots of lights."

Charlie told him about the aeroplanes and ships which Esella had mentioned. He told him about war and weaponry, but Solimo did not like hearing about these. They shocked him.

"Don't worry Solimo. All the wars are happening far away. They won't come here to the wood."

"It is not so much that they might come here, it is that they happen at all. Violence on that scale was barely known about until the Order came."

Charlie also wanted to know about Solimo's world. He was fascinated by the Order. He asked when they had arrived.

"It was hundreds of years ago. More than five hundred."

Charlie did some quick calculations in his head.

"So they're like knights? They have swords and wear armour?"

"I do not think they wear much armour anymore. But in those days, delf had never seen people dressed all in iron. The first battles were very one sided. Until the Mages came."

"Who were they?"

"Once there were delf with greater knowledge of light lore than the light doctors. They were the Mages."

"What happened to them?" Charlie asked.

"They died. Were killed. Except one. The last Mage. He was the one who let the Order into our world. He disappeared and no one knows what became of him. We presume the Order killed him too."

"But why did he let them in here?"

Solimo shook his head.

"No one knows. But many have not trusted light lore since. They say there is such a thing as too much knowledge. So our knowledge of the lore is diminished and the books that contain it are kept under lock and key. It shows how serious is this threat of the darkness that the councillors of Kyntilla let the Light Doctor read what she did."

A quiet delf was there sometimes. Charlie found out his name was Raul. His hair was usually tied back in a ponytail and he wore a coat which came down to his thighs. Solimo said he was a hunter. He came to see Charlie the first time he arrived and looked at him curiously through narrowed eyes.

"I have never met a child of men before," he said to no one in particular.

"He is a child much like delf children," said Solimo.

"You say that, but I have seen what they grow into."

"Charlie will not grow into one of them," Solimo replied.

"What are they like?" Charlie asked.

"They are scum," said Raul.

Charlie was taken aback.

"Raul, he is a child," said Solimo.

"Are the men in your world better people? Have they stopped taking the lands and lives of others?"

Charlie thought of watching the News on television and of films he had seen.

"I don't understand much about what happens. It's what the adults watch on television. But there are lots of nice people. People have been helping my Mum since my Dad disappeared."

"Your father has disappeared? What happened?"

"We don't know. He was depressed and one day he didn't come back."

Raul seemed to soften.

"So you have no father?" he said.

"I do," said Charlie fiercely. "We just don't know where he is."

One day Raul had been out, but came back with some dead animals hanging over his saddle.

"Can I see your rifle?" Charlie asked.

"My what?" said Raul.

"That," said Charlie, gesturing towards the saddle holster.

"My long-arm," said Raul. "What did you call it?"

"We call it a rifle."

"Your friends in the Order used to call it an arquebus. Do you have different weapons in your world then?"

"I don't know much about guns," Charlie said evasively. He had seen enough of Raul's distrust of humans to realise it may not be a good idea to mention tanks and rocket launchers to him.

"Well, your friends in the Order brought a weapon called an arquebus with them. When the delf found it, our craftsmen improved it. They stole the idea back of course."

He had stalked off after that and Charlie watched him go. He admired Raul. He admired him even more when Solimo told him about Evatura and Metsakant. In a way, he wanted to be like him because he seemed brave and confident and like he did not need anyone else. But this meant he was remote in a way Solimo was not and he liked Solimo a great deal.

One conversation he had with Solimo haunted him.

"Solimo," said Charlie. "What would happen if the darkness came and stayed forever?"

"Living in the dark would be terrible," said Solimo.

"But you could have candles and fires," Charlie suggested.

"Perhaps, while the candles and firewood lasted. But to live we need cosmic fire born in a light cradle. The light from a fire is but a faint echo of true light."

"A light cradle?"

"Where all the light in the cosmos is made. Without light we have terrible nightmares as the soul starves of light. Not nightmares as you have them, but dark dreams of despair. We need light like we need food."

"Aren't you human then?"

"Of course not. We are delf."

"Flowers need light, don't they? Are you like them?"

"No," he replied. Then he smiled in his gentle way. "Well, maybe a little."

Then Solimo had started to sing. He often sang, but this song gave Charlie goose bumps. It grew from haunting quietness. As he sang, pulsing sounds came and went. Each was different, but he would come back to them and pick them up again until Solimo's voice was filling the room, each sound still echoing as he began another and left that to echo until there seemed to be too many voices in the room to count. And then he realised that Solimo was no longer singing and the echoes were dying one by one until eventually there was only the quiet whirring of the pedals in the still silence of the funnel room.

One weekend he was still there when the Light Doctor came in for a shift at the funnel. The two delf pedalled side by side for a while and all shared a companionable silence. Charlie found the funnel hall to be very relaxing and he would fall into a daydream with his thoughts wandering where they wanted.

Then Solimo climbed off his saddle. He caught the Light Doctor's eye and she gave him a little nod.

"Charlie. Come and help me water the plants."

The door at the back of the funnel hall led into the corridor which led to the garden hall. Charlie had only been through it the once when the funnel hall had been dreamed through. Solimo stooped and opened a hatch in the side of his pedal station and pulled out a sponge. Then he closed the hatch, stood up straight and went towards the door at the back of the room.

Charlie followed him. The corridor both frightened and fascinated him. Solimo had now been through it many times and seemed to be used to it, but Charlie felt disorientated as it opened out into the blurred landscape of Unlembien. He went close behind Solimo, afraid to be left in the corridor alone and trying not to look around him.

They reached the far end of the corridor and Solimo opened the door. It was dark. The only light was what had followed them in when they opened the door. He could just make out what appeared at first to be a forest and dense undergrowth.

Solimo motioned with his hand and Charlie noticed a bench to his left. He sat on it.

"Shall we make it rain?" asked Solimo.

Charlie turned to him and he was smiling. He put his hand up to a rope hanging to his right and pulled it. Then he sat down next to Charlie.

"I love this," he said.

And it began to rain. It did not fall on them where they sat by the door, but they could hear it. It was a soft sound of rain on leaves. It calmed and soothed. It sounded like an evening in late summer when a rain cloud has wandered overhead and drops a light shower on the garden. Charlie turned to Solimo. He had his eyes closed.

"Are you asleep?" he asked.

"Shh. I am listening," he said.

So Charlie listened too. He imagined he was outside or camping with his Dad and there was rain. Patter-patter-patter it went, without interruption. It was mesmerising, it was soothing. It sounded like magic.

It began to ease, then fade, then it ceased altogether. They both took a few moments to open their eyes. Solimo turned to Charlie again with a smile.

"Was that not wonderful?"

"How did you do it?"

"It is rainwater. The funnel catches it anyway so we channel it off and keep it to water the plants."

"But why are they in the dark? I thought plants needed light."

"They do. I will show you something else. These are special."

Charlie's eyes had become accustomed to the dim light and he could see there was a table in the middle of the room and on it, there was a plain glass bowl.

"Come," said Solimo.

Charlie followed him to the table. He handed Charlie the sponge. It felt dry.

"This is a light sponge," said Solimo. "It collects the distilled light. A light keeper always carries a sponge of each light as they could be needed at any time, but most are kept here in the light tower. Now watch."

Solimo took the sponge in his hands. Charlie did not notice him do anything, but then the sponge was glowing and from its lower corner there was a bright light that was pouring out of the sponge and into the bowl. Like water. The room was suddenly bathed in fresh, golden sunlight. Charlie was amazed. He looked around him. The sun was in the glass bowl and every plant in the room seemed to have come alive. They had lifted their heads and their branches. They seemed to be holding their arms up to the light and Charlie imagined that they too had their eyes closed and were enjoying this bath of light as they had enjoyed the shower of rain.

The raindrops glistened and the light was the same as when the sun comes out after a rain shower. There was a smell of freshness as if all was right with the world and the growing darkness in the sky could be forgotten.

The light was just like the sun, only it was different. Charlie could not tell if it was because they were inside or because there was something different about the light. After a few minutes, it began to fade. As it did so, the trees relaxed with it, or it may have been the effect of the shadows as they dropped behind the branches.

There was no dusk, the sun had gone down.

"That was amazing!" said Charlie. "How do you get the sun in the sponge?"

"It is distilled light. I know it is new to you, but it still amazes me that in your world you can do all the things you have told me about, but you cannot distil light. It is like...concentrated light. Only it is not concentrated. It is the essence of the light. The funnels catch it."

"But why don't you just have a glass roof? This is like a greenhouse and they're made of glass."

"Some are. This one is made of stone and we bring the light in. I told you they were special plants and they are because they have been grown almost entirely with the essence of light. They need it as much as the water."

He picked up another of the sponges.

"Watch. There is more."

He squeezed the second sponge into the bowl.

"Moonlight," he said.

It fell with slow quietness. The room was filled with a silver light that took the colour out of the garden. It was black and grey and silver. It was as if they were in a different place. Charlie stared at it and as he stared, it seemed as if it moved to envelop him. He became lost in the still ghostliness of the garden. He thought of his parents again and was filled with a great warmth for them. He had to find his Dad. He would find him for himself and for his Mum. And he would find him for his Dad too, he realised. But then the moonlight was fading too as the light in the bowl ran out.

Solimo took the last sponge and squeezed it.

"Starlight," he murmured.

The light streaked out in thin lines, secret and magical. It was a light that gave no shadows, but still there were shapes in the room, although they could have been any shapes at all. What he felt most of all was presence; the presence of the garden. Ideas shot around his head. A maths question he had struggled with came to him unbidden and suddenly he knew how to find out the answer. It was quite clear. Why had he not thought of that before?

Charlie sat for a time in the dark after the light had faded. He felt unusual, but he could not explain quite how he felt. He felt as if something exciting had just happened, but he did not know what it was.

"How do you feel?" asked Solimo.

"Funny," said Charlie. "Actually, I feel like running around and shouting."

Solimo smiled. "It is rather wonderful is it not? I think it is rather like the sun coming out after months of winter. You feel as though you could answer any question if you only had the time to think about them."

Charlie thought for a moment.

"So there are three types of light? I suppose there are."

"These are the lights born of the cosmos which we cannot be without. I have heard there is also another light, the light within. Perhaps it means the soul, but that knowledge is lost with the Mages."

"But why do you catch all this light? What is the garden for?"

"You are full of questions."

"Well if you didn't want me asking, why did you show me?"

"I do want you to ask, Charlie," Solimo smiled. "Some of these plants we use in our healing. We make preparations in the laboratorium through the door over there." He pointed to a door on the far side, all but hidden by the greenery. "We eat the fruit of some of them too. We use the leaves to line the funnel itself, it helps our ability to weave, the rest..."

"Weave? What, like clothes?" Charlie interrupted.

"No. We weave light. Or some of the keepers can. I do very little. It is higher light lore and I am not so comfortable with it."

"What's it for?"

"We use it for helping people, for healing their minds. But sunlight can also be used as a weapon. Sunlight can burn. I do not like this. I am a healer, not a killer."

There was silence in the room between them for a while as both were lost in their own thoughts.

"Can I have a go at making that light?" said Charlie.

"Not today. They cannot have too much light. But maybe tomorrow."

Solimo was as good as his word. The next day, he let Charlie pull the rope that started the rain shower. Then they went to the table and Solimo handed him a sponge. Charlie tried to squeeze it.

"Ow!" he said and dropped it suddenly. "It's really hot!"

"More gently," he said. "Slowly and quietly. As if you do not want the sponge to realise it is being squashed. Ignore the heat, it will not really burn you."

Gingerly, Charlie tried once more.

He dropped it again. It burned like pin pricks of ice drilling into his fingers.

"It was hot!"

"It just feels hot. It is the density of the light. Try again."

He did, but it was so difficult to squeeze when it felt as though it were burning him. No light came. He looked downcast. Solimo chuckled.

"If it was as easy as that, everyone would be a light keeper. Do not worry. It takes time. You did very well. We have to learn. You can try again tomorrow. I had better do this one now. If you squeeze it too much you get heat, but not enough light to feed the plants."

So each time he was there, Charlie tried to squeeze the light sponge, but he found it difficult to think past the burning heat. His body would react quicker than his mind and he would drop the sponge instinctively. Then he would peer at his hands in the faint light, expecting them to be red and sore. Solimo continued to encourage him. To tell him it was not a heat that burned.

"You need to think differently," he told Charlie one day as he pedalled. "You need to think with your hands as well as your head. You need to think through the heat and the sensation. It is only the first level of thought. There are many more."

Charlie was in his usual place, sitting cross-legged on the floor against the wall.

"What else can you do?" he asked.

"Doses of light can be used as a kind of medicine. Each has a different effect. A little like what you see happening to this garden. It is life-giving to these plants."

"So it can give life?" said Charlie with awe.

"No. Not life. But in people it can bring back a feeling of joy and that is medicinal in itself. Surprisingly so."

"What about moonlight and starlight?"

"Their effect is different. Moonlight is a strange one. It brings on a kind of madness which changes from person to person. For some it makes them sad and others it makes them feel love. This is what makes the Light Doctor skilled. She knows how much of what kind of light is needed and when. I am still learning, but this is what I prefer. It is called the lesser lore, but to me it is very important. It is how Light Keepers have served the delf for as long as we can remember."

"What about starlight?"

"Starlight is the light of the imagination. It brings out ideas from deep inside where other parts of your mind block them out."

"Why does your mind block them out?"

"Because it is too busy. The artist is the one who can forget the everyday. They are like dreamers because they create new worlds. And sometimes they can actually visit them."

Charlie was silent for a while, thinking. Solimo continued to pedal.

"Are you saying I created this world by dreaming it?"

"No. But dreams are powerful things in the right hands. We have scraps of lore about dreams creating, but most of that was lost with the Mages."

"Tell me more about them."

"A Mage was one who was most skilled with light lore. They were master practitioners of our art. Light keepers live among the people, but the Mages would live to study. They would teach the Light Doctors and the other light keepers. They kept themselves to themselves in the mountains. As I told you, there are none left now."

Solimo stopped and looked thoughtful. Then he shook his head.

"It's funny that something so big in your history is a mystery," said Charlie.

"It is," Solimo agreed. "It is not much of a story when no one knows what it is. Many delf cursed him for bringing the Order. I like to think there is more to the story than we know about. Why would the Mage have deliberately brought the Order?"

"You're right. Something must have happened. Maybe he thought they were nice. Like me."

"Maybe," said Solimo. And he carried on pedalling.

Sometimes Solimo would let him pedal. This was something Charlie was good at. Solimo had been amazed.

"But it's like a bike," Charlie explained. The seat's a bit different and it looks funny, but it's pedals and cogs and gears and stuff."

"What is a bike?"

"It's like this, only it's got two wheels and when you pedal it, you go places. And you can go really fast down hills and use the gears to get up hills."

"We have horses and wagons. The Order brought those too. I do not know what we would have done without horses. People must have walked everywhere before." He smiled. "I still like walking."

"You sound like my Mum," Charlie said. "She tells me off when I want to go to school in the car when it's raining. Then Dad says that if

God had meant us to drive around in cars when it was raining, he wouldn't have given us raincoats."

Charlie smiled. Solimo did not understand the joke, but it had sounded funny and he laughed.

"I wonder where Dad is," said Charlie, the smile vanishing as quickly as it came. Suddenly Charlie looked so small, Solimo thought.

"Keep pedalling," he said. "The sun has just come out. Pedal faster. You need to make the most of the light."

Charlie awoke from his reverie, grinned, gritted his teeth and pedalled harder.

"You see! I can do it. And I'll soon be squeezing sponges and becoming a light keeper!"

Solimo laughed.

Charlie was indeed becoming better with the sponges. After a few weeks, he had a taste of success. As he squeezed, he saw a glow around his fingers.

"Look! I've done it!"

"Very good. That is the start of it. You should keep at it. When you are older, you could learn about the lore."

"Those medicines sound cool. But I can't believe you go through all this pedalling just to cheer people up a bit."

"It is more than that. There is higher lore. And perhaps lore beyond that where light and dreams weave themselves. But that too is lost now."

"But you still weave it?"

"We do, but maybe there was once more. The Light Doctor can do it. And Mondo and Esella. I am still only learning. The Light Doctor says I do not have the confidence. I suppose it is a little like squeezing the sponge. You have to think past it. Maybe I will get there in the end. The Light Doctor keeps telling me I will, but I do not think I want to master weaving sunlight. It frightens me."

"Why?" Charlie was intrigued. Solimo felt perhaps he had strayed too far. He forgot sometimes he was talking to an eleven year old. It was not that Charlie was mature beyond his years, just that they got on so well together and would chat about many things.

"I told you before. It is very powerful. The light of the sun contains the power of life and death. Before the coming of the Order, it had been little used. Now I fear it will be used more and more. It is like weaving with fire. You have to know what you are doing."

He smiled and Charlie smiled too and did not ask any more.

28

RICHARD LEANED ON the fence at the small, but busy market on the edge of a town. Around him was the noise and smell of animals. Quiet, surly buyers eyed up the stock and tried not to give anything away in their faces.

He nodded at Berwick as he walked up and took a place next to him. Together they watched quietly as farmers on the other side of the pen surveyed the six steers inside it.

"These ones should get a better price than the last lot," Richard said. "They're in better shape."

Berwick gave an easy laugh.

"You learn quickly!"

"Tilley gave me a few pointers of things to look out for and I can see for myself if any of the ribs are showing."

"You don't see many ribs on devil cattle, I'll give them that. They look after their animals."

"None of these farmers look happy with them though."

"I've never met a happy farmer," Berwick said with a smile.

"All the ones I've ever met have only complained," Richard agreed. "I can't say I blame them. It's a precarious business when you're reliant on the weather. It's not raining, it is raining. We're in the European Union or we're not."

"What be the European Union?" Berwick asked.

Richard regretted mentioning it immediately. "It's a kind of agreement to trade amongst the countries of Europe. Only it's more complicated than that."

"Many countries agreeing? We rarely have all the manors agree on anything. I don't remember it myself. They tell me things have been different all my life. That the manor lords were always feuding with each other and even the king. Things be different now. The Archbishop tells us we've got a common purpose. He's done a lot of good for Outreterre. God promised the Order the whole of Faerie, but we failed. Now be our time. The Archbishop has studied the ways of the devils for years and he knows his business, I reckon. I be lucky to be living now."

Richard felt a hand on his shoulder and saw Tilley had come up behind them.

"Gossiping to the soldier boy, eh Denham? Don't believe a word he says. They be all powder and no shot. So then, how much do you think I got for these fellers here?" he asked nodding at the cattle in the pen.

"You had nearly five pounds for the last two lots. I reckon you got six, no seven for these."

Tilley laughed.

"Six pounds and eighteen shillings. There was two old gaffers arguing over them which made us another twelve shillings. I should take you to all the markets. You've got a shrewd eye."

Richard raised his eyebrows at Berwick who smiled in return.

"Now then, young Nick, shall we teach him to ride like a soldier or a 'booter?"

Berwick went to answer, but Tilley did not give him the chance.

"Depends on whether you want to ride like a man or a woman I suppose?"

"Perhaps if I start by learning how to ride properly, I can learn to ride cleverly afterwards?" Richard offered.

"Grand idea!" said Tilley laughing. He punched Richard on the shoulder.

"Come boys, let's go for a drink."

Richard enjoyed learning again. He was riding and looking after cattle, he was sword-fighting and he was shooting. Over the next few weeks, he felt like another man. He was feeling fitter than he had done for as long as he could remember, thanks to all the exercise. Tilley kept him working. He would split wood, mend walls and help the men as they were mending a roof on one of the barns.

Every morning he woke to the smell of wood smoke as the fire in the big hall was lit. He would lie in bed listening to the sound of the dawn chorus and then the sounds of men waking up. It felt like being on tour with a rugby team.

Few of them were intelligent men and it was easy to see why Tilley was their leader. But conversations and life were simple and no one questioned his presence. He had become quietly accepted and Richard was sure to pull his weight at every opportunity.

There was only one time of day when he had time to think. Come evening, he would collapse exhausted with activity and taking on new things, he would stare at the dark wooden ceiling above him and wonder what Helen and Charlie were doing. Was this a dream he was living now or had that been the other life?

29

CHARLIE WAS AT school, sitting at his desk in history when he heard a noise outside. He went to the window. It was an upstairs window and it had a view over fields instead of the other school buildings and the paper factory next door. The blackness filled the sky. On the ground was a group of men carrying flaming torches. Then he was on the ground next to them. One of the men was his Dad. He was wearing a black jacket and had a gun slung over his shoulder.

"Dad!" he said.

His father looked past him sadly as if he could not see him.

"Dad!" he said again, louder this time and waved his arms to attract his attention.

The bed covers flew off and he lay still, his heart beating quickly.

"Charlie? Are you okay?" It was his mother. She was at the door.

"I was dreaming of Dad," said Charlie.

She smiled a faint, sad smile.

"I was too," she said. "You woke me up, I think. I knew it was him, but I couldn't see him very well. There were men with torches. I don't know why I should dream of that."

"Torches like the ones with flames?" asked Charlie.

"Yes. Not electric ones. Go back to sleep Charlie."

Charlie lay back and stared into the grey of his ceiling. He felt a surge of excitement.

He was up early, bolted his breakfast and rushed out the door. There was autumn mist in the hollows and he passed a couple of people walking dogs, but there was no one around when he climbed the fence, crossed the stream and found his way to the light funnel. He threw open the door.

Esella was pedalling. Since Mondo had been away, she and Solimo had needed to do longer shifts. She looked up sharply.

"You are early. And in a hurry."

"And you're late," said Charlie. "Where's Solimo?"

"He is coming. I suppose you may as well go and meet him, but do not touch anything."

Charlie had been through a few times. He always enjoyed it. It felt so different. It was exciting. He walked gingerly through the tunnel and its strange landscape and emerged in the garden hall, found the door and went out. It was still dark. Too dark. The blackness was overhead. He stopped and looked up at it. Solimo had not mentioned the darkness coming. Charlie could make out a band of light on the southern horizon where it ended, but all around was darkness. He trotted around to Solimo's house and found him out the back in the garden.

"Did Esella send you? I am coming," he said. "I have just finished gathering these berries. They will be our last now we have lost the light."

They started back towards the funnel room.

"Solimo, I've seen Dad."

"He is home?"

"No, I dreamed of him."

"You must dream of him a lot."

"Not really. But I dreamed he was *here*. The blackness was behind him. I think he's here."

"He cannot be here. Just because you dream he is here, does not mean he is. Most dreams are just dreams."

They entered the funnel room and Esella glanced at them, still humming.

"But Mum dreamed of him too. In the same place. She said there were men there with flaming torches. And that's what I saw in *my* dream too!"

Solimo straightened and frowned.

"Did she also dream of the blackness?"

"I think so. She said it was dark and there were men with torches. That's what I dreamed. I think he's here. Where's the Light Doctor? She'll know."

"She is not here. She has gone north to the farm at Heimo to see Mondo. She will not be back for a week. Maybe more. There have been more raids."

"Then we can go and see the Light Doctor!" Charlie said excitedly.

"We need to stay here and collect light," said Esella.

"You are right. It could be important," said Solimo. "But we need to collect light."

"I saw on the weather forecast that the weather's going to be rubbish for the next week," said Charlie. "There won't be any sun to collect."

Solimo was looking hesitant.

"Oh please, Solimo. It's my Dad. We'll only be gone a few days. I just need to talk to the Doctor."

"Your father is not as important as this light," said Esella.

Charlie decided not to answer that, but he had an idea.

"But if my Dad *is* here, what does that mean for you? If my Dad has found a way through and he's with the Order, then they could bring others through. They could bring soldiers, mercenaries with our modern weapons, like rockets and tanks."

"What are these?" asked Esella. She had stopped pedalling. Her voice was harsh.

"Charlie has told me about them. The world of men has moved on in many ways since the Order left it. They are powerful weapons."

"And you brought us to this place?" Esella said, suddenly angry.

Solimo frowned. He did not do it often.

"Charlie did not bring us here. The Light Doctor wanted us to come here. She knew enough from our own dreams that Charlie's world could be dangerous."

Esella was silent for a few moments. She looked at Charlie. He could feel himself blushing as her dark eyes bore into him, but he forced himself to look back at her.

"Very well," she said at last. "But I am not happy about it. You cannot go before this bad weather arrives. And if there is sun, I will pedal during the day and sleep at night."

He visited every day for the next three days and on the last of those days it was raining when he left the funnel room. He ran most of the way home. He felt as if the faster he ran, the quicker time would pass.

That night, he packed a bag. He put in some underpants and socks, and some tee-shirts, a jumper, a penknife, a torch and a notebook and pen.

Before he went to bed, he gave his Mum a big long hug. She hugged him back.

"It's all right," she said. "Things will be okay."

"Yes," he said. And buried his face in her shoulder.

The next morning, he wrote her a note.

Dear Mum
I've gone to find Dad. Don't worry about me. I'll come home soon.
Love Charlie.

He looked at it for a few minutes. Was it enough? He did not want her to worry about him as well. But he had said he would be home soon, so it was clear he was not running away.

He took a deep breath. He had made his decision. He put the note by the kettle where he knew his Mum would see it, then he quietly left the house.

Solimo was waiting with a horse and a pony. The darkness was unsettling. Solimo tied Charlie's pack to the saddle and helped him up.

"I've never been on a horse before."

"Do not worry. Nella is very docile. You will soon get used to it. It will take us a few days to get there. The two of us will not be fast."

They set off almost straight away, riding down the high hill on which the light tower stood and dipping along a ridge above a hollow filled with a tangle of trees and bushes.

Charlie had been looking forward to seeing more of this world, but it was like travelling at night. There was almost a smell about the darkness, it felt oily, as if some part of it was seeping into him.

"What did you tell your mother?"

"I told her I was going to find Dad and I'd be home soon."

"She will not worry?"

Charlie pondered. Maybe she would worry anyway.

"No. I told her not to worry. And I told her I'd be back."

Solimo nodded.

The darkness put them off speaking.

They rode all day through the gloomy landscape. They had joined a road which ran along high ground as much as possible, running along ridges between the hills. It was not always the most direct route, but it minimised the effort of going up and down hill.

"I feel as if there could be someone out there," Charlie whispered.

"I know what you mean. It does not seem right to talk too loud. I hope you are not frightened."

"No," said Charlie unconvincingly, but then Solimo too was fighting dark thoughts.

"Could there be anyone out there?" asked Charlie.

"No. You do not often see people when you cross the hills. And people are not going far in these dark days. There is just us."

"What about the Order?"

"Do not worry about them. If they were already this far south, we would have heard about it."

Charlie did not think that Solimo sounded convincing.

"You're worried about them," he challenged.

"That is because I am older. It makes you worry about things more."

The days and nights were uneventful, but both found they lay awake half of the night, staring worriedly into the dark and starting at noises.

It felt like a very long journey to Charlie. He had thought long car journeys were difficult, but at least you could look out of the window or listen to music or play games. Here it was just hills and darkness. They would talk of course. Solimo asked many questions and Charlie would find himself chatting about all sorts of things, from what his friends were like, to funny stories about school, to what he thought his Dad might be doing.

Sometimes Solimo would sing. Charlie liked to hear him sing, but it also worried him. He felt it made them more obvious, as if the dim light protected them from being seen and Solimo's voice only made them noticeable.

On their second night, they stopped at a small farm house with small windows. It had a wall around it and the front door was up some stone steps. The family were welcoming to Solimo, but looked at Charlie with suspicion. They had two children around Charlie's age, but neither spoke to him, although they stared a great deal. They shared a hot dinner of mushrooms in a thick gravy. It tasted much stronger than any mushrooms Charlie had ever had before.

That night they slept on the floor of the living room. It was made of stone slabs and was hard and cold. The family gave them some extra blankets to lie on. Charlie thought he would never sleep, but riding turned out to be more tiring that he thought it would be and he slept solidly until he woke to the sounds of the father preparing a kind of porridge and saw the two children watching him with large dark eyes.

The next day's riding was no easier. Charlie wondered how long it would go on. He told himself he would never find a car journey tedious again. Solimo seemed to enjoy the solitude, but Charlie was pleased when they saw the dim glow of the farm down in the valley.

In the glow of the fires, they could just make out the triangular bulk of the main buildings. They were surrounded by other fires and dark shapes and as they rode closer, quiet sounds reached over the outer wall.

They were challenged when they were far from the gate.

Solimo called a response in a clear voice.

"Solimo. From Kunnaslaki."

They heard a gate open and a figure appeared holding a flaming torch. He was standing on a wall next to the gate. They rode through and glancing at the delf with the torch, Charlie could see the wall was made of earth and stones backed by a firm stockade of wood. Part way up was a firing step, a kind of catwalk that would enable those inside to see over the wall when standing on it, but be out of sight when on the ground behind it. They rode past this outer wall and into the space between it and the stone walls of the buildings. There were tents and fires and people milling about. Smoke and smells of cooking filled his nostrils and a gentle murmur of voices bubbled in the night.

"It's like a castle!" breathed Charlie excitedly as they clip-clopped through the gate house and into the yard. It was triangular, like the yard at Kunnaslaki. Just like the area between the walls, it was full of people. They were sat around a central fire and there were wagons around the walls. Someone took their horses and they were pointed towards the kitchen.

Food was being prepared by four delf who moved between a long table in the middle of the room and a long bench down one wall. Several others were leaning over a map at the far end of the table. Charlie recognised the Light Doctor and Raul. Solimo knew Margreta, he guessed at Kurk and Olla, but did not know the other two. He assumed they were from the refugees camped around Heimo.

The Light Doctor looked up as the door opened and her eyes widened with surprise as she recognised them

"Solimo, what is the matter?" said the Light Doctor. Then she saw Charlie. "Charlie, why are you here? Solimo, you should know better, it is dangerous. Charlie, you should stay home." Then she turned to the others.

"This is Charlie. Without him, we would not have the light. He helped us dream it to the other world."

The others around the table looked at him with curiosity.

"Why are you here when we need all the light we can collect?"

Charlie opened his mouth to reply, but Solimo put his hand on Charlie's shoulder.

"We are not sure," said Solimo. "So we came to ask your advice. It could be important."

The Light Doctor raised her eyebrows.

"Charlie thinks his father is here," Solimo said. "He thinks his father has come through." He turned to Charlie. "Tell them about your dream."

Charlie felt suddenly nervous with all these eyes on him and he felt guilty that he had brought Solimo here when he should have been helping to collect light. What if he was wrong? What if his father was not here?

"Mum and I had the same dream. She told me. We saw Dad here. I knew it was here because there was the blackness. He was with men with flaming torches."

"What did they look like?" the Light Doctor asked.

Charlie was pleased because she had not seemed to doubt him. But there was something about her question that made him uncomfortable.

"They looked like men."

"Men or delf?"

Charlie thought.

"Men," he said. "Some were dressed in black coats." Then he remembered a detail he had forgotten before. "And there were apes or something. I couldn't quite tell. They were hairy and had long arms."

The Light Doctor breathed in and out, but said nothing.

"Could it be him? Could he be here?" Charlie was almost pleading. The others around the table were silent, they were looking at the Light Doctor.

"It could be true. People can pass between the worlds. You know this. He could be here."

"But he's with the Order, isn't he?"

"Charlie, I do not know. You dreamed of the Order. Or that is what it seemed. But there is little we can do about it now."

"But what if the Order has found a way to bring people through from their world?" Solimo asked. "Charlie has told me about terrible weapons."

The Light Doctor looked at Charlie.

"Is your father a soldier?"

"No," said Charlie.

"Then I agree it is strange, but if the Order is deliberately bringing people through, would they not pick people who could help them? It might be true, but I am sorry Charlie, we have other things to worry about. Our scouts tell us a strong force crossed the river and is heading south. They tell us they are coming this way. I think they are coming straight for here. You need to leave now while you still have time."

Margreta shook her head.

"Now is no time to leave. It is not safe any more. You should not have come at all," said Margreta. "But now you need to eat and rest. And you will be safer in here than you will outside in that pitch. Stay and we will see what the morning brings."

30

THE MORNING BROUGHT more darkness. Charlie only knew it was morning because he felt awake. He lay confused in the weak light of a candle at the far end of the room. Around him in the barn where he had slept were the noises of sleeping delf and quietly muttered conversations. He turned his head towards Solimo who had lain down a few hours after Charlie had gone to bed.

"Solimo," he whispered. "Are you awake?"

"Yes. I am always awake at this time."

"I'm going down to the yard."

He pushed the blanket off and stood up. He had slept in his clothes and after three days in the saddle, he felt uncomfortable and in need of a shower. He managed to weave a path through the bodies on the floor. Every building on the farm was like this one, he knew. If not crowded with people, it was crowded with animals or supplies. The door creaked loudly as he went out. He grimaced and pulled it again. He heard more people stirring in the room because of the noise, then he was outside.

The air smelt fresh, especially after sleeping with the odour of a cramped room of delf sleeping. He looked up at the sky, expecting to see moon or stars, but there was nothing.

A light was shining in the kitchen. He went across the yard and walked into the kitchen tentatively. Two delf were sitting at the big table eating something out of bowls. A young woman was over at the side, measuring something from a small sack into a large bowl.

"Good morning Charlie," she said. "I am Olla. We did not get a chance to be introduced last night."

"Hi," said Charlie, a little shyly.

"Would you like some breakfast?"

He doubted they would have his favourite cereal.

"There is porridge."

"Thanks."

She pointed to a large pot. He helped himself, wolfing down a bowl. He felt much better afterwards.

Olla put down her measuring cup firmly.

"Right. That is done." She turned to Charlie. "I am going to the gate," she said. "Want to come?"

"Okay," he said. He took his bowl up to the counter, looking for a sink to wash it up in. There was one in the corner of the room with a single brass tap over it attached to a pump handle. Olla waited for him while he rinsed it out.

She smiled at him.

"Thank you."

"Mum tells me off if I don't do it at home," he explained.

"We could do with her around here," she said.

He went with her across the yard to the gatehouse and followed her up the ladder. A delf was there, arms leaning on the parapet as he scanned the dark country. They could make out the hills around them. There was no one about in the outer bailey, just the few tents which had been erected for those who wanted more privacy and quiet than the barns allowed.

"Shh!" said the delf on watch suddenly, although neither of them had made a noise. They listened. There was a faint sound, a light rumbling. Then they caught movement over the hill. There were horses coming.

"Can you make them out?"

"Not yet," muttered the sentry, lifting his long-arm into both hands, holding it across himself ready to raise into the firing position. There were people about in the courtyard behind them now. It was clear that some of them could hear the galloping too.

"There!" said Olla. And then Charlie saw them too, about six horsemen riding out of the gloom.

"Who is it?" It was Kurk down in the courtyard below the gatehouse. Two other delf were with him. All three jogged towards the gate.

Then a cry rang from outside.

"It is Mondo. Let us in!"

Kurk and the other delf pulled open the gate and ran to open the outer one. Mondo and five others rode through. Mondo leaped down from his horse.

"They are coming. Maybe an hour behind us."

"How many?"

"Hundreds. Three hundred. Five hundred. It is hard to count in this dark. Men and cobs. We delayed them, but that was all I could do. We must be ready."

Mondo had enough time to look curiously at Charlie before Olla pointed him and his companions to the kitchen.

Soon there were people mustering. Doors were opening and candles were being lit. A few delf were quietly issuing orders and others carried long-arms to the give out to those who had none. Tents were struck in the outer bailey to clear the area. Some delf went out and manned the outer works. Ammunition was brought up, livestock taken inside.

Within half an hour, the farm was a different place. The space between the walls was empty of tents and watchers manned the walls. Although crammed and crowded, the hubbub of the reorganisation gave way to an uneasy silence. Charlie felt scared. The tense mood infected him, although he did not really understand what he was scared about. He had an empty feeling in his stomach and he followed the uneasy gaze of many eyes to the surrounding hills which now seemed pregnant with menace.

It was full daylight, or as light as it ever was under the leaden sky. The oily slick above them seemed lower than ever, the dark of it pressing down on them, squashing the air, making it stale. There was the strong background smell of animal dung, but lacing it was the musty odour of old sweat.

Charlie went into one of the upper rooms where he had a view. Delf stood at the long narrow slits in the walls. He saw Raul over to him. He felt safe near Raul. He looked calm in his silence where others seemed nervous. Charlie stood on a stool and looked through the window slit at the sullen and haunted landscape.

It felt strange to be in a room with people, but for there to be no talking. He looked at Raul and wanted to say something, but it did not feel appropriate and besides, he could not think of anything worth saying. Several delf sat on the floor with their backs against the wall staring across the room. The rest watched the landscape. The only sounds were of a long-arm knocking against a wall, a cough or a fingernail scratching at a stubbled face.

It was almost a relief when they came.

It was surreal to watch. One moment there was the dim grey of the hills against the blue-black sky, the next, the crest of the hills was lined with small points of fire. It was as if a string of orange lights had been laid along the top of the hills. Looking again and next to the lights were the small dark shapes of horsemen and infantry.

Slowly, the lights began to move, slipping down the slope as if each torch were connected, part of a single web of lights spread across the land in front of them. They made no sound that could be heard across the dim valley. Charlie tried to count the torches, but there were too many. There were certainly hundreds of them. He started again, but just as the lights reached the valley floor, they vanished. They must have extinguished their torches. Charlie peered and peered into the gloom and could make out movement. They were coming. Raul breathed in and out.

"They show us their numbers to intimidate us, then they hide in the dark. But we can see you, you lightless butchers."

Charlie looked at the wiry delf leaning calmly on the wall and watching out of the window slit. He was glad Raul had spoken. It made him feel better. It also felt better that the rocky hillock on which Heimo stood was higher than the Order as they made their way across the valley floor.

There was no challenge from the farm, no firing, but the mood in the room had changed. There were a few muttered comments.

A line moved away from the front of the on-coming army. Charlie realised with a terrified thrill that it was a cavalry charge.

Suddenly there was light. He heard gasps and he looked in the sky above the outer works and there was a human form in the sky. Its arms were outstretched into a dazzling cross. It hung in the sky, the light rippling across its form, then swooped at the horsemen.

"Wow – an angel!" breathed Charlie.

Raul turned to him as if seeing him there for the first time.

"Charlie! Get out of here, this is no place for you. Get below! Now!"

Charlie dragged himself away from the window and was walking backwards to the rear of the room and the door when the gunfire started. There were volleys from the room he was in as well as those around and the earthen walls outside. Torn between feverish excitement and fear, he ran outside and down the steps into the yard. Olla was there with a long-arm over her shoulder and a box of balls and powder charges in her hands. Charlie needed to do something. He needed something to occupy himself in this world that had suddenly erupted in noise.

"Can I help? Please – if I'm busy, I won't be scared."

Without hesitation she thrust the box in his hands. He sagged under the sudden weight, almost dropping it.

"Take that to the big hall. Make sure they do not run out. We have plenty. It is in the cellar under the kitchen."

She turned back to fetch another and he hobbled through the frightened crowd in the courtyard until he reached the great hall. Inside he could immediately smell burning and hot metal. There was a line of delf at the windows here too. He carried to them and each one put a hand into the box and thrust a couple of handfuls of bullets into their pockets or placed them beside them.

With each handful, the box became lighter and easier to carry. He took it upstairs to the top floor. Kurk was there. He beckoned excitedly to Charlie and put his big hand into the box. The firing was rapid but steady. Charlie peered through the window slit. Now there was smoke outside to add to the gloom, but he could make out horses beyond the outer works. There were a couple of bodies lying on the ground below the catwalk and a delf was dragging another back towards the main buildings.

His box was empty, ducking low, he ran back for the stairs and into the yard. He paused for breath and saw a teenaged delf unscrewing the lid of another box of ammunition. A burly woman carrying two buckets of water emerged from the kitchen. A cup hung from each by a string.

"You," she called to him. "Take these round everyone."

He put one bucket at the bottom of the steps and carried the other inside. There was a lull in the shooting. He handed the cup to the closest delf. She took quick, grateful sips.

"What's happened?"

"They have pulled back."

"Have they gone?"

The delf laughed humourlessly.

"They have only just started."

As if in response, shooting began on the other side of the complex.

"They are at the other side now!"

The delf in the room turned their heads towards the sound, although there was nothing to see but the back of the room lined with crates, sacks and bales of hay. It was unsettling to have the fighting at your back without any knowledge of how it went. Charlie was pleased that he could go, that he had no post to desert. He would look.

Once he had taken the bucket around everyone in the room, he went out and collected the other bucket. He did the rounds of the whole farm, fetching more water as his buckets were emptied.

He came upon the Light Doctor. She was standing at a window staring intently outside. He wanted to speak to her, but he felt a hand on his shoulder. He turned and saw it was Olla. She put her hand to her lips.

"She is weaving the sun wraith."

Only then did Charlie notice the sweat on her forehead. A number of spent sponges were at her feet, thin and grey, empty of light. A bag sat beside her.

So it was a sun wraith he had seen and the Light Doctor was - how did she describe it – *weaving* it from the light in the sponges!

He went on with his work, not realising how hot, dusty and smoky he was becoming. When he found Mondo, he knew what he had been doing. There was the tell-tale litter of old sponges at his feet and he was leaning on the wall by the window, focused on the battle outside. He appeared to be in some kind of trance. He too was weaving a sun wraith. He wondered what they did. He imagined one of them swooping down on him out of the grim sky and shuddered.

While he was doling out water, he found the hospital. It was in one of the cellars. Space had been cleared and small pallets laid on the floor. They were already busy. Some were having superficial wounds seen to and being sent out, but there were a number of bodies covered in sheets. Margreta and an old man were working on a patient on a table. There was blood on them and on the floor. Then he saw Solimo. He was crouched over a delf on the far side of the room near the corner. He had been wondering where Solimo was and was pleased to see him. He went over, but stopped, his stomach lurching. On the pallet at Solimo's feet was a delf. His skin appeared to be grey and his eyes were cloudy. There was an open wound on the side of his head and blood had soaked his shoulder and shirt. The delf appeared to be conscious. He was breathing in short, shallow gasps.

Solimo had reached into a cloth bag over his shoulder and pulled out a light sponge. He took a small glass bowl, held the sponge over it and squeezed gently. A few drops fell, glowing. They appeared to fall too slowly, almost to float down and Charlie had to remind himself it was not water. They splashed into the bowl and an iridescence exploded out of the vessel that lit the face of the stricken delf. His eyes cleared, like morning mist burned off by the sun, his breathing calmed.

Charlie watched mesmerised. Then as the few drops of light faded, the mist returned to the delf's eyes and they slowly closed. Charlie realised the breathing had stopped. Solimo reached out and put a hand to the delf's chest.

He had never seen anyone die before. He could hardly believe what had happened, could not fathom that the delf was no longer alive. He looked grey and lifeless, as if life had never even possessed him.

"I thought you were going to cure him," whispered Charlie, his voice catching.

Solimo noticed him and shook his head.

"No. If it had been a lesser wound, I could have given him some strength, but not that. He was always going to die."

Charlie thought of the pile of empty sponges at the feet of the lightweavers, of their desperate need for light to create those angels.

"But that's a waste," he protested. "The Doctor and Mondo need those sponges. What's the use of wasting them on someone who's dying?"

"Charlie, the light was used to bring succour to the dying or the despairing long before we turned it into a weapon to defend ourselves. Keepers carry the light on them at all times. I have told you this. One of each light. We carry it because we never know when we might come across a need. Here there is much need of light to fight with, but also to die with. His world was going dark. It is not our way to let someone go without light to see by. He went well. It was the least I could do."

He looked at Charlie still staring at the dead delf.

"May I have some water please?"

Charlie came to and automatically handed Solimo a beaker of water. The keeper took a few sips, then handed it back to Charlie.

"How about you? Have some too."

Charlie realised he had not had a drink since the attack started. He had been so busy he had not noticed how dry his throat was. He took the cup and gulped it down. Then he looked at the two by the operating table. Solimo followed his gaze.

"I think they could do with some water too."

When Charlie emerged into the courtyard there was a commotion around the gate. He ran over. Delf were running in from outside. He could just see a group stop in a mass and fire several volleys back. He put down his bucket and made for the ladder up to the wall by the gatehouse, curiosity overcoming his fear.

Through the gaps in the battlement he could just make out a horde of ape like creatures leaping over the outer walls. Bodies of their dead lay around, but still they came. A rush was halted briefly by another volley from the delf in front of the gate and in the buildings to his right. Shouting came from behind him. Raul was in the yard. He was rallying those who had run inside.

More and more apes were leaping the wall now, the firing party at the gate was wavering. A couple of delf cast an anxious look back towards the safety of the gate, then Raul was walking past them, shouting. He had two pistols and was firing one at a time.

For what seemed like an age, he was alone, the delf behind just watching, then suddenly, the group at the gate started to walk forward too and they were joined by those who had fled to the courtyard. Raul's pistol's emptied and he pulled out a short sword with a vicious blade and ran swinging it. Axes and swords were drawn by the other delf or long-arms swung by the barrel and they plunged into the mass of apes. There was howling and screeching. It was madness. Another volley smashed into the apes. Then Charlie saw cavalry again. They were coming on from behind to lend support to the cobs. Nothing was stopping them. Where were the angels? He rushed down the ladder, sped across the courtyard and back up to the great hall.

He found the Light Doctor. She looked exhausted, but was standing and holding a sponge. She went to the window again. A bowl stood on a ledge below the opening. She held the sponge over it and squeezed gently and rhythmically. Brightness trickled down into the bowl. The shimmering light scintillated around the room, then it started to lift out of the bowl. As it did, it stretched and grew until it became a radiant figure five feet high. It slid out of the window and rose into the air with the speed of a flicked eye. For a moment it bobbed in the air above the Order like a hellish kite, then it swung down, hurtling into the cavalry and the black clad soldiers beginning to climb up on the wall behind the cobs.

The men dropped back, shielding their faces from the phantasm. Then suddenly the Light Doctor fell backwards. It looked as though someone had jerked her off her feet with a rope tied to her back. The sun wraith fell to the ground and lay still in the grass. A great cheer went up and the Order came on, redoubling their efforts to climb the wall. Armed men were over and backing up the cobs.

As soon as the Light Doctor was on the floor, Charlie saw the red patch on her left shoulder. He gasped.

Two delf were immediately at her side.

"I am all right. I am alive. It will not kill me. Stand me up."

The two delf, gently lifted her. She winced and they paused.

"Lift me up. Quickly. Do not mind me, I can groan if I need to!"

They did as they were told. The others in the room had stopped to watch.

"Keep firing!" shouted someone and they turned their attentions outside once more. There were cobs and soldiers swarming over the outer bailey now, finding what cover they could.

The Light Doctor was lifted to her feet. She stood swaying. Then she squinted out of the window. The sun wraith on the grass was fading.

"Go back to your work," she said to the delf. They obeyed, but then she looked around and saw the bag on the floor. She hesitated, then started to bend over. Charlie saw what she was looking at: the bag of sponges. She could not reach it. He leaped for it and passed it to her. Slowly and deliberately she pulled another sponge from the bag with one hand. Her other hung loosely at her side. It was difficult to squeeze it. She turned to Charlie.

"You squeeze it."

He looked startled.

"Do it, it will not hurt you! Both hands. I know Solimo has been teaching you. Wring it out."

He took it. His head was full of the noise of battle. It echoed around his head as he gazed at the sponge. Solimo and the dying delf came to him. He was afraid of a little burning feeling when others were dying in agony. For a moment, the gunfire seemed to fade and he was lost in his thoughts. He twisted the sponge in his hands, then there was light around his hands and the sponge was like a rag. He pulled back from the bowl as a ball of light rose from it.

Fire streaked by the window, but it was no wraith. Burning arrows were being fired by the Order.

"They are trying to create fires. Is anyone on water watch?" asked Kurk beside him suddenly.

Charlie wondered if that meant him.

"Yes," he said. Kurk nodded. Then Charlie ran back into the courtyard.

"There are burning arrows!" he told the delf who had first given him water to pass out.

"Do not worry. The roofs are turf and will not burn. Just watch out for yourself in here." Even as she spoke, an arrow landed at her feet and clattered on the cobbles. She turned to it angrily and stamped on it. She raised her eyebrows to him.

"Keep close to the walls."

Lord Lyell watched the men climb over the earthworks and run for the walls. He knew he was exposing himself in doing it, but he needed to be able to see what was going on, as if seeing it could ward off the bullets.

"We've got the sorcerer! We've got him – look the demon's fallen! Now we'll get them."

There seemed to be a lull in the sound of gunfire from the farm. They would be crowding around their fallen sorcerer. Now was the time to make a charge.

He leaped up onto his horse again.

"Go hard! Blood! Death! Glory! Go lads go!"

They were surging towards the gate again, ignoring the gunfire and crossbow bolts from the windows. If they were to take this place, they would have to charge for the gate.

Suddenly another demon emerged from the window. The sorcerer was still alive. And then he saw another. He had seen it from time to time on the other side. Had that attack faltered as well? With two demons now the troops inside paused, confused, trapped between the inner buildings and the outer walls. Gunfire rained on them from close range.

The momentum of the attack had been stopped. Then the demons were amongst the men, swirling and lashing and burning. They leaped for cover back over the earthworks, out of sight of the hidden sorcerers. A few had managed to reach the walls and pressed themselves where the defenders could not see them.

"The whoreson sorcerer lives."

Lyell glared at the farm. This was nothing like the light towers of Metsakant: demons and broadsides of gunfire. He turned to the man next to him.

"Pull them back."

The man put a horn to his lips and blew a few quick notes. It was a well-rehearsed manoeuvre from Metsakant. Units provided covering fire in turn until they were all back out of sight and range.

There was a silence like a wheezing pause for breath amongst hacking coughs. The last demon had faded. There were cries and moans from the men and whimpers from the cobs.

An officer came over, his face grimy with sweat.

"By God that was a hard fight. There be a lot of them in there and I think we'd be hard put to prise them out, least while they've got the sorcerers."

"Aye maybe," Lord Lyell replied. "But they be all alone up here. We just need to do something more cunning against these devils."

From the farm they watched as the Order faded back across the grass to the valley sides. They hardly dared believe it was true. They watched and then they sagged. Some leaned their heads against the window ledges, others sank back onto the floor and cradled their heads on their arms. The Light Doctor stood still, then suddenly, she fainted.

Kurk was standing near her and caught her before she hit the ground. He was cradling her when Mondo came in. He too looked exhausted. His eyes were ringed and dark. He knelt over the Light Doctor and gently touched her face. She came to almost immediately and they laid her gently on the floor, clearing a space around her. A stretcher was brought and she was carried out, protesting weakly. The others watched her go in silence.

31

IT WAS EVENING. Solimo and Charlie were sat on the outer works looking out across the darkening landscape.

"Will they be back?" asked Charlie.

"Yes. I think so."

"I know so," said a voice behind them. It was Raul. "They got a pricking they did not expect today, but next time they will be ready for us. Trouble is, *we* will not be ready for that. We would struggle to fight that battle again. We have light, but that and the ammunition will not last too many such attacks."

He climbed up and sat with them.

"I left them arguing about it, but I only see one result of this. We have to leave. We cannot hold this place. We are a long way from help. We only held them today because of the wraiths and we only have wraiths while we have light and while we have weavers."

"And we do not have many weavers," said Solimo. "There are too many of us here. Kunnaslaki is barely defended."

"After the light is gone, they can just creep up in the dark," said Raul. "This place is strong, but there are too many mouths to feed and too many children."

The comment sank into the earthen wall. There was a silence which weighed on Charlie. He was one of those children and he had ridden into the most terrifying and exciting day of his life. He did not want to repeat it.

"Could you help and weave the wraiths, Solimo?" Charlie asked.

"I will administer light to the sick and despairing. Despite all this, I do not have the heart to weave the sun wraiths."

He sounded sad, but not regretful. Charlie wanted to hug him.

They walked back into the courtyard. It was busy once more with people cooking, eating. There was tired laughter and there were tears. There had been casualties and a number of deaths, although they were much lighter than those of the Order.

The kitchen door opened and Olla came out. She saw the three coming through the gate and went to join them.

"It is decided. We are leaving. The first wagons will leave before dawn."

"There was no other choice. To stay would be suicide," said Raul.

"This is my home," Olla replied. It was a mild rebuke, but mainly she was simply stating a fact.

"Everything will be all right," said Charlie.

Olla looked down at him.

"I do not know that it will, Charlie."

He looked confused. Of course everything had to be all right. How could it not? These were his friends. Things always turned out for the best. He had thought that as he looked at the bodies of the dead men of the Order who had been left behind inside the outer wall. He had been looking for his father.

Charlie was sitting on the stool in the kitchen at home playing with a loaf of bread of the kind that the delf ate. Then his Mum was there and she asked him if he had any paint left for the postman.

"It's outside," he said.

So his mother looked out of the window and the garden was full of cobs carrying torches. She swung around, a terrified look on her face. Then there was a banging on the door, a stumbling sound and Charlie was kicked in the side.

"Sorry," said the delf who was trying to lift a bag over Charlie's head. Charlie mumbled a response and tried to turn over on his mat, but the room was full of movement. Everyone was packing up. He wondered how he had managed to sleep through as much as he obviously had.

He stood and rolled up his mat. There were lamps in the room and it was still dark outside. It felt like the middle of the night. He looked around for Solimo, but could not see him, so he threw his satchel over his shoulder, found his way through the busy activity in the room and went outside.

Things were no quieter. Horses were being hitched up to wagons and wagons loaded with boxes. He ducked around people and weaved his way to the kitchen which he had soon learned was the nerve centre of the farm. Sure enough, a group was seated around the table talking. There was the Light Doctor, propped up in a high-backed chair with her arm in a sling. She still looked grey. Next to her was Margreta, her face grim. Olla had her arm around her. Mondo, Raul and the two other delf elders were jabbing fingers at a map in animated debate. Solimo was sat quietly to one side. He smiled at Charlie as he entered. Kurk came in behind Charlie.

"We will be ready to go in an hour."

"I will be the last to leave," said Margreta.

"Then I will be with you," said Kurk.

"And so will I," Olla sighed.

"I almost want to burn the place!" Margreta said fiercely.

"No mother, we will come back one day."

"The Order will look after it," said Kurk. "They will love its strong walls."

"Kurk," said Raul. "We are trying to agree how we leave. Do we go in one train, or do we split up and take different routes?"

"I think we do both at the same time. How about divide into three units, travelling in sight of each other. That way we can still come to the aid of the other if we need to, but the front and back of each caravan is not too long."

"I like that idea," said Mondo.

The others nodded their agreement.

"Then we all leave together," said Olla.

Charlie was put on one of the wagons. His pony had been commandeered as a packhorse. The courtyard and outer bailey were full of wagons, livestock and people. The delf above the gate looked down at Kurk who was astride a big horse.

"Signal," said Kurk.

The man held a lantern aloft and moved a shutter, making it blink into the darkness. An answering set of blinks came out of the distance that must have been on top of the one of the hills. He repeated the action twice more, each time in a different direction and each time he received a response.

"All clear," said Kurk. "Move out."

The first horsemen rode out through the gate, followed by the wagons. Charlie tried to count them, but he could not see clearly and surprisingly for the delf, none was carrying a light. He lost count at twenty. They trundled along the track, out across the valley floor, which only the previous day had been full of an attacking army, and up the valley sides. At the top, they split into three. Charlie watched the other two trains move away to the left as they veered right.

Their speed slowed a little as they left the track behind them, but the ground was even and they still moved faster than walking pace.

Charlie was still tired and nothing was happening to stimulate him. The weak dawn could not be far away but had not yet come. No one was talking. Faces were glum with the shame of retreat and the fear of leaving sanctuary behind for a journey across the open hills.

He was sat on the bench by the driver. The rocking of the wagon was soothing, the creaks and jingles of harness, wood and bumping goods had a delicious richness to it. They were sounds he never heard in his world. It felt like an adventure. It *was* an adventure. He realised his eyes had closed and opened them again. He was in a wagon train. A real one. He looked around at the hooded figures on horseback, at the swaying wagon in front of him and smiled. Then gradually, his eyelids drooped once more.

He woke with a start. There had been a shout of alarm. For a moment he had no idea where he was and was filled with confusion. Something fiery shot out of the darkness and thudded into the frame of the wagon in front and his confusion turned to terror. It was a flaming arrow. It was followed by two more and soon the fire was licking up the canvas covering.

The delf spurred their horses. They did not know which way to turn. They could see nothing to fire at. With the shouting and the whinnying of horses, no one heard the riders until it was too late. There were pistol shots and swung swords flashing around him. A delf fell from his horse. The driver next to him looked around in panic, reaching for the long-arm at his feet. Then suddenly there was a figure beside them. Charlie turned to see who it was and a bearded face glared at him for a moment in the trembling bright light of the burning wagon in front. Their eyes met for a moment, the man looked surprised, lifted a pistol and fired.

Charlie screamed. The driver fell back against the side of the wagon and he felt strong hands grabbing him. He was too shocked to resist, then he kicked, but he had been thrust down over the saddle bow and the horse leaped away from the wagons. Charlie saw their light fade behind him. He was aware of others around them, heard gunshots following them into the darkness, then they were down a slope and lost in the night.

32

AT LEAST CHARLIE had left a note. It sounded so cheerful. Just like Charlie. Matter of fact and assuming the best. Helen stared at it for several minutes, struggling to think.

Then she rushed out to the car and drove. She drove around all the neighbouring streets. Then through town. Then the country lanes. There was no sign of him. She slowed down as she passed every child and received some strange looks from parents. She did not care.

Panic was mounting. She pulled over by a dry stone wall and suddenly she was sobbing, gripping the steering wheel and sobbing. Charlie was gone too. Where had he gone? He was so young.

She called the police again. They asked her questions about his friends. What was he like? No, he would never have gone anywhere with a stranger, he was much too sensible for that. They went to see his friends. Where did he play? She hoped Fraser would have the best answers. Reluctantly, he told them about their secret playing place in the clearing in the woods on the edge of the moors. She went with the police while they searched. And found nothing.

It was odd that Fraser had not mentioned the building. It was large and made of stone with a huge funnel-like chimney. Most unusually, it had three sides. It was nothing like the other old stone buildings in the area. They looked in the windows, but it was largely empty apart from a set of cylinders and things in the middle of the room where the chimney came down. It was like an old factory or something. The policeman tried the door, but it was locked. He was new and not local to the area. He shrugged at her comments about the architecture.

Fraser was puzzled about the building when she went around to see them later.

"You must have gone to the wrong place," he said.

"Fraser! Don't be so rude," his mother told him.

"Well it is a secret place. She could easily have gone wrong."

"Fraser!"

"It's all right," said Helen.

He suggested the crags too where Richard had taken the boys, but there was no sign of him there either.

The police went away and she called her friends again, but there was little they could do.

She was living in fear. Richard was a grown man who could look after himself; Charlie was a just child. What did he know of the world? Where had he gone? Scenarios played out in her head which she could not switch off. She saw them over and over again. The television and radio would not blot them out; they would only provide material for more terrifying thoughts.

She realised how much she had relied on his cheerfulness and his pretence, most of the time, that his father was well.

She continued to go to work, but she was too distracted and her manager gave her time off. Work had been something for her to do. She kept the radio and the television on all the time in case there was news of either of them. She cleaned the house from top to bottom. She decided she would clear out things, but found herself sobbing over some old clothes of Richard's and some toys that Charlie had long ago grown out of but had not had the heart to throw out or give away.

She went back to the clearing. She had set off for a walk simply to be away from the house and found herself following the way that Fraser had told her and the police about. She was unsure at a few points: it is often difficult to concentrate on where you are going if someone else is leading. She thought she had it right, the no trespassing sign had been a useful marker. She reached the clearing and when she arrived at the building, she stood looking at it. It was very odd with its three sides, high windows and that wide chimney. It haunted her in a way she could not define.

33

RAUL RODE BACK into the flickering light of the burning wagon, his face a mask of fury. Delf were calming the horses which had been cut loose from the wagon. Others were desperately beating at the flames. Kurk and Margreta rode up.

"We should have expected that!" Raul spat. "Of course they did not leave."

"There was only a handful of them," said Margreta.

"And how many more over the hill?" said Raul.

"Two dead, one injured," said Kurk. "And we have lost a wagon. We need to be more watchful." He looked out hopelessly into the darkness. The wagon behind them was an island of fire in the enormous night, stretching and leaping into the infinite blackness.

Solimo rode up, he was wide eyed.

"Have you seen Charlie? Which wagon was he on? I cannot find him. Who was he riding with?"

The others looked at each other. Kurk looked down at the wagon driver whose face had already been covered with a blanket. He climbed down and pulled back the blanket and bowed his head, then turned to look up at Solimo.

"This was Kanti. Charlie was riding with Kanti."

Solimo's face sagged with horror. He felt as though his stomach had suddenly shrunk or bunched up to hide.

"Where is he? Is he out there?" He turned to look into the dark. "Charlie!" He turned his horse about and out of the firelight trying to see through the opaque black.

"I think I saw him," said a delf. He was the one with the horses.

"I grabbed the horses, but I saw one of those ironheads. He shot Kanti then took the boy. Slung him across the horse and was gone."

"Took him? Why?" Solimo had never felt like this. "He is a child, why would they take him?"

"He is one of them," said Raul flatly. "The ironheads would have seen it. They would have thought we had kidnapped him."

Solimo's mouth moved. There were too many thoughts.

"He is not one of them."

"He is a human boy. He will be safe," said Kurk as if that closed the matter.

"You cannot give up on him like that. He trusted us. We have to find him. Without us, he can never go home! It is betrayal!"

"You forget we have just lost our homes," said Margreta.

"I know that. We may all lose our homes. But he is a child, he does not belong here. This is not his world."

"No. It is not his world," said Raul. "And it is not *their* world, but they are here and they hate us. And he is with them!"

They were silenced by the venom with which Raul spoke. A calm voice spoke from behind them.

"He is a child, Raul." They turned and saw the Light Doctor looking very small and wrapped in a blanket. Kurk rushed over to support her.

"You should not be up."

"No. And you should not be arguing over this. We invited Charlie here. He helped us. We were his parents."

Solimo found his voice again.

"I will find him."

They all turned to look at him.

"You are a fool. How will you find him?"

Solimo glared back at Raul for a moment, then looked down.

"I do not know. I will follow their tracks. I will ride north. I will look for them. If they can find us, I can find them."

He knew as he was saying it that it was nonsense. Every minute that they spoke, Charlie was being carried further and further away.

"It is not that easy," Raul was speaking more gently now. "Can you track? Can you follow a horse across fields of grass in the dark? Through forests? Since when have light keepers been trackers?"

Solimo put his hand to his eyes to cover them.

"He was looking for his father!" was all he could say.

"We must move on," started Kurk. "We cannot stay here, we are losing time. That is what they want."

Solimo's hand dropped and he looked up again.

"I am not coming. I must at least try to find him." His voice was without hope.

"Solimo," said the Light Doctor gently. "We need you. There are few enough keepers as it is."

"No," said Solimo. "You do not need me. You need light weavers. This is a war. I keep the light to help others. And Charlie needs my help. I took him into my care and I must try to save him."

He looked at Raul.

"If he wants to stay with his kind, then he can stay with them and I will leave him there. With a heavy heart, yes, but he needs to have the choice to go home." He paused. "I think I know Charlie a little now. He will not stay with them." A thought occurred to him. "He may even try to get away, to come back to us. We should be near if he does."

"Very well," said the Light Doctor. "But you cannot go alone."

"This is my charge," said Solimo. "I cannot let anyone else risk themselves."

"Out there on your own, you would not last until tomorrow nightfall," said Raul quietly. "How would you be helping the boy then?"

Solimo did not know what to do. He knew Raul was right. It was suicide.

"I do not know," he said. He felt lost. "I just feel I must try."

"Solimo," said Raul. "You are very stupid. And very brave. I, on the other hand, am simply stupid."

Solimo looked at him, searching his eyes with a glimmer of hope. He found something in the reflected sparks rising from the wagon. He smiled at Raul. Raul grimaced and shook his head in disbelief.

"Let us get moving," he said.

34

HELEN SEARCHED THE internet for old buildings in the county, but came up with nothing. Bad weather hit the country and she stayed in. Then she begged work to let her go back. She said she was going mad sitting at home on her own.

She dug out their local map to search for clues about the building. The scale was too small, so she went into town one lunchtime and bought the larger 1:25,000 scale map from the Ordnance Survey. This showed individual buildings and field boundaries. There was nothing in the clearing, nor was there anything on satellite photographs she found on the internet. How could the building be new? It did not look new. Could it have simply been built with old stone?

Unable to focus on any one thing, she channel-hopped between the News and a western. That night she dreamed of Charlie sitting in a stone room carrying buckets.

It was nearly a week before she was able to go out again. The weather had cleared, but the grass was still wet and the sun came and went behind piles of untidy white clouds.

She took Fraser and his mother with her this time. Fraser had been very puzzled when she told him about the building.

"I'll take you to the right place," he said.

So Fraser led the three of them. He was over his reluctance now and looked full of importance. They climbed the stile and went down the public footpath. They climbed the wall and slipped and slid down the wet slope in the trees. They crossed the stream and passed through the hedge and into the wood. They reached the clearing. Fraser stopped, dumbfounded.

"That wasn't there before!" he said, sounding puzzled. Helen felt relief that she was not going insane.

"Fraser, how could you not notice it?" said his mother.

"It wasn't there!" said Fraser. He rolled his eyes in frustration.

"But If it wasn't there, how can it be there now?" said Helen.

"Well someone must have built it. Whoever owns this land," said Fraser's mother. "Have you looked inside?"

"It's locked and the windows are too high."

Helen moved into the clearing towards the building.

"It looks like it's been here for ages," said Fraser, frowning. He was struggling to believe the evidence of his own eyes.

"Yes, but this isn't going to help you find Richard and Charlie."

Helen did not say anything for a moment, then she vaguely shook her head.

"No," she said quietly. Then she jumped.

"What's that?"

"What?"

"There?"

Fraser leaped to where she was pointing, eager to be helpful. He picked it up. It was a badge for Nottingham Forest Football Club.

"It's Charlie's," he said.

"It is, isn't it?" she replied.

"But it could have been dropped here at any time," said Fraser's mother.

"It was on his coat when I last saw him. The day before he left. He's been here."

That night, she lay in bed thinking. Crazy thoughts were going around her head. When she awoke, a new feeling had settled on her. Inexplicably she felt as though some weight had been lifted.

She got out of bed and went into Charlie's room and looked at the bed. She searched the house as if expecting to come across them hiding from her with big grins on their faces. Then she went to the kitchen drawer, dug around at the back and found a torch and some candles. She went into the garage and found an old lantern which had been stuffed inside a couple of boxes and placed on a shelf. She put on her coat and went out to find the clearing again.

She walked around the building, tried the door then stood back, looking at it. Finding a stone on the ground amongst the leaves, she placed the lantern on it, lit a candle and put it inside the lantern.

"Charlie," she said out loud. "This is so you know I'm waiting for you. Hurry home."

Suddenly she felt foolish. She went to pick up the lantern, but stopped, her hand on its door. Then she stood up straight and left it on the stone, burning.

She had become a sad celebrity in town. Acquaintances and even some people she did not know who must have recognised her face from the media would either pretend they had not seen her or would give her an overly sympathetic smile as they went by. She ignored them and focused on her friends.

She told two of her friends about the lantern. To her surprise, they did not laugh at her.

"We could light candles too if you want," said Jo.

"Thank you," said Helen, genuinely touched. Then a thought came from nowhere. "Would you - could we...do a vigil? On a Wednesday night, the night he left?"

"Where, in the market square?"

"No," she hesitated. "In the wood."

"But shouldn't we do it somewhere more public? It could get on the News and he might see it."

"No. I want to do it in the wood."

"Why on earth do it there?"

"I don't know. It was just the last place I knew he was. I don't know where he went after that, but if it's as special a place to him as Fraser makes out... I don't know," she said finally in a tone of resignation.

For a week or two, her friends joined her in the vigil, but then they began to make excuses and stopped going. Helen continued to go. She did not know where Charlie was, but at least she felt his presence there in that place where he loved to play.

35

THE ARCHBISHOP LEANED back in the chair in his study and fixed Richard with a look that announced he had something important to impart.

"I asked you to return to Collenium because I believe I know how you came to be here." The Archbishop paused to check he had Richard's attention. He did. Richard was watching him with wary excitement.

"Oh, there be so many mysteries still in the worlds," the Archbishop continued. "I be an alchemist and a philosopher. I have made it my life's work to study these things. I have looked at our histories, but find little real evidence. It be said our ancestors put the fear of God into the mind of a devil which brought them to Outreterre."

Richard waited. He was struggling to follow what the Archbishop was talking about, but he wanted to know what he was going to say.

"I have found a way to create darkness," the Archbishop said. "Or to project darkness so that it flows. For it be said 'But with an overrunning flood he will make an utter end of the place thereof, and darkness shall pursue his enemies. '"

He paused, his eyes gleaming.

"By the grace of God, the devils themselves have been my unwitting accomplices in this. I have taken the secret out of their hands and studied it and turned it upon them."

He looked triumphantly at Richard.

"I will show you. I will show you what I think brought you here! It will mean going back to the Pits, for I believe you have already partly seen the answer."

They made a small party, just the Archbishop with Rodon and two guards along with Richard and Berwick. Most of the way was along the manor roads and they made good time in the mild dry weather which the Archbishop assured him was typical of this time of year.

They stayed in a comfortable inn along the way. It was full of wood smoke from the blazing fire and the murmuring of farm labourers over tankards of ale. Richard ate with Berwick and the Archbishop in a small, private room at the front.

The next day, mountains came into view in the distance. Eventually, they passed through a wood and emerged to be confronted by high, craggy hills covered in trees. It was just below the crest on the southern slope that the darkness began. Rising above the trees were strange, tilted chimneys. A kind of sooty smoke was pouring from each. Richard looked at them with curiosity. He had heard the Archbishop talk about the darkness, but did not know what it was. Now, at least, he seemed to be seeing it.

They continued along the road, Richard still staring up at the chimneys until they went out of sight around a shoulder of hill. They rode a mile or two more until the hill stopped in an abrupt cliff. A tunnel had been cut into it and then blocked with a gate flanked by two turreted towers which had been built into the rock. They were of the same stone and it was hard to see where one stopped and the other began.

As they rode up, the gates swung open and a burly man jogged out to greet them, bowing as he ran. He wore a brown jacket, belted at the waist. Richard knew him. He was the first man he had seen when he had arrived in Outreterre.

"Your Grace! What a delight, an honour to be gifted and honoured with your presence. You do us a very great honour and service to visit our establishment. Everything be well. I wish we were better prepared. Word did not arrive of your coming."

The horsemen rode through the short tunnel with the man walking quickly beside them to keep up.

"Thank you Silver, but you know I dislike fuss. I be here on a short visit. You will remember our guest. We be doing some investigations into his arrival."

He gestured at Richard. Silver looked at him and smiled ingratiatingly, but there was curiosity in his eyes.

"But of course. I be glad you be well. And that Your Grace has, has... found him to be..." he was lost for words, "a friend." He finished weakly. "But let me lead you inside, I shouldn't be keeping Your Grace waiting." He turned to a stooped, grey-faced man in a smock who was standing nearby holding a bucket and broom.

"Henry! Open up His Grace's chambers."

"Thank you, Silver."

"Nothing but my duty," Silver bowed.

They had ridden into a courtyard. Richard looked around. There was what he assumed to be a guard on the gate. He was wearing a thick brown coat like Silver's only it appeared to be too big for him. A long-arm was leaning against the base of the left hand tower next to an open door. Through it, he could see a hammock had been strung up.

They were in a small natural amphitheatre around which rocky grey hills rose steeply. In places, a manmade wall had been built so that man and nature had combined to make a dreary grey courtyard. Long wooden sheds lined the base of each wall and on the far side was a large stone building three storeys high. A set of wooden doors studded with iron had been cut into the base of the rock. Another man was slouched in a seat next to them and he jumped to his feet at their approach. He was a youngster, a teenager, with an apology for a moustache struggling under his nose.

The Archbishop turned to Richard.

"I want you to see things quickly, before you are too tired as   you would be if we waited until after dinner. We can freshen up afterwards. And it will give us time for Mr Silver to air the apartments."

"Oh very well, of course," said Silver. "And I will make sure you eat well tonight."

"I expect you will need to purchase something. Here, take this." He dropped a small bag of coins into Silver's hand.

"I'll see to it right away, Your Grace," said Silver then turned to the lad at the doors in the rock face.

"Turley, you dozy layabout. Fetch the key and open the doors." He turned back and rolled his eyes at the Archbishop while Turley went to a cupboard hanging off the rock and brought out a key.

"I will have fires lit for you," said Silver.

"You have a house here?" asked Richard.

"I would not call it a house," smiled the Archbishop, gesturing at the stone building. "I have stayed here to perform some experiments. The rooms be comfortable enough. You will find them more uplifting than these drab surroundings."

Turley unlocked the doors. They opened into a cave mouth which led into the hill. As they opened, Richard felt as if some phantasm rushed at him out of the hill, a dark breath which drifted past him. Goose bumps prickled over his shoulders.

The two soldiers stayed in the courtyard while Berwick and Rodon accompanied them inside. Silver led them along the uneven floor and they soon came to the set of steps which Richard recognised from before which led down to the hallway chamber. Beyond this, the rough-hewn corridor grew narrow and the air became cooler. Once inside the hill, the air stayed at a constant temperature. Reaching the chamber, they were already deep under the hills, but now the set of steps began to ascend. They were even, usually of stone, but sometimes of wood where the rock vanished into a profound darkness. By now their eyes were accustomed to the light from the few torches on the wall.

As they climbed, Richard remembered it all. This was where he had first arrived, where he had woken from the dream and been pursued. It had been night then. He had not recognised the courtyard in daylight.

"I remember it now," he said to the Archbishop.

"Yes," the Archbishop replied. "This be where they found you."

Richard was walking more and more slowly. He felt as though he were wading in mud. The gloom was reaching out at him from all sides. He felt trapped, lost. He knew this feeling. It was coming back and even as he felt it, he feared it. He looked about him. All he could see was the flickering torch in the Archbishop's hand. He realised he had stopped walking. He did not know how long he had been stood still. The Archbishop was watching him again, watching him intently and with a wide-eyed triumph.

"You can feel it! Yes, I knew you would. You be falling back into it, be you not? You remember it from when you came here before. I feel it too, but I have my faith to defend me." He looked at Richard strangely and Richard's mind went back to their conversation in the cathedral. He felt as though he were being judged. "You can feel their despair, can you not?" the Archbishop asked. "It be tangible!"

It *was* tangible. There was something in the air. He felt the Archbishop's hand touching his back, gently guiding him forward.

"Come, Richard, you be safe with me," he said.

He went on, like a child led by the hand. They reached a wider lobby. There was a snuffling sound and a couple of shapes emerged from the darkness. It was the ape creatures, their flapping ears monstrous in the light from the torch, their eyes wide and a pale green. They stepped back at a gesture from Silver.

"You remember our cobs," the Archbishop smiled. "They are not without intelligence and like the darkness. They make very useful servants down here."

"Light the pit below the gallery," said Silver and without a fuss, the two cobs turned and loped back into the dark. Ahead was an open doorway. Just inside they could see a low wall and darkness was beyond it. Silver led them through.

Richard struggled against the feeling of the darkness. It was cloying and pulled at doors in his mind which he had managed to shut in the weeks he had been in Outreterre. He put his hands on the top of the wall. There was a sense of space beyond.

"I strove to make the darkness stay and not fade in the light of the sun," the Archbishop whispered loudly in his ear. He was gripping Richard's arm now.

"And once more the Lord inspired me by telling me that 'the children of the kingdom shall be cast into outer darkness: there shall be weeping and gnashing of teeth. '"

The Archbishop laughed.

"Weeping and gnashing of teeth. Imagine – the spawn of Satan hating darkness! Without light, they despair. It keeps them meek. We must always keep them with little or no light or they may summon demons."

"I need to go," said Richard quietly. Despite the grip on his arm, he turned. The Archbishop held him.

"Of course. I understand, we shall go back up in a moment."

Richard gripped the top of the stone parapet, trying to retain his composure. He felt tearful and frightened.

"But you must hear the final beauty of it, Richard," said the Archbishop, still at his elbow. "By chance, I had some of these devils in the same dark place I was using in my experiments. I noticed a heaviness to the air, this same you feel now. Their despair was perceptible. It reaches out. Do you understand? Of course you do! It permeated the darkness itself, it made the darkness almost a living thing."

Yes, that was it. The darkness was wrapping itself around him, suffocating.

As they looked, they could see the two cobs carrying torches emerge into the chamber two storeys below them. And as the light entered the chamber, they saw the occupants.

Scattered in groups across the floor and disappearing into the gloom were delf.

This time, the Archbishop roared out into the cavern: "'The children of the kingdom shall be cast into outer darkness: there shall be weeping and gnashing of teeth!' "

Dozens of eyes looked up at them blankly and stared. All were sitting. Most did not move at all.

"You see there was never any need to fear these devils. They can be tamed. These have been here for years, captured in the Tanglewoods and northern Metsakant. We keep them out of the light and they become quite malleable. In the endless dark of the Pits and the moonless nights, they built this place. Now we keep them here." He turned to Silver. "Show him the funnels."

Silver pulled his arm back and launched the torch out into the cavern, sending it arcing into the air. As it flew, it lit structures on the ceiling like huge trumpet mouths. They saw them only briefly, the light from the torch causing the holes to appear to move as the shadows rolled with the moving light. The torch fell amongst the delf on the floor. A cob loped in amongst the delf who moved out of its way as it ran for the torch, scooped it up and moved at an easier pace back to the wall. Richard could hear it snarling.

Silver was grinning, enjoying the slow revelation of the chamber's secrets. He turned back to the cavern and shouted down.

"Enough. Make dark!"

"And the dark feeds their dreams." The Archbishop's voice was insistent. "It feeds them until even their dreams be places of darkness and they dream no more of light. Sleeping or waking, their world be a world without light. They see how far they are from God and they despair. And that despair fills the air and fills their dreams." The Archbishop was thrilling at what he had created, but Richard was trying to comprehend it, the enormity. This was something that was very wrong. Still the clergyman continued.

"Oh Richard, I had no idea the power of it could be so strong. It reached across the worlds and found you in your dreams of despair. And you walked into their dreams and into this darkness."

Richard's mind was reeling. Already bowed down by the palpable blackness, he was appalled at the idea.

"And that same darkness, drenched in despair and the darkness of the soul *stayed*! It did not fade. It became a thing. And it be never ending! You can project darkness and still there be more to take its place. In a place without light, darkness be infinite. And now I spread that darkness across the lands of the heathen. It be already causing their downfall as they lose their powers. Now they shall all fall into despair as their sorcery be destroyed. Without light, they can summon no demons. The Knights of the Order of St Collen will descend upon them like the wolf on the fold!"

A chill ran down Richard's spine. Was this the same kindly man with whom he had sat in the garden and enjoyed meals? He was horrified. He already felt as though he had been living with his own misery for a lifetime. He could not believe that hundreds of delf had been trapped down in these caves for years.

He did not hear the conversation around him. He was looking inward. He felt the darkness around him. He tried to ignore it. If he walked quietly and firmly down the steps, it would not notice him, he could avoid it.

He felt an arm around his back. It was the Archbishop. He was saying something. He could not hear what he was saying. The Archbishop was smiling. Richard looked at him blankly. He could not focus on any sounds. He looked at the Archbishop and he saw only the hollow, empty eyes of the delf in the pit. Then words started to come through.

"Look at what it does to you. Richard, can you see it now? This be how you came through. Their despair found yours in your dreams. It dragged you here, dragged you into the pit and now it tries to take you down again. They pulled you between the worlds! Oh, this be fascinating. We shall discover great things together, Richard!"

36

CHARLIE DID NOT know for how long they rode. All the while there was a hand resting firmly on his back.

"It be all right, you be safe now, lad, safe now," the man was saying. He kept repeating it.

"They weren't expecting that," said another voice, away to his right. It was hard for Charlie to tell where it came from, slung over the saddle as he was. Then another voice, further off.

"Ha! They'll be on edge all day waiting for another strike. We should do it again!"

"Maybe, maybe not. But that felt good! The rats running away. Makes up for yesterday. I wist they wouldn't last in there!"

"Ned, you be a liar. You were doom and gloom last night saying they were holed up till Judgement Day," his rider laughed gruffly.

"Well this be bloody Judgement Day, Ragga, you arse! And we've made those devils a hell on earth now. They'll be jumping at the breeze all day and all night."

Charlie could see a little now, the sun must have come up.

"Ragga what have you got there!"

One of the other men must have seen him.

"I was going to show you once we were away from the devils. Hold up now."

The horses stopped and they gathered around. Two hands gently swung him upright.

"By God, it be a boy!" said one.

"He was with the devils?"

"He was," said the man that held him who was called Ragga.

"Boy, when was you captured?"

Charlie looked fearfully at the faces around him. They were all bearded or unshaven and looked fierce under their steel helmets. He had no idea what he could say to them.

"Speak boy, you be safe with us."

He looked around wide-eyed.

"He be terror struck, poor lad," said another. "What did they do to him? Be he marked?"

"Can't tell. He seems fine."

"He doesn't look fine. Lad, tell us what happened."

"He's been struck dumb, I reckon."

That's right, Charlie thought. He would pretend to be dumb, then he wouldn't need to say anything. And he could work out what he would do. How he would escape. He relaxed a little. He realised these men were not going to hurt him. They thought he was one of them.

"There. He be looking better. You be looking better already, lad. You be safe with us. We won't let those devils near you again."

"What will do with him, Ragga?"

"I wot not."

"I think you'd better take him back to Outreterre. His mother will be pleased to see him back."

"Aye. You should. We can spare you. Ned, you go with him."

"Ah what? I wanted to have another crack at those devils."

"You'll have another chance. We'll need you back for the full advance. And there might be more in these hills and it'll be safer with two of you and just as fast."

"Aye, corporal. We'll take the lad home."

"Come on lad, we'll take you back to your mother. Don't you worry."

They found a place to camp soon afterwards. Charlie was shocked to find Ragga had tied himself to him.

"Don't worry. It be not to harm you," he said as gently as he could. "It be just that I know you be a bit frightened and I don't want you running off into the night. You stay with us and you'll be all right."

He was given blankets to sleep between, but they smelled of horse and the ground was cold. Even so, he slept, waking to the bleak, dim light of morning.

The men took little time to strike camp.

"It'll be a blessing to get back to Outreterre and the sweet light of day. If we push on we could be over the border before nightfall."

"Aye well there's no use lying around here. Captain, we'll catch up with you before you reach Kyntilla. We'll be back before you know it. Save some devils for us!"

Ned passed Charlie up to Ragga who placed him in front of him astride the horse and. Charlie saw little point in struggling. He had nowhere to run to. He was lost.

There was a ragged range of hills on the horizon now, steep sided, forested and with rocky summits, they stretched across the horizon above the hill country.

The hills came closer during the morning. He was handed bread as they rode.

"We won't stop til we cross the Styx. You'll be home then, home and safe," said Ragga. "And look, we be almost out of the dark too!"

The sky was bright ahead of them. When they reached the edge of the darkness, Charlie looked up. It had almost no form, it was just black and a little swirled as if someone had been playing with a black water colour.

They entered a narrow winding valley and came eventually to a river. Despite its width, they forded it easily and entered the mountains beyond, zig-zagging amongst trees and rocky outcrops. Charlie felt happier now they were out from under the darkness, but still miserable. There was a smell of autumn under the branches, leaves had already fallen and those in the trees were turning yellow. The smell reminded him of autumn at home and he suddenly felt a long way away. He began to cry. He cried silently, but his nose began to run and he sniffed and rubbed it with his arm. Ragga noticed.

"That be right. You be home. Don't cry. Ned, he be crying. I wonder what those bastards did to him."

"I wouldn't want to think about it. Something horrible."

Charlie wanted to retort. He wanted to tell them that the delf had not done anything horrible to him. They had been kind and hospitable. He found these men confusing. They thought they were being kind to him, but they had killed that delf sitting next to him, the driver of the wagon. He had been too tired to even ask his name. Who knew how many delf they had killed.

They rode along the edge of the trees for the rest of the day. That evening, they took him down from the horse gently and with rough tenderness wrapped him in a blanket and made him something to eat. To his embarrassment, they both insisted on giving him the best slices of dried meat. He found it chewy and salty and would have spat it out if he could, but they looked at him with genuine concern and he was hungry.

The next day they rode out of the trees and crossed a wide valley. Climbing up the other side, they came into a country that looked quite different to the land of the delf and more like what he was used to. It was farmland, split by thick hedgerows. There was stubble in the fields fresh from the harvest. They passed farm houses and a couple of small villages. There were copses and scattered patches of woodland. He almost felt at home, apart from the high rugged hills on their right. They had been following a track initially and at some point it turned into a firm road made of small stones or cobbles.

Towards the end of the day, they heard noise which seeped over a low rise ahead of them. It was the sound of voices.

"What be that?" Ned asked Ragga.

As they crested the rise, they saw pennants and then the first riders. A column of horsemen was wheeling and falling out of formation. Many were in shining breastplates over buff coats. There were hundreds of them. An officer was shouting orders. Behind them loped hundreds more of the cobs.

Three riders broke off and rode towards them.

The first wore red stripes around his cuffs.

"What be you doing here?" he asked.

"We found this boy taken by the devils, sir. We be taking him back to see if we can find his mother. But we'll just leave him with someone and get right back, captain. Be this the army?"

"We be the Gala'shire contingent. This be the mustering point. And we be first as always. Which county are you?"

"Per'shire. Begging your pardon, captain, but we be already across the Styx."

The man frowned.

"What be your names?"

"Edward Smith, sir," said Ned.

"Thomas Ragstone, sir," said Ragga.

"Good. I'll be checking up on you."

With that, the five horses wheeled and returned to the main column. Ragga and Ned relaxed.

"Bloody stuck up Gala'shires," said Ned.

"Whoreson officers. Did he think we were deserters? 'Good I'll be checking up on you'" Ragga mimicked. "I hope a demon fries his ballocks. No offence kid, but we won't be hanging around once we get you home. We don't want to miss out. But you'll hear about us."

They passed more horsemen and behind them were wagons and packhorses, and, Charlie gasped, there was a cannon on large wheels behind a team of six horses. Surely that would have made mincemeat of the farm's defences. As if he had read his thoughts, Ned exclaimed:

"So now they bring in the artillery. We could have done with that the other day!"

"Ours was supposed to be a surprise attack. You can't move cannons that fast."

"Did you like the look of them, lad? They be a grand sight, don't you worry. And wait til you see the boys of Percival."

They rode past the end of the column. He shivered. He could not believe these were humans like him. It had not occurred to him that the delf were not actually human.

In the late afternoon, the range of mountains which they had been following dipped and the darkness became visible again.

Charlie saw a building ahead.

"I always get thirsty when I see a pub," said Ned.

"That'll be the Crossroads Inn then."

And with that thought in their heads, the men pricked on their mounts.

"I'll have me a gammon pie."

"I'll just settle for a pig steak as big as my thigh!"

"You be a greedy bugger. How do you live on rations?"

"I don't call it living, I call it surviving!"

The pub was a few hundred yards ahead and did indeed stand at a crossroads. It was made of wood and stone and looked as if it had been there for a few hundred years. It was what his father would have called a proper pub. He thought about his father again. Could he really be here in the same strange world as him?

Ragga helped him off the horse and led him inside. There were only two other people, the landlord, an older man with a drooping mop of hair and sagging cheeks, and a burly man with a small belly. He turned small blue eyes on them as they entered and his hand, which had been stroking a small brown beard, rose in a salute.

"Soldiers of the Order! Welcome, welcome! Off to fight be you? Let me buy you a drink to send you on your way."

He was wearing a heavy brown coat and had a long wooden truncheon and a pistol tucked in his belt.

"That would be very kind, sir, but we be on our way back from the war for a short spell before we return again."

"Even better if you've been there already. You can tell us about it as you drink. Bob, pull two."

He cocked his head at Charlie standing half behind Ragga's legs.

"And you'll have small beer for the boy?" he asked the landlord.

"Of course."

"You be a kind man, sir," said Ned, then turned to the barman and put a couple of coins on the counter. "And if you've got a gammon pie and a plate of pork and neeps, you'll make us happy men."

Bob nodded and took the coins, then pulled the beer from a barrel set on a rack against the wall. He placed two foaming mugs on the bar and followed them up with a smaller cup for Charlie.

"There you go lads, drink up with the best compliments of Jack Silver!"

Charlie was unsure about his drink. He sometimes had a sip of his Dad's beer, but he had never had his own before. Would be get drunk? Ragga saw him hesitate.

"Drink it lad, it be just small beer."

Charlie tested it. It tasted a bit like the beer his Dad drank, but with a distinct but watery flavour. It was not the best, but he thought he should drink something as he was thirsty.

"So tell me, how goes it? Although I know it be early days an' all." Silver's eyes glittered and his mouth hung open with anticipation.

"Early it be, but we've had our first scrap and a hard one it was I don't mind telling you. The good of it be, we had them on the run the first chance they had to escape."

"That be good then," Silver nodded. "Oh you be brave boys. I wish I could be out with you riding down the heathen. Cheers!"

The soldiers nodded without saying anything and took swigs of their beer.

"Yes," he continued. "I'd like to be out riding with you brave boys, but I have duties keep me here. Important ones I suppose they are – though not as important as you lads in the new crusade!"

Ned wiped his face on his sleeve.

"What keeps you from the war then, sir?"

Charlie thought Silver looked as if it was precisely the question he wanted them to ask. He hesitated as if wondering whether to answer.

"Oh no, I think I can tell you boys." He looked conspiratorial. "I be beadle at the Pits."

He followed the statement with a meaningful stare.

"The Pits. I've heard of them I think," said Ned. "You heard of them, Ragga? Didn't we hear them officers talking about the Pits?"

"Aye, we did. But I can't say I know what they are."

"Well my fine fellows. You may not know what they are, but you know their purpose well enough."

He gave them a sideways look that was meant to be cheerily engaging. The soldiers looked at him stupidly and expectantly.

"Oh I can see it's become a bit of a secret. Well boys, I know there be no harm in telling you." He leaned forward and stared hard at them as if he was about to impart the most wonderful news.

"The Pits be where we make the darkness."

He sat back in his chair and looked at them in a satisfied way.

"You make the darkness?" said Ned in awe.

Silver nodded slowly with a slight, smug smile on his face, enjoying the moment.

"What be it made of?"

"Darkness," he said. "Really, tis no jest. It be made out of darkness."

His conspiratorial look ended and he changed the subject.

"So what be you doing back here then? If you don't mind me asking," he added quickly. "Needn't say anything if it be a secret mission."

Ragga laughed. "They don't give me and Ned secret missions. No, I don't mind telling you, sir, it be on account of this lad."

Silver looked down at Charlie with renewed interest. Charlie looked him in the eye and then looked away. There was something about him that Charlie did not like at all.

"You see, after that battle, I told you how those devils had run at the first chance. Well, we set to harrying them as they went. Keep worrying them like a fox on the chickens. Just hit and run like, to keep them on their toes and stop them from sleeping."

"Oh yes, good, good. Can't let the devils sleep. Keep them on the run. That be what we like to hear."

"And on the raid, we found this lad. So we rescued him and brought him with us so we can give him to his mother. If we can find her!"

Jack Silver looked appalled and cocked his head to one side when he looked at Charlie.

"What was he doing with the devils?"

"We wot not. The boy's dumb. Hasn't said a word since we took him."

"Poor lad!" said Silver leaning forward and ruffling Charlie's hair. Charlie backed off.

"Hmph. He be a little jumpy."

"Wouldn't you be after a stay with devils?" said Ragga. "I keep telling him there be nothing to fear, but he keeps looking frightened. I wish he'd learn there be nothing to be scared of now."

The man's eyes suddenly brightened.

"You could show him."

He clearly enjoyed saying things which required a new question. Ragga was not slow in asking it.

"What could we show him?"

Silver opened his arms, his palms outward.

"You could bring him to the Pits!"

His audience continued to look blank.

"Look. I could take you. If he be afeared of the devils, he won't be by the time he leaves when he sees how harmless they be in sooth. And we've got room for you in the barracks which will save you another night out. It be too cool these nights for roughing it."

He paused again.

At that point the barman came out with two large plates of food.

"Now that be a sight you don't see on campaign!" chuckled Ned.

"Good eating to you. Enjoy your food and we should go. As beadle, I be captain there. I can come and go as I please."

It did not take long for the two soldiers to demolish their meal and they passed pieces to Charlie who took them hungrily. All three men had a few more mugs of beer before they left.

They were already losing the light when they took the other road at the crossroads and headed towards a clump of low hills in the lee of the mountains. They were once more going towards the darkness, but it seemed to start at the hills and spread out from them. Was this what Silver had meant about making the darkness?

They trotted the few miles in a jolly mood, Silver calling Ned and Ragga brave fellows and talking about how important he was at the Pits. Charlie wondered what they were. Perhaps it was a coal mine and the darkness was smoke from the coal.

They were still amongst the trees when they caught the first sight of the tops of the hills. Charlie saw the darkness swirling up into the sky and flowing south. He tried to remember what coal smoke looked like. Was it this dark, this polluting? He thought back to old history books of early factories. The skies always seemed so dark over the towns and terraced streets. It must be coal smoke.

Silver raised a hand to the hills like a showman.

"It is written: 'And the Lord said unto Moses, Stretch out thine hand toward heaven, that there may be darkness over the land of Egypt, even darkness which may be felt. And Moses stretched forth his hand toward heaven; and there was a thick darkness in all the land of Egypt.' And so it is here, my friends."

They continued along the road, until they came to the tunnel mouth with its gate.

"Here we be. The Pits," announced Silver proudly.

There was a small door in the main gate. Silver unhitched his truncheon and banged it on the wood. A window slid open and an old face peered out.

"Oh it be you, beadle. Who be that with you?"

"Never mind who it be, simpleton, let me in. Can't you see these be soldiers of the Order come to inspect the Pits of His Majesty?"

The gate was opened and the old man pulled off his cap as they rode in.

"Good evening, gentlemen," he said. He was wearing an oversized, thick brown coat like Silver's.

"Where be the others?" demanded Silver.

"Oh in the barracks and at the Pits. The cobs are all below."

As they rode through the tunnel and into the open beyond, Silver looked over his shoulder at the soldiers behind him.

"I must apologise for our unmilitary ways. Our care be focused inwards rather than outwards as you'll see. Most of the younger lads have gone to the wars, but we still have the old and the wily on guard here."

"What be you guarding, friend?" asked Ragga.

Silver made as if he did not hear and led them between the sheds and buildings in the yard and across the gravel towards the end wall with its door.

"Still loafing, Turley? Where be His Grace?"

"He's in his rooms, beadle. Resting."

"Good. Open the doors."

As they descended and climbed the steps behind Silver, Charlie felt his spirits droop. Where were they going? Where was this man taking them? Would he ever find his way out? He would never find his father.

His thoughts turned ever more inward. Ned and Ragga had stopped talking and joking. Silver turned to look at them. He gave a short, gruff laugh and looked away.

Charlie was confused. A feeling of gloom seemed to have settled on the party which had been so garrulous before.

They came to a hallway and were led through a door to a stone balcony. Below them, cobs appeared carrying torches. They lit people a cavern, groups of people huddled on the floor. Charlie could not believe his eyes. He could not believe they were delf. He felt sick. He could not think, he could not move. Ned and Ragga felt differently.

"That be astounding. Who would've thought you could do that! You see, Ned. That be why we be just humble private soldiers. We don't have the brains to think of that. You really do make the darkness, sir!"

Silver beamed in the flickering light of the torch. Then he reached over and patted Charlie on the head.

"You see, son. Nothing to worry about. Just harmless rats in a hole."

Charlie suddenly felt sick. He needed air. He needed light. He turned and bolted down the steps.

"Oi, get back here!" Ragga shouted. "You'll hurt yourself! The boy be mad!"

He ran. He was aware of nothing else but his feet pounding down the steps. He had to get out. He had to get away from that sight inside the mountain. How could they do that? How could they do that to *any*one? He could hear them coming up behind. His breath was going fast. He had to keep going. He was being pulled by the light outside. He wanted to hear birdsong again and see the branches of trees moving in the breeze. He heard a curse and stumble behind him. He did not know how many steps there were, he just kept going, his thoughts only on the doorway and being outside again. He must be nearly there. He looked up and caught light on the level above him. One more flight. He put his head down, the breaths becoming harder. Then he was at ground level.

The door was open, even late afternoon light was bright and blinding after the near darkness of the stairwell, but he could see there was someone just beyond the doorway. It must be that sentry, Charlie thought. Turley wasn't it? He did not know if he had enough breath left to keep running. As he emerged, the man did not move at first, but then he felt hands grab at his sides, catching him under the armpits, lifting him. He wriggled to free himself and, as he did so, looked at the face of the man who had picked him up.

"Charlie!" said the man in astonishment.

"Dad!"

37

CHARLIE'S FATHER SET him back down on the ground.

"What are you doing here?" he asked, still with that note of amazement in his voice. Then he hugged him, the strength of it almost squeezing out what was left of Charlie's breath.

Charlie was overwhelmed. While he at least had already convinced himself that his father was in this world, he had not thought about how he might actually find him, or even less, simply bump into him. With a start, he remembered that at any second, Ned and Ragga would run out of that doorway. The young sentry was simply watching, looking puzzled.

"Dad, we need to get out of here."

"Why, what's wrong?"

"It's the delf, what they're doing to them, it's wrong."

His father looked at him, his mouth looking as though he was going to say something, but it was prevented by Ned and Ragga erupting from the door. They stopped when they saw Richard holding Charlie and leaned, puffing on the doorway.

"You got him. You got him. What...what were you doing, lad? What be the matter?"

"I'm sorry," Richard said, confused. "What's going on?"

His tone was suspicious, ready to pounce.

"Thanks for stopping him, friend. I didn't know what was going on when he bolted. Come on lad, me and Ned'll look after you, but you be a strange one."

"What are you doing with him?"

"We be trying to find his parents if you must know. And who be you to ask?"

"I'm his father."

Richard put Charlie down and Charlie retreated a little behind his father's legs. He noticed another young soldier standing just behind his father. Ragga and Ned looked straight at Richard. Then they looked at Charlie.

"Be this true lad?"

Charlie nodded.

At that moment, Silver appeared at the door. He was red faced and puffing.

"Bloody child, running off like that, what..." then he stopped and took in the scene in front of him.

"How can this be your son?" asked Berwick, who had watched the whole scene unfold from just behind Richard.

"I don't know. I don't know how I got here and I don't know how Charlie got here, but we're both here." A thought occurred to him. "Where's your mother?"

"At home."

"He *can* talk!" exclaimed Ragga.

"Could someone tell me what's going on?" said Richard.

"We rescued him from the devils a few nights ago."

Something told Charlie he should not attempt to correct them. He was still uncertain of what was happening himself. In his dream, he had seen his father amongst the Order, but he was not prepared for him being on friendly terms with them.

"We brought him back over the border. We were going to leave him with someone so he could find his parents again. We brought him here so he wouldn't be so scared of the devils after what they did to him. It was Mr Silver's idea," he added, gesturing over his shoulder.

"What did they do to him?" Richard asked the soldiers, then turned to Charlie. "What did they do to you?" his question was urgent, there was anger in it.

"Nothing, nothing!" said Charlie crossly. "They were very nice to me."

No one said anything, but just looked at him.

"Dad, I want to go."

"Where?"

"Away from here. It's horrible."

"What were you doing in there?" Richard asked Charlie, but it was Silver who replied.

"We were showing him how harmless those devils really be. Thought it would do him good after his ordeal, poor lad."

"What ordeal? Charlie?"

"You be welcome to stay here, gentlemen," said Silver. "There be space in the barracks since some of the men went off to the muster."

"I don't want to stay here," Charlie hissed at his father. Richard squeezed his shoulder.

"I know."

"I hate this place."

Richard looked down at his face, then nodded.

"If you don't mind, could we stay somewhere else?"

"There's the inn at the Crossroads," Berwick suggested. "But we should tell the Archbishop if we be leaving. I think he wants you to stay longer."

"I'll do it. Charlie, wait here. I won't be long."

Richard knocked on the Archbishop's door.

"It's Richard."

The Archbishop called him in. He was sitting at his desk and he looked up at Richard with a frown of concern.

"Richard, I apologise for not seeing you all day. I had things to do and I knew you would need a rest after yesterday. You still look unwell. I be sorry if I distressed you yesterday, but I needed to be sure of the effect the Pits had on you."

"I understand," said Richard. "But I can't stay here."

There was wonder in the Archbishop's face. Even, Richard thought, some delight.

"Be the effect that strong?"

"I hear there's an inn not far from here. Berwick said he would take me to stay there."

"That be a good idea. I have more work to do. You could return to Collenium from there, or you could follow the army into the land of devils as I intend to do."

"Let's see how I feel."

"Very well." The Archbishop looked down again, then lifted his head. "And take care of yourself."

"We'll ride with you," said Ned when Richard returned to the courtyard and told them he had the Archbishop's blessing to leave. "We need to get back to join Lord Lyell."

They all mounted up, Richard pulling Charlie onto his horse in front of him. Charlie eyed the long-arm in his father's saddle holster. His father had a gun. What was he doing with these people?

Silver waved them all off, shook his head and shouted at the young sentry at the door to the Pits to shut it, then he walked off to one of the barracks.

Only once they were out of the main entrance did Richard pull Charlie around to face him.

"Charlie, how did you get here? This is amazing. Are you really here?"

He kept prodding him, hugging him.

"It's a long story. How did *you* get here?"

"That's a long story too. But I don't really understand it. We need to get home."

"I know how to go home," Charlie whispered.

"What? You do? How?"

Richard gripped Charlie.

"I can't tell you. Not here. Not with them. Dad, what are you doing with them?"

"They've looked after me since I got here. They've been very kind. What were you doing with the devils?"

"Stop calling them devils! They're delf. I like them!"

This was not how Charlie had imagined meeting his father. He enjoyed the feel of his father's arm around him, supporting him on the horse, but he was confused because he did not know what he could tell him, what was safe to tell him. Was this really his father? How could he be with the Order?

The sun had set and dusk was fast turning to night. They entered the trees and the canopy closed over their heads as they went deeper into them. Charlie closed his eyes and leaned back into this father. Suddenly he was aware that all the horses had stopped.

"Alice?" said Ragga.

Charlie followed his gaze and his eyes widened and his skin crawled. There was a bright, misty spectre hovering in the air a few feet in front of them.

"It's your mother," said Richard with a mixture of horror and wonder.

"What is?" asked Charlie.

"There!" his father whispered in response.

"That's not Mum," said Charlie, but the four men appeared to be mesmerised by the apparition.

Then a quiet but commanding voice came out of the darkness.

"Charlie, climb down."

Charlie looked around. There was no one to be seen.

"Charlie, quickly," the voice came with greater urgency. "We do not have long!"

"Who is it?"

A figure emerged briefly from under a tree into the moonlight. It was Raul, a pistol in one hand. Charlie was delighted but terrified.

"Get back – !" he started.

"They cannot hear me, now, but it will not last. Climb *down!*"

"I can't. This is my Dad."

"Your father?" There was a moment's hesitation. "Then we take you both."

He stepped out and took the horse's bridle and pulled it to the side of the road. Then he ran to the other horses. He pulled the long-arms from the soldiers' saddles, then looked uncertain about what to do next. He looked briefly at the still shining apparition, then leaped at Berwick, grabbing him by the arm and pulling him from the horse. Berwick cried out, a confused cry. Raul's arm went up and came down, clubbing Berwick on the head with the butt of his pistol. At the sound, Ned and Ragga stirred. He felt his father jolt too. Then everything happened very quickly.

There were two gunshots. Ragga fell from his horse, but Ned stayed on, his horse wheeling round. He realised that his father was looking at Raul and reaching for the gun at his saddle.

"Dad no!"

Raul turned.

"Father of Charlie. I am your friend. I will not shoot you."

"Dad, he's my friend."

Richard's hand stopped. At that moment, the apparition began to fade. Ned was still looking at it, but his focus seemed to be shifting. Raul turned and ran for Ned's horse. Holding its head, he muttered something to calm it. Then he pulled at Ned with both hands. Ned came off, the horse ran. As Ned lay still dazed on the ground, Raul clubbed him as he had Berwick and the soldier lay still.

"Are they dead?" asked Charlie with horror. He did not want them to be.

"No," said Raul. "But they will not be following us."

There was a sound behind them and Richard and Charlie jumped around. Another figure was coming out of the shadows.

"Solimo!" exclaimed Charlie with a smile. He ran to him and hugged him. "That was you – making that...thing?"

"A moon wraith, yes."

"I didn't know you could make them! Is it like a sun wraith?"

"No, those are beyond me. They need controlling. This can just be created."

"But that was my wife," said Richard incredulously.

Solimo turned to look at him. Charlie watched him. He wanted these two to like each other.

"Who are you?" asked Richard. "What's going on?"

"Dad, this is Solimo. And Raul."

"You're dev- delf!" said Richard, wide-eyed. He paused. They were not like the other delf he had come across.

"I am pleased to meet you," smiled Solimo and pressed his hand to his chest. "You thought it was your wife, but it was your mind that made it your wife. It is the effect of the distilled moonlight."

Richard frowned, but it was the look of someone once more grappling to understand the strange twists of fate of which his life was full.

"I am sure that is all very interesting, but could anyone help please?" asked Raul testily as he dragged Ned from the roadway. Then he rummaged in their saddle bags until he found some cord and tied their hands and feet.

"What about their wounds?" asked Richard. He went over to the unconscious Berwick and felt his pulse. He had a bump forming on his head and blood in his scalp. Richard was relieved. He could not help but like the young soldier. If he had been fooled by the Archbishop, why would someone like Berwick not be?

"We do not have time for this," said Raul frowning.

"Charlie's father is right. It is the least we can do," said Solimo.

"They would not do it for us."

"Even more reason why we should do it for them."

Raul made a sound of exasperation, but returned to the saddle bag and found some cloth. Solimo reached down to Ragga who was still in the road and pulled open his jacket. There was a blood on his shoulder and a larger exit wound. Solimo delved in his coat and took out a small leather pouch. He opened it, showing a line of small bottles in their own pockets. He selected one and tipped some drops onto the wound. Then he took a water bottle from one of the soldiers' saddles and washed where the bullet had entered and exited Ragga's shoulder. Raul passed him the cloth and helped Solimo to tie it around. They sat him up against a tree. The other two were unconscious. They would have sore heads when they woke.

"Now, we need to go. Someone may have heard the gunshot."

"No, we can't," said Charlie. "We need to go back."

"What? You were saying we had to get out of there?" said his father exasperated and clearly uncomfortable with the night's work.

"The caves, the Pits, they're full of delf. In the dark. We've got to get them out!"

"Charlie what are you talking about?" said Solimo.

"They use them to create the darkness. The Pits are creating the darkness. I think they're using light funnels. I saw them!"

"Can they do that?" Raul asked, looking at Solimo.

"I – I do not know. The Light Doctor would know."

"But she is not here. You are. Come on, Solimo."

"All I know is about light funnels. Charlie, what did you see?"

"There are caves inside the mountain. They took us in there – with Ned and Ragga. And I saw them, hundreds, maybe thousands, I don't know. It was too dark to see properly. And I saw the bottoms of light funnels were poking into the cave. No, the *tops*," he said, suddenly realising. "They were upside down!"

"So they are collecting darkness?" said Raul.

"And pumping it back out!" said Solimo, breathless with fear and wonder.

"It's true," said Richard. "They told me themselves."

"But why do they have delf in there? Why do they need slaves?"

"They keep them perpetually in the dark, break their spirit and that somehow makes the darkness."

The two delf were looking horrified, but the face of the one called Raul was quickly becoming angry.

Richard's stomach felt as if he had just missed his footing. He felt as if he was about to hear something he did not want to hear, yet knew was coming. They were about to go back. They were about to go down into the Pits again. He did not want to go back. These two delf seemed to be looking for trouble. He was as disgusted by what he had seen as they would be, but he could not go back.

"We have been there. We went as close to the gate as we could," said Raul. "How are we going to get in?"

"Were you following us?"

"We have been following you for a couple of days. Ever since Raul picked up your trail," smiled Solimo.

"I don't think they've got many guards," said Charlie excitedly. "That man, Silver – I don't like him – but he said lots of them had gone off to fight. I saw two, one was old and one was young. And there are cobs."

"If this place is what you think it is, and they have hundreds of delf there, there will be more than three of them, you can be sure," said Raul grimly.

"What about the gate?" asked Richard. He had spoken before he realised it. What was he saying?

"The gate?" asked Charlie. Then his eyes lit up. "Solimo and Raul could dress up as soldiers."

"But how do we get into these caves? The night will only disguise us for so long before they realise we are delf too. There must be a way."

"But you've got to destroy the funnels or the darkness will carry on. You need to blow them up or something."

"And how do we get in, let alone what we blow them up with?" asked Raul.

"I don't know."

They were all silent for a few moments. Then, hesitantly, Solimo spoke up.

"What about the starlight?"

"What?" Raul was impatient.

"In light lore, we use starlight for inspiration. I have a sponge of starlight. I brought one of each. I just used the moonlight. We could see if the starlight helps us."

"Is this some kind of drug?" asked Richard suspiciously.

"Dad, don't be stupid."

"It is the distillation of the essence of starlight," said Solimo gently. "We gather it. We use it. Starlight helps you to think. It makes the most of your creativity."

"Let's use it!" said Charlie.

"I'm not sure we should," said Richard. This was becoming more like the devilish works he had heard so much about. Who were these people? "And you're certainly not, Charlie. You're far too young."

"Richard, let me assure you, it is quite safe," said Solimo.

"Look, I don't even know who you are and I don't trust you."

Solimo looked hurt, but said nothing.

"Dad, they're not going to hurt me. These are my friends. You'd like them if you knew them better."

Richard looked down at his son. He wished it was not so dark so he could see the look in Charlie's eyes.

"It works very well on children. They have such active imaginations. I know Charlie has one of those. He told me lots about your world and the floating cities and flying ships. I thought he was making it all up."

"Most of it was true, but the horses driving tractors wasn't," Charlie said sheepishly. "Dad, you've got to let me!"

"All right," Richard said slowly. He was feeling his way again, trying to work out what was right as a parent; trying to work out what was right at all when the world you thought you knew has fallen away and become something else. "But the moment I don't like the look of anything, I'm stopping it."

"Then it will not be stopped," said Solimo with a smile, "because you will love this."

He led them out of the trees and away from the tied up men, hidden in the shadows. The four of them sat together. Solimo pulled out a small bowl from his jacket and placed it on the ground.

"We should wait a short time. The moon will go behind the darkness and we will just have the starlight."

The edge of the darkness was indeed very close to where they were.

"I think we should lie down and look up at the stars too. Starlight by starlight. I always like to look at the stars when I am thinking. I can see the stars when I am in bed," said Solimo.

Richard cast a quick sideways look at Charlie. He could not be quite sure, but in the gloom, he thought he saw Charlie smirk back at him. Raul, Solimo and Charlie all lay down. Richard looked at them, then awkwardly lay down too.

The sky was full of stars. Even the moon did not hide them. They filled Charlie's vision. The more he looked, the more he saw. Then the moon started to go behind the darkness. With every moment that passed he could see more and more stars.

"Wow," he breathed. Then the moon was gone and he felt as though he were in space, looking out at the universe. He had never seen so many stars. At home there was always some sort of light pollution from nearby houses or a city a few miles away. Here, it was as if someone had taken a bag of sugar and sprinkled it across the night. Out of the corner of his eye, he saw Solimo take the sponge and squeeze.

It was like grey light, it fell, floating, into the bowl.

Charlie could feel something behind his head. It must be the starlight, he thought. Then it seemed to pass into his head. His head felt as big as the sky. He could no longer tell whether he was looking at the night sky or looking at the inside of his head. It was amazing. Then he tried to focus on what they were doing. He should not be enjoying himself, he should be thinking of how they were going to rescue the delf. But whenever he tried to think about it, his thoughts would wander off somewhere else. He was remembering the faces of the delf in the dark. He thought of the Light Doctor looking serious, then of a sun wraith forming in front of her and shooting out of the window. He imagined one going for that Mr Silver. Charlie was in a spaceship riding into the stars. He reached out a hand and waved it in the stars, hiding some with it, seeing how many he could blot out with his own small hand. He thought of his Dad playing football with him and of his Dad sitting staring at the wall in his chair. Then he remembered the delf in the caves again. His mind would not stay on a single thought. He felt as though he were falling into the stars, or were they coming towards him?

"Charlie?"

"Shh."

"Is he okay? It's your drug."

Charlie focused on the voices. Then he realised the others were all sat up and looking at him.

"Sorry, I was thinking. Wait til the starlight's finished."

"It has," said Solimo. "It faded a few minutes ago. You looked lost in your thoughts."

"I was. Did anyone have any ideas?"

"Well I thought Solimo could be our prisoner," said Raul. "What about you?"

"Not really," said Charlie. Then he looked up in surprise. "Yes! I do have an idea! I do!" Suddenly his face fell. "But we'd need to leave someone behind. Someone who could pull the garden hall through in their dreams."

"What do you mean?"

"Well I was thinking that we need to bring light to the Pits. You moved the funnel room, so couldn't you move the garden room too? It would still be connected to the funnel room and to the light."

"I'm sorry, Charlie, what are you talking about?" Richard asked.

"Go on," said Solimo.

"Well if we brought the garden into the Pits, then you could bring light directly from the funnel. There would be light and you could make sun wraiths. We could free the delf and destroy the Pits at the same time!"

Solimo's eyes were shining.

"Charlie, that is a wonderful idea."

"But to dream it into the Pits, we would need someone to pull it through at the same time as it was being pushed," Charlie said sadly.

They sat in silence for a time. Richard did not understand the conversation, but the others seemed to, so he simply waited and watched. Solimo in particular appeared to be wrestling with something.

"I will go," said Raul finally.

"No," said Solimo. He turned to Raul and smiled at him. "You have already done enough for me in bringing me this far. I would never have found Charlie without you. They need you now to guide them back to Kunnaslaki. The delf in the Pits need me. I am a Light Keeper. I can dream the light."

He patted his coat.

"I have one sponge left: sunlight. I can use it to help me dream and maybe to help the other delf dream too."

38

THREE RIDERS APPROACHED the gate in the moonlight. Richard was in the lead and he leaned forward and knocked on the gate. After a few moments, the same old sentry peered out.

"I thought you were leaving."

"We are," said Richard. "We have a present for you. We found him in the woods." He tugged on a rope and the horse behind him walked forward a few steps. Solimo was sat with his hands behind his back.

"Where did that devil come from?"

"One of yours, you said they were all locked up!" said Charlie in a hurt tone of voice.

"I'd best get Mr Silver," said the sentry.

"Let us in first, I don't feel safe out here."

"Where be the other two?"

"Gone on to the inn to warn them there might be delf about," Richard replied. "We think there are more of them. So let us in."

"I be opening."

The sentry opened the gate and shut it behind them. He led them through the tunnel and into the courtyard.

"Wait here til I fetch Mr Silver."

They waited while the man walked briskly to one of the barrack blocks.

"That's the entrance, over there," said Charlie, pointing at the doors under the overhang, barely visible in the shadow from the moon. The door opened in the barracks and Silver and the sentry stepped out and started to walk towards them. Silver was carrying a lighted brand.

"Henry says you found a devil in the woods," said Silver before he had even reached them. He noticed Solimo and gave him a hard look, lifting the brand towards his face. Raul bent his head so that his borrowed helmet would shadow him.

"Hmm. How did you get out, you whoreson devil?"

"Look Mr Silver, we need to get this devil back into the Pits where he'll be safe."

"Oh he'll be safe."

"Should we tell the Archbishop?" asked the sentry.

"I don't need the Archbishop to tell me how to do my job. Get back to the gate."

"We'll take him back down," said Richard.

"You sure? You seemed to take on badly last time."

"I was surprised at what happened. I'll be expecting it this time."

"Yeah. That be how we deal with it. We know to ignore it, not like those fool devils. I'll let you all in right now."

"We can't stay long. We need to meet back at the inn tonight."

Silver opened the doors himself and led them into the staircase. Richard tensed. He felt the darkness closing around him again. He gulped for air.

"Dad?"

He felt Charlie's hand around his. He gripped it. No one else seemed to have noticed. They continued down the steps into the gloom. It seemed to be closing in around him. It was a too familiar feeling. He realised how free he had felt before this and now the feeling was coming back. In the final hallway, he tried not to show his fear as the cobs loomed out of the deep shadows and then melted away as Silver waved his hand at them.

He glanced at Solimo. He looked frightened. One of them at least did not need to act. Raul had his hand inside his jacket and his head down, but Richard caught the flash of his eye in the torchlight.

Silver had been talking the whole way. Richard had no idea what about. He was about to open the door into the delf chamber. As he did so, Richard felt a wave of darkness break over him. He stopped again.

"Mr Silver," said Charlie. "Can we look from up here? I don't want to go down there with them."

"Of course, young man. I wasn't thinking."

"Dad, will you come with me? There's a balcony."

He knows I can't go in, Richard thought. Charlie led him over to the double doors. Raul, Solimo and Silver went down the steps. Charlie opened the doors for his father and almost had to push him inside.

"I know what's here," said his father. He could barely walk. He fell towards the balustrade in front of him and looked out. He could see nothing, but he could feel an immensity of despair. It rocked him. It cried out to him. He groaned. He felt Charlie press up against him, he felt his son's confusion and reached out his hand to him, cradling his head, ruffling his hair.

He saw the fiery light of a torch emerge from a door in the wall below him as Silver led out the two delf who stopped dead in their tracks. Behind Silver's back, he saw Raul lean forward and whisper something into Solimo's ear, saw a slight nod from Solimo, felt his son squeezing his hand and something wet. His son was crying. He reached down and pulled Charlie up and hugged him close. He was heaving great sobs out of his body.

"We can't leave Solimo, we can't!" he was saying.

"Shhh. You said it would work yourself."

Solimo walked slowly forward amongst the other delf. Then he turned around and looked up at where Richard and Charlie were standing. Charlie met his gaze. These two are friends, thought Richard and felt sorry for his harsh words to him earlier. Then Silver struck Solimo with a truncheon.

"Get over there devil, you've done enough! You be lucky I don't kill you now. Get in there."

There was a gleam. Richard realised Raul had drawn out a long knife. He was going to stab Silver!

"Come on now, let's get out of here," Richard called, barely getting the words out. Raul whipped the blade out of sight and turned, Silver followed and darkness fell on the cavern once more.

Going back, Richard had to stop himself from running, from fleeing the feeling that grabbed at him. The entrance did not come fast enough. Silver was prattling; something about how bad it was down there, but you got used to it, ignored it, knowing it was the devils' self-destruction. He was laughing. Richard caught Raul's eye when they passed a torch and looked away quickly at the rage he saw there focused on Silver's back.

In the doorway, Silver turned to them.

"You'll stop for a bite to eat? Surely boys?"

"No we can't. We must get back. The others will be worried. And my boy's asleep on his feet. He'll sleep well on the horse. We'll be off. We'll be back at the crossroads before midnight." He hoped he had kept the desperation out of his voice. He tried to speak in a slow, measured tone. He felt exhausted.

They were a few minutes out of the gate before any of them could speak and the first to speak was Raul.

"I would have killed him."

"How could we leave Solimo there? Can we get him back?" sobbed Charlie suddenly.

"No," said Raul. "We need to keep to our plan. We need to get home. And we need to go now, before any alarm is raised at those soldiers going missing."

"We should check on them," said Richard. He felt guilty about Berwick who had befriended him. At the same time, he wanted nothing more to do with him now he had seen the Pits again.

They reached a bend in the road.

"Is this the spot?"

"It is," said Raul.

"So where are they?"

"Looks like my knots were not good. I am usually trussing up a dead animal not a live one," Raul cursed. "I wonder which way they will have gone."

"There's a manor town north of the crossroads," said Richard. "They will have gone for that."

"That makes sense," Raul agreed. They would never think we went back to the Pits. We need to go. Across country. They will be thinking we are hours ahead, not behind them. We have a little time so we are going to make the most of it."

They kept to the road until they judged they were nearing the crossroads, then they turned off and struck across country, hoping to meet the road again south of the crossroads. They slowed down so that the horses could find their way over the uneven ground in the dark. Once Richard was almost knocked from his horse as a tree branch appeared to leap at him out of the night. Then they were back on the roadway again.

Charlie was sat on the horse in front of his father and the regular movement of the hooves soon lulled him to sleep as his father had predicted.

He woke because they had stopped. He was being lifted off the horse and laid on the ground. He was half aware of his father pulling a cover over him. The next thing he knew, he was cold. He was not sure whether he had been asleep. He could smell leaf mould. He opened his eyes. It was dark. He was aware of trees above him and his father next to him.

"Dad?" he said.

"I'm awake," said his father.

"Where are we?"

His father rolled over so he was facing him.

"In the woods on the mountains. We need to cross the Styx."

"The Styx?"

"The river. The border. We're up a hill and off the road. Raul is already up and has gone to scout. I was just waiting for you."

They stood up. Charlie looked at what had been his bed, a pile of ferns and light branches, two military blankets and his father's coat.

"Is there any breakfast?"

"I don't know what your friend Raul's got, but I've got some bread and cold pork. Want some?"

Charlie nodded, and thrust his hands deep into his pockets.

"Is it morning?" he asked as his Dad rummaged in his saddle.

"Soon, I think. Raul wanted to sleep under stars, but there was no cover."

Richard cut some pork and slid it between two doorstops of bread.

"I don't think Raul likes me very much," he said.

"I don't know. He doesn't like men much. I mean people who aren't delf."

Charlie took a bite out of the sandwich.

"This is good bread." He chewed for a moment. "Dad, what were you doing with the Order?"

His father was making some food for himself.

"They found me when I...arrived here. They looked after me."

"How did you get here?"

"How did you?"

"I asked first."

His father sniffed.

"I don't know. I went to sleep. And I woke up in those caverns."

"In the caverns? We didn't know where you'd gone. You went out for a walk and never came back. Mum called the police and everything. But I knew you were coming back."

"I did come back to the house. Maybe you didn't hear me. I went up to bed. But I woke up here."

"That's how you got here then. You dreamed in."

"*Dreamed* in? What do you mean?"

"I'm not really sure. Solimo and the Light Doctor told me about it a bit. They said the worlds are joined by dreams. Makes sense."

"It doesn't. How can worlds be joined by dreams?"

"I don't know. But they are."

"I suppose I'm here and that's weird enough."

There was a pause.

"Dad?"

Richard sensed some hesitation.

"What?"

"Are you still..."

"Depressed?"

He could see Charlie nod slightly.

"I don't know. I don't think so, so long as I keep away from those Pits. But I was terrified I'd never see you or your Mum again. That felt different. I think I focused more on that than... anything else."

There was a low whistle. Richard tensed.

"It's Raul," said Charlie.

From out of the dark, Raul's darker shape came towards them.

"Hey sleepy. Good to see you up."

"Want some bread and pork?" asked Richard.

Raul glanced at it and shook his head.

"It will be daylight soon. We should be on our way. I went down to the road. There were twenty or thirty riders along recently, but they are ahead of us. We will go a little further with the horses, then cross the mountains on foot. It will be too dangerous to use the passes even if we are behind the pursuit."

"But we need to get to Kunnaslaki quickly," said Charlie. "Won't we need the horses?"

Raul winked. "How do you think we got here? Ours are on the other side of the river."

They rode on a little further until they reached a place where the hills rose steeply under the trees. They dismounted and loaded as much as they could into sacks slung across their backs. Then they slapped the horses and they trotted off back through the trees.

Raul led them up the forested slopes. It was hard going, but they felt fresh and ready for the day. They padded softly through the trees, the only sound the occasional snap of a branch or the rustle of fallen leaves. Light began to seep into the woods.

They reached a narrow ridge. The ground dropped away before rising once more on the far side. They paused for a few moments to gather their breath. Charlie was breathing hard but his Dad stopped and leaned on a tree.

"Dad, you're so unfit! Watch me!"

Charlie ran off down the slope, dodging trees as he went. Richard watched for a moment, then stood up straight and charged down the slope after his son. Charlie heard him coming.

"Can't catch me!"

He reached the base of the dip and started climbing the other side, soon slowing as he lost the momentum of his downhill run. He looked over his shoulder. His Dad was bounding down the slope.

"I'll get you, boy!" he called. Then he was coming up behind him. Charlie could hear him breathing hard. He looked back and laughed. His Dad was floundering. Charlie reached for a rock to pull himself up a steeper section and to his surprise the rock came away in his hand. He only had one foot on the ground, so he toppled sideways and back and landed at his father's feet.

"Less haste more speed," said Richard. Then he bent down suddenly and tickled him. Charlie started to laugh.

Raul caught up.

"As much as this is a delightful scene, you would do well to keep quiet. And not to use up all your energy. We have got at least a full day's climbing to go."

Raul was a hard task master, although he was clearly going slower than he could have gone alone. Charlie was the slowest, but they settled into a slow steady plod uphill. Richard found it easier to keep looking at the ground or to watch Charlie's feet ahead of him. That way it came as a pleasant surprise to see how far they had climbed when he looked back.

They neither heard, nor saw anyone all day. There was little conversation as they saved their breath for climbing, but they had plenty of time for thought.

Richard was haunted by the cavern. He marvelled at the physical sensation of darkness, of emptiness, that he had felt. It had seemed to make it hard even to breathe. Here outside, amongst the trees, he was relaxed. The light was dim, but it simply felt late in the day and under the trees it was easier to forget the oppression of the Pits.

He watched his son ahead of him. Charlie seemed so relaxed in this world. He took it in without questioning it, as if dreaming yourself into another world was like taking a train. Normally he would have been worried about Charlie spending days with complete strangers, yet here in a war zone in another world, he found it did not bother him. He smiled to himself. He was with his Charlie. They were together. And the best part of it was that Charlie said he knew a way back home.

The trees were becoming shorter and the soil thinner, exposing roots and making it more necessary to watch the ground to avoid tripping. There was no path, but they were heading generally up and west. Sometimes Raul would zig-zag on a particularly steep section, or they would rest from the constant climb as they sidled around a tall rocky outcrop. On one these, they stopped for lunch.

Richard kept thinking they had reached the limit of the trees, but they were false promises caused by shallower inclines. Then he saw the rock ahead and realised the trees really were thinning. Raul gestured for them to stop, then trotted on, hunched low. He reached the edge of the trees and lay down, crawling to see what was beyond. He went beyond the trees, then came jogging back and beckoned to them.

They emerged onto an easy slope. Around them were high rocky crags and the odd stunted, wind savaged tree. There was grass and stony ground underfoot. They were in the middle of mountains and the darkness filled the southern sky. It filled them with gloom merely to look at it. Richard's heart sank further when he looked and saw in their direction of travel that there seemed to be another valley. Would they need to go down and climb up again?

Raul pointed to their west to a rocky knoll on the ridge. It appeared to be the highest point around.

"Keep low," said Raul pointing to its summit. "Look."

He pointed west and they could both see a tall building on the ridge in the distance. Two lights were shining from small windows, bright under the dark sky.

"A guardian tower," said Richard.

"We need to keep out of sight of it. Our way lies over there."

He pointed south to where the ground dipped down about a thousand feet. With relief, Richard saw this was the head of the valley he had looked into before. On the far side, it climbed up onto the next ridge.

"That is where we are going tomorrow," said Raul. We should be at the horses tomorrow night if all goes well. We will spend the night back in trees out of the way. No fire again tonight. Or any night until we are back at Kunnaslaki."

They found an area of grass on turf largely without tree roots and prepared a simple meal. Raul offered food from his own supplies, but was reluctant to take any of Richard's.

Richard wanted to ask Charlie questions about his time with the delf, but did not like to ask with Raul there. For the same reason, he did not want to talk about his time with the Order, so their evening was spent discussing the climb and what the next day would have in store for them.

Richard dreamed of darkness. He whirled around searching for light and in the gloom he saw a single face. It was Solimo. But he looked like Charlie.

39

SOLIMO LAY IN the darkness. No one came to him. No one seemed to know there was a newcomer amongst them. Or if they did, they did not care. He scrabbled for food with them when the cobs brought bowls of scraps of vegetables and stale bread. They pushed and pulled at him because he was in their way. These were not delf as he knew them.

He slept on his own, away from the others. He found a place over by the wall. The darkness was heavy around him. He yearned for light. He had never slept without candlelight in his life. He was scared of the impenetrable blackness, the void full of undelf. He needed to feel something more than the ground. He slept with his back pressed up against the wall, something solid in this eternity of darkness.

How long had passed? When should they dream? How could he track time? How long would Raul and Charlie take to return to Kunnaslaki? What if they were caught? The chances were very high. He could be in this cave until the end of his days. He had signed his death warrant. He would go mad like these poor creatures around him. He had walked willingly into insanity.

The plan had seemed so simple in the starlight, so convincing and he had been optimistic. Now he had time to think about it, too much time, and he began to think of all the things which could go wrong.

He started to count. He counted for hours. The numbers were like a mantra, a rhythm. He chanted them, holding onto them. But he lost track of time when he slept. Then he had to guess from how he felt on waking. Each time he awoke, he would blink with surprise into the darkness, for it was all the same whether he opened them or not. He was still there. Surely this was some kind of dream, some kind of nightmare. How could he have left the sunshine through the high windows of Kunnaslaki, his hill of green? How could his world have vanished into this pit? His dreams faded quickly when he awoke. He groped for the memory, but they slipped out of his grasp when he opened his eyes.

He told himself stories he remembered from his childhood. The tale of the giants in the great ship; the year the moon vanished; three wooden bowls and two spoons; the town that was made of sand; the stones that walked; the trees and the moss; the fish that dreamed of flying. He recited them, he added in every detail he could remember he had ever heard. He was a child again.

They distracted him for a while, but then his fears would return. He wondered how he would know when to dream. He wondered if his dreams would turn dark. Up until now, he had been able to see in his dreams. There was always light even if he could not see its source. He would have one chance and what if he failed? He would fail everyone, not just himself, but Charlie, Raul, Mondo, Esella. He would fail the Light Doctor. She had said she believed in him. He would fail these delf around him. It was too much responsibility.

40

WHEN RICHARD AWOKE, he lay still for some time. He could hear his son breathing beside him, a calm, steady rhythm. If they ever got out of this, he would take Charlie camping properly. They would have warm sleeping bags and a tent and they would go somewhere sunny. He felt something crawling near him and automatically flicked it away with his hand. The night was moonless and he could see almost nothing, although he knew he was surrounded by trees. It was unnerving. He was listening, listening for anything, listening so hard there was no way he would go back to sleep.

"You are awake," Raul whispered.

"How did you know?"

"Your breathing was different. And you just moved your hand."

"You have sensitive hearing."

"Hearing is all I do on these black nights. Delf need the light. I sleep out often, but never get used to it. The dark fills me with fear. Even more so when it reminds me of their sick darkness."

"*You're* afraid of the dark?"

"Why are you so surprised?"

"It's just that you seem so confident."

"Perhaps I look calm. All delf need some light. I have camped in forests for as long as I can remember, but the Ironheads' night is like nothing I have ever known. No moon, no stars. Just dark."

"Why are you telling me this?"

"So you do not rely on me too much."

Richard was silent. He was unsure how to respond.

"Thanks for telling me." It sounded rather a weak response. "It actually makes me feel better."

"What?"

"That we're both afraid of the dark. The funny thing is, I don't know if Charlie is."

Raul snorted a quiet laugh in his nose. "Why be afraid? He's got us to look after him."

"Thank you for following him. You risked your life following him into Outreterre."

"It was Solimo. Charlie was in no danger from his own kind, but I could not let Solimo go on his own. He would have got himself killed. And he probably has anyway."

"You don't like men do you? Humans? You don't like me."

"You are Charlie's father. I like Charlie."

"But you don't like me."

"What do you want me to say? You lived with them, you ate with them. You dress like them and ride with them. Have you fought with them?"

"No. This isn't my war. Look, I came into this world confused and…and I was in a dark place before I even came here. They're not bad people. I know they're from somewhere else. But that was hundreds of years ago. They don't know anywhere else now. This is their home. They just need somewhere to live."

"They murdered my entire family."

Raul said it so matter-of-factly that at first Richard did not realise what he had said.

"I – I'm sorry," he said.

"They rode into my town. Over twenty years ago. Those they did not kill they took off to slavery. Some of those delf in the Pits could have been my people. I did not want to look at any of them in case I knew them. And did you hear about Metsakant?"

"I did, but I don't know much about it. They said they had attacked it."

"They used delf prisoners to hide behind. They dressed them as Ironheads so that our light keepers would not recognise them from a distance and would attack them with sun wraiths."

"I don't know what to say. I don't understand this world."

"That is the truest thing you have said."

"Raul, you never told me they'd murdered your family," said Charlie.

"How long have you been awake?"

"Not long. Is it morning yet?"

"No. About another two hours."

"How can you tell?"

"I start counting when I go to bed. Go back to sleep. We cannot do anything in this darkness."

They all stopped talking, but only Charlie slept, the two adults were lost in their own thoughts.

Raul heard it first. His hunter's ears were sharper than ever as they reached out into the darkness around him. It was only a slight sound, but he knew he had not imagined it. A cold fear swept over him. There was something out there.

He heard another noise. It came from the other side of them.

"You hear something?" whispered Richard.

"Shh. Yes."

"Is something out there?" he asked, even quieter this time.

"Wake Charlie."

"I'm already awake. What's going on?"

"We don't know. Something's in the trees," said Richard. He felt helpless in his blindness.

All three were straining to see in the dark. Charlie felt very afraid. His stomach seemed to draw inwards. He felt cold and shivered. He put his hand out for his father. Richard felt it and gripped it. They heard a couple of clicks next to them as Raul cocked his pistols.

"If only I could see. We need fire, to light a torch. I should have made one."

Charlie had a moment of clarity.

"I've got a torch!"

He had suddenly remembered packing one the night he left the house. He felt for his backpack and groped inside it, his hand closing around the plastic case.

"How will you light it?" Raul asked.

"It's electric," said Charlie, realising Raul was confused. "Magic from my world. It's a good bright one. I can just switch it on."

"I do not understand what it is, but do not light it yet. Point it at the sound. I am sure it is coming closer. Something knows we are here. Cobs probably, if they are tracking us in the dark. They can smell us – and probably hear us too now."

Charlie had never felt so awake. His ears felt like they were exploding in the black silence. Richard realised he was gripping his long-arm.

There was a faint snap, a fainter rustle. Charlie was holding his breath so that the sound of it did not obscure any sound around them. There were definite sounds now and they were much closer.

"Light. *Now!*" said Raul through his teeth.

Charlie fumbled for the switch and the torch shone. It lit trees. There was a louder noise.

"To the right!" said Raul.

"Charlie swung the torch and caught three figures in the light. As the light hit them, the cobs stood stock still, their eyes shining green, like cats' eyes.

Raul's pistols fired at the same time. One cob fell, the others sprang to the side. Charlie jumped at the discharge and in his fear, he forgot he was holding the torch and was no longer pointing it at their attackers.

There was a bang from his other side; Richard had fired at the creatures too. There was a howl, then Charlie was searching for the beasts again with his torch. He found them, but as he did, he heard a sound behind him as something broke through the undergrowth.

Even as Raul's guns went off again, he whirled around to face what was behind him. Two more were loping at them, only a few yards away. Richard had turned too. The long-arm was at his hip. He fired wildly and one of them fell. Now his gun was empty and he was fumbling to reload. Charlie shone the torch in second one's eyes. For a moment it froze, then it gibbered and leaped to one side, dodging behind a tree.

Something knocked him sprawling. The torch flew from his hand. There was snarling, Raul cried out. Charlie jumped and groped for the torch. He fell short, but his hand found something else, the wooden handle of a pistol. Raul's? He stretched out his arm for the torch and something gripped his ankle and dragged him back. He screamed.

There was another bang, followed rapidly by two more, then a click. The grip on his ankle loosened. He wriggled forward and found the torch, holding the pistol up in front of him and lighting a tall figure.

"Woah!" shouted his father, turning his head away as the light struck him. Charlie lowered the pistol instantly. He had nearly shot his own father.

The snarling and struggling was stronger and in the edge of the beam were figures grappling on the ground. Another cob lunged up, one arm hanging loose. Richard stepped back, his long-arm clicked again. It was empty. As the cob came towards him, he swung the weapon around by the barrel. His first two swings missed, but the cob wavered. Charlie pointed the torch right in its eyes. Its good arm went up to protect them, Richard moved forward, clubbing wildly. The cob was knocked off balance, then fell over the still struggling pair behind.

Charlie could see Raul was underneath, his face turned to one side, his teeth clenched together and his hands around the throat of the final cob. He seemed to be holding it back, but it was still snarling and trying to shake itself free. Charlie levelled the pistol at its head.

"You'll hit Raul!" shouted his father.

The gun went off. The recoil surprised Charlie and he fell over, the torch swinging up into the branches. Out of the corner of his eye, something had leaped up. He had dropped the pistol. He saw a movement. It was an arm driving down again and again. Then there was silence.

Silence except for hard breathing. He sat up and shone his torch at the scene. Raul was knelt over the body of the cob, still holding the handle of a knife which was in the belly of the creature. His jacket was torn and his face and neck were bloody. He was trying to calm himself. Richard was standing staring at the carnage around them, there was blood on his coat too. His father had been injured.

"Dad! Are you okay?"

His father looked down dumbly.

"I don't think it's mine," he said.

Raul raised his head. His teeth showed through the blood on his face as he grinned wildly. He put the hand up to his own face.

"Their breath stinks."

He withdrew the knife and pushed himself up from the ground.

"Point that magic away from me, Charlie, it is blinding me. That saved our lives tonight."

"Are there more?" Charlie stammered.

"Who knows? But hand me my pistol. I do not know whether to brain you with it or hug you."

"Did I get it?" Charlie asked.

"You blew its nose off and shot the one your father had already killed. And you missed me by inches."

His father looked at him, opened his mouth. Nothing came out, then he made two steps towards him and dropped to his knees, hugging Charlie fiercely.

"Let us move camp," said Raul. "Can your torch guide us?"

They walked for perhaps a quarter of an hour, before settling down to sleep once more. But they did not sleep. They all lay in the darkness listening with thunder in their veins.

The morning saw the three of them leaving the trees as soon as it was light enough to see. They cut around below the rocky knob they had climbed the previous evening and made their way to the head of the valley, out of sight of the guard tower.

The sunrise was hidden in cloud and soon became lost in the darkness to the south. The walking would have been easy had it not been for the poor light. They had to look out for stones on the ridge, but the ground was even as they dipped down and then along the grass and bare rock at the head of the valley. Where they slowed was on the other side as the ground rose again and they climbed onto the next line of the range.

From its top, they looked onto a tumbled landscape of rocky pinnacles and trees. Beyond it, they could dimly see the lower, grassy hill country of the delf, grey under its polluting mantle. On either side, just below the ridge, chunks of limestone jutted out here and there. In front of them was a large boulder which must have rolled down from the heights behind them some lost time before. Below it was thick grass and bushes before the forest began again.

"Stay low, I will look ahead," said Raul and went slinking through the grass in a low crouch. He was half way across when he flung himself flat amongst a patch of bracken. They could not see what he had seen because it was hidden behind one of those slabs of rock. Richard and Charlie lay down on the ridge. They felt very exposed. Richard twisted his neck to see if there was better cover nearby and saw the boulder down the slope ahead of them. He looked behind him, but the ridge was too wide to be able to make it back to the cover of trees out of which they had come. Besides, if they did that, they would lose sight of Raul. Richard grabbed Charlie's hand and they rushed down the slope. Just as they reached the boulder, men on horses came into view.

Richard pulled Charlie down next to him and they sat with their backs against the rock, listening. Soon they heard the sound of horses' hooves and jingling bridles. Which way were they going? They heard a couple of voices. The sounds were coming closer.

"Dad, they're coming this way!" whispered Charlie.

Richard nodded and pointed to the side of the rock, away from the horsemen, then he looked to his left, the side they were coming from. He waited, judging the sound of the hooves, then grabbed Charlie and pulled him around behind him. He peered back and saw figures on horseback, six of them, then pushed Charlie around further until they were on the opposite side to where they had started and the same side as Raul. Richard quickly scanned the ground for him, but he was nowhere in sight. If the horsemen turned around, they would see them if they made for open ground. They were still a few seconds from the top of the ridge. He made up his mind, pointed at where they had last seen Raul and tugged Charlie.

They ran. It seemed so far. With every step, he expected to hear a challenge from behind. He turned to look for Charlie, but Charlie was only just behind him. He dared not look around further as it would slow him down. Then he felt his foot catch and helplessly he was tumbling forward. He knew he was going down, he knew there was nothing he could do to prevent it.

Instinctively, his hands went out to break his fall. He felt the shock jar his arms and his shoulders. Immediately he was scrabbling with his feet to stand up again. Charlie had stopped and stood indecisive, looking at his father, looking at the ridgeline. Then Richard was off again, Charlie too. There was the bracken. They both slid feet first into the vegetation. Richard rolled, put his arm over Charlie and lay still. They were both panting hard, fighting to breathe, but fighting to keep it quiet too. His chin pressed to the earth, Richard looked up. He could just see over the top of the rock. There was no one there. Where had they gone? Then he saw them as they reappeared, riding towards the ridge from the other side. Reaching the crest, they turned east, to Richard and Charlie's right now, and continued riding.

"A fine bit of running," said Raul grimly. He was all but obscured by bracken a few yards from them. "Come on, let us get down into the trees before any more come along or they turn back."

They gratefully entered the cover of the woods and started down. The pressure on the lungs when going uphill, transferred to pressure on the knees from the relentless downhill walking. But now at last they could talk about their time in this new world. It seemed odd that they had not yet done so, but they had been conserving their breath for climbing.

Richard asked first and Charlie told him how Solimo had talked to him in dreams. He told him about the light tower, the dreaming of it, the fight at the farm and his capture. Richard told Charlie about his first meeting with Silver, his adoption by the Archbishop and Berwick and his time with Tilley's men. His near-death experience at the hands of the sun wraith which left Charlie wide-eyed at how close his friends had come to killing his father.

They saw no one for the rest of the day, but the hill was interminable. A few times there was the relief of a short uphill or the bliss of a flat stretch which would last barely a minute. At times it was so steep they were going hand to hand on the trees to stop themselves from slipping. Then Raul was guiding them to the left. He paused, thinking, then tried to the right again. They came across a dry gully and Raul relaxed.

"I was trying to find out where we were. Come on. This way."

He led them along the top of the gully to a point where it was narrow enough to cross. Then the ground flattened and he took them through the trees and onto a rock platform which projected from the hillside. It was about thirty feet long and eight feet wide at its deepest. It gave a view of the river at the feet of the range and the stone country beyond it. In the distance they could see the hills which disappeared into the gloom.

"Almost there," said Raul.

They went back into the forest and continued down. They heard water and all of a sudden, there was the river flowing darkly beside them. They kept to the trees as they made their way to it, then walked downstream. They stopped at a wider pool where a small waterfall, all but hidden by low hanging branches, tipped over a ledge and joined the main river.

"Time for a short swim," said Raul. "Watch me and follow. Head for the waterfall, then go behind it."

He pulled off his clothes, rolled them in a blanket and stuffed them into his bag. Then he dropped into the river with a sharp intake of breath as the cold hit him. It was waist deep. He waded into the centre. When it was too deep to walk, he lifted the bag over his head and swam on his side, straight for the waterfall. He was there in less than a minute. He swam to its edge. Charlie could hardly see him through the trees, then he disappeared.

Both Charlie and Richard glanced about as if expecting to see Raul appear on the bank, but there was only the narrow bank and rock walls rising behind it.

"Up here!"

They followed Raul's soft call and saw him standing on the rocks above the bank. There was no sign of how he could have climbed up.

"Just do what I did. You will see when you get there. Hurry."

They both stripped off and wrapped their clothes as Raul had done. Richard slipped into the water first. He grimaced.

"If you're not awake already, this'll do it" he smiled. "Come on, I'm not standing in here all day."

Charlie dipped his toe in, then pulled it out. The water felt freezing cold.

"Do not dawdle. Solimo is waiting!" urged Raul from above. Charlie needed no further encouragement. He jumped in. The water was up to his chest. He cried out then plunged his shoulders under and pushed out swimming immediately for the other side. He found it hard to look ahead while swimming on his side with his bag lifted. His father overtook him and came back without his bag, took Charlie's and Charlie was able to swim the rest of the way.

They had reached the waterfall and Charlie saw that it fell over an overhang. Below it was a small cave. He pulled himself into it, his father pushing him from behind. The floor was wet in places.

"Follow my voice," said Raul.

Charlie crawled. He was so focused on what was ahead of him that he almost missed the junction. A wide crevice reached down to the tunnel he was in. He felt it first as a cold draft on his left shoulder. He looked up and could see Raul, bending over and beckoning. He looked around for handholds and footholds. He soon found some and was easily able to climb up the near vertical shaft with his bag over his shoulder. It went for about twenty feet, with a wider ledge part way up where he rested for a moment. Then he was out on the bare rock at the top next to Raul. His father was up behind him and soon they were drying themselves off and shivering in the chill morning air.

Charlie felt very awake.

"How did you know that was there?" asked Richard.

"I found it years ago," said Raul. "In the spring and summer, the water is usually higher and the cave is flooded. Now, the best thing to do is walk quickly. You will warm up."

He was right. They trotted along the bank for about fifteen minutes until they came to a dense patch of woodland. Raul led the way in and they soon came upon the tumbledown remains of a dry stone wall, over which they climbed. The trees thinned towards the middle and there, cropping grass, were two horses. They looked up and whinnied as Raul approached. They walked over to him casually, sniffing him. He stroked their necks. Then he went to a thick bush and pulled away some loose foliage to reveal two saddles.

"Some more food in here too," he said. "We will make a start into the stone country and lie up before the hills. That will give us a head start. There is little cover out there and we want to make as much ground as we can before it goes completely dark at nightfall."

They were soon under the darkness and their conversation petered out. They rode in the long dusk through rough tussock and bronzed bracken, dull and dry in the failing light. Here and there across the land were clumps of rock and stands of silver birch. They looked grey and forlorn, the few leaves on the trees hanging on grimly in the grey light. It was to one of these that Raul led them. A few hundred yards off, he stopped and turned to them.

"Wait here. I will make sure no one else is in there."

He drew his pistols and rode towards it, disappearing into a break in the rocks. A light breeze picked up and blew around them. Richard put his arm around Charlie who leaned on him, snuggling into the large coat. A few moments later, Raul rode out again. There was someone with him. And another. Then they realised they had not come from within the rocks, but from around behind it where they had been hidden. More and more horsemen rode into view. Richard wondered what to do, where to go, but they were stood out in plain view. The one at the front pointed in their direction and they all trotted over. They did not look as though they were in a hurry. There were perhaps as many as thirty. They were men. As they came closer, Richard realised who they were. Tilley was unmistakeable with his shaggy hair and red beard. As they came closer, Richard and Charlie could see a broad smile spread across his face.

"Richard of Hadbury! What in God's name be you doing out here, man?"

Charlie looked quizzically at his father. The man knew his father. Was this the man he had told Charlie about? Both of them realised that word of their flight had not reached units south of the border range or Tilley would not have been so friendly. Over their shoulders, he thought he saw something move on the top of the rocks. Was it Raul?

"I came over to have a look for myself," said Richard.

"Where be that guardian angel of yours?"

"Nicholas? He stayed behind."

"Haha! Feeling a bit more confident now eh?"

"Well I trained with the best didn't I?"

Tilley laughed and held out a leather gloved hand.

"Well it be good to see you. And who be the little man?"

"This is Charlie. My son."

"Your son? But you told me you'd left all your family behind."

"That was what I thought at the time, but it seems Charlie followed me."

"That sounds like a story. Come, ride with us. We heard that the boys over the Styx had a prize and we were going to meet up. We're just looking for a camp site and those rocks behind us look likely."

Richard glanced at the rocks, thinking quickly. Raul must still be amongst them.

"Those? We were hoping to go a little further, perhaps into the hill country itself."

"Yes," said Charlie. "The delf have all gone since the battle."

"You know about the battle eh? We were sorry we missed that one. I heard the devils could still summon demons. But there be still a few of them loose up here, so you should come with us. We be on our way to hack at their cowardly running backs. You be right, we should get into the downlands. We can ride in the night. You be a good lad Charlie. Come, your story can be told by the campfire and you'll be as safe with us as you would be in Outreterre."

As they rode on, Charlie tried not to look at the rocks to see if he could see Raul, but he knew Raul would be watching them.

41

SOLIMO WAS LOSING his dreams. There was a time when he always remembered them, but no more. Sometimes they were out of reach to memory except for knowing there had been a dream. Now even that was going. He would wake and not be sure if he had dreamed.

He sang songs; all the songs he knew. He sang rhymes he had grown up with. He sang the songs he liked to sing when he was pedalling at the light funnel. He knew many songs. There were some long ballads: the reiver and the lost horse, the maid of the mountain, the farmer's sheep, the porridge pot and the worm. He sang wedding songs and sad songs, drinking songs and harvest songs. He began to make up words and music.

It was while he was singing that he noticed a difference to the delf. Where there had been quiet mutterings before, there seemed to be more silence. He felt there were bodies closer to him now. He knew they were moving towards him, not close enough to touch, as he reached out with his hand. But when he went for the food, followed the sound of the clanking bowls, he would bump into bodies sooner than before. The songs, the music seemed to draw them in somehow.

Was it the nearness of these lost souls that was making him lose his dreams? He was no longer dreaming. He was sure of it. He went to sleep in the dark, he woke up in the dark and in between there had been simply dark nothing. Had it been a day or weeks or months? Should he stop singing? Would that drive the delf away? Would he then regain the ability to dream?

He began to count again, but the monotony of the numbers leading off to infinity was like the darkness itself. He fell quiet. No more songs, no more stories or numbers. He would lie still. He would focus on nothing. He could not track time. He did not trust the regularity of meals. Some of the gaps seemed so long. No. He would simply lie and wait. He must have missed the time. Surely he had been there an age in the blackness. He was too late.

He slept again.

42

CHARLIE AND RICHARD rode with Tilley's men into the hill country in the last shreds of grey daylight. They found a defensible hollow near a hilltop and camped on the northern side so their fire was invisible from the south. Tilley organised sentries and food was prepared.

Charlie was made to tell his tale, so he told of how he was captured by the delf as he wandered confused in the hills, how he was looked after through the battle and how he was rescued by Ragga and Ned who took him to be reunited with his father. Charlie warmed to his tale as he told it and was careful to talk about how he was well treated by the delf. He may have to lie, but he would not paint his friends in a bad light. Tilley wanted to know more about the battle, but Charlie said he had been kept in a cellar throughout. He did not want to describe his friends to these men.

As Richard made Charlie a bed from blankets and coats, he whispered to him.

"They don't know about what happened at the Pits, they can't do. And if they don't know, we should be safe unless they meet some others. We need to think about how we can slip away or find an excuse to leave. Think about it as you go to sleep. I've told Tilley I'll do a watch for him and I'll think about it too. I'll be back in a couple of hours. Try to get some sleep. You're safe with these men."

Charlie nodded and snuggled into the blankets, his head up against a saddle. He listened to the mutterings and low laughter of the men around him. He could only see them now in the glow of the fire, but they frightened him. They were like the kind of men who he would sometimes see hanging around in the middle of town, drinking cheap cider and shouting things drunkenly at passers-by. At least these did not seem to be drunk, but they were dirty and dishevelled. Freebooters, his Dad had called them. Wasn't that another name for pirates? They weren't soldiers, he could see that, but they were heavily armed and had the confidence of soldiers and more. He listened to the jingling of bridles and the occasional snort and stamp of hooves. The invisible sky seemed to lie flat across them tonight, the noise of the men helping to keep it at bay, perhaps because they were so comfortable with it. But it was they and people like them who had created it.

The next morning, they struck camp with the minimum of bother and continued to ride southwards. From time to time, Charlie would look around to see if he could see Raul. He was sure he would be tailing them. He would not have followed him all the way into Outreterre only to leave him on the way back south. But Raul was nowhere to be seen, there were only bare hillsides, bleak in the grim morning.

They rode briskly, scouts always out in front and to the sides. He and his father said little to each other as they rode. Charlie looked out for anything in the landscape that would be familiar, but he had not been this far north in daylight, or what passed for daylight. It was only when they came to the top of a ridge in the late afternoon and looked down into the valley beyond that he realised where they were. The stone buildings of Heimo stood on the high ground in the middle of the valley. He could see movement there and for a moment, his heart leaped – the delf had retaken it. But even as the thought occurred to him, he knew it could not be true. The behaviour of the men around him confirmed it. These were not men riding to meet an enemy, but those with a safe haven in sight.

Raul had been right when he had said that the Order would like the fortified farm. None of the buildings had been damaged and the place was busy with soldiers. They rode through the gate in the outer turf walls, then they were through the main gate, the man on watch merely nodding at them and shouting something with a grin as they rode in.

It was strange to be back there so soon and in such a different situation. They clattered into the courtyard where horses were mustering. A powerfully built man walked out to meet them.

"Ah the scum have arrived," he said with a guffaw. "Tilley you dog, I hope you have some fine wines with you. The devils left nothing behind worth pissing."

Then he saw Richard.

"Well, well, well, so you decided to come down after all. I heard you were riding with Tilley's company. And you could have ridden with mine!"

He laughed again. Charlie's Dad merely nodded his head with a faint smile and said: "Hello, Lord Lyell."

"I suppose you've just come to see if there was anything here worth 'trading', eh Tilley?" Lord Lyell continued. He put an emphasis on the word trading and smiled as he said it with a raised eyebrow.

"I wot right well that where the Order goes, all trade has vanished by the time I get there," returned Tilley, swinging off his horse and handing it to one of his men. "I admit I came out of curiosity." The man waited for Richard to dismount too then took his horse with him.

"So you've heard about my witch have you?" asked Lord Lyell. "I thought the Archbishop himself might come down to officiate."

"He be coming with the army soon enough. I don't think you should wait. If you've got a witch, you should burn her as quickly as you can."

Who was this witch they were talking about, Charlie wondered.

"She be not here. They caught her further south on a raid of their wagons. We be going to meet them to see it done right, then we'll start on their light towers. You be welcome to join us. It could be all over before the rest of the army arrives."

Charlie's stomach felt suddenly hollow. There had been more raids on the wagons. When he was taken must have been just the first. And they had taken someone prisoner. A woman. Why did they have to call them all devils and witches?

"We'd be delighted, your lordship," said Tilley with a mock bow. "Just as soon as we've rested."

"I hope you brought your own food," Lyell responded. There be nothing to eat here unless you eat dung."

Time no longer mattered to Solimo.

He sat in the dark.

Breathing occupied him. It was all there was to life. He breathed in and felt his lungs fill with the cool stale air of the pit. He could smell the odours of the other delf as he inhaled. He had never been aware of being able to smell others before, but then he had lived on a bright hilltop washed by the winds and the sun. But that was so long ago.

He exhaled. He felt his body deflate. Sometimes he tried to hold onto the breath. He was afraid that when he breathed out, he was breathing out his life. Perhaps his soul too would be sucked out into the impenetrable blackness around him. But then, perhaps that was the best thing that could happen. He had stopped waiting, but he had no idea how long ago that had been.

43

THE HILLS SPREAD before them in endless, dull layers until at last they saw a darker mass in a valley. It was a wood and Charlie thought he recognised it. Surely they were close to Kunnaslaki now. He looked up and peered into the gloom at the hills ahead and there he saw a group of buildings that looked familiar yet different without the familiar shape of the light tower on the crest of its hill. He could not believe they were so close.

Across the valley on the hill facing Kunnaslaki, but still a mile or more away, he could see a couple of horsemen. Their company rode down into the trees. There were soldiers camped amongst them, their horses tethered.

"Hey boys, you be just in time to watch the witch burn!" called one of them who was just hitching up his saddle.

Lyell leaned over to the corporal riding next to him and said something to him. The corporal raised his arm and called a halt.

"Fall out!" he called. "But don't wander off or you'll miss the spectacle and be ready to mount up fast."

"Tilley, your men can do what they like," said Lyell. "But I be going up to check on preparations and take a look at that tower."

"Both of those sound like I shouldn't miss out on them," grinned Tilley.

"Dad, can we go too?" whispered Charlie. His father looked at him.

"I don't think you should see this."

"No, we're really close now. To the tower. We're here. We're almost home." His voice was low, but insistent. Richard nodded.

"We'll come up too if you don't mind," he said.

"Whatever you like," returned Tilley. "I know you don't get witches where you be from, so this will be new sport for you."

"Corporal," said Lyell. "Give the men an hour, then bring them up."

The four of them rode through the wood and climbed the other side. There were half a dozen men gathered around something on the crest of the hill. Charlie tried to make out what it was in the darkness. As they reached it, he saw it was a pile of branches from the wood. With a lurch of horror, he realised what it was: a pyre to burn the witch. Several of the men were still arranging the wood, their coats and helmets laid on the ground nearby. Charlie jumped off the horse and went to the woodpile, looking it over.

A man in a wide brimmed hat folded up at one side came over to the head of their troop and saluted Lord Lyell.

"You've made good time, your lordship.

"Thank you, captain. Do they know you be here?"

"They've must have seen us by now, but no one's ventured out. We don't know their strength, but we know some of the wagons continued south. I've every confidence that we can take them now you've come up. We'll have done half the work before the rest of the army arrives!"

"Good work. Where be the witch?"

"They be bringing her up now. We were waiting for you. Once we've burned her, we can take their tower. We had thought it was a light tower, but it must be another farm. There be not even a gate. When they see us burning their witch, any heart they have left will leave them."

Lyell looked back down the hill and the others followed his cue and turned as well. Charlie could see a small party coming up the hill on foot. As they came closer, he could make out a small figure amongst them. She appeared to be tied and was stumbling. In the gloom, he could not see who it was for the soldiers around her until they were almost at the top of the hill. And then he felt as though all his breath had been punched out of him. He had been hoping his suspicions were wrong. It was the Light Doctor.

He stood stock still, his mouth open, not knowing what to do or what to say. He tried to catch her eye, but her glance passed across him. Would she think he had gone over to the Order?

The soldiers who had been at the wood pile left it and walked away, as if afraid to be so close to their witch. The Light Doctor was led towards the pyre. The captain went over and spat at her.

"Summon your demons now, witch. The only light you'll see will be that bonfire and the fires of hell when you die. And your people in that tower will see our fire and wonder what the beacon tokens. And it will be a sign of their doom. We have your bag of charms, witch!"

He held aloft what Charlie knew to be her bag of light sponges and hung it on a scrubby bush next to him and still in her sight, as if to torment her.

"Dad," said Charlie.

Richard looked down at him. He appeared troubled, confused. Richard knew what he was watching was wrong, terribly wrong, but felt powerless to prevent it. No. Not powerless. He was frightened. He knew what he had to do, but he feared for the consequences. He would fail. How could he succeed? Who was he to prevent this? He was nobody. He had to remember that.

"You be not so proud now, witch," said Lyell.

"Where be your fairy gold?" asked Tilley with a sneer.

"Dad, you've got to do something," Charlie moaned.

Charlie. Charlie was looking at him. Richard could not look at him again. He had looked once and those imploring eyes had stabbed him. There were tears in his eyes. Charlie wanted him to do something. What could he do? Why was Charlie asking him to do something? Things don't always work out, Charlie, he thought. I can't make everything all right. They aren't all right. Life isn't like that, sometimes life is just horrible. People are burned. People lose their jobs. People are wasted and thrown aside. These just happen and you can't stop the people who make it happen.

"Dad..."

He could not resist the tone of voice. Richard looked at him. Charlie's face was begging him. There were tears running down his cheeks. He was expecting his father to do something.

"You're not – " croaked a voice. "You're not going to burn her are you?" Richard realised he had spoken.

Lyell and Tilley turned their horses to face him.

"She be a witch," said Lyell. "Don't they do that in your world any more either?" he laughed.

Richard said nothing.

Lyell turned back.

"Tie her to the pole."

Two of her escort grabbed her roughly by the arms. She winced and let out a small cry, half stifled, not wanting to give them the satisfaction. Tilley laughed and as they passed Lyell, without warning, he whipped her across the cheek with his pistol.

"Bitch!" he said. "Leave your crying and whimpering!"

"Stop."

It was Richard's voice again. Charlie's eyes widened. In his father's hands was the long-arm from the holster on his horse. The others did not notice at first. Richard had done it without conscious thought. One moment he had been in a state of mental turmoil, the next he was pointing a gun at the two men in front of him. He felt suddenly calm. The decision had been made and there was no going back.

"Leave her alone," he said.

That was when Tilley and Lyell turned and noticed the gun levelled at them. Richard could feel Charlie staring at him. He could sense Charlie's sudden terror.

"What be you doing, man?" demanded Tilley. "Has your world gone soft?"

"We don't burn women" said Richard. "We don't burn anyone."

"Put down your weapon!" Lord Lyell said with stern outrage.

The soldiers had stopped their work around the pyre. Several were looking confused and wondering whether to reach for their own guns, but without looking at them, Lyell raised a hand to stop them.

"Put that down," Lyell said again.

"No," said Richard.

"You be a traitor to your people. Has Satan taken you too?"

Charlie felt as though his heart had stopped beating. He could not take his eyes from the three men in front of him, but even as he was gripped by the new drama his father had created, he felt an urge to turn towards the Light Doctor. She was staring at the bag of sponges. It was just in front of Charlie.

"You wouldn't use that," said Tilley to Richard. "You never shot anyone and you be not about to start."

"You didn't see me the other night," said Richard. "Let her go."

"I'll burn myself before I let her go," said Lyell and he turned his back on Richard. There was a gunshot and everything seemed to speed up and slow down at the same time, yet Charlie was aware of everything: a trooper right next to Lyell tumbling backwards; Tilley's face frozen in amazement, staring at Richard; Richard's own confusion. He had not fired. Or had he? Had he just shot a man? Had time just stopped?

Another gunshot. Lyell was looking around as another soldier fell. He was drawing his sword. A horseman was galloping, riding towards them out of the trees on the ridge brandishing a pistol in each hand. It was a soldier of the Order. He had fired on them.

Lyell was ignoring Richard now, turning to face the danger. Tilley wrenched his pistols from his belt. The men on the ground were groping for their long-arms and swords. Tilley was watching the rider. Richard fired at Tilley, a half-hearted shot that missed Tilley, but hit a soldier behind him who cried out and fell holding his arm.

The horseman galloped closer. Tilley pointed one pistol at Richard. Richard dug his spurs into his horse's sides. Why was he going towards the gun? He should run away. He was swinging his long-arm.

There was confusion, another gunshot. Tilley looked around, then back at Richard just in time to see the long-arm swinging at him. He cursed and ducked, losing his balance and tumbling from his horse. Then the other rider was upon them, slashing to right and left with his sword. The thicket of troopers could not move freely. Lyell was cursing. Hands were reaching out in the mayhem, Richard no longer knew what was going on. His body was tense and tingling, expecting some kind of blow or shock or he knew not what. And then they were bathed in light.

It was the bright light of the sun and all were blinded by it. A burning figure stood before them. Charlie was kneeling at its feet, a sponge in his hands, crouched over one of the discarded helmets. The sun wraith moved suddenly as the Light Doctor lifted it, a blaze of angry light and the soldiers around fell writhing from its burning touch.

Charlie felt a hand grabbing him roughly and pulling him onto a horse and they were riding. All was a blur, a mess of actions. His father's arm was around him.

"The Light Doctor!" he called.

There was another group of horsemen coming after them. Charlie could not see the Light Doctor, but he could still see the sun wraith. It rose into the sky. It quivered and hung. He could hear gunshots. They galloped down the hill. He tried to twist around to see in front of him, trying to see the light tower. He looked back. There were more soldiers on the hilltop, there were more horsemen. He thought he would fall. He was across the front of his father's saddle. He was slipping. He could see their pursuers and then he heard other horses ahead of him. They were being cut off, outflanked.

"Dad!" he called out, but he was winded, he could hardly breathe.

Then there were horses on either side of him, riders going the other way. He waited for the end, but they did not stop. There was more firing. They rode on. He could see the light tower now. It was closer. The horse that had been following pulled passed them. The Light

reloading their long-arms. Another was sprawled on a roof. Raul swung about looking to see where there was support and where there was a threat. There were so few of them.

A volley of shots cut short his thoughts and bullets pinged off the walls around him. There was a cry from above. The delf on the roof was face down and motionless. His long-arm clattered across the tiles and dropped to the ground. Raul ran over to the wagon, jumped up and peered over. Horsemen were milling beyond it, preparing to charge. He could hear other gunshots coming from the cottages behind him. He needed to fetch more delf from that side. The wagons were their most pressing need to defend. He tapped the nearest delf on the shoulder.

"Where is Mondo?"

"On the other side. Esella was on this side."

"Does he not know she's gone?" he said. Then he raced across the yard and crashed through the door which had only been pushed shut. Across the simple room, a single delf stood beside the window. He turned, startled, his long-arm raised before he recognised Raul and turned back to the window.

"Shut the door, you are silhouetted!" he hissed.

Raul did so.

"We need to guard the wagons. They are about to charge. How many of you are in here?"

"Just two upstairs. The rest must be in the other cottages."

"Where's Mondo?"

"Next door."

Raul cursed.

"You must come outside, the others can hold this side a little longer. If they come through the gap, it will not matter how many are in here."

The delf looked at him, then nodded sharply.

His eyes jumped to the staircase.

"Mikko! Topi! Come down. They are heading for the wagons!"

Seconds later, there was a thundering on the stairs and two young, wide-eyed delf appeared.

"Come on!" said Raul and he was already heading out the door and back into the courtyard and to the cottage next door to find Mondo. With alarm, he saw a massed bunch of horsemen suddenly lurch forward. There was a blaze of sound. Bullets thudded into the wagons. One of the delf behind it spun around, his face blown apart. Others simply collapsed. Raul and the three delf from the cottages ran to the wagons, kneeling by the wheels to gain a little cover.

They fired a volley into the body of soldiers. Several fell, but still the rest came on. They would have only one more chance to fire before they were upon them.

They fired again. There were simply too many.

"Back to the cottages!" Raul called.

They retreated and made the door just as the first horsemen reached the wagons. The soldiers leaped onto them from their saddles, then jumped down into the courtyard, looking around quickly at the new environment.

Raul realised he had left the door to the garden room unguarded. It led first into the small laboratorium, but that was all that lay between any attacker and his friends in the garden room beyond it.

A soldier ran for the door of the laboratorium. He tried the handle, found it was locked, then threw his shoulder at it. Raul raised his long-arm and fired. The man fell. He saw two more raise their own weapons towards the window and he pulled back. One shot hit the wall outside, but the other entered the room, ricocheting dangerously onto the floor.

Two more men were now throwing themselves at the door. Others were pushing the wagons out of the way to let in more horsemen. He saw the door give. Just as it did, a sun wraith tore down into the courtyard. At last, Mondo had arrived! He did not think any more. The only cover he had was the birthing room in the middle of the courtyard. He pulled the pistols from his belt and ran out of the door firing. He was ready to dive behind the birthing room if he needed to, but the soldiers had not expected the double assault. The men at the gate scattered or fell to the wraith. Raul hurtled across the yard and flung himself at the two men who had just forced their way into the laboratorium.

In that slow-motion instant, as Raul expected at any moment to feel the hard shock of bullets hitting him, his own pistols raised, he saw one of the men turn to face him. Then he felt as if his legs had been swung from underneath him and he had been hauled upside down. The room spun and he was reaching out to hold onto something for support. He had a last sensation of the two men in front of him groping for air.

There was only darkness and gunfire. Every muscle in Richard's body was tense. There was only one thing which he held onto and that was

Charlie's calm. His face looked urgent and a little fearful, but there was something else there which spoke of confidence.

Suddenly there was light, Richard sank back into its warm glow. This was insane. Maybe it was all a dream after all. He would wake and this battle, this world, this madness would all be the fevered memories of a night.

He dreamed of Charlie in the forest. The guns were fading now. He could hear birdsong. He remembered playing hide and seek with him when he was little. He could hear his laughter, joyous peals of giggles as they ran from tree to tree, jumping out from behind the trunks to surprise each other. It was an innocent time, a lost time, a wondrous time. He had forgotten it. But still there was Charlie. He could see him following him, older now.

"Go on," he seemed to be saying. "I'm with you Dad. It's okay."

There was a breeze and the creak of a branch and shifting of leaves as they rustled together, rippling in the gentle sunlight. But then it was fading. A darkness loomed out of the trees, out of the deeper wood. The branches were gnarled and bent and twisting and reached out tangled claws. Leaves were a dense, heavy pall, sound was muffled. He was in a corridor, that long corridor again. His world was spinning out of control. He was losing it.

Then it was fading until there was only a hint of light, like a cloudy morning before the sun rose. He floated alone and fear began to seep into his thoughts. He was adrift and falling in a great, grey void. Where were the others? Where was Charlie? He needed something to hold onto. He needed someone.

Helen, warm beside him, her smile, her eyes. She had supported him through everything. She was always there. There were trees outside the window, there was a flickering of light from behind branches and leaves. The light was spinning. It shook in front of him.

44

A SPARK.

Solimo did not realise at first. A blurred spark. Was it a torch held by the cobs? He walked towards it. It was no spark. It was a leaf. A single green leaf. It was shining. There were more leaves. The darkness was pulling away. He could see something made of stone.

He sat up. Awake. He had dreamed. He had *dreamed*! He stood suddenly and almost fell. He reached out a hand to the wall to support himself.

"Delf of the dark!" he called. "I am Solimo Keeper of Kunnaslaki."

There was silence at first, then a murmuring. Then a voice spoke out of the gloom.

"Was it you that sang?" It was said hesitantly, dredging up the memory.

"I did."

"We had forgotten."

There were the low sounds of mumbling, then silence.

"I am a Light Keeper," said Solimo.

"Then you are a ghost. Sing to us again."

"I will tell you a story, a true story, but I must tell you quickly. I have come to you from Unama. The Order is spreading darkness over our land. They have spread *your* darkness over the land. You make it in these pits. Your despair. It pollutes the darkness and the darkness hangs in the sky and blots out the light."

"There is no light."

"Dreams are dark," said another voice.

"Dream of light again. I need you to dream with me. I need you to dream of the coming of light."

"Our dreams are of the dark. There is only dark."

"I will show you the light. I want you all to dream of light, of hope and if you do, I promise you, it will bring light to this place, to your lives. The light I am about to show you will fade, but you must remember it and dream of it and it will bring more."

As he spoke, he pulled the last sponge from his pocket and the small bowl from his other side and he squeezed the sponge gently.

In the darkness of the cavern, the light was almost blinding. The area of cave around him was bathed in sunshine. He saw hundreds of faces around him, dumbstruck and looking at the light with awe. Some even looked up at the roof of the cavern as if expecting to see the sun shining down from a blue sky.

There was a sound. It was a sound beyond hearing. It was the sound of tears welling up in the eyes as a lost memory surfaces, it was the sound of a sigh, the sound of the feeling of sliding into hot water after a long day's work. It was the sound of a forgotten smile, a generation or more old. It was the sound of hope rising out of a dark sea. The sound of hundreds of souls waking out of a deathly sleep.

"Dream of the light!" said Solimo. "Dream of the light towers, dream of the sunlight pouring into the light funnel and filling your heart! Dream with me!"

He could feel the light filling him, he felt as though he were catching the light in himself, reflecting it back. He felt as if he were giving off light. The delf fell to the ground.

And then the impossible happened. The light began to fade.

Solimo stared wild eyed. It must not fade. He looked around. Had the light tower come and he had not seen it? Was it here? There was only a twilight in the cavern now and it was fading fast. Then it was gone.

The darkness was blacker than it had ever been. It was deeper than anything he had ever known. Solimo fell to the ground. He was gasping for air. He had survived on hope, the hope that the light would bring the light, would bring his friends, would bring liberty from this hell. But now the truth blinded him in a way that even the light had not.

How could he have been so foolish? How could they have hoped to bring together two thoughts divided by distance and events he could not even imagine? Charlie, Raul, Richard. They were most likely captured, or dead. There would be no triumphant reunion, no glorious rescue. Those were dreams, false hopes. Now they were gone and he was faced with the plain, brutal reality. He had walked into this nightmare prison freely, this pit of despair. What a fool he had been. Here he would end his days. He would go as mad as the sad vestiges of delf around him. They were too far from hope to grasp it. They could make nothing of the light he had shown them. He could see that now. It had blinded them and terrified them. He had promised them light and hope and all he had given them was a deeper darkness than ever before.

"I am so sorry!" he cried out and then he was sobbing. Deep, painful gasps of air. It was over. He had lost. He was a fool, a simpleton. He had failed. All that was left was despair. It mingled with the air.

Drowning in his self-pity, he did not hear the stir that tingled in the room. He did not see what caused it.

Shining down from the ceiling was a narrow blade of light.

Charlie stirred and next to him his father grunted, opened his eyes and blinked. There was darkness in the windowless garden hall.

"Are we there? I can't hear the guns."

They lay listening. There was no sound.

"Is that a bird?" breathed Esella. "Are there birds?"

"Of course we've got birds," said Charlie. "I'll go and look."

"You'll stay here. I'll look," said Richard. "We don't know where we are."

He stood up. The Light Doctor was already on her feet.

"First we will see if we have joined up with the funnel room," she said.

She walked to the door which led to the corridor. Richard was behind her and Charlie had followed regardless of his father's instruction. The Light Doctor opened the door. There was no longer the strange blurred vision of Limbo, but simply the stone walls of the short corridor to the funnel room. They walked through it, opened the other door and there was the funnel room, sunlight pouring through its high windows and making bright patches on the walls.

We've done it!" said Charlie. "Let me see!"

Before anyone could stop him, he had run past them, unbolted the door and opened it.

"It is! We're there!"

The Light Doctor shook her head.

"I did not believe it were possible. We have pushed through to the other world."

Richard opened the door wide and stepped out. He was home. He breathed in the fresh smells of damp autumn woodland. Above the trees, the sky was a rich blue framed by yellowing leaves.

"Richard?"

He looked around for the voice.

"Charlie? Is that you?"

Someone was peering from amongst the trees.

"Mum!" shouted Charlie.

She was there, a startled, white face. She was coming out from behind a tree.

"Mum! I found him. I said I would!"

They ran to her. She stood still. Her face was a contortion of fear, anger and joy.

She scooped up Charlie and ran at Richard, grabbing him fiercely and holding him tight. She was crying and laughing at the same time. Her boys were back. They were back.

Finally, she loosened her grip.

"What...?" she said. She was looking at the garden room which was now in its position next to the funnel hall. Only the cottages remained in Unama. "I was asleep..."

A thought occurred to her. Her look of surprise turned to one of anguish.

"I'm still asleep. I was dreaming of you. I'm still dreaming. You're not here."

"We *are*. Mum, you must have pulled us through!"

The Light Doctor and Esella were at the door.

"Who are they?"

"They're friends of ours." He turned to the two delf. "It's my Mum! She was asleep and dreaming of us! She must have pulled us through!"

"What do you mean, I pulled you through?" asked Helen.

"Charlie," said the Light Doctor. "We need to go. We need to find Solimo."

She was right. Solimo had waited long enough. Who knew what could have happened to him.

"Come on," he said to his parents.

"Wait a minute," said his father. "We don't need to go."

"We do. It's Solimo. He came back to rescue me. We need to rescue him."

"What do you mean?" asked Helen. She was bewildered.

Her husband opened his mouth as if to speak, then closed it again. "I don't even know where to start," he said.

"Oh Dad, it's not that hard. We need to go to another world. The Light Doctor and Esella are delf and they live there. You can only get there by dreams and they can make you dream. They use light..."

"Charlie, stop," Helen said. "I don't understand a word you're saying."

Richard wondered how he could possibly explain it to her. Then he knew. He needed to show Unama to Helen. It would always be a void between them if he did not, something he and Charlie had lived through, but somewhere she did not believe in, no matter how much she tried or wanted to.

"Helen, come with us. Charlie and I need to show you something. It will explain everything: where we've been, who these people are. I can never explain, not unless you come too."

Helen looked at him. She had never been so confused before. She could not tell if she was awake or asleep. They had been away and suddenly they were back, but nothing they said made any sense. She looked at the silent pleading eyes of her son. She took their hands and walked with them into the building. She looked at the two women. There was something unusual about them. One was short and greying, the other slim with long, thick black hair. Their skins were a dark copper colour. They looked – she was embarrassed to think about it in this way – but they all looked simply so *foreign*.

She followed without thinking, simply assuming that something would happen to explain it all. She went into the funnel room and looked up blankly at the funnel dominating the room. She followed them into the garden hall and there she hesitated in the darkness.

"What have you been doing?"

"We're all going to lie down and sleep," said Richard. "This is the only way I'm going to be able to explain this."

Helen looked at him as if she was about to say something, as if he were mad.

"I know that sounds odd. You've got to trust me. You've got to trust Charlie. Just this."

"I need to sleep," said Helen vacantly. "I've hardly slept since you went away."

"Then sleep," said Richard.

45

THE ARCHBISHOP WATCHED as Rodon stowed the crate of books into his carriage. It was the last item to be packed.

"Be you sure you don't want me to go with the carriage?" Rodon asked.

"Yes, yes, quite sure. My notes can look after themselves on the way to Collenium. I want you with me when we join the army. I would not cheat you of this moment. You have waited all your life for it. It be the crowning moment of Christendom in Faerie. The Lord be smiling on us and will finally reward us with the land he promised us. At last we will deserve it."

He went over to Rodon, held his shoulders and looked into the younger man's eyes. He was a little taller and his gaze was downward.

"Thomas, you have been the most faithful of servants and friends. You have lived through all of this as much as I. You will come with me."

The door to the Pits was flung open. Two cobs erupted from the doorway and loped towards the stone building, chattering madly.

The Archbishop's party in the courtyard looked around at the animals, then turned to the Archbishop as if he would have all the answers. He watched them calmly.

"Most unusual," was all he said. He did not move, but watched as they flailed at the door of Silver's lodgings. Silver was just emerging from the Archbishop's apartments with his final valise. At first he looked irritated and barked a command at them, but they pawed at him and waved their arms. He hesitated, then looked across to the Archbishop.

"Your Grace, they say there was light in the Pits."

"Light? Torchlight, they mean."

"No. They said it was sunlight."

"Impossible," he replied. It should be impossible, he thought, but he also realised this was a field of knowledge that was still expanding for him. He knew only too well he was feeling his way and that serendipity and imagination had been his friend as much as logical deduction. It could be true.

"I be sure it be nothing to disturb us, but you should go down there and see if you can see aught." He turned to Rodon. "We shall wait until they return before we leave," he said.

"Your Grace!" said Rodon with alarm and pointed suddenly.

The Archbishop looked. All looked. All saw. Above the hill, in the midst of the fresh darkness was what looked like a lone star in the night sky. There was a tiny white patch of light. A narrow ray of light fell at an angle from the dark and into one of the inverted funnels.

"What be that?" Silver asked slowly, fearfully.

"I will come with you," said the Archbishop. "I want to see what betides. Perhaps my notebooks will see more entries after all."

Silver ran to a bell by the doorway and started to ring it. Men came stumbling from the huts, pulling on jackets. There were perhaps a dozen of varying ages, tripping over their weapons and each other. The two soldiers looked questioningly at Rodon who nodded at them. They pulled long-arms from their saddles, then the whole group of them walked briskly to the doors and inside.

There were still the few flaming torches flickering on the walls and there was no sound above their thudding footfalls merging as the men descended the steps, the cobs running ahead. At last they reached the hallway at the base. A body of cobs had gathered in a crowd, waiting for their masters.

"I will look first," said Silver gallantly, then motioned several cobs ahead of him into the doorway onto the balcony. He looked about and only one thing had changed. A thin line of bright daylight shafted down through one of the funnel mouths in the roof. Silver turned to call for the Archbishop, but he was already at his shoulder.

"It be coming through a funnel," said Silver.

Over their heads, above the hill, the black smoke of despair continued to roll out of the funnel mouths. It drifted across the hole in the darkness. The light blinked and went out.

Down in the Pits amongst the delf, all was dark once more. There was silence again. In the dull, blankness of their minds, it was not even clear if it really had happened. They barely noticed the sound of men and cobs on the balcony. It was not unusual. They sank back to the ground where their customary sleep took them. Sleep had ceased to be a refuge, but in the dark it was all there was to do.

"That be it then," said Silver.

"Be that all it was?" asked the Archbishop, half to himself. "Silver, would that have frightened your cobs in that way?"

"They be simple creatures," said Silver.

"Not that simple, Silver," said the Archbishop. "Where did it come from?" Something was not right. He could sense something. It nagged at him.

"How did it happen?" he asked himself. "Go down and search the devils," he said to Silver.

"Of course, Your Grace. At once." He made to go, then turned back. "What be I seeking?" asked Silver.

"I know not. Something unusual."

Silver took some of his own men and the cobs. They carried torches and a man went with each cob into the pit amongst the delf. Each cob sniffed and snorted, scurrying amongst the huddled delf. As the beasts came towards them, they did not move, but slept, oblivious to the world around them.

Except this time was different. This time there was something else in their dreams. There was a spark. And in their dreams they stared at the tiny white fire and were drawn into it, or perhaps it grew. The haunting shadow of which they usually dreamed was being pushed back.

They were watching the beam of light. They knew it was light. They would have known it was light even if there had not been that moment of incandescence which the singer had brought.

Silver did not know for what he was looking but he knew he had to find something. A change had occurred. The cob in front of him stopped, twitched its head and moved to its right. It started to grab each delf as it went and sniff it, then push it away. It did this with three or four. Then one it held. It chattered to Silver.

"Bring it," he said.

The cob pulled the delf out. He was limp. It dragged the delf to the front of the room until they stood below the balcony.

"I've found something, Your Grace," Silver called up. "This one be different." He lifted the torch nearer the delf and lit the terrified face of Solimo freshly woken from the temporary oblivion of sleep into hell again.

"Look at its cloths. They be cleaner and in good condition. And the cobs say it smells different. It smells of trees. And men."

Silver leaned in closely.

"It could be the one which escaped. What be you doing here?" he snarled, then he struck Solimo, a sharp backhand across his face.

"What do you mean, the one which escaped?" asked the Archbishop.

Silver suddenly regretted not saying something before. He tried to sound causal.

"Your man Richard brought him. Found him in the forest. Brought him back."

"You did not tell me."

"I did not want to bother you, Your Grace." Silver wondered if he had done the right thing. He redoubled his efforts to interrogate the creature.

"Tell me, filth. You be different. What be you? How did you escape?"

Solimo was limp as he was flung away from the man. His head struck the wall and he crumpled helplessly to the floor, dazed. He was exhausted. He had no will to fight this. He had no way out of this. He lost consciousness, he slipped down into the dark and met a wave which rushed out of the pit. Light was cascading all around him. It bubbled and frothed, it took him with a surge towards the sky.

He dreamed of Kunnaslaki, of the garden, of rising in the fresh morning, of the glow on the horizon as he made his way to the funnel hall. He dreamed of the tower against a blue sky, of Charlie laughing, of his garden, of the hill. He dreamed of the sun, then all was brilliance.

Raul shook his head. He was not sure if he was awake. He did not remember falling asleep. He had thought he was awake and then he was awake again. Outside the laboratorium the gunfire had stopped. When had that happened? Then he remembered the two soldiers he had followed into the room. He climbed to his feet and looked around. The soldiers were there. He could hear them, feel their presence, but there was no light now from under the door. He had slept. The men too seemed to have fallen and were picking themselves up. He groped for his pistols.

If the fighting had stopped outside, that could only mean the other delf were dead and he was alone between the group in the garden hall and the soldiers. But if he had been asleep, what could that mean? Perhaps everyone was dead. His hand found one of his pistols and he grabbed at it.

"I suggest you sit down. Slowly. Or I will shoot you both where you stand," said Raul. "The room is small. I will not miss."

"Be this witchcraft?" asked the younger of the two.

"Oh yes," Raul smiled with menace. "So this pistol is the least of your worries."

The door of the garden hall burst open and there was a blinding beam of light. The three in the laboratorium did not know it, but it was the light from Charlie's torch which Richard was holding.

For a moment, nobody moved. It was Richard who spoke first.

"Nicholas!" he said.

He was looking at one of the soldiers. The other one suddenly pointed at Charlie who had appeared behind him.

"The boy!"

Esella pushed past Raul to open the door to the courtyard.

"Do not go out. The Order is out there!" said Raul.

He saw the eyes of the two soldiers open wide. He could not help himself; he turned too. He had expected daylight to flood in, but there was nothing.

Something had happened. The air had changed. The Archbishop did not believe his eyes. The light from the torches was blotted out. He did not remember it happening. He heard jabbering. Something big was in front of the balcony, something big and dark.

"Sorcery!" cried a voice. It was Silver's.

The Archbishop reached out and his hand and touched stone. His stomach felt cold. Sorcery.

"Kill them all!" he shouted suddenly. "Kill them! The devil be come!"

Rodon and the soldiers did not need to be told twice. They turned and ran to the steps into the great cavern.

In the laboratorium there was confusion. They heard the shout. Raul realised where they were. He looked back at the bemused troopers.

"Move and you die!" he said, but the two men were still too stunned to do anything.

"Richard, what...?" began Berwick. "This be the devil's work!"

He groped at his neck and pulled out a cross and brandished it at Richard. Then he looked at the open doorway and knew he was in Hell.

In the shifting dark orange of flames, there was a crowd of the damned. He heard snarling and the pattering of feet and saw the cursed souls shrink back. Then hairy fiends were running amongst them, slashing and snarling.

Two women swept past him from inside the building. The smaller was carrying a bowl. The cobs were already reaching at those delf nearest to them as they stumbled over each other to escape.

The Light Doctor carried the bowl out into the cavern, set it on the floor and squeezed out light.

The cobs paused, ever sensitive to changes in the light. The murmuring turned to crying, but not the sound of sadness and misery and despair. This was a sound of hearts too full to express themselves. All were once more bathed in light. The roof of the cavern became visible. Right above their heads was the wide opening of a funnel. The light lit its polished insides.

The ball of light spread and reformed. It began to rise. The cobs stopped and look up blankly. Then the sun wraith swooped down from the ceiling of the cavern.

Some of the cobs held their arms over their heads, others ran, a few snarled and swung their arms at the air and the diving spectre.

There was more light. Solimo turned and there was Esella. She was squeezing out another sponge. The rough stone walls of the cave were bathed in a sunny glow which washed over the squalid floor. He could see other funnels in the roof, their insides were reflecting it. The darkness had been torn into shadows separated by a terrible, dancing light.

The cobs at the door wavered. Both sides paused, the delf of the pit hovering in confusion. Some cowered, but others stood and stared at the light or the shape of the stone building which had suddenly appeared in their midst.

Solimo sprang up and ran forward. His face was radiant with joy.

"I cannot believe you are here! I cannot believe you are here!"

He went to hug them, then there were four short, crashing sounds of sudden thunder. Gunshots. They echoed around the chamber. Delf fell.

The Light Doctor and Esella looked about them. They could not see where the shots had come from. The sun wraith hung in the air as she looked. Then there was another gunshot and the Light Doctor was thrown to the ground. She felt arms dragging her back inside.

"Is she dead?" asked Charlie. He turned to his mother who was staring at the wounded delf.

Solimo looked distraught.

"I do not know," said Esella.

Raul was still in the laboratorium. He did not know which way to turn. His mind raced.

"Take her into the garden," he could not watch the two men and deal with those outside. He pointed his pistols at them.

"No!" said Richard.

His pistol clicked. It was out of ammunition. He threw himself at the open door, shutting it. Even as he did so, there was the thump of bodies throwing themselves against it from outside. He could feel the wood shake with each blow. He did not think it would hold long.

"That way!" said Richard, pointing into the garden room. The two soldiers looked at each other. Their minds were still struggling to understand what was happening. Richard pushed them out of the door and they found themselves seemingly in a forest lit by the residual glow as the light from the dreaming faded. Charlie's eyes met those of Ned, his erstwhile kidnapper. But others were entering the room. Stooped, hooded shapes were coming from the corridor into the garden hall.

At first Charlie thought they were delf from the pit, but then they lifted their faces. They were grey, birdlike and so gaunt as to be skulls. Lank hair fell onto naked bony shoulders and they stared out of dark holes in their faces, swaying. Charlie's hair stood on end. His father shuddered and began to back away into the trees, his hand reaching out to Charlie, pulling him towards him, then protectively behind him, all the while looking for Helen.

A man emerged from the darkness of the Pit, grim and bearded. Rodon lifted the gun again, his face livid in the light of the motionless sun wraith. He ran at the door and behind him there was a roar of fury. The Archbishop was holding his cross aloft and brandishing a pistol in the other. He fired wildly into the delf.

"I be the wrath of God! Turn, vomit of Satan! Get thee back to the pit!"

The clergyman saw the frozen Silver and grabbed his arm and turned him towards the funnel room.

"Fear not Hell, for the Lord be with us."

His voice was warm and confident. His two soldiers were beside him. The cobs peered up at the sun wraith, then followed the Archbishop to the building. Together, the soldiers and the cobs started to hurl themselves at the door.

Raul was knocked backwards, men barged in. Rodon swung his long-arm violently across Raul's head. The delf crashed against the wall and crumpled to the floor. Then Rodon was through the laboratorium and into the garden. Behind him was the Archbishop, still dragging the hapless Silver, and the two soldiers.

They stopped and looked about the room. Esella and Helen were knelt over the Light Doctor to the left of the door under the bough of a tree, but Rodon too had seen the mysterious figures. More were crowding into the room. They came without haste, but they came slowly and relentlessly.

"Have you raised the souls of the damned? I fear them not!"

Then the Archbishop stopped. He turned slowly to look at Richard.

"Bird people," he said slowly. "These are the bird people you told me about."

He looked around the room at the two women.

"You witches have opened a gate into Limbo."

Esella said nothing, but glared fiercely at the tall man, her hands holding the Light Doctor's.

Helen was convinced she was in the middle of the most vivid, terrifying nightmare she had ever had. Knowing it was a nightmare did nothing to still her fear.

"Thomas, the first knights journeyed through Limbo to reach here." There was wonder in the Archbishop's voice. "The way back to Christendom lies through that door."

"And through those spectres," said Rodon.

"They be but lost souls in Limbo. 'Yea, though I walk through the valley of the shadow of death, I will fear no evil: for thou art with me; thy rod and thy staff they comfort me.' The Lord will protect us."

He turned and glared at Richard and then at Solimo. Then he walked over to Richard.

"So Judas, we are met again in the pit from whence you came."

His eyes narrowed.

"How very circular. The Lord has delivered you into my hands after you betrayed us. Betrayed our hospitality, our friendship. And for what? You betray your own kind to fight for the children of Satan!"

"I went to be with my son. That is only natural."

Richard could feel his heart beating. He had never imagined this could happen. What had he done to bring his family to this? They could have stayed at home, but he chose to bring them back.

The Archbishop looked down at Charlie, his eyebrows sliding up his forehead.

"Well, well. You be coming with us. You, this devil and the child. You will show us the way."

"I will not," said Richard.

"Then I will kill your son," said the Archbishop.

"No!" screamed Helen who was on her feet and running at the Archbishop. Rodon grabbed at her and held her.

"Mum!" Charlie cried.

Richard jumped forward too, but the two soldiers were upon him in a moment. One of them jabbed the barrel of his gun into Richard's belly and he doubled up, winded, struggling to breathe. Ned and Berwick went to help Rodon. Charlie watched in horror and did not know what to do, tears sprang to his eyes.

"She be a woman!" said Ned.

"This be your wife?" asked Berwick.

Rodon relinquished his hold on Helen and turned and said something in an urgent whisper to the Archbishop, but the Archbishop shook his head.

"The war will be won. Our soldiers will be victorious. We have turned your trick back on you. You cannot breach our darkness, you devils! You were born in darkness, but you cannot stomach it!"

He turned to Ned and Berwick.

"Pick up your weapons and follow us. We go into history. The king lords will finish the conquest of Unama. *We* will go back to the world of men and then we shall return here with glory and power."

Ned and Berwick picked up their long-arms.

"Silver, secure this building and lock up these women. In the dark. Send for a detachment of troopers to support your guard."

"But what of these..." asked Silver faintly, gesturing at the cadaverous figures. There were dozens of them now.

"Lock them in with the devils."

He turned and to the two soldiers behind him and to Ned and Berwick, gestured to Richard and his family.

"Bring them."

Richard was pulled forward, Charlie went too.

"Helen!" Richard called out. His hand was raised imploringly. He had wanted to show her wonders and had led her into Hell.

Ned looked at him strangely, but said nothing. Berwick would not look him in the eye. The other soldiers pulled up Solimo. He looked back at Esella. Her eyes gave nothing away.

The Archbishop marched towards the spectres, his cross aloft.

"Make way!" he called out to them.

The figures did not move, but a way appeared amongst them. The Archbishop walked along it looking straight ahead, with Rodon on his right hand, his face expressionless. The four soldiers looked distrustfully at the silent creatures, but their faith in their leader was strong. Berwick looked towards the Archbishop and Rodon at the front, then glanced around him.

"Come on, let's move," he said. He took Richard by the upper arm and guided him forward. Richard turned to Helen as he was shoved with the butt of a long-arm.

"I'll come back! I'll find you!"

Then he went, his hand on Charlie's shoulder. Charlie shrank into him. The last sight of his mother was as she was pushed from the room by Silver.

Solimo followed blankly. He had gone from utter despair to euphoria and back to despair again. All had been for nothing.

Part 3

46

THE DOOR STOOD open. Charlie could see nothing as they went towards it, he was simply aware of the strange creatures that crowded around them, silent and doleful. His chest was tightening and his heart pounding and he could feel his father's hand tight on his shoulder. The knuckles were white. Around him he saw grubby, black wings hanging from the bodies of the dark spectres and then they were into the corridor.

He was stunned. He had expected the redbrown dust and the pink sky, but it was all changed. A grey sea churned, choppy waves riding up into one another under heavy black cloud that reeked of storm. The ground was stony.

The company stopped. To their right, jagged rocks lay at the base of a cliff. They looked as if they had tumbled down from the height and been tumbling for centuries into a jangle of boulders and rocks and precarious pinnacles.

Scattered about, balancing on fingers of rock and fists of boulder were the carrion figures, voiceless, immobile; their loose rags limp in the still air.

"My God," whispered Richard. "I know what they are. They're the dreams of the delf in that pit. I saw them when I came here."

"They are going to meet their dreamers," murmured Solimo.

"What will they do?" Charlie asked.

Solimo simply shook his head. Charlie looked up at him.

"Where are we? This isn't where the corridor went."

"I do not know Charlie. This is all new to me. We have not strayed into the Unlembien for hundreds of years. That is why we stayed so carefully in the corridor. It is wonderful. And terrible."

Then a cry leaped out across the soundless air.

"Rejoice!"

They looked up at the Archbishop. He had clambered onto a rock and held up his hands to the creatures.

"Rejoice. Go forth from Limbo and know thy Saviour! I give you a second chance. Go this time and walk in the path of the Lord!"

"What's he talking about?" asked Charlie. "What's Limbo?"

"Somewhere that's neither Heaven nor Hell. Where souls waited for the end of the world, or something," said Richard.

"Are we dead?" asked Charlie, his eyes widening.

"No. But he seems to think we're in Limbo. And maybe we are."

"This is Unlembien, the dreams that hold the worlds together. And keeps them apart," said Solimo. "We are not dead."

Their guards were watching the Archbishop. His arms were still extended and he watched the creatures as one by one they drifted towards the entrance to the corridor. Rodon stood at the foot of the rock, impassive, but watching the dark shadows of Limbo.

"Go! Rejoice!" said the Archbishop again. Then he turned to the group behind him. "You shall see great works! I shall free all the souls of Limbo as we travel to Christendom! See how your vile acts conspire against you in your corruption!"

Rodon offered his hand to his master, the Archbishop took it and descended from the rock. He looked ahead and a narrow, gravelly path led up the rock face, twisting amongst the stones. Up this the Archbishop led them. As they climbed in the muffled silence, Charlie looked back down. There was still a crowd of the ragged nightmares, but they all looked at the door through which they had come and none showed any interest in them. He wondered where they were going and fear stabbed his guts as he took a last look at the doorway, the last link with his mother.

One of their guards took a last look too. Berwick was taking up the rear. He had paused, then turned again to the group and walked again. As he did so, he saw Charlie watching him and their eyes met for a moment. Charlie knew Berwick had been thinking the same as he was. At least Charlie was used to there being two worlds. A third one was not too great a leap. Perhaps Berwick really believed he had entered Limbo populated by the dead.

There was thick grass at the top of the cliff and it led into fog. Visibility was little more than thirty or forty yards before the world was drowned in blank grey. The group stopped. There was no knowing what lay through it. Everything was still.

Then to their left, there was the faintest stirring in the whiteness.

"The Lord shows us the way!" exclaimed the Archbishop and plunged into the fog. The rest of them followed.

At first Charlie thought that they might fall over the edge of a cliff in the fog, then he realised they always had a circle in which they could see, but not see beyond. He began to wonder if they were walking in circles and started to search the grass for something he could remember; a particular thick tuft or patch flattened by their feet in some way. Sometimes he thought he saw something he recognised, but then he doubted himself. Their passage did little to disturb the grass. And so they kept walking.

Richard had become quiet. He seemed calmer and he walked with his arm around Charlie's shoulders. At some point, Charlie realised he was no longer afraid. He was simply bored. There was nothing to see. No one was saying anything. Everyone seemed lost in their thoughts. Lost in their own fog, he thought.

He looked around him. He could not see the faces of those in front, but the Archbishop kept up a steady pace. Rodon walked beside him, almost gliding, his head held alert. Solimo was a little ahead of him and Richard now. He seemed to feel Charlie's gaze because he turned to look at him and tried to smile, but it was an uncertain smile and it had faded before he even turned back.

Charlie looked at the soldiers on either side of them. These were the two he did not know. The one on the right was a small, wiry man with a hooked nose and a rough beard and he chewed at his bottom lip. He too noticed the boy looking at him and stared back unblinkingly until Charlie turned away embarrassed. The other soldier was an older man with a leather waistcoat over his heavy black coat. He had grey stubble on a lined face. His lips were moving constantly as if muttering to himself. Charlie strained his ears to listen. "Thy rod and staff they comfort me," he thought he heard. He was praying.

He risked a casual glance behind him. Berwick looked lost in his thoughts and did not notice him, but Ned met his gaze and stared into it, puzzled, before Charlie turned forward again. He noticed for the first time that Ned was wearing a bandage under his helmet. He felt a pang of guilt at how Raul had set on them.

He was aware of shapes looming out of the mist again. It was more rock, dark grey with damp. They showed first as darker fog before suddenly forming into jointed rock walls. It sloped up away from them and Charlie saw the shape of a small twisted tree part way up.

They followed the way that was easiest, finding the lowest rock steps to climb, moving to the left and right as they climbed the slope. Finally they reached a flat area.

Rodon signalled a rest and they sat down, while he went over to talk to the Archbishop. They could not hear what he said, but he gestured back at the group of them.

"God will provide," said the Archbishop in a louder voice.

After a few minutes, they set off again. The ground dropped away and there were rocks on the grass. The fog was thinner and eventually they dropped beneath it and were walking in clear air.

They were in the bowl of a valley filled with grey rocks amongst the grass. Stretching across it from where it began on the hillside away to their right, they were surprised to see a huge viaduct, supported on many grey arches. It reached right across the valley to the distant far side. Charlie wanted to explore it. He wanted to walk along it. Then he looked at the valley again.

"Dad, are those houses?" He was pointing at the rocks in the valley floor. They lay and leaned in what seemed at first to be odd angles, but now Charlie began to think he could see some sense of order amongst them.

"They do look like houses."

"I think they are. Or were," said Solimo.

They were overheard by their guards. The one with the hooked nose grabbed Solimo roughly by the collar.

"Who lives there, devil?"

Solimo looked fearful.

"I do not know. I know no more than you do about this place."

"You gave it a name before."

"So did your Archbishop..." began Solimo.

"Don't get clever with me!" snarled the man.

"Leave him be, Colman," said the silver haired soldier simply. "You're making a lot of noise."

Colman looked sideways at the older man, but released Solimo, pushing him away with a jerk.

"I don't like the look of it," said Rodon. "We'll cross the valley by the viaduct."

They trudged left along the ridge to find where the viaduct began. They saw two great towers rising above the hillside. As they neared it, they could see the towers were made of huge rusted girders, bolted together. The towers were buried into the hillside and great spans reached out and carried the roadway out above the hill, across the wide valley and onto the shoulders of the first set of arches. These grew higher off the ground the more the valley sides dropped away, until they were at their tallest above the ruined city.

They stepped onto the bridge, Rodon as ever keeping a watchful eye around them, but they seemed to be alone in this world. The bridge was narrow, barely the width of a single lane of a road. Crumbling low parapets ran along either side and here and there grass was growing out of cracks in the stonework. The surface of the road itself seemed to be reasonably flat, so their progress was at a good pace. Charlie thought the bridge looked old and unstable and he wondered what he would do if it did fall. Would he fall with it and just land on the ground still on the paving stone on which he was standing?

"This is the straight and narrow way," said the Archbishop. Then he turned and looked Richard in the eye.

"'Enter ye in at the narrow gate: for wide is the gate, and broad is the way, that leadeth to destruction, and many there be which go in thereat: small is the gate, and narrow is the way, which leadeth unto life, and few there be that find it.'"

He looked at Richard some more, appearing to wait for a reaction. Richard felt uncomfortable, but could think of no response. The Archbishop eased his pace until he drew level with him. Charlie was forced to hang back a little way.

"I have been waiting for you to ask forgiveness."

"For what?" asked Richard.

"For what? For what? Do not play with me, sir. You have your chance to redeem yourself, Richard of Hadbury. I am saddened and angered by your betrayal. Were you spying on us all this time? We showed you great hospitality!"

"I told you. I went to be with my son. We just want to go home. Now you've kidnapped my wife."

"Your son had allied himself, against nature, with these creatures!" he gestured vaguely at Solimo. "Allied himself against his own people. And you went so easily. And as for your wife, she should never have strayed here. And nor should you." His eyes were searching Richard's face, but Richard decided not to respond. It did not seem to be helping and he was unsure where this conversation was going.

"Be this the way of all your people? What has happened in the hundreds of years since we left? Did Satan come among you? What has happened to men? You were always coy when I asked you questions about how the world be now."

The Archbishop's eyes lit up with a sudden realisation.

"You were ashamed, weren't you? Have all men sunk in corruption? Be you typical? Weak of arm and counting friendship cheap? Have you exchanged the ways of war for an easy peace of luxury and sloth? Your hands be so soft, the hands of a sluggard."

279

The Archbishop stopped in his tracks.

"Your world needs medicine to heal it. Now I see God's purpose! I will see this decay for myself, anon. The Lord has cast me to save the world while there is still time!"

He looked around at them all now.

"Yes, friends," he said to Rodon and the guards. "We have been shown this way, this path through Limbo for the Lord's purpose is to return the light to the world which has lost it."

He looked back at Richard, a wild look growing in this eyes.

"I had wondered why you came to us, Richard. Now it all makes sense. You were a sign withal. You betoken what has become of mankind. I had thought my purpose was to finally claim our inheritance over the devils, but I see it be far greater. Their destruction was merely to show us the way home."

"Your Grace!" called Rodon suddenly. "Look!"

Charlie looked over the side and saw they were no longer over a valley. The viaduct was now crossing churning waves. He looked around for the hillsides, but they had vanished in fog and all they could see below them were grey waters.

The entire party was in fear and confusion. All four soldiers looked to Rodon and the Archbishop for some words of explanation. The Archbishop merely smiled.

"You see. We took the high road and we be above the wrath of the waters."

"There's something in the water!" called Charlie. "Look!"

He pointed down and all of them crowded to the edge and peered down, even the Archbishop could not help himself. A shadowy shape was gliding beneath them towards the arches which were now braced against the mysterious flood. Charlie could not make out what kind of shape it was, except it seemed huge and frightening. Then the shape changed, it seemed to shorten. Whatever it was had angled towards the surface. He wanted to stand back, to hide himself from the edge, but he could not move in the fascination of fear.

Then it broke the surface. It was eyes and teeth and sea pouring from its mouth and down its neck. It seemed to keep rising towards them, seemed as if it would never stop coming, its eyes fixed on them, a tongue flicking amongst sharp pointed teeth.

All stood transfixed.

"Be gone, beast of Hades! I command you in the Name of the Lord!" The Archbishop was roaring and holding aloft his cross and a sword.

As he said it, the beast stopped coming. It seemed to hang in the air for a moment, then crashed back into the sea in a churning storm of spray. And vanished. There was no shape beneath the waves, just the waters running against the feet of the stone arches and the empty air between.

All were visibly shaken, except the Archbishop whose eyes were gleaming. Even Rodon's face looked uncertain.

"Where did it go? Will it come back?" asked Charlie, his voice shaking uncontrollably. His father said nothing, but hugged him.

"It went back from whence it came. The monsters of the deep cannot harm us. 'The Lord with his hard and great and strong sword will punish Leviathan the fleeing serpent, Leviathan the twisting serpent, and he will slay the dragon that be in the sea.' We go on God's errand."

Uncertainly, they moved on, but the soldiers looked at the Archbishop in a new light, almost with awe.

"There was nothing there," said Solimo, finally. The Archbishop rounded on him, swinging his arm across the delf's face in one fast movement.

"Filth! Unbeliever! Devil!"

Solimo was knocked back off his feet and fell against the parapet. The Archbishop was onto him and clutched at his coat front with both hands, the knuckles whitening. His face was a few inches from Solimo's and he spoke through clenched teeth, spittle flying into Solimo's face.

"Do not try me! Do not deny what all of us have seen! You see now how pathetic be your witchcraft compared to the power which I command! The power of the Lord your God who you deny and reject. But his wrath is great as you shall discover!"

Solimo tried to stare back at the Archbishop, but the ferocity in the man's eyes was too much for him and he looked away.

"Your Grace," said Rodon gently.

The Archbishop let go of Solimo and stood up straight, looking around at his soldiers as he recovered his composure. They looked stunned. The day was becoming quite overwhelming.

"Let us go on," he said. And once more, they set off.

The straightness of the bridge was mesmerising. Its vanishing point seemed to come no closer, but they kept walking as if on a treadmill. Their only feeling of movement being the stones they passed on either side.

The fog began to lift.

"The sea be draining!" exclaimed Ned. He was walking on the side and he pointed down at the waters. They all looked and the water was indeed vanishing, sliding away from the bridge as if the world was being tipped up. The hills reappeared out of the fog. They seemed a little steeper this time, or perhaps only closer.

Charlie was looking at the city. It was clearly a city now, a city of spires and blocks and domes. They looked like model buildings made huge. From where he was standing, he could see right down into its streets far below him. There was no sign of water, but he could see movement.

"There are people."

There appeared to be shapes, but they moved as blurs and vanished. They were scattered about the streets, sometimes in twos, but usually singly.

"They look like flies," murmured Ned, half to himself.

"I be glad we be up here," said Berwick.

Colman shivered, then looked at the older man.

"Doesn't it bother you, this place?"

"It be just another place. If there can be demons, there can be cities of flies. I'll take what comes my way."

Colman stopped and leaned on the parapet, craning to see into the streets below. Suddenly he cried out. The others turned. The wall was crumbling in front of him. He tried to push himself back, but this simply pushed the already weakened wall further until he was flailing at air and teetering frantically above the city.

Berwick froze, then jumped forward, but it was Solimo who was closest. He leaped immediately towards the frightened trooper whose arms were wind-milling as he desperately tried to pull himself back from the drop. Colman leaned further and further until he could hold his balance no longer and he passed the point of no return.

It all happened so quickly and yet so slowly. Solimo dived at the break in the parapet as Colman's legs disappeared from view. Solimo landed and seemed to be pulled forward across the roadway to the edge.

Charlie watched his friend in blank horror. It seemed nothing would stop him from following Colman over the side of the viaduct. But he did stop. His upper body was hung over the edge and his left arm was wedged against the piece of wall to his left. His grip was visibly slipping, his hand sliding helplessly back along the wall to oblivion.

Berwick reached him and flung himself across the delf's legs. Then Ned had reached the parapet and looked over.

"He's got Colman!" he said and immediately bent down beside the delf at the gap.

"I cannot hold him!" cried Solimo.

"Sit on my legs!" Ned shouted as he lay down beside him. Richard, the corporal and Rodon were already behind him. They could all hear screaming now.

"Don't let me go! Don't let me go!"

"I've got you!" said Ned. "I've got him! Pull me back!"

The three on the roadway took Ned's legs and slowly inched him backwards. Soon they could see he held Colman's ankles in each hand.

"Hold on," Rodon said to Richard and the corporal, straining on his legs, but Berwick had already jumped up from Solimo's legs who was no longer encumbered by Colman's weight. He took one of Colman's feet in both his hands and pulled too.

Then Colman was up and there were seven bodies lying gasping on the road by the broken wall. Ned aimed a slap at Colman's shoulder.

Colman was struggling to speak. He had lost his helmet and nodded, his mouth moving. Then finally he said "Thanks, mate."

"It was nothing. It was the devil caught you." He tilted his head at the still prone Solimo.

Colman's head stopped nodding. He looked confused. Then the Archbishop was there.

"The devil did not save you!" he spat. "It pushed you then dangled you over the abyss!"

Solimo stood up and shuffled across the bridge to the other parapet without looking at the Archbishop.

"See, it knows its shame!" said the Archbishop following him with his eyes. Then he turned back to Ned. "God bless you, soldier for your quick thinking."

Ned looked quickly at Solimo, then back at the Archbishop before he nodded, embarrassed. He pulled himself up and put a hand out for Colman who accepted it silently. He too looked at Solimo as he stood. Richard gazed around him in bewilderment. He was about to say something when Rodon put a hand against his chest and shook his head.

The group gathered themselves into their usual formation, although Colman was still shaking and stayed in the middle of the road from then on. Richard briefly put an arm around Solimo's shoulders.

Only Charlie noticed the stolen glances the soldiers gave to the downcast delf from time to time as they walked in silence.

They went on across the viaduct, a blank grey sky overhead, the city passing beneath them, greywhite like the sky. The bridge seemed to go on forever, the city never seeming to end.

"Stop!" said Rodon suddenly, raising his hand for them to stop. "There be something on the bridge ahead."

He unshouldered his long-arm and walked on.

Charlie could not see clearly, but there was something on the parapet of the bridge. The more he looked, it became clearer. It was a man in a raincoat. He was sitting with his knees tucked up under his chin. He turned his head to look at Rodon, but his face was blank, downcast. Then he turned back towards the view – and vanished.

"Ghosts!" said Rodon.

"The souls of Limbo will not harm us," said the Archbishop.

The members of the group looked at each other. Two of the soldiers made a sign of the cross.

"Was that really a ghost, Dad?" Charlie asked.

"Unlembien is made by dreams," said Solimo before Richard could respond. "So all that you see has been dreamed or is being dreamed. Dreams that are still or moving, dreams that are happening or past."

"We're in a dream?" Charlie asked. "How?"

"That I cannot tell you, Charlie. We are in the space between worlds. I know very little about it and those who can are gone."

Walking did feel like a dream. They moved, but went nowhere. Sometimes they would look over the parapet and they were over that city of shapes, but other times they were over fields or desert or something like endless corrugated iron. Often they would disagree about what they were seeing or its colour.

After a time which they could not have described, they saw the end of the bridge. There were two tall crenellated stone towers. They came closer and closer, growing gradually as the group approached them.

They walked in silence. Talking seemed a foolish thing to do here. Everything seemed unreliable.

The towers loomed over them now, as if bending their heads to watch as they came towards them.

"It's a big church!" said Charlie.

"A cathedral," said his father.

The towers were enormous, larger than any cathedral Richard had ever seen. Between them was the main entrance to the cathedral. It was lined with crudely cut statues guarding a great oak door studded with black painted iron. They heard a sigh escape from the Archbishop. He put his hand out and touched Rodon's arm.

"I have dreamed this," he breathed.

They continued walking until they were dwarfed by the size of the towers. The Archbishop put his hand out to the doors and they opened easily.

Inside, it was immense. Four lines of pillars soared up to the stone ceiling. Light streamed in from windows high in the walls. Charlie did not remember seeing the sun outside. He had expected the inside to look like the cathedrals his father had taken him into. He had expected it to be full of more statues and ranks of wooden pews. Instead it was a vast and empty except for one thing.

At the far end was a single stone box. They slowly followed the Archbishop up the centre aisle, passing the pillars one by one. There was no sound and even their footfalls were silent. As they neared it, it became apparent that the box was a tomb. On its top in pale grey stone lay the statue of a knight in full armour, his eyes closed, his hands clasped in prayer.

At this far end of the cathedral, Richard noticed that the walls were closer together and the ceiling lower as if the narrowing perspective they had seen from the main door was a physical reality.

Richard realised he was standing in the cathedral of St Collen in Collenium. Clearly the soldiers recognised this too. The tomb in front of them was of the founder of the Order, William, Earl of Allingham.

"Who's he?" whispered Charlie.

"He founded the Order. This is just like the cathedral in Collenium, only bigger."

There was puzzled wonder in Richard's voice as he looked around them.

"Interesting," said Solimo.

Then the statue moved.

Its eyes opened. What had been a stone mask became a face, alive yet blank. It unclasped its hands, moved them to its sides and sat up. Everyone jumped in fright or took a step back. Everyone, apart from the Archbishop. As each part of the statue moved, the armour glinted like steel, as if its plate armour had been beaten out of stone.

Rodon and the soldiers were stunned. Their icon had come to life in front of their eyes. The Archbishop felt no similar feeling. He appeared to have been expecting it. He rushed towards the knight.

"It be true!" he cried and knelt at his feet. The knight's sightless eyes turned to focus on the kneeling man in front of them. An arm dropped and gently touched the Archbishop's shoulder. The cleric rose and looked into the face of the stone knight.

"Take the world," the knight said. There was no emotion in the voice.

"I will, my lord. We be on our way."

He turned to face the party.

"Here at last, be final confirmation. I have seen Lord Allingham in my dreams. This," he gestured wildly about him, "this was in my dreams! I was destined to come here. There he urged me on with these very words. I thought it was the world of the devils that he was telling me was ours for the taking. But now I realise it be the world of Men fallen into sin. Yes! There we shall go. There we *must* all go."

He turned to the statue knight.

"Will you come with us? Come with us, guide us!"

The knight said nothing, but it turned.

"Let us waste no more time. The soul of Lord Allingham himself be with us."

In the farthest wall, where the altar would have been, was a small wooden door. Following the knight, they passed through it and out onto the dull green grass of the hillside.

47

THE SKY WAS darkening. Perhaps it was night, but it was not the true darkness of night. High mountains of a shadowy purple lay beyond the hills. Charlie found he was wondering what had lain beyond the hills before. He could not remember there being anything there.

"What are you seeing Dad?"

"We're walking towards mountains."

"I see them too. I can see snow."

"I just see shadow. They're almost purple, but very dark."

The ground ahead was suddenly bright as if lit by the sun, yet there was no sun in the grey sky. In front of them, the knight, the Archbishop and Rodon were all starkly lit against the bulk of the mountains.

"There's light behind the mountains. Is that the sun?"

"I just see cloud."

"We all see mountains, but they look different. To me they look like the mountains on our border with Outreterre," said Solimo.

They walked in silence for a few minutes.

"Do you feel tired?" Solimo asked.

"No," said Charlie.

Richard thought for a moment and when he spoke, there was surprise in his voice.

"No," said Richard.

"How long have we been walking?"

There was a pause for thought again. Richard and Charlie exchanged looks, each realising neither had an answer.

"I don't know," said Richard. "We were in that fog for...I don't know. When did we arrive? It feels like days ago."

"There is no time here," said Solimo slowly, turning the thought over as he spoke it.

"How can there be no time?" asked Richard.

"This is a dream. How does time pass in a dream?"

"Well things happen, time must pass."

"Often I've had a whole dream and only been asleep a few minutes," said Charlie.

"But how can there be no time?" Richard insisted.

"I thought it was just me," said Ned.

"Stop your chatter and get over it soldier. And move away from the prisoners," said the corporal.

"How can you just ignore it?" Berwick asked.

"Because it doesn't matter to me and it shouldn't matter to you," the corporal replied.

"Who cares?" said Colman.

"What be this jangling?" said the Archbishop rounding on them.

The soldiers fell silent. A couple of them looked at the corporal as their natural spokesman. He shifted on his feet.

"They be saying they don't know the time. How long we've been here."

The Archbishop's eyebrows went up and his eyes flicked from side to side, searching his own experience.

"You be right. How long have we been here?" He thought some more. "Thomas, we shall stop here for...a while to make an assay on the passage of time. For fifteen minutes, shall we say?"

The knight's statue had also stopped walking. It did not turn, but simply stopped where it was and stood facing the distance. The others sat where they were.

"I want you all to tell me when you think fifteen minutes be done," he said. "Even you," he added, looking at Solimo, Richard and Charlie.

They sat. Charlie leaned against his Dad and looked out at the country around him. The plain was covered in small, sandy coloured rocks. They went on until they reached the mountains. He leaned further into his father.

In front of him, in the middle of the playground was Max Thorpe. He was in his grey school shorts and a blue sweater with a V-neck. He stood there staring at him. He looked angry. Charlie did not know what he had done to make Max angry. He could see his fists were tightening. The knuckles were white.

"Injured," said Max.

It frightened Charlie.

"Injured," said Max again. He still did not move.

They were in a field of short grass. It was a little like a playing field. The grass was a yellowy green. The sky was flat and grey. There was no one else about.

"Injured," said Max.

Charlie felt the urge to run. Something about Max, about his voice. It was all focused on Charlie. There was an intensity, a strangeness. Max was a monster that looked like a child. Charlie felt terror stirring within him.

He turned around. Max was behind him.

"Injured," said Max. It was toneless.

Then there were more Maxes. They were all around him.

"Injured," they said together, but it sounded like one voice.

He tried to run. He was glued to the spot. Then they were right next to him. Their still, brown eyes were boring into him, their flat faces enormous next to him.

"Injured," they said.

They opened their mouths and displayed rows of jagged white teeth. Suddenly they were biting his shins. He felt a sharp pain.

"Charlie!" said someone.

They were shaking him now. He struggled to free himself. He lurched forward and his father caught him.

"Charlie!"

He was awake. He had been dreaming.

But there was Max in front of him.

"Injured!" said Max.

His Dad was lifting him up. Solimo was by his side. He was still dreaming. Was he?

"I was just dreaming of him," he said.

"They just appeared," said Richard.

"You summoned these?" cried the Archbishop. The soldiers had raised their weapons.

"They be all the same!" exclaimed Berwick.

They? Charlie looked around. It was just like his dream. There were a dozen Maxes around them. Their heads looked a little too big. He shrank back into his father.

"Tell them to go away!" he said.

"They be just children!" said Ned.

"Those be devils! Look at their teeth!" said Colman. He fired his long-arm. One of the Maxes went spinning back. He spun as if in slow motion, he kept spinning wildly, his arms flailing like some grotesque dance.

"Hold your fire!" barked Rodon.

The remaining Maxes stepped towards them in unison. One step. Two steps.

Solimo looked at Charlie, then at the Maxes. Their mouths were open now. As Colman had said, they did have jagged white teeth, just like in Charlie's dream.

"We've got to go!" Charlie said.

"You did not mean to summon them, did you?" asked the Archbishop, genuinely interested. "You just dreamed them?"

Charlie nodded, speechless with fear.

"And they came."

Several of the Maxes suddenly lunged at him. Richard lashed out with his arm. It struck the nearest Max on the side of the head and it stopped.

"Move away slowly," said Rodon.

"We should kill them," said the corporal.

"Maybe," said Rodon. "But we don't know what they be or what could happen."

The Archbishop looked at the one Colman had shot. It was still spinning but revolving into the distance.

"No. We should kill them. Shoot that one," he said, pointing at the one behind the one Richard had hit.

Colman did not need to be told twice. He fired a shot into the Max. It staggered, but did not fall. Then it started to walk towards Colman. He fired again and the thing merely faltered. Rodon drew his sword and swung it. It lopped off the left arm, but still it came on. He swung again with both hands on the hilt of the sword and this time caught it in the neck. The head toppled to the ground, the body paused, then collapsed next to it.

"Your Grace, we should go. Let's leave these. If they follow us, we think again."

"Very well, Thomas."

They began to back away from the Maxes. The Maxes stood still and watched them. The group began to speed up.

"Go. Walk, don't run. I'll watch our backs," said Rodon. The others turned and walked away quickly. Charlie peered back.

The crowd of Maxes stood still there. The sky was pink over their heads. He could still see their white teeth.

"Injured," they said. The word passed around them like an echo, but an echo that faded as they left them behind. Rodon continued to back away, then he turned and jogged after them, looking over his shoulder every few yards.

They went until they could see them no longer, then they stopped again and all looked back into the distance.

"That was weird," said Richard. He had no other words for it, that he was prepared to share. He did not want Charlie to know how the strange Maxes has frightened him too.

"I was just dreaming about him and then he was there when I woke up. It was just like my dream."

"You created them," said the Archbishop simply. "You dreamed them and you made them. You have done witchcraft, boy. That be the work of Satan."

Charlie looked at him astonished.

"We are *in* a dream!" said Solimo under his breath.

The Archbishop stalked up to the delf and thrust his face at him.

"Silence devil," he hissed. "We be in Limbo and soon you will be in Hell because you be damned. You have no soul."

Solimo looked down. Charlie could see he was upset. He had no experience of the kind of hate and anger which poured from the Archbishop. It was something he did not understand. Charlie took Solimo's hand.

"Just ignore him," he said quietly. "That's what they always told me about Max bullying me."

"And at last I have met him," Solimo replied, brightening a little. "He did seem a little hard to ignore."

"Yes, Charlie," agreed his father. "Don't go to sleep again."

"Perhaps none of us should."

They walked on. It did not become dark, but they found they were in the mountains and climbing amidst dark slabs of rock. Their surfaces had a dull sheen and their edges were sharp, as if they had been chiselled, but the whole mountainside was covered in them, large and small.

"There is always a path," said Solimo. "I think it is the corridor."

"But why is it so long?" asked Charlie.

"Perhaps the worlds move around."

The sky was a deep and violent purple and had a texture of cloud without any defined shapes of them. Their way took them uphill, but there was no feeling of climbing. There was no summit in sight and the path, which seemed curiously even, did not seem to reach any ridge or point from which they could see.

Charlie turned around at one point and any view of the land from where they had come was lost amid the pillars and slabs. He began to wonder where they really were and where they were going. Were they really on their way back to their own world? How could the Archbishop know the way? He seemed demented, but he was certain of where he was going. What if they were stuck in this world forever, or was he really only asleep? Perhaps he had been asleep the whole time? He tried to think what being awake felt like. It was something like this, only, perhaps not quite. Things did not feel right. He felt neither awake nor asleep. But he had just slept, he reminded himself. Just slept? That had been a long time ago. He could not remember having slept in a dream before.

A savage scream rent his thoughts. In a shattered second he took in the shiny blueblack creature in front of him, its fine-boned limbs, its hood-like crest of sharp points and its wide, blue mouth of needle teeth. It put its head back and screamed again. There were gunshots. The soldiers had wasted no time in giving vent to their fear. The creature leaped back behind the rock next to them.

"Follow it!" said Rodon, gesturing at Colman and Ned. With long-arms levelled they crept around the rock, fear on their faces like a mask. Then the mask melted into confusion.

"There be nothing here. It's gone!" Ned said.

There was nowhere for it to have gone. It had simply leaped out of nowhere and vanished as quickly. Rodon himself looked, finding himself unable to believe what seemed impossible.

"'Resist the devil and he will fly from you.' The Lord be with us on our road. We go on!" said the Archbishop, but the rest of the group were very nervous. All were watching the rocks around them, their nerves on edge as they caught movement out of the corner of their eyes only to find it was more of the blurred shadows flitting that they had seen before.

They left the slabs behind them and stopped abruptly when they reached what appeared to be a vast mirror. Deep bluegreen sky was filled with bubbling cloud and it was both above and below them. A causeway of white gravel reached out onto the surface. Here they paused, uncertain, but the Archbishop led them out along the causeway. He reached its end and hesitated, just for a moment, then he stepped out, tentatively, as if expecting to fall downwards into the sky. His foot rested on what appeared to be nothing and ripples went out, like stepping into shallow water. The others followed. Each of them took a nervous first few steps, trusting their eyes more than what they could feel with their feet.

Charlie looked around him. They were suspended in a world of sky where distant islands floated. They fell naturally into a long line as they crossed the strange surface, following where those in front trod, unwilling to trust their own footing. Charlie felt giddy. He tried looking down, but it made his head spin and he would feel his father's hand on his back, steadying him.

The floating islands resolved into a line of rocky hills. They focused their gaze on them and tried to ignore the void at their feet. The feeling was sickening, so high they could see nothing below, yet their feet fell on something firm.

The islands came closer and closer and then they were ashore and gratefully climbing the rocky hills. They were nearing the summit, walking across patchy, short, dry grass which covered the undulating terrain over which they walked.

"Your Grace." It was Rodon. He was standing on the summit of the hill above them. He went into a crouch."

"Your Grace, you should see this." He voice was slow, dull and quiet. Ominous.

The Archbishop cast a look at his three prisoners to show he would not forget them, then walked the last few steps to catch up with Rodon. As he approached, Rodon waved him to crouch as well. The Archbishop did so, and froze.

The others were drawn to the hilltop with them, bending low as they went. They dropped almost onto their bellies.

Below them was a wide plain. But it was barely visible. Seeming to fill the plain were people. Thousands upon thousands of people, tens of thousands. There was a countless multitude. It was the most breathtaking sight Charlie had ever seen. But it was not simply a crowd. It was an army bristling with spears, lances and pikes. It stood in massed legions. Most frightening of all, was that amongst all those armour-clad men in shades of grey and black, chain mail and plate, from the foot of the hill on which they lay to the hazy distance where the host's regiments ended, Charlie could see no movement at all. The dark army was still and silent.

They stood in a huge ring and in the centre of it rose a fortress of brown stone. A ring of outer walls was studded with towers and a stocky gatehouse. From their vantage point, they could see the walls made a great triangle. Inside the curtain wall, more walls rose higher to grey tiled roofs. These too made a triangle, inverted inside the larger. Inside these rose another tower, much higher than all the rest and from its top sprouted a huge light funnel.

Charlie looked at Solimo whose face bore an expression of disbelief. Then Charlie's eye was caught by something bright. Way up high in one of the tallest towers of the inner buildings, there glowed a tiny light. He did not know if anyone else had seen it. He looked around. The corporal was near him, but no one was watching him. All eyes were fixed on the plain.

Below them, a pennant on a lance stirred. It stretched out briefly to reveal a silver sword on a black field.

"The Order!" said the Archbishop, the words catching in his throat.

48

RAUL OPENED HIS eyes wide on the second gunshot. He had no idea what he was hearing. He closed his eyes again. His head throbbed with pain. He tried to open his eyes. One opened, but the other stayed closed. His one eye opened to near darkness. There was flickering and some dim movement. He closed it again. The pain in his head seemed to decrease.

He was lying down. His right leg was tucked uncomfortably under his backside, while his left stretched out in front. He attempted to move his leg. Nothing happened. He tried again and managed to pull it out from under him. He lifted his right arm and put his hand to his face. He felt a stickiness on his forehead and a swelling. His eye was sticky too.

He tried to remember where he was; what was happening. He concentrated. He had a memory of entering the light tower, but of nothing after it.

He felt his head again. It must be blood. He tried to lift himself. He pushed with his arms and heaved himself up the wall until his back was leaning against it. He took a deep breath. He lifted his sleeve to his eye and wiped, then he tried to open his eyes again. He felt the eye peel open, pulling at the last stickiness of blood. He waited for the world to focus, then he tried to work out what he was looking at. It was the stone wall of the laboratorium. He could tell from the shelves along it. The shapes, he realised, were shadows. They ranged around the walls and from the half open doorway came the sound of muttering and moaning and some shouting.

Then something walked past him. He froze. It was dark, ragged and stooped and seemed to be shrouded in rags. It went through the door into the pit. Then another passed him. A feeling of damp gloom settled on him. In the flickering light, he thought he could make out a beak. He must have made a sound as he sat up, but they had ignored him. Or not seen him. They continued to walk through, right past his feet.

He looked back at the floor. Both his pistols lay where he had dropped them. He stretched out and felt their reassuring weight in his hands. He tucked them firmly in his belt next to his hunting knife. He took a deep breath and pushed himself up the wall, grabbing halfway up at a bench to pull on. Another bent creature went past as he did so, but was as oblivious to him as the one before it had been. He stood for a moment in case he was dizzy, then moved away from the wall, his muscles tense. Another went by, brushing his shoulder.

He inched towards the door into the garden hall and peered around it. There were dozens of figures, dully lit by grey light from the open door into the corridor. They were coming out of that door which would have led to the funnel hall. This meant they were either coming from the world of men, Charlie's world, or from Unlembien, from out of the dream. He had no idea what this could mean.

He quickly searched the garden room with this eyes. There was no sign of the others. Then his eyes flicked back to a patch of blood on the floor. Next to it, almost hidden by some bushes, was the handle of a canvas bag. Boldly he walked towards it, feeling self-conscious, but also more confident the further he went as none of the figures made a move to stop him. He bent down and picked it up, flicked it open and shut, then put the strap over his head. As he had hoped, it was full of light sponges. It must have been Esella's. Was it her blood? He was surprised at the lurch in his stomach.

He had to find out what happened. Were they all dead? Was it all too late? Pushing the thoughts away, he stepped behind one of the tall, ragged creatures and followed it out into the cavern.

The darkness was lit by a few flaming torches. They were being held aloft by guards standing at the front of the cavern. They shouted at the cobs who loped around the cavern pushing the confused delf into trembling huddles. He looked around to see how many there were. He could count three men. Silver was not among them. Clearly things had not gone well.

He wondered about taking them all on. At least some of the guards did not look too confident, but there were too many cobs. As for those birdlike creatures, he did not know what to make of them. The delf were looking at them in horror as they walked into the crowd. Cobs and men backed away, but the figures ignored everything.

Then he saw a strange sight. One of the figures was standing behind a delf and had its wings wrapped around him. The delf's face was frozen in anguish.

He tried to clear his mind. He rubbed his face and scalp furiously, trying to remember what had been happening. Were all his friends dead? Had they been taken prisoner? He needed to find out. He was torn, but he would have to leave the pit. Dealing with the horror in there would have to wait.

He glanced at the door. It was open, but one of the men and a cob stood by, guarding it. They stood as close as they could to the door, as likely as not, both feeling the same sick feeling of despair that was washing over him. He knew it must come from the creatures, he knew it was not his own despair. He fought the feeling, then without thinking, he stepped out of the line of creatures walking into the crowd of delf and, at the same slow, deliberate pace, started to walk towards the guarded door, his shoulders hunched over.

The man noticed him coming towards him almost at once. To him it appeared that one of the bird creatures had picked him out. In the lurid light of the flames, Raul saw the man look around him, then look more frantic. This creature *was* coming for him. The cob snuffled and moved awkwardly. Raul knew he could fool the man for much longer than he could fool the cob: even if the cob's green eyes could not see him more clearly than the man could, its sense of smell would sniff him out for a delf and then he did not know how it would react. He would have to count on it being confused by the man's reaction.

The man began to back away.

"Go away!" he called out, his voice wavering. "I be no delf, you've come for them, not me. Go back!"

Raul's hand was moving to his knife and one of his pistols. He would have only one chance. He watched the man's face, knowing his own was in shadow. He was still further away than he wanted to be when he saw the man's face change to one of realisation. At that moment, Raul broke into a run. His pistol was out and he fired at the cob which fell back into the wall. The man was levelling his own pistol at Raul, then a wave of dizziness hit him, he stumbled, the man's pistol went off. Raul caught himself and realised his trip had probably saved him. The man was readying the weapon again when Raul reached him. His knife hand swung round and into the man's body, in and out, then he pushed the man down with his hand and without waiting to see what had happened to him, he was out of the door, across the hallway and onto the steps.

Behind him there was confusion. Everyone had heard the shots, but no one had seen who had fired or the result until Raul was well up the staircase.

He stopped, his head spinning, and collapsed on the steps. He listened out for the sounds of pursuit, but there were none yet.

Then he was up again, moving more slowly, following the stairway as it went up and down inside the hill.

"Steady," he said under his breath. He concentrated on a regular rhythm, stopping frequently to listen. He was almost surprised when he reached the door. It was shut. He went to it, put his ear against it and listened. Nothing. He pulled out both pistols, cocked them, then with one hand, he started to turn the handle. He pushed slowly. He had been expecting daylight, but night had fallen.

He peered through the crack. It was too narrow to see anything. He pushed it a little further, still nothing. A little further, a cob, no, two. The door moved again, it creaked. The cobs turned. He leaped out, discharging both weapons as he dashed into the courtyard. A door opened across from him, light spilled onto the ground. A man ran out. A second almost ran into the first as he stopped, his eyes unused to the darkness. Lucky for him he only had guards not soldiers to deal with.

He ran at them, firing again. One fell, another staggered, grappling with his weapon. He could hear the snarling of one more cob behind him. He flung himself at the man, knocking him over. Then he was inside the room they had come out of, wildly throwing himself back against the door. In a moment, his wide-eyed glance had taken in the interior. There was a table, a chair and four people.

The Light Doctor lay on the floor. She looked pale. Beside her, their legs tucked under them and their hands behind their backs, presumably tied, were Esella and Helen. The man called Silver also stood there, pointing a pistol straight at him.

Even as he stood there, feeling as if his time had come, he was thrown forward by a tremendous shove at the door from outside. A cob burst in just as Silver's gun went off. Esella shouted and the cob howled as it was flung back out of the room by the force of the bullet.

Raul rolled at Silver's legs, grabbing at him. Silver ineffectively tried a kick. Raul twisted, his pistols and knife skidding across the floorboards towards Helen and Esella. He grabbed at Silver's leg and pulled. Unbalanced by the kick. Silver tumbled over.

The door swung open again. Cobs and men stood there, hesitating at the two bodies wrestling on the floor. Then there was another gunshot, loud in the confined space. A man staggered back looking surprised before collapsing. Another gunshot and a cob went down. Raul glanced up. Esella was holding a pistol in both hands. Her face was fierce with hatred. Helen cowered next to her. With renewed strength, Raul twisted. Silver flailed, trying to escape. Raul wrenched at him, pulling him back, punching him in the neck and the side of the head. The man went limp.

The doorway was empty. No one was going to rush them, but they were trapped in the room now.

"The bag!" the Light Doctor croaked.

The Light Doctor was looking at him, Raul's hunting knife in her hand which she had used to cut Esella's ropes. Esella crawled past him and took the bag of sponges from the table.

Raul took the knife from the Light Doctor and cut Helen's bonds. Then he looked at the unconscious Silver with murder in his eyes.

"Leave him. You have better things to do," said the Light Doctor.

She coughed.

"You must go back down. Both of you..."

"We cannot leave you here."

"You must. You must go into Unlembien and find them. You cannot take me there. I cannot even walk. Rescue the delf from the pit. Send them out. They will carry me as far as I can go."

"But we are in Outreterre."

"Near the border. We will travel by night. Leave me some of those sponges. They may help a little."

"There are more in the garden hall," Esella swallowed hard.

"No, I have them," said Raul.

"Then you keep yours," Esella said to the Light Doctor.

"Go. Find them. Help them. The way could be long. We moved the rest of the light tower, so now where it passes through Unlembien could stretch between distant points. The corridor could be very long, but from what I have read, the path will still be clear. Just follow it. If I know anything else, I do not have time to tell you. Time runs fast in a dream and so too in Unlembien. Go with the Light and maybe we will see each other again."

"We will," said Esella and took her hand in both of hers. She had tears in her eyes.

Helen was looking between them as they spoke, trying to take it in. She felt as if she were invisible.

"I'm coming with you," she said.

The delf looked at her.

"It will be dangerous," said Esella.

"My son and husband have gone there!" Helen exclaimed fiercely. Who was this girl? Had she no sense? "You can't stop me."

"Of course you must go too," said the Light Doctor. "If you want to. Go on all of you. Be off. Free the delf from darkness and send them to me. Go!"

Esella dropped the Light Doctor's hand and stood up. She spun on her heels, caught Raul's hand for a moment and looked him in the eyes. Then she let go and with Helen at their heels, they ran towards the door to the pit. The Light Doctor watched them disappear through the door, then she sighed and lay back exhausted.

49

THE STRANGE, VAST host of the Order stood on the plain in their silent ranks while the eight humans and one delf looked on.

"Your Grace, how can they be the Order?" asked Rodon, as they lay on the edge of the hill.

"Just look at their pennants!" said the Archbishop.

"They look hundreds of years old," said Berwick. "They be in full armour."

"Be they ghosts?" asked Ned.

"Souls!" said the Archbishop, his eyes flashing. "Souls of our fallen brothers in arms down the ages, gathered here in Limbo!"

The soldiers looked awestruck, but they could not help casting an eye at Rodon who was looking a little more uncertain.

"Your Grace, may I speak to you?"

He beckoned the Archbishop away.

"Keep out of sight," he said to the group as he and the Archbishop moved down the hill out of earshot. Charlie watched them. Rodon appeared to be quietly remonstrating, but the Archbishop was smiling and he placed his hands on the younger man's shoulders. Rodon made a final comment, the Archbishop looked him in the eyes, then gave a brief nod. With that, Rodon came back up the hill. He pointed at Ned and the corporal and gestured them over.

"Go down there. Get close to them. See what they be like before they disappear like the others we have seen."

Both men hesitated, but both went, picking their way down the slope to the right into a gully where they were hidden from the view of the army. They would stop from time to time, clearly looking to see if their descent had been noticed, but the nearest ranks of the army continued to face the other way, towards the great light tower. Eventually they reached the base of the hill and both crouched behind a boulder, peering out. They watched as Ned levelled his long-arm at a group standing about sixty yards from their cover and the corporal stood and walked towards the group.

A first he went slowly, tentatively, unsure of whether to creep or walk normally. The further he went, the bolder he became until he was walking upright, purposefully. He was about ten yards away when the group turned to look at him. They showed no surprise, but simply watched him come on. He paused, said something to them, then began to walk away again. Two followed him. Ned was keeping his long-arm trained on them, but as they approached him, the corporal waved him to lower it. Ned watched them go past then brought up the rear as the four of them started to climb up the gully.

Back on top of the hill, the group watched their progress with interest. Colman was agitated.

"Why bring them up here?"

The others too were unsure. Only the Archbishop and Rodon looked calm. When the corporal's head finally appeared, the Archbishop rose to meet them.

The two soldiers from the vast army presented an unsettling appearance. One was tall and wore a cloth tunic over a chain mail hauberk. Under a high crowned helmet, his unshaven face had long features and a drooping moustache. His eyes were dark and strangely vacant. His companion was shorter and broader. His face was gnarled and his eyebrows bushy. His teeth were oversized and seemed to fill his mouth. He wore badly beaten armour which looked as though it may once have been black. Both were armed with knives and a sword.

"I bless you in nomine Patris, et Filii, et Spiritus Sancti," said the Archbishop and made the sign of the cross. The two men started. Their eyes seemed to come to life, but they said nothing.

"They be Christian souls," he said.

Rodon tilted his head quizzically.

"They do not fear the sign of the cross," the Archbishop continued. "I know we be safe among them."

The Archbishop rushed back to the summit and looked down on the mass of soldiers below. Out of nowhere, a breeze came towards them from beyond the fortress.

"Look!" he called and pointed. Pennants had shifted in the breeze and in stirring, they revealed themselves. The silver sword on a field of black could be seen right across the host.

"It be the sign of St Collen! These be truly souls of the Order! So many! So many brave soldiers have died over the centuries, yet they be gathered here in Limbo. An army still, loyal in death."

He raised his eyes to the stone tower rising out of the plain.

"They surround a fortress of the devils. How long have they besieged it and what be within? What they have held at bay for so long, by the grace of God, I will destroy."

"Your Grace," said the corporal. "If such a large army be daunted by storming that fortress, perhaps there be something truly fearsome in there."

The Archbishop's face took on a look of thunder.

"What bewitches you, corporal? Have you so lost your faith in the Lord that you would doubt He be with us? Even after all that we have been through in the world of Limbo? Has He not brought you here alive though devils and fiends assailed you on the path? Has He not brought you to this very place? It is a test. Our ancestors failed the last test and we have been punished ever since to squabble amongst ourselves like children without parents. We will not fail Him this time. We rise to the challenge. We all will rise to it."

He dismissed the corporal with a wave of his hand.

"Thomas, we shall descend and pass through this great army and we shall enter that castle."

Rodon pre-empted any mutterings from the others with a stern look. The soldiers gathered their prisoners and moved behind their leaders. As they did so, there was a sudden movement from the two strange men from the host. They were drawing their swords and advancing. The soldiers of the Order were confused, but raised their long-arms automatically. This had no effect and the Limbo footsoldiers came on.

Solimo felt their eyes on him as they continued to walk forward. He knew he was their target and he felt an overwhelming urge to back away. The troopers did not feel they were the focus of an attack, but they could see an attack was about to happen. The Archbishop turned around.

"What passes here? Put up those swords!"

The two men at arms stopped immediately and sheathed their swords, but still stood glaring at Solimo. The Archbishop turned thoughtful eyes on him.

"So, they recognise a devil when they see one. Very interesting. But now be not your time, devil."

The troopers looked sideways at him.

"Soldiers of the Order of St Collen, lead the way!" declaimed the Archbishop and the two armoured soldiers turned and started to descend the gully up which they had come. The stone knight, which had been as still as a statue since they arrived on the hilltop, moved to join them and walked ahead over the edge of the hill. The party followed the creatures of Limbo and wound its way down the hillside.

Charlie watched the sea of people below, his heart pounding. He could sense his father's fear and that worried him more than his own. He felt himself slowing down as they reached the flat ground, but Colman gave both of them a shove and they carried on.

It was the stillness of that great host which was the most disturbing thing. The silence of a multitude seemed more silent than that of a desert. He looked at Solimo and the delf was pale with fear. He saw Charlie looking at him and tried to smile, but the incident on the hilltop had clearly unnerved him and now he was descending into thousands of the same creatures. Charlie tried to smile back, but he could not make his mouth do what he wanted.

Then they were down and walking towards the rear ranks of the army. The Archbishop raised his arms, his sword in one hand and his long cross in the other.

"Knights of the Order of St Collen, make way for the soldiers of the Lord."

Heads turned their way to look at them. As the Archbishop went forward, they gently broke ranks and formed a lane amongst them so that the party could walk through. Charlie could see that their own guards shared his apprehension rather than the Archbishop's confidence. Yet the host of Limbo did nothing but stare. And that stare was directed at the delf in their midst. It was blank yet malevolent. Solimo kept looking straight in front of him, into the back of Rodon's head.

The army peeled apart as they walked forward and, above their heads, Charlie could see the brown fortress coming closer and closer. Still they walked and he risked looking at the army around them. Some of them appeared to be men, while others had strangely blurred or blunt features as if their faces had begun to melt. His stomach lurched, sickened. Were these really men? What were they? Yet here and there were faces that looked real, if strangely lifeless. He realised that there was a great similarity amongst some of those faces. It made him start to search out the more real faces, gave him something to look for around the mutated ones.

Charlie risked a look at the others. All of them were watching the strange people around them, their weapons held ready, nervously.

"No one do anything stupid," muttered the corporal, but not so loud that Rodon or the Archbishop ahead could hear. Apart from the corporal's comment, their walk had been in silence broken only by the occasional clink of mail or weapon.

Only Solimo avoided their gaze, but their gaze was always directed at him.

The walk seemed to be taking forever. They went slowly, carefully, avoiding making a sudden move lest it break whatever spell rested on that great, strange army. Ahead, the bodies parted to let them through. Charlie and he turned and his stomach lurched again at what he saw. Behind them, the ranks closed silently, their faces watching after them as they went. They moved as if inside a bubble through the mass.

Charlie looked at the fortress. They were closer now. Its outer wall was clearly visible and in it was a great gateway in a barbican and behind it, the keep rose in its monstrous pile of stonework.

Some bodies had parted and, at last, there was only stone ahead of them as the host kept a distance from the outer walls.

They halted at the gate and looked up. The walls were devoid of life. Charlie searched the windows of the keep, but could no longer see the lit one he had spotted from the hilltop. Their guards half turned to watch the force at their backs.

Rodon turned to Berwick.

"You be young and fit. Climb that wall," he said.

Berwick seemed relieved to be doing something. He handed his long-arm to the corporal and walked to the great wooden drawbridge which was drawn up to the gate. Strangely, there was no moat over which it would rest if lowered. He looked at it, then beckoned Ned to him, said something and Ned bent down. Berwick climbed up onto the large man's shoulders and steadied himself as Ned slowly raised himself until he was standing. Berwick crawled his hands up the walls as he too raised himself, stretching up until his hands were groping for one of the great bolts embedded in the gate. Then he put his other hand on a piece of stone and pulled. As he did, he put his foot out and then he was off Ned's shoulders and hanging from the wall like a fly.

Ned stood under and watched him as he put his hand out, found another hold and pulled, pushing with his feet at the same time. His grip was precarious, but higher up, there were larger gouges in the stone and he was able to put fingers and feet into them, then he stretched to his right and his hand caught the top of the drawbridge. As he did, his feet slipped, his other hand was pulled away from its hold and he was hanging by one hand from the top of the drawbridge. All of them jumped, their minds briefly distracted from the multitude.

Berwick hung there for a moment, then his other hand moved up to the drawbridge. He paused for breath, then dragged himself up slowly until his shoulders were above the drawbridge, followed by his chest. He sagged as he threw one arm over the back, then pulled himself so that his body lay along the top of the drawbridge. There he paused, breathing hard.

After a few moments, he pulled his feet up onto the top and faced the wall, moving his hands until he was standing again, then feeling above his head for something on which to hold. He found it and heaved himself up a little way. He found a lip of stone that provided a much surer hold and with that he pulled himself again until his flapping hand found the parapet, positioned itself into a firm grip and pulled. Once he had a second hand on the top of the wall, he was able to pull himself over faster. Then he lay across the battlements for a second, slipped over and vanished.

On the ground, there was nothing the others could do but wait. There was no sound. What could lie within the castle? Was there something even more terrible inside?

They all started together at a grinding screech. One of the gates was opening. Charlie looked over his shoulder, but there was no movement from the silent army.

The gate swung open. Berwick stood in the gateway.

"Come!" he called. "Quickly!"

The Archbishop was not to be rushed.

"Your Grace, the army..." started Berwick.

"The army will not move," said the Archbishop.

They walked forward through the gate. Charlie slipped under it as soon as he could, Richard and Solimo quickly following. The three soldiers moved quickly. Rodon, the Archbishop and the stone knight stood still, waiting as the others went through. Then they followed, the Archbishop walking with exaggerated calmness into the bailey of the light tower.

Ned went to help Berwick close the gate again. No one spoke until the unseemly screeching of the hinges had stopped and once more there was an oppressive silence.

They looked around. They were alone. The courtyard was bare and empty. It had a desolate, windswept feel.

Inside, everything was different. The hills and the silent host had been shut out. Their world was now the brown walls, the sandy ground, and the keep towering over them. There was no sign of life anywhere. They stood just inside the gate, the soldiers hefting their long-arms ready for they knew not what. Rodon looked at the corporal.

"Circle the keep. Two men each way."

The corporal nodded, then looked at Ned and Berwick.

"You two that way. Colman, you be with me."

The two pairs went in opposite directions, each craning their neck up and looking around them. When they reached one of the towers in the outer wall, they would peer inside then one would walk in, coming out a few seconds later. Charlie watched them all as they continued in this way until they passed out of sight around the sides of the keep. The five of them stood waiting. Rodon did not watch the prisoners, sensing they were in no mood to try to run away. The statue stood a little way off. They all waited without looking at one another or saying anything. They were used to losing track of time, but they had never been out of sight of one another. Charlie did not feel like a prisoner. He simply missed the company of familiar faces in this strange place. His fear of the army outside and the unknown inside this fortress was greater, he realised, than his fear of the soldiers of the Order, or even the Archbishop, whose focus seemed to be on other things.

Berwick and Ned were the first to appear.

"All clear this side," Berwick said.

"You saw the other two?" asked Rodon.

"We did."

All faces turned to look at the empty courtyard on the other side where they expected the corporal and Colman to complete their circuit. Where were they? Berwick started to walk around again. He was half way to the corner when the two other soldiers appeared.

"What took you so long?" Berwick asked crossly.

The corporal ignored him.

"Nothing to report. There be no one out here but us." He looked back at the keep. "It be what be in there that's worrying me."

Opposite where they stood, a set of steps without a handrail led up the front of the building to a door.

"That would appear to be the way in. Be that what you want to do?" Rodon asked the Archbishop.

"We have not come all this way to turn back here. We were led to this point. We be meant to come here. And we be meant to try the defences of this fortress. The armies of Limbo have let us pass. I see not what could be in here that we should fear."

He turned to the statue of the knight.

"Lord Allingham will lead the way."

Rodon cast the statue an ambiguous look, but nodded.

Charlie wondered if there was some sort of unspoken communication because, without any apparent signal, the knight lurched into movement and walked across the bailey to the steps and started to climb. The Archbishop followed, so Rodon, who had initially hung back, walked briskly until he was ahead of him and followed the statue up the steps. The corporal shrugged, then turned to the remainder.

"No use loitering here. As His Grace said, we've come this far..."

Inside the keep, Charlie realised he had been expecting it to feel cooler, just like when he had been in other castles, but there was no change. There never seemed to be any change in this place. He felt neither hot nor cold.

"Solimo," he said suddenly. He had just realised something.

"There's no sun."

Solimo looked as if he were thinking about something, then nodded slowly.

"You are right."

"So how can we see?"

"This is a dream, Charlie. It's not like the world."

There was a small room inside the door. Another room led off it and contained benches, a couple of low beds and a sword hung on the wall. There was a little light from the narrow windows. On the far side of the entrance chamber, another set of steps led up and around a corner. The knight walked straight over to them and began to climb. They climbed steps and walked along corridors. Sometimes they would pass a window and Charlie would strain to look out because they were too high.

"What can you see, Dad?"

"A bit of wall," he would say, or once "The hills."

They passed rooms, most of them empty, but occasionally one would contain a few pieces of wooden furniture or an old chest. Nowhere appeared to be lived in, none of the furniture appeared to be arranged; it simply looked as though it had been left in the room. There was no sign of life. The light tower seemed uninhabited. Charlie felt as though this should have given them confidence, but instead everyone appeared to be more tense. They moved in silence, weapons ready, the only sound was their feet on the stone floors.

Charlie noticed the Archbishop and Rodon in quiet conversation. It ended with the Archbishop nodding and Rodon calling a halt.

"There are too many of us to go prowling around here together. We will split up. Ned, take the devil and the boy and find a room on this corridor to take yourselves. If you feel unsafe, move. We will find you."

Ned did not look pleased with the arrangement.

"What do I do if you don't come back?"

Rodon ignored him.

"What about Dad?" Charlie asked.

"He comes with us. He can be of use."

And so they were left in a bare room with a high, narrow window out of which they could see only sky. The corporal muttered a few words of advice to Ned and Berwick slapped him on the shoulder, then the others were gone. Charlie listened to the noise of their receding footsteps until they disappeared.

Everything was very quiet. Ned seemed to have been listening as well because after a few moments he felt the need to fill the silence with conversation.

"So. Boy. Charlie. What be this all about? What happened at the Pits? Where be you from?"

"That is many questions," smiled Solimo.

Ned glanced at him with annoyance, but surprisingly did not respond.

"I'm from Hadbury."

"But you be from Christendom?"

Charlie looked blank.

"England."

"Yes. And so are you. Or your family. Ages ago."

"What be it like?"

"Well. Quite nice," said Charlie, wondering what to say.

"Be it different?"

Charlie opened his mouth to speak, thought of too many answers and closed it again.

"What be you smiling at, devil?" Ned demanded. He turned to Charlie again.

"Why do you like these devils? Have they bewitched you? The Archbishop says you be a traitor and a sinner."

"I'm not a traitor!" said Charlie, rather more stoutly than he was expecting. "They're..." he searched for the right word, but there was only one word for it. "They're my friends. They're nice people. You'd like them too if you got to know them and stopped shooting them."

Solimo looked at the floor. Ned looked surprised, but was silent for a time.

"I've never heard any good of them."

"Well you wouldn't would you? I bet you've never heard one of their songs. Solimo, sing one of your songs."

Solimo glanced up, not because he was expecting an invitation, but because he was afraid of Ned's reaction. To his surprise, Ned was staring at him.

"They sing? You sing? What songs? Go on. Sing us one now. I can't stand this silence."

Solimo was startled.

"Go on," smiled Charlie. "I can't stand the silence either. Nothing can hurt us if you're singing."

Solimo nodded, pondered what to sing for a moment, then began.

He chose a song of the dawn. It was one he sometimes sang at the start of his shift. It began quietly, the first notes seeping over the horizon until they burst into a firmer tune, clear and bright. Through the song, Charlie watched the man's face. It faded from challenge to a small frown to surprise and even disbelief. The song ended on a high note in Solimo's rich tenor voice.

The silence that followed still seemed to hold that note. Solimo looked down, embarrassed and afraid now that his performance was over.

"I am sorry. That was too loud."

"No," said Ned. "I liked it." But then he stood up and went to the door, looking outside and listening for a moment.

"I don't like it in here," he said. "I feel trapped. There be no way out if we be in here. We need to find somewhere else."

He looked back at the others as if waiting for their response.

"Let's go somewhere else then. Where shall we go?" asked Charlie.

"I don't know, but I'll know it when I see it," he said.

It seemed to be an invitation, so they stood and joined him at the door. He took his long-arm and held it ready. Then he stopped, looked at Solimo and pulled the knife out of his belt. He held it out to Solimo, handle first. Solimo looked at it, then shook his head.

"No. Thank you. I do not like weapons."

Ned looked at him quizzically for a moment, then shrugged, slid the knife back into its sheath and walked on into the corridor.

There were two rooms off it and a staircase at either end, one leading upstairs, the other down. They looked in both rooms. Both were small, one with only a small, high window and the other with nothing at all. They went up the steps. It was where the others had gone. Their feet fell with a muffled smack on the stone and when they reached the top, they were in a higher, wider hallway. Two staircases led off from rounded archways at the far end and on either side of the hallway was a door into a large empty room.

They entered the one on the left. At the far end was a fireplace jutting out from the wall and with a mantelpiece at Ned's shoulder height. There was nothing else in the room. Charlie walked right in. The room seemed to draw him into its empty space. He wandered towards the fireplace. Something caught his eye. There were three symbols above the mantelpiece in the familiar triangular shape. He looked up at them. Solimo saw him looking and came and stood at his side. He reached out and touched them.

"The triad of light," he said. "Star, moon and sun."

He looked at Charlie.

"What say you?" asked Ned.

Solimo hesitated. "These are delf symbols," he replied.

"And that looks like a cloud!" said Charlie.

Solimo looked at where he was pointing, into the back of the fireplace itself. There, in the darkened stone was something that could have been a cloud.

"I have seen that in books," said Solimo. "The light hidden by a cloud. A secret."

He looked around, searching. Charlie peered around him too, not knowing what he was supposed to be finding and walked to the left, to the side of the chimney breast. Ned watched them.

Charlie ran his hands down the wall. Solimo started tapping. And then the wall opened.

Just a small patch of wall. It slid away from the chimney right in front of where Charlie was standing.

Ned jumped and raised his gun.

A spiral staircase was revealed. They all exchanged glances, then Charlie began to climb, Solimo followed. Ned hung back for a moment, but seeing his charges disappear from view, he followed. They wound up and up as if they would never stop.

They ended in a room.

It was large and rectangular and hung with vibrant tapestries which showed hills and landscapes and creatures. Charlie recognised lions and tigers and elephants and deer, but there were also more fanciful creatures: dragons and animals he did not know. There were rugs on the floor and tables lined the room piled high with books. They were large ones, bound in dark leather, some of which were open. There was black writing and bright pictures around the text. Behind the tables and in front of the tapestries were racks of lit candles. They did not flicker, but stood still like photographs of candles.

"Ah. You have come at last," said a voice.

She must have fainted, the Light Doctor thought. She was being gently shaken. She opened her eyes expecting to see Esella, but a strange, thin face with hollow cheeks leaned over her. His eyes seemed overly large in the shrunken face.

"Are you the Light Doctor?" it said.

She blinked.

"Yes." She tried to pull herself up. "Who are you?"

"I am...I am..." He looked puzzled, straining to remember. "I am Talo Baker," he said.

"What has happened? Where are Raul and Esella?"

"They have gone into Unlembien," he replied. "This has been a day of wonders."

He spoke haltingly.

"We thought all the light in the world had gone and all that was left was despair and fire."

A tear trickled down his face. And then he gently put his hands under her and helped to sit her up. She could see past his shoulder now and out into the courtyard. It was full of delf, hollow eyed, gaunt; more bones and skin than body, but delf.

"Are you all out?"

"Some are dead," he said.

"What happened?"

"Your friends brought light and blood. The men were frightened. I have never seen a frightened man before. They fired their guns wildly before they died. And the cobs fled from the light. Some of them died, but I do not know if it was all of them. And our nightmares..."

He stopped, his eyes dropped and he swallowed before slowly raising his eyes again.

"...the nightmares clutched at us. One clutched at me. It was suffocating me. I had no breath. But I looked at the light. I looked into the eyes of the sun wraith. I saw hope where the others saw terror. I saw the sunshine. And then I could breathe. The nightmare was gone."

"They vanished?"

"I did not see where they went."

"But the rest of you are safe up here now. We are close to the border. We must go south, escape Outreterre as quickly as we can."

"Some went with your friends. They would not face the land of the Order. They would rather face Unlembien. Should we have gone with them too?"

"No. We must face dangers we understand."

The Light Doctor had not expected it, but there was nothing she could do now. As poor a protector as she was, she needed to shepherd these waifs south.

50

AT THE FAR end of the room was a figure. He was tall with long dark hair, flecked with grey. It hung down to his collar. Charlie could not tell how old the man was. Older than his father, but not as old as his grandfather. He could go no further than that. He had fine features, dark eyes and a reddish olive coloured skin. His clothes were rags, tattered, worn. They were loose robes, but reminded Charlie of his father's gardening clothes. They had seen better days and those days were an age ago.

Solimo caught his breath. He was looking at one of the tapestries. Charlie followed his gaze. There was a representation of hills and on the top of the highest was a building. It was unmistakably a light tower. Then his eyes had already moved to the figure at the end of the room. Solimo realised instantly and Charlie knew it when he felt the light touch of Solimo's hand on his shoulder. He was delf.

The delf saw him and a look of surprise passed over his face too.

"What is this? Did you not expect to see me? Did you not sing for me? And what are you doing with this man? And a child?"

Charlie felt Solimo's hand gripping his shoulder tighter and he turned to see Solimo sinking to the floor, his mouth open in wonder, his face amazed and sad.

"Don't move!" said Ned, his voice wavering in confusion.

"I take it that is a weapon. It reminds me of an arquebus. What are you doing here if you were not looking for me?"

"We were brought here," said Solimo.

"Who by?"

"Don't say anything!" said Ned nervously.

"Not by him."

"Ned, I think it's alright," said Charlie.

The delf surveyed them.

"I will not harm you," said the delf. "Unless you try to harm me of course."

The threat was said quite casually, but with confidence. Ned slowly lowered his long-arm.

"Man, delf and child. Man child. What *are* you doing?" he asked again, musingly. "Lost in a dream."

He said it as if it was a conclusion. A true one, thought Charlie.

"And how did you get through my army?"

"Your army?" asked Solimo.

"They are my nightmares. Have you slept here yet? Have you dreamed inside the dream? You have, have you not, little man? I can see it in your eyes."

Charlie shrank back into Solimo.

"Do not frighten him," said Solimo.

"What say you delf? What are you doing here? Are you their friend? What has happened? How long has it been?"

"You aren't like those other dreams," said Charlie.

The delf fixed his bloodshot eyes on him and Charlie wanted to look away, but could not.

"Clever boy."

"Who are you?" Charlie asked.

The delf looked at Solimo.

"Ask him. I think he might know. Is that flattering, I wonder, or heart-breaking?"

He fell silent, watching them for a moment.

"I knew you were here. That someone was here. I felt the breeze. I do not know how long it has been. It feels like it must have been a long time. But I still remembered what it was when I felt it. I can feel it even in here. A change in the air that does not change."

The delf paused. He was still staring at Solimo.

"How long has it been?"

Charlie saw Solimo's mouth was moving, forming words, but it was a moment before sound came out.

"Nearly six hundred years," he said. They were almost an echo of a sound that had not been spoken.

"Six hundred years," the delf repeated, slowly. "I did not think it would be that long."

"Are you six hundred years old?" asked Charlie.

"Witchcraft!" cried Ned, raising his long-arm again.

"Not witchcraft," snapped the delf quite suddenly. "Merely the result of playing with something I did not understand." Then his anger died as quickly as it had flared. "But I have had much time to think about it. Much more than I thought."

He suddenly looked old, his head dropped and he staggered to a chair and sat down. He looked so helpless that Ned lowered his weapon again.

"What did you play with you didn't understand?" Charlie asked.

"You ask a good many questions, boy," growled the delf without looking up. "I played with dreams. And I fell in love with your world."

"You've been to Earth?"

"Of course I have."

"Are you the last Mage?"

The delf looked up at him. His anger had died again.

"Is that what they call me? And you have heard of me?"

"Solimo told me."

"And you are Solimo I presume?" he asked turning to the younger delf. Solimo nodded.

"So I am not known of on 'Earth'. It is the same planet you know. Well, almost the same."

"So we're on Earth now?"

"We are in a dream. Surely you know that if you are here."

"But how come?"

The delf sighed and put both his hands to his forehead and rubbed his face. Then he massaged his temples.

"Fools. Fools like me."

Then he looked up and spoke so viciously that spittle flew from his mouth.

"What are you doing here? Do you want to be trapped here for six hundred years too? Do you? Cursed to thrash around in a rambling tower for eternity? And who knows what kind of a hell you would create for yourselves when you finally fell asleep!"

"You be real!" Ned blurted.

The Mage stopped his rant and stared open mouthed at the soldier.

"Congratulations you knock-kneed gimberbrain! I am glad to see you have an ounce or two of porridge to think with still hiding inside that helmet."

To Charlie's surprise, Ned chuckled. Somehow, being abused by the delf had made him less of a threat.

"You need to talk to me," the Mage said, returning to a business-like voice. Charlie was beginning to find his rapid mood changes quite disconcerting. "Where have you all come from?"

Solimo looked over at Ned, but Ned simply nodded.

"We came from Unama," said Solimo. "We are going to the world of Men. We were brought here by Men."

"Are you trying to get home?"

"I don't know," said Charlie.

"The Archbishop says this is Limbo," started Ned. The delf stood up so suddenly, all three of them jumped.

"Archbishop? A snake is here? Is he? Did he bring you?"

Ned nodded despite himself. He was used to taking orders and this delf seemed used to giving them.

"Where is he?"

"In the castle."

"Here?" The delf was looking about him madly as if the Archbishop were about to walk in. Then he relaxed. "Then let him come. Let him come. Go call him. I am sick of all this."

He sank back into his chair.

"Looking for a way home is he? Well I can show him. And maybe there is a way home for me too. Call him. Call him. *Call him!*" The last was a barked order.

Ned stood up, backed away, then turned and walked out of the room through the opening in the door. After a moment, the Mage looked up quickly. A mischievous look was in his eye.

"He has gone. He is the snake's is he not? I can tell. But I can trust you. Now tell me. Where are the entrances?"

"Do you not know?" asked Solimo. "You are a Mage!"

"I am, but I am in here. If I step outside those gates, I would be torn to pieces by the goblins."

"You said it was your army."

"Only in that I created them."

"Is the other door far?"

"I do not know how far it is. It has seemed like far, but I cannot tell. No. The breeze is strong." He was almost talking to himself. "There is an entrance not so very far from here. Maybe it is time. Maybe it is time."

"Time for what?"

"Time, time to leave. How did you get through the nightmare outside?"

"The army?"

"Yes, yes, them."

"I do not know. While the soldiers were around me, they did not touch me. The Archbishop seems to command them. But they watched me all the way here. I was terrified. What are they?"

The Mage looked affronted.

"The Archbishop could control them? But they are mine. I dreamed them. I dreamed them in my fear when I could stay awake no longer. I try not to sleep, but then I do. I cannot help it. It is six hundred years. And when I sleep, I have nightmares. They feed on themselves. I dream of their Order. Of their soldiers. As time goes on, my memory of them fades in precision, they blur, but I still dream of them. And they are created blurred. Goblin men from the pit of my soul. And what are you doing dabbling in things you do not understand?"

"Mage," said Solimo. "I am a Light Keeper. A student of the light."

"I know you are. I can see it. I am a Mage." He waved his hand dismissively.

"We had never dreamed a Light Funnel into the world of men before. Had not dared to. But we needed their light. This Archbishop had made our sky dark."

The Mage spat.

"Made it dark did he? How? How? Did he invert the funnels? Did he? Did he? He did. Yes. He would have done. That is what he would have done."

"He did. But Mage, you have been here for six hundred years. How did we find you? You are right, we are playing with what we do not understand, but we did not want to play with it this way. We were brought here under threat. This boy too. And his father. Tell us, how are we here with you?"

"Well I have had much time to study this, to think on it. Dreams create worlds. Some dreams are stronger than others, closer to the worlds than others. You stepped into mine. I had been dreaming it a long time. It was an island floating in the stream waiting for bridges to join it to the land."

"But what happened all those years ago? Many think you betrayed us and the lore was lost."

"They can think what they like. I was tricked. My friend betrayed me to the snake of a priest. I never trusted him. I *never* trusted him. I could not stop them going through. They killed my keepers. All I could do was dream away the bridges and leave them there. At least no more could follow. And I could not leave."

"Could you not leave the way you came in?" asked Solimo.

The Mage gave a gentle laugh.

"No. Of course not. This is a dream. There is no light in here. That is not light you see out there. That is a memory of light, nothing more. To dream through, you need your feet on solid ground or you need light. Here I had neither."

There was a sound of stone on stone and they all turned to the entrance. The stone knight stood there. The Mage did not so much as stand as drift to his feet.

"Is it you? Is it you old friend? What has happened to you? Alas, are you stone? So much time has passed?"

Rodon came through the opening with Ned, Berwick and Colman right behind him, followed by the Archbishop, Richard and finally the corporal.

The Mage seemed oblivious to the men who had just entered the chamber. He was looking at the stone knight.

"They have gone and made a statue of you and now you walk in here. Have you waited all this time to command the creatures I created?" His eyes filled with tears. "I forgive you my friend. It is all behind us now. Death is here at my door. But let me embrace you."

The delf stepped forward and put his arms around the knight. Charlie heard a noise and turned to see the Archbishop's eyes bulging, his mouth moved in a splutter.

"Devil, do not touch him!"

The delf seemed not to have heard, he stood with his eyes closed embracing the living statue, then he started, his eyes opened and he stepped back. The knight was crumbling. As they stood there, its form began to disintegrate and collapse down on itself until it was simply a tower of dust giving way onto the floor.

The Archbishop charged forward.

"What have you done, fiend?"

The delf seemed to notice the group by the door for the first time. They had not moved as they watched the scene playing out in front of them.

"He was my friend," he said simply.

"Villain! Do not call him your friend!"

"Ah but he was. He never stopped being my friend. Even after our last meeting."

"You lie, creature! You are damned!"

"I am damned. And now I know my world is damned too, my misery is complete. There is nothing you can do to me now."

"I know who you be!" exclaimed the Archbishop. "I know. I know why the Lord led me here. I know why Lord Allingham came here. It be his final atonement. Thomas, it all makes sense now."

Rodon tilted his head and looked at his master.

"Lord Allingham was a sinner. That be revealed to us now. He led the Order, but he was ensnared by Satan. Look, he has become dust. It be because of his perfidy that the Order never conquered Faerie. That was the punishment for our sins."

He turned to them all, his eyes blazing.

"But now our purgatory be over and the Lord has chosen me to lead the legions of Limbo."

"Legions of Limbo you call them do you?" said the delf. "They are *my* legions." It sounded almost like pride or like petulance. Then it turned to a voice of heartbreak. "My friend is dust. But what of you, eh? What of you?"

He stepped forward around the dust. The soldiers raised their weapons.

"Hold your fire!" said Rodon quickly.

"But you could not kill a dream anyway. If I am a dream. What do you know of this world? Much, if you are here."

He seemed to have gained some confidence. He surveyed them.

"No. No, you are just playing here. You are lost are you not? How will you find your way out?"

"I have followed a road here. I have been guided here to your door, devil, here to where you sit besieged by a million souls of the Order."

"They are not souls of the Order, sir priest, Sir Snake."

Now that he was closer, Charlie noticed his eyes for the first time. They were wild and bloodshot.

"They are my nightmares. Have you slept here yet? Have you dreamed inside the dream, like the little man has?"

Charlie shrank back into his father.

"Who is he?" asked Richard, voicing the thoughts of the newcomers.

"He be the devil who betrayed his world," crowed the Archbishop. "Why did you not plunge straight to Hell?"

"This is Hell enough, Sir Snake."

"The serpent calls the hand of the Lord a snake!" The Archbishop let out a snarling laugh.

The Archbishop walked up to the delf slowly, put out his hand and touched him. The delf watched him curiously, but did nothing to stop him.

"Six hundred years and the first flesh I feel is that of a snake."

"You be real in sooth! You be alive. How can this be?" breathed the Archbishop. "Do all you devils perish like this?"

The delf suddenly threw back his head and laughed wildly.

"What fools have blundered into a dream here then? You did not come looking for me."

"Do not flatter yourself. Once more the Lord has given us a sign. So, do I leave you here in your living torment or do I throw you to the Legions of Limbo?"

The Archbishop looked hard into the reddened eyes.

"If I were to leave you here, why was I shown the way here?" He walked around him. The delf did not deign to watch him. "But be this Hell enough to live in Limbo forever? I will think on this, devil. I will pray and the Lord will answer me."

Richard was trying to work out what was going on. The four soldiers were clearly at least as confused as he was. He wondered if they would do anything if they tried to escape. But where could they go? He looked at Rodon, a man he had found enigmatic since they had first met. The man was silent, but he was watching. What was he thinking? All of them were watching this bizarre conversation between a ragged delf and the clergyman and not a single one of the ten people in the room appeared to truly understand it.

"Your Grace," began Rodon. "We should talk to the devil. He will have great knowledge."

"Consort with the damned? Trust his words? Thomas, have I taught you nothing? He would lead us a dance, a hot dance into brimstone and fire. He would bewitch us."

He went to the window and looked out.

"You have a fine view, devil. A million souls waiting for you."

"They have waited a long time," said the delf. "And you know a way out, do you not? Your way in is still open."

The Archbishop snapped around at the window.

"Our way be open, devil. But there be no way out for you. I do not need to pray. The Lord has answered me. The answer be before me. This army be held here because of you. If I free them from that task, they are at liberty to do my bidding."

"Your bidding?"

"They know me as their master."

"They know your cross and your sword, Sir Snake. I gave them that much. I gave them bloodlust and barbarity. Such were my nightmares. Oh do not sleep, Sir Snake. What demons you could conjure up."

"Your Grace, what say you?" Rodon spoke for all the men of the Order in the room whose eyes were darting amongst the speakers.

"This great host the Lord has given me to purge the corruption from the earth," the Archbishop replied. "I will lead them into the depravity from which this man Richard Denham and his child have come and when we have swept it clean, we will return to conquer all of Faerie at last."

Rodon's mouth opened, but he seemed to think better of it and instead moved closer to his master and said something more quietly, his arm moving to rest gently on the Archbishop's arm. The Archbishop shook it off.

"Thomas, question not the Lord's intents. We be his tools. His healing fire. We be the Great Flood to wash away the sins of the world."

"No!" It was Charlie, crying out despite himself. The Archbishop turned on him.

"Oh yes, child. You be too young to understand. And you will never be old enough."

Richard blanched. He could not believe what was happening. Of all the things he had experienced over the last few weeks, this was the most insane. This was not happening.

"Your Grace..." It was Berwick. The words died in his throat as the Archbishop turned to look at him.

"Soldier of the Order, do not quail at your duty now. Not when the hour of glory be at hand. Go down. Open the gates and let them in that they may feast on the blood of the traitor. The author of the doom of his own people." He turned back to the Mage. "How often do you labour to defeat yourselves!"

"Your Grace," said Rodon. "Be that safe?"

"Thomas, Thomas, do not question me. Did I not lead you through their hands? They be here for the devil."

"Then why do they not storm the walls? There be something deeper here."

The Mage laughed.

"You look too deep. They simply do not know how. I gave them hatred not intelligence."

"Then once more you devils create your own destiny. Thomas, take him away." The Archbishop's eyes had been caught by one of the open books on the table next to him. He walked over to it. "I will watch from here," he said vaguely.

Rodon nodded.

"Everyone outside," he said. "Take the devil."

Colman and Berwick took one of the Mage's arms. The Mage took a last look at the place that had been his home and his prison for centuries. His eyes played over books and papers that had become familiar, but now looked new and interesting again. He would never see them again. All that he had learned would die with him. He inhaled, turned away and was led outside.

"Hurry back, Thomas," said the Archbishop absent-mindedly. "I think you will find these books interesting."

They walked back out through the empty room and into the corridor.

"What's going on?" asked Richard.

"Be quiet," said Rodon curtly. They were dragged down the flight of stairs to the corridor where Ned had been left with his prisoners. There he stopped, looked at them intensely and spoke with quiet urgency.

"His Grace be not well. He does not mean to lead that army into Christendom. I will go back and talk to him."

He looked at Richard.

"If I fail, you need to warn your people. You must go back."

"But I don't know the way!"

Rodon grabbed his collars.

"You must know the way. You came here."

"Not this way. I don't know this way."

"I will know the way," said the Mage. "I can follow the breeze."

Rodon turned to him.

"I do not trust you, devil."

"They're not devils! They're just people!" exclaimed Charlie suddenly. The others looked at him and he reddened.

"They have been our enemies for hundreds of years," said Rodon darkly, glaring at Charlie. "We throw them both outside the gates."

"You can't!" said Charlie. He had tears in his eyes. He threw himself at Solimo and hugged him. "He's my friend!"

The Mage drew himself up and looked directly at Rodon.

"You have never known your own world. I have and it was beautiful." He turned to Richard. "Is it still beautiful?"

Richard nodded.

"I would not have it ravaged by what I have dreamed. Only I can close the door into this dream. Only that will stop them. You must come too or you will never go to the world of your ancestors."

"I do not care for that world," said Rodon. "That be not my home."

He stopped. He looked the Mage in the eye, they stood like that for many moments, each holding the other's gaze.

"If they be your creatures, you will know. Tell me truthfully. Will they harm a man?"

"They did not harm you, but I cannot speak for what your master may do with them."

Rodon turned to the corporal.

"Take them all out. Hold these..." he paused, looking at Charlie, "...these delf close to you. I will stay. I will not see you again."

The corporal looked as if he were about to say something, but Rodon simply put his hand on the soldier's chest and shook his head.

"Just go. Now."

51

THEY WERE RUNNING. Down stairways and corridors they went. Charlie simply followed. He had no idea if they were going the right way. He did not remember the way they had come. But the Mage seemed to know and the others followed him.

They found themselves in the bailey, standing beside the gatehouse through which they had first come. They all looked at each other. None of them was feeling confident.

"What if it was just because of the Archbishop?" asked Berwick.

"If you came through unscathed, I think it was because you are Men. If he came through unscathed," the Mage said pointing at Solimo, "it is because he was your prisoner. You need to do the same thing to us this time as you did before. If you do not, we are dead, and either you are trapped in here or your Archbishop unleashes my demons onto an innocent world."

"Form up around them," said the corporal taking control. "Denham, take my sword and go on the right, Berwick, the left. Keep the boy in the middle. Colman, stay at the back. Ned, you and me will be in the front."

All of them were quiet as Ned and Berwick pushed open the gate. It swung slowly, with the same rasping clank with which it had opened before. When it stopped, the noise of the silence was tremendous.

The massed ranks of the creatures from the Mage's nightmares faced them. Charlie felt as though thousands of eyes were on him and him alone. It felt like a nightmare, but a nightmare from which there was no waking. This was a real, living nightmare. He could not move.

"We can't close the gate again," said Berwick. "What will happen to the Archbishop?"

"He can look after himself," said the corporal. He turned to the Mage. "Which way?"

The Mage raised a cheek, turned his head and pointed in the opposite direction to the one from which they had come.

"March," said the corporal.

The corporal and Ned stepped forward, but Charlie did not move. They stopped and turned.

"What be you doing?" the corporal hissed.

Charlie did not say anything. He was utterly pale. He was beyond crying.

"Come on Charlie," his father said gently. Then he bent down and hugged him. "Come on Charlie. The sooner we start, the sooner it'll be over. Think of it as being like a visit to your Mum's aunty."

The Mage's mouth curled. Solimo bent down to Charlie's ear.

"Let us go back to your wood, Charlie. Show me the sun in the leaves."

Charlie tried to move his leg. It dragged forward. His other followed, then the others were moving around him and he was swept along in their movement. He tried to look ahead of him at the backs of Ned and the corporal, but each time, the army about them lured his eyes away. Their dead faces and empty eyes watched them as they walked. Their heads turned slowly, following Solimo and the Mage as they went by.

Charlie focused on the sounds their coats made, their boots on the ground, the slight squeaking of the leather in their belts, the knocking sound as the butt of a long-arm brushed against the pommel of a sword.

The eyes were still watching. If he ever survived this, he would see those eyes in his nightmares. There was simple hatred in them, calm hatred. Only their heads moved. If only they had made some noise or moved like real people, he could have borne it more easily. This behaviour was unearthly, unhuman. He felt his father's hand on his shoulder, gently guiding him forward. Then he heard a voice. It was the corporal. He was chanting, or was it some sort of poem? Was it a prayer?

"The Lord be my shepherd and nothing shall I want.
He sets me down in pastures.
On the waters of rest he brought me, my soul he turned.
He leads me on the streets of rightness, for his name.
Though I went in the midst of the shadow of the dead
I shall dread no ills, for thou be with me.
This rod and thy staff they comfort me.
Thou has laid a table in the sight of my foes.
Thou anointest my head in oil; and my cup is bright with drink.
And thy mercy shall follow me all of my life.

And I will dwell in the house of the Lord all the long days. Amen."

"Amen," echoed the other soldiers.

There was silence again and only the sound of their movement. The corporal's gruff voice had been strangely comforting. Charlie wanted to hear it again. He willed him to say it again.

"The Lord be my shepherd and nothing shall I want," the corporal began again.

The Archbishop was deep in a book. He raised his head and realised Rodon was standing in the doorway.

"Ah. You be here. Perhaps we should watch from the window. I have heard nothing yet. I presumed I would hear something,"

He stood and walked to the window across the room. Below him were thousands upon thousands of dark shapes. He had never seen an army so vast.

"I cannot see clearly from here. Be there another?"

"I will look, Your Grace."

Rodon went to look in other rooms in the apartments. They were littered with books and tapestries. In one room he found piles of papers containing notes and sketches. There were clothes on the floor in a heap and in a wardrobe whose door hung open, another pile of clothes folded impeccably. He passed through an archway and there was a large, leather covered chair with arms and a low table beside it. It faced a doorway in the wall which gave onto a stone balcony shielded by a wooden awning. It looked out directly onto the sea of bodies surrounding the castle. He could see a ripple of movement within it, a tiny group moving forward in a bubble of space that opened up in front of it and closed again behind. They were making their way through. They appeared to be safe, at least he assumed they were all there. He squinted. He had spent too much time peering at books by candlelight. Yes, he thought they were all there.

"Have you found anything?" called the Archbishop. He was standing in the doorway. "Ah yes."

Rodon wondered what he would make of the sight beneath him. He wondered if he could delay the Archbishop, but the cleric was already walking towards the balcony. He walked out and stood next to Rodon and rested his hands on the balustrade.

"Look at that army! I wonder if ever there was such a power gathered. Not even before the walls of Troy was there such an army. And the Lord has given it to me as my instrument!"

He drew his sword and took up his cross and raised them in his arms.

"Soldiers of the Order!" he called. "Soldiers of the Order of St Collen!" he called out again, this time more strongly.

"You have waited in Limbo for centuries for a moment to do the bidding of the Lord. You have waited for a sign, for a messenger. You have waited long enough for that sign. The Lord has chosen me, his humble servant, to be that sign. I am the priest of St Collen. I bear the silver sword of the saint on my robes. I am a priest and a knight of Christ. We are the of same blood, the same bond, the same brotherhood. He has chosen me to lead you out of Limbo. He has chosen you as His scourge on the nations who have left His path, who have sunk into corruption, who consort with devils and stray from the way. The Lord has brought us together in this place to march into glory. You be His holy warriors, His sword of vengeance and I am the mailed fist who will wield it!"

He stopped. There was no sound from below, but tens of thousands of faces were looking up at him. If he had done nothing else, he had their attention. Had they even understood him? He stood holding aloft the sword and cross. And looking down, he saw movement. Those closest to the front were raising their arms and in their hands they were holding swords. And as each one began to raise their swords, there arose a sound. At first it sounded like a distant wind, but then it became an audible groaning. The creatures below were opening their mouths and responding in perhaps the only way they knew how.

His eyes widened with delight, tracking across the bodies beneath him as they raised their swords and lances and banners high. Throughout the crowd, they were responding. In their thousands, their tens of thousands, they were responding to his call.

His eyes swept over them and were caught by movement towards the edge of the great host. A circle of space was moving outwards towards the plain beyond. He knew at once what it was, it was familiar.

"What passes there? Who be that? Thomas, where be the others?"

"I left them below with the devils, Your Grace." He could say no more. He would not lie to his master.

"Did you not tell them to throw those devils into the hands of these?"

"Those were your orders, Your Grace."

"Why be they taking them through? What passes here, I say?"

He looked back at Rodon in horror.

"He has bewitched them! That devil! Was this all a trick? Have I been deceived? Then it be his last act of sorcery."

He turned again to the multitude gathered below the walls.

"Soldiers of St Collen! Your first duty be before you. Even now, amongst you be a disease spawned by Satan, the great enemy. It tries to flee, it disguises itself and moves amongst you. But see there be devils and false-hearted men who would trick you and destroy you if they could. You must root them out. You must destroy them for the glory of God and for the honour of the Order!"

52

AS THE PARTY of delf and men passed through the host, they could hear a voice ring out across the silent, alien landscape.

"It be the Archbishop!" said Ned.

"Keep moving!" the Mage snapped.

"Be he calling us? Be he calling us back?" asked Colman.

"No," said Berwick, who had younger ears. "He be calling on these creatures around us."

"But can they hear?" asked Richard. He looked at the Mage next to him. "Can they hear? Can they understand?"

"In my nightmares, they were the Order of St Collen. They knew in their creation what the Order was and all its signs. I am sure the snake will say enough to raise them. And they can kill. I have seen it. They can rend a delf into scraps so they could do the same to a Man."

"But they will leave us be," said Berwick. "Because we be men...Wait – what be that sound?"

A groaning had begun. It was running towards them like the wind moving through treetops, only it was the sound not of leaves rustling, but of the wind winding amongst rocks and caves on a desolate moor.

"God help us," muttered the corporal.

"We are almost at the edge of the circle. Keep moving."

Charlie felt a cold wave surge over him as his hair stood on end. They were almost there. He could see beyond the bodies now.

"He speaks again," said Berwick, "but I can't make it out any more."

Then they were out. Berwick could not resist turning around. The creatures were still looking towards the light tower.

"Go faster!" urged the corporal, but they had already instinctively increased their pace.

"I can't keep up!" said Charlie, tripping.

His father reached for him.

"Get on my back."

Charlie was not a large boy, but he was heavy enough. He gripped his father's shoulders. They trotted on around a spur of the hills and a desert land opened up before them. He looked back for any sign of pursuit, but the dark hordes still stood immobile around the fortress. They hurried on and soon the fortress was lost to view behind the pink rock. His father set him down again.

They skirted a red lake. Odd shaped objects flickered across the unmoving surface. They crossed into a plain ringed with mountains which looked like volcanoes. Boulders were strewn down their sides and into the distance.

"They be behind us," said Ned.

They all turned. On the far side of the boulder field, the Mage's nightmare legions were crawling like an infestation.

"How far is it?" Richard asked.

"How long is a nightmare?" the Mage replied.

The land turned to small, pale stones and a plateau surrounded by slopes of loose stones stood before them. As they hurried around it, the impression grew that it was an ancient city that had been obliterated in some cataclysm.

Mountains stretched across their path. Their flanks were like crimson glass and their summits were topped with snow.

"Tell me we don't have to climb those!" said Colman.

The Mage looked at him crossly.

"There will be a way. Follow the breeze."

There was dust rising behind them as they entered a ravine which wound into the heart of the range and both their pursuers and the peaks above them were lost to sight. Now they were amongst the rock, the sides looked like curtains hanging in long folds to the ground. The ground began to rise. As they climbed, the rock underfoot became like long, slabbed steps with several strides to each one.

They reached a pass from which they could look back on the way they had come. It was a red jagged maze, but behind it was obscured by a wall of dust which hung above the land. There was no sign of the following legions.

"Are they still there?" asked Charlie.

"They are," said the Mage. "We can do nothing but go on following the path. We have a head start. I hope it is enough."

The others looked at each other, searching for assurance in the faces of their companions. They found little. Charlie's hair prickled on his neck as he turned his back on the valley and they started to descend again into a dusty brown country.

They entered a world of rock which grew like monstrous trees in twisted brown clumps. These grew as they went on, extending into long high hedges of melted stone, shattered in places with some giant axe. The land tended down a long slope to a yellowish green plain. They looked back. Their pursuers were in sight again. The ground was swarming with their dark mass. A sound came from them. It was a moaning like the wind through rocks, rising and falling.

"They be closer, eh?" said the corporal with calm resignation. No one spoke in response, but all stared for a moment in silent agreement, before turning once more and picking up the pace.

"Where does this corridor end?" Charlie asked, his voice trembling. "Will we find it?"

"Of course," said Richard automatically, but he looked at Solimo as he said it. Solimo met Richard's eyes with his own dark ones, but the look was inscrutable.

Ahead, a storm cloud was piling across the sky like spilled ink, flashing lightning and rumbling ominously. Tendrils of cloud reached out over the land ahead of it. Blurred shadows buzzed silently in and out of existence on the ground below it.

The track turned from dust to stone until they reached the marshy green valley floor. As they followed the valley, its sides became higher, steeper and narrower until they were hemmed in by high cliffs.

"They're gaining on us!" said Charlie.

The valley felt as though it were closing in on them, funnelling the goblin horde towards them. Charlie and his companions were was jogging now. Ahead of them, the cliffs ended abruptly and as the gap came closer, he tried to see what was out the other side. The gap did not seem to be coming any closer, yet every time he turned to look behind, the goblin men were nearer.

Suddenly they burst from the canyon. Behind them on either side, cliffs stretched from horizon to horizon, while in front was a great wide stony plain scattered with clumps of yellow grass. Which way to go? They stopped, looking about fearfully for a clue. They looked at the Mage for inspiration, but he too was searching.

Charlie and Richard felt Solimo's hands on their shoulders. They turned to him. He was staring straight ahead.

"Look at that tuft of grass," he whispered.

They looked around. There were several tufts of grass amongst the stones. They followed his gaze to the tallest which was waving in a breeze, then both turned uncomprehending faces back to him.

"The breeze is stronger here," he said.

Suddenly Charlie's face lit up with understanding.

"It must be coming from the other doorway. To home! It must be close!"

"Yes, I can feel the breeze now," said the Mage. "It is on my cheek. This way. Turn this way."

They wheeled to the right. Charlie could feel it too now. He could see the plain and a cluster of rocks. Now that they were moving, there seemed to be a path in the dust, a straight line.

Their delay had cost them. Racing to the end of the canyon were their pursuers. Charlie knew his father could run faster than he, but he was always behind him, quietly urging him on, with desperation in his voice. Fear filled all of them, it flowed from one to another as they ran.

As the Mage's nightmares emerged from the rock, their front ranks began to extend on either side. They were close enough now to make out individual figures.

"They are going to try to encircle us," said the Mage.

"Charlie, climb on my back again!" called Richard. They stopped just long enough for Charlie to leap up and wrap his arms around his father.

Berwick looked from them to landscape around them, searching for cover or a way out.

"What be that on the rocks?" he asked.

There was something standing on the rocks in front of them. It had not been there before.

"Be there more of them at the rocks? We be doomed."

"I can only see one," said Ned. "I'll shoot it."

"You'd have to stop to hit it. Keep moving," said the corporal.

The groaning was louder now. Charlie turned. He gripped his father's shoulders.

"Not so tight Charlie. Charlie, not so, what - ?"

Richard turned too.

"They're coming!" he said.

"It is in those rocks," said the Mage. "I can see the door."

He seemed to be the only one not fixated on the nightmares circling for the kill. Solimo followed the Mage's gaze.

"I see it too," he said.

Charlie could see nothing. The rocks were a hundred yards away, maybe more. And the figure resolved into two, still waiting, as if ready to pounce. There was something familiar about them.

The creatures were moving faster now. And the moaning sound was becoming more intense. It was changing from a wandering wailing to a deeper, more certain tone. They could hear the clank of armour and weapons.

More figures came out of the rocks, they moved slowly.

"A trap!" shouted Colman.

The rocks were closer. Without anyone saying anything, all of them suddenly broke into a run. Charlie clung on. His knuckles were white. His fingers dug into his father's shoulders, but Richard did not feel them. The figure on the rocks was climbing down to join those on the ground. The soldiers readied their long-arms. They would not have much of a chance to shoot.

As they watched, the two figures strode to the front of the group. There was a grim smile on the face of one and a look of stern fear on the other.

"Raul! Esella!" said Charlie. He was almost screaming.

"I thought I would be pleased to see you, but I fear that pleasure will be very short," Raul said, looking over their shoulders.

"We know we are near the door," said Esella. She was nearly in tears. "But I cannot find it."

Then Charlie realised who was amongst the crowd at their back.

"Mum!"

She whirled him up and held him close. She said nothing, but over his shoulder, she was watching the army approaching. She put herself between Charlie and them. The closest of the creatures were near enough now that they could see their faces, if faces they could be called.

Confused, but relieved the newcomers were not more goblins, the soldiers turned towards their enemy for a moment.

"There be too many!"

"Shoot!" said the corporal. "Don't just watch them!"

Four long-arms were raised to shoulders.

"Fire!"

The guns cracked and there was smoke. Several of the creatures stuttered as they came, but did not fall.

"Can they die? It be hopeless!" said Colman.

Charlie felt no terror now. He felt nothing at all. The moment had become quite unreal. He was aware Esella was holding out a small sack to Solimo. Solimo shook his head, but the Mage pushed him aside and plunged his hands into the sack, his eyes rolled back and he closed them.

"It has been so long," he breathed

The nightmares were upon them. The soldiers had fired again and one of the Limbo goblins had veered away, apparently confused. Then the four troopers drew swords and swept them around themselves. They met the blades of the host with sharp clangs.

The corporal was the first to fall. He clutched at his arm, then staggered as a lance entered his side. Charlie watched in horror as the creatures stepped on his body. The three remaining were retreating now and the creatures were encircling them. This was death then. His father had snatched up a fallen sword and was slashing and hacking with a madness, an intensity which Charlie had never seen. But like the others, he was being forced back.

Ned staggered and fell onto one knee. He tried to push himself up and cut with his sword, but as he lifted it, he became unbalanced and toppled. He vanished under flailing arms and weapons. Charlie saw the dead eyes turn on him. There was a glow from behind him. Was he dead now? Was this what death was like?

Suddenly the goblins paused and raised their eyes. There was a light on them all, the light of the sun shining through a break in the clouds. It shone on them for a moment, then the sun wraith swept down, cutting a burning path across the front ranks before rising again. More of the legion came up, densely packed, and the sun wraith hurtled down again, spinning backwards and forwards amongst them, faster than any Charlie had seen in battle before.

The creatures paused, their motion halted by the wraith. The group of men and delf saw their opportunity. They turned and ran. Richard's eyes met Helen's and a lifetime of words passed between them, then he took Charlie from her and ran with him, Helen at his heels. They were at the rocks.

There was little time to wonder about Raul and his companions. A thought crossed Charlie's mind that perhaps Raul and his mother were merely creations of a dream he did not remember. He shook the thought from his head and turned his attention to the rocks. He looked at them desperately. Where was the door? Where was it? The Mage walked straight to a slab of stone and put his hand to it. It was like looking at one of those illusions that you think is a vase and then realise is also two faces staring at each other. As he did so, Charlie could see it was a door, with a handle. The Mage touched the handle, almost caressed it for a moment, then turned it.

The door swung open. There was the funnel hall. He could see the forest outside the windows. It looked so unnatural, so strange, so new that none of them moved for a moment. Then they bundled through and shut the door behind them.

53

THERE WAS SILENCE and stillness in the funnel room. Richard's head was spinning. One moment he was in a living nightmare fighting for his life and the next he was in a quiet stone room in the woods near his home with his son. Perhaps he really had been dreaming.

He looked around him. There was Charlie and Helen. For a moment the Denhams looked at each other. Then they fell together in a hug. They were home.

Richard looked around at the rest. There was a group of hollow-eyed delf, perhaps twenty of them. There was Raul, Esella, Solimo, the Mage, Colman and Nicholas.

He had watched both the corporal and Ned fall.

"I didn't even know the corporal's name," said Richard.

"John," said Colman. "John Biston." He was staring at the floor. "He'd been a soldier a long time. It was a soldier's death."

"It is not over yet," said the Mage. "They are beyond that door. They can come through it, if they can find it."

"What can we do?"

"Hope they do not find it. And dream this tower away and break the link to that place."

Dream the tower back? But they were home now, Charlie thought. Surely the nightmare was over?

"Do you have more sponges here?" the Mage asked Solimo.

"Yes, in the corner," said Esella pointing. "Why was the corridor so long? I thought it would be a short walk, not a walk across half the world."

"Because you dreamed it completely out of Unama. You lost its place. The dream worlds do not stay still, they float. You cannot put your hand in the same river twice. Now then, we need more sponges to dream and more to hold off those outside. Solimo, prepare the room. I will do what I can with the wraiths."

"How can we take it back without anyone to pull it?" asked Solimo.

"I am a Mage, Solimo and there are two keepers of Kunnaslaki here. The room can return."

"How long will it take them to find the door?" asked Charlie.

"Time passes much more quickly in a dream and therefore also in Unlembien. I need to delay them."

He took a sponge and a sun wraith erupted from it, curved up, then down, slid under the door and disappeared. Esella watched with awe.

"Can you control them without seeing them?"

The Mage did not respond. A second wraith leaped out of a second sponge and followed the first under the door. Only then did the Mage relax and say to Esella without looking at her.

"Of course. I am a Mage, Light Keeper."

"Let's go home," said Helen. She led her little family outside. Solimo watched from inside, a smile playing across his face.

The Denhams stopped and were talking. Charlie seemed to be pleading. His mother was looking angry and Richard was holding her arms and talking calmly but intensely to her.

"What is going on out there?" asked the Mage impatiently. "We need them in here."

"Charlie's mother did not know where they had gone. They had been away for weeks. She thinks it is over," said Solimo.

"And I have been away for centuries!"

The Mage walked outside and went over to the Denhams. Helen watched him, taking in his wild, exotic appearance.

"Everyone inside."

"And who the hell are you to order us around?" Helen demanded.

"Women have not changed in six hundred years then," he said.

"We're not coming," Richard said. "We're home now. I have my family back. It is over for us."

"It is not over. Beyond that door are a million nightmares about to descend on your world. We can only close that door by dreaming this building back to Unama."

"Then do so. You don't need us," Richard said.

Helen interposed.

"I thought I had lost my husband and son but I waited for them here and they came back."

The Mage frowned.

"How long did you wait?"

"Weeks," she said. Her eyes filled with tears. Weeks of fear and anger and heartache and loneliness.

"And why did you wait when you thought you had lost them?"

This was the most foolish question Helen could remember hearing. Clearly this was a man who had never lost anything.

"Because I knew they would come back," she said.

"But you could not know," the Mage said, with a jut of his chin. "You cannot see the future. There are many futures ready to be born at any instant. You cannot know, you can only hope."

"Let them go," said Solimo, who had come to the door. "This is not their fight, they have done enough, seen enough."

"This *is* their fight because it was their ancestors that started all this. I came to visit, to discover. They came to invade, to conquer and plunder. They will help me put it right."

"Dad," said Charlie. "We have to help them."

"We don't have to," said Helen gently.

"There is more," said the Mage. I hope we can dream this tower away. We need to sever the dream. But then my nightmare army will make for the other exit. If the snake cannot enter this world, he will enter mine. He will finish what his ancestors started. I will not let that happen again. That is why you have to come with us."

"But why?" Charlie asked.

"Always questions, boy! It is quite simple. We need to reach the garden room before they do. We need to sever that end of the dream so they cannot come through. To do that we must bring the garden room out of our world and back to yours. You can only dream between the worlds, not within one. Only then can we reunite the whole light tower by dreaming it back into *our* world. When we bring the garden room here, then you can go home."

"You sound very certain of this," said Helen.

"Oh I am not," said the Mage. "But I hope, for hope is the only weapon against despair, do you not agree?"

Helen said nothing, he was looking at her with satisfaction at his own argument. It annoyed her. He looked away and glanced around the clearing. His eyes lit on the small mound of earth and the lantern.

"Is that yours?" he asked.

"Yes."

"Do you have more candles?"

"Of course," she said, irritated again. "In the bag." She pointed to where it lay just behind the lantern.

"Bring them. We have no time to lose."

"Who do you think you are?"

"I am the last Mage and therefore the last person who can stop the end of the world."

Even as she was outraged at his pomposity, she could not believe she could walk home now with her husband and son once more. Her life did not feel as though it had just knitted itself up. She was looking at a group of people she had come to know through experiences she had not had a chance to understand and maybe never would. She looked at Charlie and she knew what he was feeling. She put her hand on his shoulder.

Richard looked confused. Berwick and Colman had come to the door now. They were looking around.

"They have trees here too," said Berwick. He sounded like a child.

"I will go," said Richard. "Alone."

"No!" said Charlie and Helen together. Charlie surprised even himself. Only minutes ago he had been terrified. Now he wanted to go back to more danger. Richard too felt a strange desire to see it through. He had lived through so much with these people that he could not leave them to go through more and not know what happened to them. He could not explain it clearly to himself.

The Denhams looked at each other. It was a moment of unreality and complete, mutual understanding. Then all three turned and walked into the funnel hall.

"Now, lie down and sleep!" said the Mage.

The two soldiers were looking uncertain.

"Be this witchcraft?" asked Berwick uncertainly.

"No," grinned Charlie. "But it *is* magic."

"Nonsense," snapped the Mage. "There is no such thing as magic, merely philosophies you do not understand."

The two men lay down reluctantly. Just as they did so, there was a hammering on the door. The Mage conjured two more sun wraiths and sent them under it. The banging stopped abruptly and the Mage nodded to Solimo.

Solimo arranged Raul, Berwick, Colman and the Denhams on the floor with their heads centred on Esella's bowl. There was a pile of light sponges next to it. The Mage walked over to the centre.

"Dream of Kunnaslaki," the Mage intoned. "Dream of green hills. Woman, follow your husband and son. We dream together."

"No, not Kunnaslaki. We do not know if it is safe!"

"I will make everything right," the Mage replied with confidence.

Then the door swung open. Two nightmare soldiers stood there, frozen for a moment. Behind them were more. The Mage moved with lightning speed. It was almost as if he pulled a wraith from the sponge in one hand and flung it at them.

Light washed around them, it rose up. Charlie was startled by the horror at the door. How could he sleep when they were coming to get them?

"Sleep!" came another voice. It slid around the rear of his brain like a cushion. "Sleep. You are safe. Safe as the sea and the sky. Safe as the sun and stars, safe as the moon..."

Charlie seemed to rise and feel, rather than see, below them, a thousand twisted faces vanish into the light. Then there was a feeling of being far away and close at the same time. He was spinning and felt like he was hanging in an unimaginably vast space with a cloud of murky purple shifting beneath him.

The Archbishop, with Rodon standing helplessly behind him, had watched the monstrous army begin to move, a rippling motion as a segment on the far side broke off towards their former companions and begun to follow it. They watched until it went out of sight. Then they had waited for a very long time, neither speaking. Time did not seem to matter here.

"What was that? Something just happened," said the Archbishop. Rodon noticed it too. It was as if a background hum they had not noticed before had suddenly stopped or a shadow had fallen across the world. "There is a difference in the air."

They waited. It was like floating in thought. Rodon found he could stare without thinking. The section of the army that had pursued the Mage and their former companions appeared again across the plain. A smaller group came through the main host towards the Light Tower, a small disturbance rippling through the sea of bodies. When they reached the outer wall, they stopped, then turned back. They had left something on the ground by the gate.

Rodon and the Archbishop stared down. It was two bodies and both of them wore the uniform of the Order. Beyond that, Rodon was not prepared to speculate on who they were.

The Archbishop took a deep breath. He was quiet for a time.

"I do not think the others dead," he said through his teeth. "I think they have closed the door against us."

"Then the plan has miscarried," said Rodon. "We must leave this host and return to Outreterre."

"Leave the host? Walk away from God's intent? Never. This army has been given into my hands. It shall wash the worlds clean of their corruption. If they have closed the gate to the world of men, then they will not close the way to Outreterre as well."

He looked through the doorway that led into the chamber where they had first met the Mage.

"Perhaps in those books is the secret that will unlock the way into the world of men once more. Never fear, Thomas. We shall be victorious."

"But what could this army do in Outreterre? Suppose you could not control it, just think – "

"Thomas." The Archbishop put his hand on his assistant's shoulder and looked into his eyes. "Do not doubt the gift of the Lord. The hand of the Lord shall find out the guilty. I see now, I have spent too much of my time in my books. I have not been a good shepherd to my flock. They have wandered. They consort with the wolves. But I shall purge Outreterre of evil just as I destroy the devils. The whole of Faerie shall be the Lord's and no longer the realm of superstition. There are other lands beyond what we know. We are bound in by the mountains and the sea. Once Unama has fallen, we will cross the sea like our ancestors did of old."

"But they never returned. They likely perished."

"Whether they did or did not, there is something beyond the sea and that too shall be the Lord's. Nothing shall stop us. Our trumpets shall sound across the world. With this host at my back, nothing can withstand us. The devils will be crushed and those who consort with devils shall be trodden beneath the boots of the righteous. I will make Faerie tremble at my name, for I shall be the vengeance of the Lord."

Rodon looked back into those eyes. Was this the same man he had served and worked with for so many years? When had he become like this, hating even his own kind?

Rodon had known doubt before, but he had prayed, he had talked to the Archbishop and the Archbishop had talked gently to him, prayed with him. The doubt had been about his worthiness of the love of God. He was a sinner, a small man, a mere speck in the mind of God. His scholarship with the Archbishop had only made this suspicion grow. God had not created just one world, he had created two, close together, yet far apart. If he had thought himself insignificant before, this made him even more so.

The Archbishop was like a father to him. He had told him that everyone had a purpose in the mind of God, even if he never understood it for himself. Even as he looked past the Archbishop to the dark ranks beyond the walls, Rodon knew he had stumbled upon his purpose.

He had to warn his people. He would try to find a way to close the last door into Limbo. He had to escape.

"If you be so decided, we need to see for sure that the gate to the world of men is shut or whether they be dead," said Rodon. "I will go and see,".

The Archbishop turned his head sharply.

"You do not fear them as the others did?"

"I fear them as weapons of the Lord," said Rodon, "but I trust in the Lord's protection and help."

"Good, good then," said the Archbishop. "You be a good man and a faithful servant. Go and I will see to these books while I wait."

As Rodon walked from the room, he felt a heaviness dragging at him. He fought an impulse to turn around and run back to the Archbishop and ask on his knees for forgiveness. His mind circled back to the thought that had been swimming for the surface since they had entered Limbo. The Archbishop had lost his way. Perhaps, as Lord Giles had said, he had spent too long in the devils' books. He needed to his help his master, but he first had to warn Outreterre, if any there believed him.

He found his way through the stairways and corridors until he was out of the keep and through the still open gate. The two bodies were there. They were mutilated, hacked at countless times, but he could recognise sturdy Ned and the little corporal by their size. This was not the work of delf. Devils they may be, but they did not kill in this fashion. This was the work of other devils, of the goblins created by the fear of the Mage. Why were only these two bodies returned? In his mind, he was sure this meant the others had reached the door to Christendom. It explained that strange feeling he and the Archbishop had experienced. The way to the world of men had been shut. If he had doubted his decision, he doubted it no longer. He turned towards the hill from which they had first observed the host. He walked upright, his heart beating quickly in his chest. He walked alone through the ranks of the goblin army.

Just as they had before, they parted as he walked. He knew he must not run. To run was to show the guilt he felt. He was still torn. Should he turn back now and serve his master? No, the Archbishop had become insane. Some fury had seized him. Surely it could not be God's will. He looked about him at the human and goblin forms around him. They horrified him. The Mage had said he had created them in fear from his own nightmares. What a place was this where the very act of dreaming could create horrors?

At every moment he expected to be discovered. He expected to hear a cry from the keep. Surely the Archbishop had seen the fear and distrust in his eyes? Surely he could see what he was thinking? He would be called to account and feel the daggers of the unholy plunge into his back. His skin crawled as he walked. He dared not look back. He had to keep walking.

He was at the edge of the army now. He could see the gully down which they had come. He needed to follow the path back. It did not seem so clear now. Only at the top of the hill on the edge of the plain did he allow himself to turn and look. The army still stood there. He took one last look, then began to run.

54

The Archbishop sat at the books, his head rested in his hands and every now and then one hand would move to turn a page. It was fascinating, but the sense sometimes eluded him. He only needed time, then he would understand. He read on.

He reached the end of the book. He would read it again. He looked up. How long had passed? It was impossible to tell in this infernal world. He stood and returned to the room out of which he had looked before.

He searched for Rodon. There was no sign of him, no tell-tale movements within the army of his passing through them. He must already be coming up the steps to inform him. The Archbishop returned to the room of books and sat down once more, picking up another tome and opening the cover.

He skimmed the writings, running his hands over them. There was such lore here, such evil and sorcery and power, if only he could understand what it said. The pages turned beneath his eyes.

It was only when he had finished that second book that he realised Rodon had still not come. Where was he? He stood again and went to the window. He looked out. He returned to the other room and scanned the landscape. Nothing. He went to other windows until he had looked out at every side. There was no sign of his assistant.

What had become of him? Had he been killed by the legions? Surely not. Not unless he had shown himself to be unworthy of trust. Could that be? He had shown doubt. He had tried to dissuade him. He had taken that as faithful challenge, perhaps a test. But where was he? And if the others had been bewitched, why had Thomas not noticed it? He was with them at the gate, he would have supervised the ejection of the devils to meet their doom. If he was there, then he was complicit. The evidence swam before his eyes. Surely it could not be true. Thomas was faithful. He was loyal and devout. Surely he could not fall too? If Thomas could fall, any of them could.

The world had become a cistern. He was alone; betrayed by them all. He hammered his fists on the table. He roared with rage.

How could they betray him? How did they dare to betray him when he had this army at his command? They mightiest army that had ever been. He would sweep down on Outreterre and overturn it in all its corruption. And then he would find a way into the worlds. He would fill them all with darkness.

He was leaning on the window now. He raised his head to look outside.

"You offspring of vipers, how will you escape the judgment of Gehenna?" he roared. He raised his hands above his head. "Knights of the Order of St Collen, your time has come. Arise and seek the Lord's vengeance!"

Below him, thousands of heads turned to his voice like dogs to their master. He turned back into the room. The books lay strewn across the long table. There were tears in his eyes. He rubbed his hand over them.

"Judas!" he said. He sank to the table. He was so tired. He had the weight of responsibility on him and him alone.

"Grant me some rest, Lord, before I lead Your army to victory. Grant me but a little sleep, then I will ride forth in Your glory."

He bowed his head and, with an open book for a pillow, he slept. He dreamed. And in his Limbo dreams he raised his sword at the head of a mighty army.

The journey back seemed interminable, but still Rodon went on. What was this world where hunger and thirst did not touch you? How many days had he walked? Or was it minutes? Time held no meaning. He walked through the wastes, every moment expecting the path before him to vanish or the world around him to dissolve into something else or even nothingness. Sometimes he ran, sometimes he walked.

He came at last to the cathedral and passing through it, he came out onto the viaduct, its length stretching out before him to the distant valley side. No floodwaters surrounded the viaduct this time, no beasts lunged out of their depths at him. He was crossing a desert where the city now seemed desolate and empty. He was alone. He wondered if he had gone crazy. Perhaps it was all in his mind. Maybe he had misread the Archbishop and this was a fool's errand. Perhaps the Archbishop was right? Or perhaps he had gone mad and he was gibbering on some street corner imagining himself in this world without time, wind or sun.

He was almost at the end of the viaduct when he thought he heard a wind. He turned to look at the hills behind the cathedral. They lay in a blue swathe across the horizon. But across their tops something was moving. A darkness was crawling over their summits. The nightmare host was on the move. It was swarming in his wake, following him. It was coming. He was running out of time. Outreterre was running out of time.

The Light Doctor winced as the delf led her horse into the trees. They were slow, so slow, and she was struggling to hold on. They should have taken more horses, but none of the delf could ride. It had been foolish. She could never ride a horse in her condition, let alone across the range. If they tried to carry her, all of them were weak and while she was small, she was still a weight to carry into the steep, forested mountains.

"You cannot take me," she said. "You need to move quicker than I can go."

"But we cannot leave you," said Talo.

"I was supposed to protect you, but I am a burden. I am slowing you down."

"We will take her back down. We will go the long way," said one of the delf who was carrying her. "We can cross the river at the ford above the Great Gorge. It is autumn now, the waters will be low enough."

"You cannot carry me that far, it would take many days," she said.

"But it is flat. It will be much easier. And who would be looking for us?"

"Perhaps you are right," she agreed. "It would be completely mad. The army has gone and they will not be looking for a few delf walking in the fields of Outreterre."

They turned back. There were five of them. Talo watched them disappear downhill into the trees.

Rodon had reached the cliffs. Below him the grey ocean seethed. The door was still there. It seemed so small now. The Archbishop's army would struggle to come through that door, but still they would come. They would mass and swarm and fall upon Outreterre like locusts, devouring everything.

Something had happened while he had been gone. The Pits were empty, and there were bodies of men, cobs and delf. Those of men and cobs had been lined up in the pit. Many bore the characteristic burn marks of sun wraiths. The delf had been brought up into the open in the compound and left covered in blankets and rugs. What had happened? The sun caught him in a beam of light as it found a way amongst the clouds and through the gash in the darkness over the hills.

He quickly searched the buildings. In the Archbishop's quarters he found Silver, slumped on a bed. There was blood on his head. At first he thought he was dead, but he started as Rodon entered.

"They have escaped," he said. "They brought demons. There were hundreds. There was nothing I could do."

"Where are they?"

"Out there," he gestured vaguely with his hand. "I don't know. The guards are all dead, maybe the cobs too. There's only me now. I don't know why they spared me. I fought. Perhaps they thought I was dead. There were too many."

"You must leave. You must come with me. There be a greater peril coming from Limbo." He was dragging Silver from the bed. "The demons be nothing to what I have seen. All of Hell be loosed."

"Where be the Archbishop?" Silver asked.

"I came on ahead to warn Outreterre," Rodon said, ignoring the question. "We have little time. Come! Be your horses still here?"

"I don't know. They would have taken them."

But some horses did remain. There were four in the stables, none of them in prime condition.

"Why did they not take them?"

"Maybe they left in too big a hurry. Maybe four horses are of no use to hundreds of devils."

They rode out from the tunnel gate and into the wood. Rodon was pleased to be riding again, moving at speed, feeling the wind in his face.

"Whither?" Silver asked.

"We find the army. We must warn them."

"I don't understand," Silver wailed. "But if peril comes, perhaps I should go to Collenium. To warn them."

Rodon had never liked Silver. He would not miss his company and the city should be warned. They parted at the crossroads and Rodon rode on west alone.

The figure of the Archbishop emerged from the doorway to the Pits into the courtyard, looked around and cried out.

"See the work of Satan! He be among us! He be unleashed and does his filthy work. Arise souls of Limbo! There be work to be done!"

The goblin men started to come up behind him, making their way in their thousands up the steps from the Pits. A crowd was around him now. He was lifted by the moaning mass and they half marched, half ran out of the gate and onto the forest road.

55

HELEN AWOKE AND immediately reached out for Richard. He was there. She relaxed. It had been a dream. She felt rested for the first time in weeks. Then she took in her surroundings. And remembered. She was inside that building with the strange funnel chimney. She sat up and watched the irritating ragged man moving amongst them. He was shaking each one of them excitedly.

She went to Charlie and hugged him again, then she hugged Richard. She knew the others were watching, but she did not care. She said nothing. Words could not contain it.

The refugee delf were rising too. She had no idea how long she had travelled with them. It had been a journey of wonder and fear. Indistinct shapes had moved in the distance, shadows had loomed over them with nothing to make them. Sometimes it had felt as she was not walking through a landscape, but that the landscape was passing by her. It had been very disconcerting.

In all the time she had spent with the delf from the Pits, they had barely spoken. They had looked about them with wonder, but they were still finding their voices after years in the dark. After their dreams of despair, they had seemed to accept any surroundings. Now when she looked at them, there was colour in their cheeks that had not been there before, a spark had entered their eyes.

"Hurry," said the Mage. "I do not want to be the first out of the door. I have travelled through time to be here and I may shock someone."

"Last time we were here, we were fighting each other," said Raul. "I do not know what we might find outside the door."

"We would have won," said the younger man. He was young, new to manhood, but wearing a dark heavy coat that looked like a kind of uniform. "We outnumbered you."

"Numbers do not always matter, boy," said Raul. Helen wondered if there was going to be a fight.

"Then we go out together," said the young man. "You and me. But be prepared to be a prisoner."

They all stood. She looked at the other soldier, a smaller bearded man with a face she did not trust. They all looked tired, especially the oldest one, the ragged delf, whose hair was greying. He looked like a drugged-up tramp, yet he moved with purpose and confidence.

The soldiers picked up their weapons. They were made from wood, like old-fashioned guns. They frightened her. The others in the room looked tense. Then the younger soldier opened the door.

They were no longer in the wood. It was like the time before, but this time, she tried to think about it. How had that happened? Outside was a courtyard. It was empty. There were broken windows, smashed tiles on the ground. It seemed to be night, or late evening. The sky was strange. At first it looked like cloud, but then not. It was too grey for a night sky and there were no stars.

"How long have we been gone?" asked Raul.

"Hours? Days? Weeks? I do not know how long you were in the dream," said the Mage as if frustrated at the other's question.

The group of them gathered outside the building. It was the same one or, at least, one very like it. What had happened while she slept? Where were they now?

"We need to search," said Raul. "We need to find out what happened. Then we will know what to do with each other."

He looked at the two men in black coats meaningfully. Solimo, the younger delf with long dark hair broke in.

"Raul," he said. "These men are our friends. Between us the war is over. Whatever has happened, nothing happens to Colman and Berwick."

Raul did not look convinced.

"Solimo, you will be the death of me," he said slowly. "So we should go and see if we can find out what happened, you and me, Solimo, each with one of our new friends. Is that good with you...friends?"

The two men nodded, but they looked him in the eye as if searching for a truth. Helen leaned into Richard.

"What's happening? Do you know what's happening?"

"When we left here just before we found you there was a fight – here – between the delf and the men. We don't know what's happened. We need to find out."

He squeezed her with his arm. "I'm sorry, Helen. It must be hard. I need to try to explain to you. There's been no time."

"Raul and Esella told me some. Richard, am I dreaming? Is this real?"

He smiled. "Somehow."

"I'll help look," said Charlie, standing forward.

"You will not!" said Helen.

Solimo smiled gently. Helen liked him.

"Indeed you will not, Charlie. You need to stay with your mother."

He turned to the others.

"We will not be long. I think the rest of you should wait inside."

The two pairs went left and right in the courtyard. The rest of them went back inside the funnel room. Charlie looked at the floor, then he turned to his father.

"Dad," he said with a thoughtful look. "Are Ned and the corporal dead?"

"I think so, Charlie," Richard said.

Helen was jealous of their connection, of what they had lived through together. They were talking about the same men who had pushed them into that Limbo world and now there were tears in Charlie's eyes. The ragged man tossed his head and looked at them.

"They are dead just as the last of my friends are dead. Years ago. Years ago. I did not think I made them with hate for their own kind. Even after centuries I do not understand." He was talking to himself.

"Where are we?" she asked. She had listened to Raul and Esella as they talked to her, but it had made little sense. She had so many questions. There were too many to ask. "Is this..." She felt stupid asking the question. "Is this another planet?"

"No," said the Mage. "You have woken up in Faerie." His eyes widened as he said it. He was mocking her, but she did not know why. "But there is no magic here, no more than there is in your world. Or have you found it yet in your age?"

She did not know what he meant, but Charlie seemed to.

"No. We can do a lot with light, but not what you can. And you can do really cool things. You're even cleverer than the Light Doctor."

"That is because I am a Light Mage. And I have had six hundred years of dreamtime to study." He sighed. "I miss my books. They were my only friends."

A low whistle came from outside. They opened the door and there were the two search parties, but they were not alone. With them were about a dozen delf women and ten children. They looked uncertainly through the door. Some looked frightened. It was the men in black coats who seemed to scare them.

"We found them hiding in one of the cottages," said Raul. "And outside, just down the hill, were two carts. They were full of bodies. Delf and men."

"What is happening?" asked one, the tallest. Then she looked at Helen. "A woman. Do you follow their army?"

"We told her we are all friends," said Solimo. "Naturally they do not believe us."

"Believing is hard when they were only here yesterday shooting at us."

"*Yesterday?*" said Solimo.

"Now you start to understand," the Mage said, his eyes wide.

The delf who had spoken gave him a puzzled look.

"How can you be friends?" she said, looking at the soldiers.

"We have been through much since yesterday," said Solimo. "Do you know what happened here?"

"When the tower disappeared, the soldiers were frightened. They ran away. We were frightened too when you came back. We hid. Those soldiers rode all the way back to the valley before they stopped and watched. Mondo kept watch, then we arrived."

"We?" asked Raul.

"Kyntilla. We came with the gathering that the council called. The keepers sent sun wraiths ahead and they ran from our numbers. The Order turned tail and headed north."

"Where is Kyntilla?"

"Gone after them. We stayed here to bury the dead. Then we will go north and bury more. There will be many more when the army of the Order comes from Outreterre. This time they will fight until there is no one left."

Raul turned to Berwick and Colman.

"Now is that not interesting?" he said to them.

"Raul," said Solimo with a note of warning.

"Do you think they should hand over their weapons? They are our prisoners now."

"Raul, our war is over."

"Perhaps. But it is not over for anyone else," said the Mage. "And nor is it over for their priest. She is right. This is the final battle for them. This is the last chance for Unama and perhaps this whole world. We must stop it. I have been given a second chance."

"What is this war about?" Helen asked. She had asked the same question of her local member of parliament only a few years before. To her surprise, the women looked at her with astonishment, perhaps even scorn.

"They stole our land and enslaved our people. And at last we are all fighting back," said Raul. "And now they are coming again. They send the darkness and another army."

"You devils have been marauding for years," said Berwick, raising his weapon. "You kill our children and corrupt the souls of the innocent with your devilish ways. This land be God's gift to us!".

"Stop!" said Richard. "This isn't getting us anywhere. Nicholas, put that down."

But Raul was laughing.

"Is that what they tell you? Is that really what they tell you?"

"None of that matters now!" exploded the Mage. "None of you understand what is about to be unleashed upon you. Even you who have seen it!" He turned back to his companions. "The feud between the delf and the Order must stop. You have seen what that foul host of Limbo did. They are the enemies of all of us now. We must stop them. We must stop them *together*."

"How do we stop them?" asked Solimo.

"Through the light of the soul," said the Mage. His voice softened. "This lady has shown us its power."

"Me?" asked Helen. "What have I done?"

"You dared to hope."

"Hope for the best?" scoffed Colman.

For a moment, Helen thought the Mage was going to explode.

"Yes," he said with studied calm. "That is precisely what we must do. The time for talking is over. We must find the armies before they fight. We will all go."

"These people are not fit to travel!" said Raul, gesturing at the refugees who were peering out of the windows of the light tower. "Limbo was more than enough. You will be taking them into great danger."

"They have survived a great deal and I am sure they can survive this. And if we fail, here will be no safer than there. Besides, the fresh air will do them good. Can you feel it?" He stopped and took a deep breath, filling his chest. "Now, we need wagons and horses. Where did you say your wagons were?"

"They are full of bodies," said the woman.

"What is your name?"

"Heka," said the tall woman.

"We shall help you bury the bodies, Heka. Then we will all travel north together."

Helen stood back with Charlie while they buried the bodies. She would not let him watch.

"Mum, I've seen bodies before. I was in a battle!"

"Charlie, don't talk like that, I don't like it."

"But I was."

They were on their way before long. Solimo had gone to the cottages and returned with sacks of food and bottles of water which he loaded into boxes attached to the sides of the wagons. There were horses which had been left behind and they took these. She was surprised to see Richard climb onto one.

"You can't ride," she said.

"I can," he said with a smile.

"Catch!" said a voice. They turned and Berwick was holding up a long-arm. He lobbed it at Richard who caught it and slid it into a holster on the saddle.

"No!" she said. "You don't need that. You won't fight."

"I'll only use it if I have to. To protect you."

"Have you used it before?" she asked, almost afraid to hear the answer.

"Yes," he said.

"Did you kill someone?"

"Not a person, no. I'll tell you about it."

"Look!" said Raul. He pointed to a lighter patch in the sky far away to the north. "The Pits have stopped spitting darkness."

"Your doing?" asked Solimo.

Raul smiled grimly. "Esella too. Or we would have caught up with you sooner."

Rodon had ridden the horse hard. It was sweating and wearying. He had paused only to stop at farmhouses and order their inhabitants out. They looked frightened and confused, unsure whether to believe his ravings. It was not the kind of news they were expecting. They knew the army had marched on the devils, so how could devils be marching on them?

With the Guardian Range on his left, he crested a rise and looked back. He could hear it. They were coming. He could see smoke rising into the air. A new darkness was filling the sky of Outreterre as its farms began to burn.

Up in the hills, Talo also saw the smoke. As the last delf filed slowly past him into the trees, he wondered what it could be. Perhaps Raul had returned. He turned back to the delf. Somehow they had become his charges. Feeling responsible was an old feeling. He watched the delf from the pit walking slowly into the trees. Perhaps one day they would go home.

The wagons rolled north from Kunnaslaki, a desultory group under the leaden sky. Helen did not feel comfortable in that grey landscape of endless hills. They wound through them on rough tracks. There was scrub in the valleys and bushes grew untidily on some of the hills. The Mage did not look happy either. He frowned and looked about him. Finally he called to Solimo who was half asleep in the back of the same wagon.

"Where are all the orchards?"

"Hmm?" said Solimo, waking from his dozing.

"This is northern Unama. These are the Orchard Hills?"

"They are not called that often these days." And then realisation dawned. This had all happened since the Mage's time. "When the Order came, they burned the orchards and the vines. They wanted to starve us."

"But some of those trees were hundreds of years old!" said the Mage.

"And that is why they did not replant."

"So what do the people do?"

Solimo smiled.

"The Order themselves provided the answer. Many of their animals escaped from their camp as they retreated north to Outreterre. The animals bred quickly on the hills, so the northern delf became stockmen and herders."

The Mage shook his head sadly and rubbed a hand down the side of his face. He did not ask any more questions, but stared sadly at the landscape.

Helen felt sorry for him, he looked so sad.

"It wasn't your fault," she said.

He turned to look at her. His face had paled and his eyes were glassy with tears.

"It was," he said. Then he looked away again. She did not want to ask any more. She wondered if Richard and Charlie knew what he meant. She was fascinated by what they had told her, fascinated but frightened. Had they really done all these things? If she had not lived through Unlembien, they would have seemed so fantastic. Yet her husband was a different man to the one who had disappeared from their home. He had a confidence she had forgotten he ever had. And it warmed her heart to see the renewed bond between him and Charlie even as it made her jealous that she did not share their experience.

She tried to think about their future. She had always been able to imagine her future before. Here she could not. She felt lost. At the mercy of she knew not what. She had lost her reality, but clung onto Richard and Charlie. They were what she loved the most and they were all together. That was what really mattered.

"They look so sad, don't they Mum?" Charlie said. He had been sitting next to her behind the driver's bench at the front of the wagon.

"Who?"

"The children."

The delf children were walking and following the wagons silently. It was nearly full dark, the time in the day when spirits usually sank.

"I'm going to cheer them up," he said. He climbed into the back and rummaged in his mother's bag until he found her box of matches, then he picked up the lanterns from each corner of the wagon, lit them and gave them to four of the children.

"Come on," he said and jumped out. He ran back to the other wagon, climbed up and lit its lanterns too. "Take one," he said. Four of the women took one.

"Get out of the wagon. Follow me."

He looked back. None of them were following him.

"Okay then," he said, rolling his eyes. "Watch me."

He delved into his pocket and pulled out his torch and held it up in front of him. Then he turned back.

"Watch," he said and began to whirl his torch around so that the blur of light created circles and patterns.

"Do this," he said.

Everyone was watching him. He felt foolish.

"Come *on*," he said.

Blankly, the children slid out of the wagons and walked up to him as he walked.

"Now follow me," he said. "No, in a line."

Obediently, the children went into single file, each holding up their lantern. It created a line of bright dots beside the wagons.

"Follow me now," said Charlie, breaking into a trot. The delf followed suit and Charlie began to snake about. The bright dots snaked too. He weaved around and doubled back and so did the dots. The smallest child who had been left on the wagons began to laugh. The ones with the lanterns started laughing too and soon everyone was smiling at the mad dance of light that followed them across the benighted land.

The mood soon evaporated under the suffocating sky. It became even darker at night and Helen huddled close to her boys. She made sure Charlie was between them and held Richard's hand so she could not lose them again.

56

RODON'S HORSE COLLAPSED under him. He would find a new one or he would walk. There was no time. They were coming.

A few people were walking in the distance. They would be from the farm which lay a field or two beyond them a short distance from the woods. He would need to warn the farmer and his family. He was so tired. He looked back and his heart sank. He was too late. A company of goblins had emerged from the trees to his right.

They came slowly, purposefully. The group of people up ahead had also seen them. He was too far away and what could he do anyway against so many? Two people from the group broke away and began to run, or rather hobble away from the wood. They moved with agonising slowness. The others began to move towards the farm house. A man came out carrying a bucket. He moved around the side of the house oblivious to the danger and began to load up the bucket with firewood from a log pile under a lean to. He straightened when he saw the creatures coming out of the trees.

Rodon was running now. He saw the three in the fields begin to run too, but they were running towards the farm. They ran slowly. He realised one of them was being supported by the other two. Then the goblins began to run. The man at the farm had noticed something was amiss because he dropped the bucket. Then the howling began. The hobbling group, stopped and turned to face the creatures. Almost instantaneously, a demon appeared. It burst into life from in front of the small group. They had to be delf, but how he did not know. The demon flew into the ranks of the running creatures. They fell in its path, but more kept coming, heedless of the onslaught.

Rodon was closer now. He recognised the sorcerer, the woman they had captured. He discharged his pistol into the head of a goblin which veered towards him. Its skull disintegrated and it simply collapsed onto the ground. He could see the man from the farmhouse. He was a sturdy man in his mature years. He had run inside and re-emerged with a heavy old long-arm and a sword in his belt. He fired it, then started to reload it down the muzzle. The goblin at the front took the shot to the body with only a stutter, but it slowed it.

Rodon fired his own weapons until they were empty. He had no time to reload. He drew his sword and began hacking around him. He felt blows hitting him. He could feel blood, but no pain. It did not matter. He saw the two delf start to run before being overwhelmed and disappearing beneath the mass of bodies. The sorcerer was trying to weave another demon. A creature with a melted face stumbled towards her, wielding an axe. The farmer charged it down with a pitchfork. For terrible moments they grappled, the goblin held back by the man's strength and the prongs in its belly. Then a newborn demon took it, incinerating its top half. The farmer sprang back and turned to face new threats. The demon whirled into a thick group of goblins which burned and smoked like dry wood. It did not burn them all. One came through the smoke. It swung its sword at the Light Doctor. She was caught in the chest and shoulder. She fell back and for long moments the demon hung in the air. The creature swung again, but merely flailed at where she had stood. Then it stabbed down at her and turned towards Rodon. A group of its fellows were advancing on him and it moved to join them.

Rodon swung about him wildly. Nothing existed beyond this moment. His blade cut into bodies and he pushed and thrashed at the creatures around him in frenzied madness.

Suddenly he realised he had no more enemies. The goblins lay hacked or smouldering in the fields. He was the only one standing. He was panting, sweat pouring from him. The farmer lay across his threshold, a livid gash across his face.

The sorcerer lay with her eyes wide open. She was still breathing in rapid, urgent gasps. He went over to her and knelt at her side.

"You tried to help them," he said. "You tried to help us. You could have run away."

"What...are...they?" she croaked.

"Goblins from Limbo. Living nightmares dreamed by accident by your Mage."

The Light Doctor's eyes rolled to look into his. Her next words tumbled out in a single breath, desperate to come out.

"You saw the Mage there?"

"He has escaped. With your friends. The Archbishop brings the nightmare legions to destroy Outreterre. To destroy all of Faerie. You be a sorcerer. How can we stop him?"

She tried to spit away frothing blood from her mouth.

"Close the way to Unlembien...to Limbo."

"It be too late for that."

"Then pray for the Mage. It is - " she coughed violently again. "Too much...for me. Mage. Only hope now."

She lay back, her eyes rolling up and her last breath left her as a wheeze. He put his hands on her eyes and closed them. Then he looked around. He was still alone. There would be more soon as they gathered at the Pits. He pushed himself up and stood uncertainly. He was so sore. He limped towards the farm house and pushed open the front door. A woman sat there looking terrified.

"Your husband be dead," said Rodon. "Run for the hills. Stay there for as long as you can. Go now."

Without waiting for an answer, he limped out. His leg must be injured, he thought. In the barn, he found four horses. Two of them were plough horses, but the other two looked as if they could be ridden. He threw a saddle on one, buckled it and pulled himself up. Then he was riding again, riding as if Hell were behind him.

57

LORD LYELL HAD ridden in that evening, bringing word of the arrival of the delf army. They set their wagons into a wall around the camp and posted pickets beyond them. Lord Lyell and the manor lords were sitting over their evening meal in his tent.

"I must say Lyell, you made excellent time back. You be quite nimble when the devil's at your heels and a witch be loose!" smiled Lord Giles.

The others chuckled and Lyell allowed himself a smile. Giles was an irritating man with a drooping moustache who slouched languidly in his chair like a leopard asleep on a branch.

"Even the devil has a fierce bite and I thought I'd be better served nannying you than throwing my men to the wolves. Now I have brought them out into the open."

King William watched them both. "Will they attack tonight? I would know that at least."

"Devils dread the dark," said Lyell dismissively. "They cannot function. You know our men are struggling to keep their spirits up under this darkness, so the devils will be feeling it even more. I've seen it in Metsakant."

"And it would be a shame if the Archbishop missed it all," said Lord Giles. "I thought you had sent for him, sire."

"I did. We sent another rider yesterday. The way be long. If he misses it, he misses it. He will be in time for the mopping up and for the burnings."

The king watched Lyell playing with his cup of wine, tipping the dregs around in the bottom of the bowl.

"Lyell, be something troubling you? I think you have spent too long under this sky."

Lyell did not acknowledge hearing the comment, but continued to look at his cup. The others too noticed something was wrong.

"I worry about something we saw," said Lyell slowly.

"Ah, be this the mysterious vanishing house?" Giles said.

Lyell gave him a brief, but dangerous look.

"I merely repeat the gossip of the camp," Giles added with a shrug.

"I have not heard any camp gossip," said the king and looked at Lyell expectantly.

Lyell put the cup down carefully.

"I wasn't sure what to make of it. I was thinking of how to tell you because I knew you wouldn't take me seriously. We were inside the walls of the light tower. I was sure we had them. It was only a matter of time. But then the main building...disappeared."

"They blew it up?"

"No. There was no explosion. There was no sound at all. It simply faded away, taking even its foundations. I've not seen the like. I can't say I'm familiar with all of the devil's sorcery, but that was something new."

"That sorcery be recorded," said the king. "None of you have the benefit of my library, so you may not have read of it. When the Order first entered Faerie, sentries reported the gates of Limbo suddenly vanished."

"And?"

"Our ancestors were left with no way back."

"So what does this mean?" asked Giles with an attempt at interest.

"We would need to ask the Archbishop."

"Well I do wish he would hurry. I am a pile of impatience," said Giles. "Be there any more of this excellent wine, Lyell?"

"I just think we need to be careful around these devils. They might have sorcery we do not know of," said Lyell.

"We have seen no evidence of it for years if that be the case," Giles responded.

"Enough. We shall be on our guard," said the king. "Now, I agree with Giles about another bottle."

The Order was camped below them. From where they sat on their horses they could see their fires in the darkness. They dared not go closer for fear of running into their pickets. Mondo, Margreta and Pava Councillor turned their horses and trotted back to their own lines with the two scouts who had brought them this far.

"We could attack them now, with sun wraiths," said Margreta fiercely. "They would not know what had hit them."

"It is risky," said Mondo. "We do not know how many there are or even if they are all in that valley. We need some light to see by. Yes we would do great damage with sudden assault by wraiths, and they might scatter, but if they are in more than one place, we could end up surrounded and out of light."

"I see your point," the councillor nodded.

"So we should wait," said Margreta, disappointed. "But tomorrow we do a reconnaissance and then – "

"And then we will see," said Mondo.

58

THE ARMY OF the Order woke early in the darkness before the distant northern sky showed any signs of light. The women began lighting fires and cooking up a hearty breakfast for the troops. No one knew when they would have another chance to eat. Children ran around on errands and the men made final preparation to their weapons. Orderlies allocated ammunition to different units and carts were loaded with crates of bullets to follow up the soldiers. Troopers fed their horses, patting the necks of their mounts and talking into their ears as if they understood every word. The cobs were camped separately from the rest of the army. They had slept in huddles. Their keepers were distributing sacks of food. The chatter and clatter of the army preparing sounded clear in the quiet morning. On the hillsides about, sentries on picket duty had been posted in pairs to help keep them alert under the effects of the blackness across the sky. They scoured the darkness for movement and strained their ears for sounds beyond the noise of their comrades in camp.

Lyell was addressing his officers outside his tent. His coat hung open and he was pacing up and down as he finished his orders.

"Finally, make sure the men break their fast quickly. The army will move forward and the baggage train needs to be ready to follow so we can pursue the devils south. I want every man kept busy with no time to brood."

After the officers had walked off to their units, Lyell paused and looked around him. His footman stepped forward.

"My lord, some breakfast?"

"Yes," he said absently. "Damn this darkness."

He turned and looked to the north, but there was no light showing there yet either.

An hour later and there was a glow on the horizon. The women were clearing up pots and putting out fires. Wagons were being harnessed. Soldiers were forming up. Lyell watched as his tent was dismantled. He was dressed in a dull, steel cuirass over his jacket. His helmet was tucked under his arm. He lifted it onto his head, adjusted his sword and pulled himself up onto his saddle. He settled himself, then set off to find his men.

Around him, troops were mustering as the other manor lords formed up their regiments. He stopped to chat to a few of his veterans who were sat easily on their horses, gloved hands resting, wrists crossed on their pommels. He laughed at a comment and slapped one on the back before continuing on his way.

A group of cobs were still asleep, curled up with each other. One moved in its sleep, flapping an arm about. Lyell caught the eye of the cobmaster.

"I wonder what cobs dream of?" he said. "Let them sleep a while longer, they have nothing to get ready."

The cobmaster grinned, showing only half a mouthful of teeth and Lyell rode on. He passed the infantry sitting on the grass and reached the baggage train. There he found his wife issuing orders to the women of the manor.

"Come on woman, the pots be not yet stowed," he smiled.

"Get back to your playing with guns and I'll mind the pots, Lord Lyell," she shot back. "Now get out of the way of the girls."

He backed his horse up as two kitchen maids stuttered past carrying sacks.

"Those girls be stronger than some of my men!" he chuckled, then turned his horse and trotted back up to the front of the regiment. He would be waiting for the king's contingent who would follow him up as the lead formation. Far over to his right, cobs were being herded into lines.

"They look so unsoldierly," said one of Lyell's captains.

"Aye. But they be good in a hand to hand scrap."

A trumpet sounded. He nodded to the trumpeter waiting behind him, who blew a response. Then Lyell spurred his horse and the column moved forward.

Away to the west, a much smaller party was trundling along a ridge.

"Look there! There's something?" said Charlie.

"The benefit of young eyes," said Richard.

"I see it too," said Berwick. "It be the Order."

He glanced over at Raul, who saw the look out of the corner of his eye but chose to ignore it. Instead, he searched the land to the south and soon saw what he was searching for.

"And there is Kyntilla. We have overshot them both."

"Who's that then?" Charlie asked.

They looked where he was pointing. There, still ahead of them was a third group.

"Looks like wagons, from here," said Richard.

"Aye," said Colman. "It must be our baggage train. If they've left it behind, it means they be expecting to fight today."

"Well they are both so close, I do not see how it can be avoided!" said Solimo, sounding troubled.

The delf driving the wagons pulled them to a halt.

"No," said the Mage. "We must not stop. I know it sounds foolish, but we must go on. We must reach those wagons."

"We have only just escaped from those men. And now you take us back."

The Mage turned around to face the delf who had spoken.

"Yes," he said, his voice barely a murmur. "Peculiar who can turn out to be your friends. Will the wagons be armed?"

Berwick and Colman looked at each other.

"Why do you ask that?" Colman asked.

The Mage barely suppressed annoyance.

"Because if a group of delf arrives when they are expecting a war, we are going to be shot at."

Colman raised an eyebrow, but conceded the point.

"There will be guards, yes."

"Then you two need to ride in first to make sure they do not shoot any of us."

Colman grinned.

"And after all we've been through…"

With no further word, the two wagons rolled forward once more.

The distant glow behind the army of the Order seemed to cast a grey light on their way as they went. Behind him, Lyell heard the sounds of the army on the move. Horses' hooves, jangling harness, men chatting and the calls of waggoners. At regular intervals, a horse would gallop out of the gloom from the outriders and report that all was well.

When the messenger rode up from the back, Lyell took him for one of the scouts. One look told him otherwise. Even in the dim light, he could see the man was covered in blood. It had caked and dried on his jacket and trousers. His stubbled face wore a wild look.

"Hell be coming!" he said.

The man's face commanded Lyell's attention, despite the cryptic ejaculation.

"I be Thomas Rodon. They be coming!"

Lord Lyell knew Rodon; he looked again. It *was* Rodon, covered in the grime of the road and blood, but it was Rodon.

"Who be coming, man? Make sense! What passes?"

"An army. An army of devils."

"The devils be south of us."

"The devils be north of you in sooth. They be not delf. Limbo has opened. They will destroy Outreterre. Forget the delf, they cannot be our enemies now."

"Where be this army, you speak of?"

"Only a few miles behind me. I have been riding hard."

Even as he spoke, his horse trembled. It was clearly near to collapse.

"I will send some men back to see."

"Very well," he said, then fell from his horse.

"See to him," Lyell said and two of his men jumped down. "Take him to the king."

He turned to his trumpeter.

"Where be Tilley?"

Tilley's men rode together, glad to be away from the army where they had felt constrained to ride in a more soldierly way. Free once more, they larked about and bantered with each other as they rode.

"If the devils be burning our farms, we'll burn them one by one in front of each other," Tilley spat. He pointed his horse's head at a tall hill in front of them.

"Up here lads, we'll get the view and save a ride."

They picked their way up the slope, hurrying to satisfy their curiosity. The summit rolled towards them and the valley beyond it opened up.

"God's blood!!" breathed Tilley.

The land below them was filled with a vast host. A dark army of enormous size was swarming through the land. It bristled with banners and lances.

"Who be they?" asked the rider nearest him.

Tilley shook his head in wonderment.

"I wot not."

He was not a man who ever admitted to fear and rarely felt it, but he felt his skin prickle and his stomach felt hollow.

"Let's go," said the rider next to him.

"Wait. Can you see their banners?"

"Black. Something on it I can't see from here."

"I think we'll be able to see them soon enough."

Tilley whistled, raised his arm in the air and pointed the way back. They wheeled their horses and galloped down the hill, looking anxiously from side to side, expecting at any moment to see the vanguard of the mysterious army spilling around the edge of the hill. They had reached the bottom when it happened. They dug in their heels, riding like they had never ridden before.

Forcing their heaving mounts on, they pulled away from the strange army and it was lost to view behind the undulations of the land.

The king was surrounded by his advisors. All the manor lords were there as well as Tilley and Rodon.

"But who be they?" demanded the king. He was like a petulant child.

"Your majesty, once again, I don't know. I just know they be beyond number and they be coming this way."

Tilley was struggling to remain calm.

"Your majesty," said Lyell pointing to a ridge to the south of them, "we need to reach that hill at least. Caught down here in a column we are vulnerable. We need to pick a favourable position to fight if we need to while we still can."

"You cannot fight what we saw," said Tilley.

For a few brief seconds the king stared hard at his manor lords.

"Where be that Archbishop when I need him?" he seethed.

"If he got in the way of what we saw, you can stop worrying about the Archbishop, sire."

"The Archbishop be gone," said Rodon. He was leaning hard on Lyell's shoulder. "Forget the Archbishop."

"Be he dead?"

Rodon breathed deeply. He wondered what to tell them.

"He be lost," he said finally.

There was a pause filled with barely contained impatience.

"Forward at the double," said Lyell. They could worry about the fate of the Archbishop later. "Move the units across a broad front. Re-form on the hill. Facing north. Keep the scouts out to the south."

"What of the baggage train? We'll need to send them word."

"They cannot reach here quickly. They must stay out of sight. We will rejoin them as soon as we can."

The manor lords hastened away. Trumpets were sounding and the manor regiments broke away from the column like spreading wings and started to jog for the hill which had been chosen as their standing point. Few knew why they were advancing at speed, but men guessed the delf were close by and excitement and anticipation began to mount.

To the south of the same hill, another force was moving. It was smaller in number and it moved with less military precision. All the delf were mounted, either on horses or in wagons. The only ones in any sort of uniform wore the sash and helmet of the Kyntilla Guard, the rest wore earthy colours. At the front of the main body rode Mondo, Margreta and the three Councillors. Scattered across and ahead of their front were border skirmishers led by Kurk. He rode in the middle, watching to right and left, scanning in the gloom for any sign of the Order. His riders were the youngest and sharpest eyed.

A shout went up from his right. He looked over and saw a delf pointing away ahead. He followed the pointing arm and saw a couple of distant horsemen. Almost immediately there was another shout from his left. Another group of horsemen had been seen. The sighting was clearly mutual. Both groups wheeled suddenly and rode back behind the hill. Kurk knew the Order were close. The rider next to him looked at him expectantly.

"Tell them we need to make that hill. The Order are to its north."

The rider nodded, peeled away and rode back to the main body.

The Order reached the northern base of the hill and began to climb. The cobs loped up the slope easily and gathered on the flat summit behind the armed men. Tilley and the freebooters turned as soon as they had any height to see if they could make out the host they had witnessed. Tilley hoped they had been mistaken, that it had been a trick of the grey light, but they had all seen it.

"There!" said a man up the hill from him. Across the land was a dark mass. It could almost have been a forest, but if they looked for a minute, it could be seen to be moving towards them.

Lyell rode up next to him.

"My Christ!" he said. "What be it? What devilry be this?"

Lyell realised he had never really known fear before. He had experienced apprehension before a battle, a kind of nervous excitement, but not fear. He did not understand what he saw.

"There must be tens of thousands," he said.

"At least," Tilley replied. Then he pointed. "Look!"

A bulge was forming out to the western side of the host.

"They've seen the baggage train!"

Tilley did not know why he did it. He turned his horse back down the hill. His men saw him, frowned, but followed.

"Tilley! Whither go you?" called Lyell.

"The train," he called back.

"What will you do?"

"God wots it, not I," came the fading shout thrown over his retreating shoulder.

Lyell watched the freebooters descending the hill amongst the stragglers of the army for a few moments, then kicked his horse and continued to climb.

Berwick and Colman had ridden ahead and now they were turning and waving the others in.

"Can we trust them?" Raul asked as they approached the baggage train. Men stood on top of the wagons, long-arms held ready at their waists. They were older men, too old for active service, mostly in their daily clothes. Only a few wore any aspects of uniform. Their faces showed suspicion, fear and curiosity.

"Yes," said Richard. "I think they're more worried about whether they can trust *you*."

"There are women and children in there!" exclaimed Helen as the people amongst the wagons became clearer. "They took them into a war zone!"

"Camp followers," said Richard. "Part of armies for hundreds of years. Who else does the washing and cooking?"

They heard the sound of the host before they could see it, a low moaning. The refugee delf huddled together. Charlie shrank inwardly and his mother pulled him close to her. The men on top of the wagons turned to face the sound.

"What be it?" asked one, a grizzled man with long grey hair tied back in a ponytail.

"What we told you," said Colman.

And then they saw it, a moving mass.

"My husband will know what to do," said a well-dressed woman, Richard recognised as Lady Eleanor, Lord Lyell's wife.

"You look familiar," she said to Richard.

"I know your husband," Richard replied. "We need to leave. Now."

"No," said the Mage. "There is nowhere to go. You cannot outrun them. We join the others."

"That's insane," said Richard quietly. "We'll all be killed."

"Insane am I?" the Mage growled. "I have lived longer than you ever will. I have seen more things than you ever will. I understand things you never will. I have looked into the heart of light. I have seen the light cradle where all light is born!"

He paused, perhaps for effect, perhaps to compose himself.

"I created those monstrosities and I can destroy them. But I need *your* help and I need *their* help," he nodded in the direction of the baggage train. "I need delf *and* men. It is time to stop fighting each other and to fight what can really harm you."

"Who be you?" demanded Lady Eleanor.

"Apparently I am the Last Mage. And indeed your last hope." He paused. "Beyond your own."

The man with the ponytail turned to Colman.

"Why be we bandying words with a devil?"

"Sir, we do not have time for your questions," the Mage said. "Now, you are going to have to choose between certain death...and possible life. Do you have candles?"

Tilley's men were riding. All he could hear was his breathing. The grass seemed to rock beneath the pounding hooves, but he was not aware of any sound as they approached the host. Part of it was breaking off from the main body and starting to head in the direction of the baggage train. He needed to divert them somehow.

They were clearer now. He could see individual shapes of men, their banners. He looked at the banners, saw the sign of the silver sword, the sign of the Order of St Collen. He slowed, puzzled. Where was this army from? Then the spreading limb curved its tip towards the freebooters.

The delf reached the hill. It was steep, too steep to make an attack. There were whistles of command and signal. Delf jumped down from wagons and a few started up the slope on foot, unslinging their long-arms to hold them in their hands. The main body went to the west, while a smaller, scouting unit went east to warn of any attempt to outflank them.

On the summit, the Order was forming up. The king stood in his stirrups to try to see what his force was doing and cast an anxious eye at the black cloud on the land. It was like a plague of insects. A rider came pounding up the hill heading directly for the king's standard.

"Your majesty!" he shouted as soon as he was within earshot. "The devils be here. They be south of the ridge and coming around the flanks!"

The king whirled around. They were trapped! It was all a trap. Devils to the north, devils to the east. They had been lured out into the open and into the maw of their sorcery.

"Be you certain?"

"Your majesty, we saw them."

"How many?"

"I could not tell. Not in this light."

The king turned away from the messenger.

"Form up north and east!" he called to an officer nearby. "You! Put your unit across there. Watch the eastern slopes."

Lyell rode across the small plateau to the southern side even as the order was given, and sure enough, there below was a mass of figures. Some were forming up on a lower hill just to the west of them, others eddied around the base of theirs, perhaps searching for a way up. This gave them a little more time because he knew the easiest way was from the north. From what he could see, they were inferior in numbers to the Order, but with the strange host to the north, that mattered little now.

The Mage dropped from his horse and sat on the ground. He rubbed his forehead with his left hand, then scratched at his scalp furiously with both.

"How can I convince you?" he began. "Look at *us*," he gestured to those who had come through Unlembien. "Are we not together and united?"

He received blank looks, but no one was interrupting. He shook his head and made an irritated noise.

"You all know of the light of the sun and the moon and the stars. You know, or have heard, of the ways the delf harness those lights. But there is a fourth light."

He looked around at his audience. The delf were attentive and, strangely, most of the men and women seemed to be listening too. It occurred to him that they would never have heard a delf speak. He needed to use that curiosity.

"You have heard of it; you just cannot see it. There *is* an inner light. It is in every newborn because every birth brings with it the amazing possibilities of that new life."

They were listening. All of them.

"You sometimes call it hope, but it is the living essence of a being. The determination to survive and to grow. In most of the beasts it is merely an instinct, but we delf – and I discovered long, long ago – men too, have evolved it to be far more distinct, more conscious than a mere instinct. We are able to create a will to live, a will to succeed. We can even *change* things."

The delf were nodding.

"This be sorcery and nonsense!" cried the man on the wagon.

"*Listen* to him," said Berwick. "We've seen many strange things these last few days. You see out there the strangest and most fearsome thing for yourself. This delf offers us help."

Richard almost smiled. He felt a warmth of affection for Nicholas. He had changed. They had all changed. So much.

"Thank you, young man. It is good to see wisdom in the young." He turned once more to both humans and delf. "I am going to give each one of you a candle. Look into that candle and at nothing else. Fill yourselves with hope."

Lady Eleanor studied the wild man.

"You want to stop the fighting?"

"Lady, in all the worlds, I have never seen fighting achieve anything except misery."

"Amen to that," she said.

"Then fetch me candles."

"Can we beat them?" asked a boy.

The Mage looked down at him and his eyes softened.

"Oh yes. Of course we can. I created those creatures out there. I will not call them men. They are the shadows of a mind in despair. They were born of despair. My despair. They will not, *must* not withstand hope."

Solimo handed the boy a lit candle and another to a delf girl.

"Do you remember the light in the Pits?" he said to her. "Do you remember how you felt?"

"Oh yes," she said. "And the singing. The singing before it."

Solimo blushed.

"Singing was there? Yes, you must sing again, Solimo," said the Mage. "You must all be part of a miracle."

"Come on then," said the boy. He punched Charlie on the arm.

Charlie suddenly felt brave.

Solimo took the Mage by the arm.

"I cannot sing, Mage," he said quietly.

"Then who did I hear in my light tower?"

"But surely you are the best one to sing. You understand all this. I am merely a healer. I cannot even weave a sun wraith."

"I have other things to do. And six hundred years did not improve my singing. No, mine is for private use only." He gripped Solimo's arms and thrust his face into the younger delf's. "I see in your eyes some fear I do not understand, Keeper. Whatever it is, we do not have the time for you to indulge it. We do not need weapons. Look around you, there are plenty of them. This world needs healing and I need you to do your part! Sing to the children of the worlds and show them what is deep in their hearts!"

59

KURK HAD HIS long-arm resting across his saddle, ready to use as they came around the side of the hill. Around every hump in the land, he expected a shot to ring out or a group of the Order to leap at him. Even if he had been making his main stand on the summit, as they seemed to be doing, he would have left smaller units below to harry and delay the delf. His suspicions remained until he finally reached the northern side of the hill.

The first thing he saw was a troop of horsemen riding northwards from the hill. Following them with his eyes, he blinked, clearing them to see through the gloom. They seemed to be riding towards another army. He looked again along the huge body of men expecting it to come to an end, but it did not. The dark line laced with banners seemed to go on and on across the vale. It was an army so vast, he could not comprehend it. He had no idea that the Order was so powerful. He had to warn Mondo. He raised his arm to signal the others and turned tail.

He met the forward units of the Kyntilla force and the commanders. He told Mondo what he had seen.

"Impossible. If there were really that many of the Order they would have invaded years ago. Surely you are mistaken?"

Kurk shrugged.

"Come with me then, but our situation is hopeless. There is nothing we can do against a force that size."

They rode back together.

"What is that sound? Is it wind?"

Mondo gasped. The strange army was closer now. The troop of horsemen of the Order which he had seen had ridden off to its left flank which seemed to be distended. That flank began to curl out towards the horsemen. When this happened, the horsemen suddenly turned and began riding furiously back to the Order's line. Just as they did, lights emerged around a fold in the hills. Looking again, Mondo could see the lights were mounted on wagons. These too were heading for the ridge on which the men of the Order were arrayed.

Richard watched Charlie from the back of his horse. Charlie was carrying a candle. The oldest boy walked next to him holding another and behind them walked the delf and baggage train children, each with their own candle. From the back, the only difference between them was their clothes. They had quickly overcome any fear of the other. The wagons all came behind. Out at the front walked Solimo. And Solimo began to sing.

He had a clear, tenor voice and it soared in the still air, ringing clear against the incessant moaning that rose and fell from the nightmare legions. The tempo quickened as the song went on. The tune was like a mountain stream skipping amongst the rocks, or sunny dapples caressing thick, green grass. It was like waking up on the first morning of summer. It was like seeing Charlie again. Richard felt a wave of goose bumps roll over him. It was like when Charlie was born. He looked at the candle in his own hand. He listened to the music and gazed into the flame.

Behind him, Raul rode closer to Esella until they were right alongside each other. One hand was holding the candle. He held out his other, not taking his eyes from the flame. He felt Esella's hand take his, her fingers closing gently around it. The flame of his candle seemed to dance.

Mondo watched Tilley's horsemen. Even from the distance, he sensed fear in the way they rode. He watched as figures from the dark army began to run. He thought he heard the faint sound of shouting.

Tilley did not think of fear any more. He thought only of out-running the pursuit. He had seen the wagons emerge and had seen the enemy turn to meet him. He knew they were the enemy. They had ridden close enough. These were not human. He had called the delf devils all his life, but these were far more demonic, these goblins. He knew they could not outrun them, but he would race them as far as he could.

He saw figures around the bottom of the ridge. More of the Order must have come to help. They should flee, he thought. Then a bolt of flame appeared amongst them and rose into the sky. It was not the Order; the delf had come. He was caught between the devils and their servants. Well he would die fighting.

The sun wraith tore up through the sky, punched a hole through the darkness and disappeared. A shaft of sunlight dropped through the hole. Bright and pure, Tilley thought it was the most beautiful thing he had ever seen. Then another ray of light appeared in front of him. He looked up to see the wraith descending.

Lyell was trying to rally his men, but they were mesmerised. They had forgotten where they were. They watched the baggage train snaking slowly across that wide gap between hill and host. Why was it carrying lights, why was it making itself so visible?

When the sun wraith went up, his heart sank. They had completely under-estimated the delf. He raised his sword.

"Front rank! Take aim."

Standing with the king, Rodon watched the sun wraith with anticipation. What was happening?

Few of the men moved.

Lyell was still holding his sword high as the wraith disappeared through the layer of darkness and first one, then two rays of light stabbed down at the scene as the wraith dropped back through the blanket of the dark and bore down on the fleeing Tilley.

"Front rank!" he barked again. "Take. Aim!"

They shook themselves.

"Aim at the sorcerer."

"No!" called Rodon. He spurred his horse and began to ride towards Lyell.

The wraith shot over the heads of the horsemen and swung into the front ranks of the strange army, cutting an arc across its face.

"Hold your fire!" Lyell shouted in amazement.

Confusion filled the faces of the soldiers, but they lowered their weapons. The king was riding down to the front. Rodon had almost reached him.

"The devils be attacking them," said Lyell.

"I told you!"

"It be not their sorcery."

Two more bolts of flame lifted from the ground below them, arms outspread, but this time, they came from the baggage train. Two, then four more narrow blades of light cut through the dark blanket. They too shot into the host like Greek fire.

"Who be in those wagons?" said Lyell, half to himself.

"I think I know," said Rodon.

Tilley could not believe it. He had given up on life and the death he had expected had passed over him. He could not cheat it forever. He looked to his right and saw the wagons trundling oh so slowly with their lanterns bobbing. He did not understand how demons could come from their own baggage train. More of the goblins were rushing out at the wagons now. They had attracted their attention. Were those children in front? They were insane.

His horse was sweating, its eyes rolled back and mad in its head. They would never make the hill. This was one ride too many. His mount suddenly fell and he flew sprawling from its back. His long-arm was nowhere to be seen. He pulled out his sword and a pistol and watched as the infernal hordes came at him. He screamed a wordless war cry and began to slash around him as the moaning tide flowed over him.

Mondo heard trumpets from the top of the hill. He was at the head of the delf army now. All had come around the hill. Then he thought he heard singing. It seemed to be coming from the Order's baggage train, but he knew the words. He frowned. It was a delf song. Clearly there were light weavers there. He knew of only one it could be, it had to be Esella, but she was weaving wraiths like no one he had ever seen. Alderman Pava rode up beside him.

"That army has stopped moving," she said. "Something is holding it back."

Solimo was still singing. He went back to the same songs. He could think of no others in the moment. Staring at the candle flame had ruined his night sight, but he saw the sun wraiths and the sunlight coming through the dark. He saw the Mage weaving the wraiths, but knew that they had few sponges left. He heard the moaning, but it did not seem to be any nearer. Still singing, he looked up from the flame and buried his eyes in the gloom. His eyes adjusted and he could see the goblins.

The ones facing them stood motionless; no longer advancing on the baggage train. He could see them spreading up the far side across the valley and towards the Order on the ridge. He could no longer see the troop of horsemen. Everywhere else, the goblin hordes were moving, but no longer were they moving towards the baggage train. They simply watched.

He found himself singing louder and behind him, the high voices of the children were joining in. He had sung it so many times, they had learned the tune and some of the words. He quickened his pace. He felt tall.

The Mage rode down past Esella and Raul.

"Solimo is singing wonderfully," said Esella. "But I do not understand, Mage. Is this all through the light of the candle?"

"It is not the light of the candle that has the power. The candle merely focuses the thought and it is the thought which has the power."

He smiled.

"And it helps to avoid the distraction of impending death."

Lyell and Rodon watched as a shape bearing lights broke away from the baggage train. As it came closer, it devolved into two shapes: riders. They watched them moving across the grey landscape. Behind them, the host came on. The shafts of sunlight shone onto its seething masses. The horsemen were riding on a diagonal in front of the ridge bearing the order and the lower one around which the delf were gathered.

Rodon looked at the delf force below. They were moving, forming up on the lower slopes to the north now, but not facing the Order. Instead they were looking northwards. A single figure on a horse broke away from the delf army and rode out towards the two horsemen.

"Make sure they hold their fire!" said Rodon. "This be our chance."

"Our chance to do what?"

"Our chance to save ourselves. I'll ride out to meet them."

"Hold your fire. Let through the parley!" Lyell called, then he turned to Rodon. "I will come too."

Rodon nodded and together they rode out in front of the troops.

As they picked their way down the slope, they heard singing from the direction of the wagons. The host had become distorted in shape, part seemed to have stopped, but the rest of it was boiling forwards, black banners rippling soundlessly.

Lyell and Rodon reached the plain and galloped out. There were five horses aiming for a meeting point. They reached the space at the same moment. Rodon took in the two riders from the wagons. They looked as surprised as he at their meeting.

"The Mage!" Rodon breathed.

Lyell glanced at him and then noticed Berwick with surprise. He was accompanying a strange, ragged delf with wild hair and a wilder look in his eyes. The delf was grinning maniacally.

"You I did not expect to see," said the maniac looking at Rodon. "You escaped from the snake, but now he comes anyway."

"You know this creature?" Lyell asked.

The Mage looked at the other delf who had ridden from the delf army. It was Mondo. his strong, serious face framed in silvering hair.

"Do you have candles?" the wild-looking delf asked.

"Of course," said Mondo.

"And what of you?" the Mage asked the two men.

"There will be candles," said Rodon. "Every soldier carries them."

"Now listen to me," said the Mage. "We are all about to die. Everything you know is about to be destroyed, unless you do as I say. Light your candles. Everybody light them. And dare to hope. That is all you need to do. See what we have already achieved today and yesterday and you can achieve more."

"He speaks truly, Lord Lyell," said Rodon. "I saw things in Limbo I thought I would never see."

Lyell looked at Berwick. The lad's eyes were burning.

"My lord, it be astounding. We share a power!"

"What power can we share?" Lyell asked, pulling on the reins to control his horse that was beginning to step nervously.

"The power of hope." He waved his arm behind him. "It protected the wagons. It can do more."

"What be that army?" asked Lyell.

"Goblins from Limbo," Berwick said. "They be here to destroy us. This...delf...understands much."

"Yes. I do. And I understand we have no time for tittle tattle. Light your candles, all of you. Here now is an end to your wars and a new day. Here. Now!"

Then he turned and trotted straight at the oncoming horde. Rodon suddenly rode forward and grasped Mondo's hand.

"I have met your sorcerer. A small woman," he said.

Mondo eyed him, trying not to show any emotion, trying not to show what he was thinking.

"She be dead," said Rodon. "She died protecting a farm in Outreterre. From them."

"The Light Doctor?" asked Mondo, unable to control his reaction. "She is dead?"

"I was with her when she died."

Mondo and Rodon continued to grip each other's hand. Each wondered quite what passed between them at that moment.

"I will never again lift my arm against a delf," Rodon said and let go of Mondo's hand.

"Nor will I!" said Berwick reaching out to shake Mondo's hand. The lad's face was pale, but his dark eyes were deadly serious.

Lyell was sitting on his shifting horse and trying to think. Something had happened to Rodon, something terrible had happened to the Archbishop, that now seemed true. Next to the clergyman, the man who knew the most about the witchcraft of the devils was Rodon, yet here he was pledging friendship. He glanced to the north. The Mage was still walking his horse towards the huge army. It did truly look like the army to end all armies.

The armies of Men and delf, tiny by comparison, looked on at the strange scene below, this parley of men and delf. Then Berwick raised his hand to his helmet in salute. Rodon followed the gesture with a bow of his head towards the delf, then both abruptly turned their horses and rode them back towards the ranks of the Order. Mondo sat watching them go for a moment, nodded at Lyell, then he too wheeled his horse and returned to the delf forces.

The soldiers of the Order gazed in fear at the oncoming horde. They struggled to understand what was happening.

"Devils have taken our wagons," said one.

There were murmurings. Rodon heard them. He jumped from his horse and began to shout at them.

"Then why did they protect Tilley's men? Why?"

He looked men in the eyes as he asked.

"Is that the action of an enemy? These delf are not what we thought. I have fought alongside them. They have risked their lives and lost them for the sake of those we left behind in Outreterre."

Many of them knew him. He was counting on the respect he had amongst the men of the Order.

"Take out a candle and light it. Each of you. Take it out and pray for our future. Pray that what protects the delf and men, women and children on those wagons will also protect us."

Men on that hillside looked fearfully at the line of wagons that carried the families of many of them. They looked like a rock about to be engulfed by a great wave.

Charlie watched, dazzled as dots of light spread amongst the two armies. Hundreds of little fairy lights coming on one by one as the candlelight was passed along the lines of fighters.

The keening of the host was swelling towards him like a flood. A voice rose up from a lone horseman in front of it. It was the Mage. Charlie had watched him ride back and stop, alone. The delf and Order were to his rear, the legions to his front and the baggage train to his left. Then he turned his back on the host and faced the armies of Faerie. His voice carried across the dim landscape.

"Men and delf! After centuries of war, I bring you hope. After blood and distrust, I bring you hope. Fathers, your children can live in a new world. Mothers, your children can know peace. Watch how the spawn of despair balks at the hope of children. Look at how it fears song. These are goblins from dark dreams. Though they are a multitude, you can defeat them. But not by force of arms. Put up your weapons. Think what could happen if you could live without guns and the sword between you. Look on one another with light."

As he said it, two sun wraiths appeared from his hands, hovered for a moment on either side of him then shot upward, rising like twin kites in a brisk wind. Seconds later, four new pillars of sunlight were reaching from the sky to the ground as they broke through the dark and shot down again into the front ranks of the goblin host which was coming dangerously close to him.

"There is a light inside us all," he called out. "Sometimes it is buried deep. But reach inside now. Reach inside for your children. Be the light of the candle."

His tone changed. The voice of declamation ceased and in its place was one of savage mischief.

"Words are very fine. Perhaps actions will help."

A light appeared above the baggage train. It was like a glowing fog. It started to flow towards the Mage. As it did so, little patches of the same misty light began to appear in places above the delf. There were some in front of the Order as well, but less solid. It all began to stream towards the single figure.

Charlie could hear a screaming like a rant coming from the nightmare legions. It was a single voice. He could not make out the words.

The Mage stretched out his arms to take in the delf, the Order and the wagons. He began to glow.

"I am the light funnel! You are the candle!"

Mondo watched this delf from the past standing there. The unreality of the moment seized him even as he was caught up in it. A host of creatures dreamed in Unlembien were in Unama under a thick sky of despair and there, standing between them and this peril was the Last Mage, somehow returned to them from the depths of the past. A thrill of excitement when through him such as he had not known since a young delf and he had first seen the light woven by a light doctor who had come to his farm. He glanced about him. The eyes of the delf were shining in wonder. And over to his left, those who should have been his enemy had not raised their weapons against the delf. Instead, they faced a common foe. If all this could happen, what was there that was not possible?

The misty glow deepened around the delf. It began to tumble from them as thickly as it did from the baggage train.

Charlie had never felt such excitement. It was almost palpable. He wanted to shout. He felt no fear whatsoever, only expectation. The mist was growing.

The Mage groaned in a kind of ecstasy. His body wavered where he stood.

"Ah, I fear you no longer," he said, then with a shout of joy. "I do not fear my fear!"

Nothing in Rodon's studies had prepared him for this. Even after all that he had seen and experienced in Limbo, what was before him was a thing of terrible wonder. Something was happening with the men too. He had seen fear in their faces. Never before had they seen such a host arrayed before them. The older ones would remember pitched battles amongst the manors and the raid on northern Metsakant. All the younger ones had known was the invasion of Metsakant and border raids into Unama. Now the delf beside them were forgotten, at least as enemies. He had heard their cries of anger turn to murmurs of surprise as the demons raised by the delf sorcerers had plunged into the nightmare host rather than Tilley's riders. It was with amazement that they had realised the demons had been trying to stem the nightmare tide that had engulfed Tilley and his men.

And what of this Mage, this wild, mad, raggedy delf who stepped out of their own legends and history? What did he understand that they did not? What did he understand that he and the Archbishop could never have known from the few books they had managed to gather together? Rodon realised then how little they knew about the light, indeed, how little they knew about the delf who had been their neighbours for centuries. What had they missed out on all that time? What could this Mage do that would give them all another chance?

He looked at the glowing figure once more, standing alone against the bristling ranks of Limbo. He heard again the Mage's fierce joy.

Rodon's eye was distracted by a dim glow about his arms. There was a faint mist there. He could feel it too. It felt as if it were coming from inside of him. The ethereal light was around him. He felt a flame inside.

"Outreterre!" he bellowed. "Outreterre! Unama!"

Soldiers around him were looking at him. He returned their gaze with fire in his eyes. He raised his arms, his long-arm held high.

"Outreterre, Unama!"

He was shouting it like a question, like a command. The mist about him was moving, it was flowing away from him out onto the plain where the Mage stood, his own arms upraised.

Those closest to him were repeating his words. It was growing louder and as it grew, so did the number of voices.

Then Rodon noticed something. There was a pale grey mist appearing around all the men of the Order. Their chanting grew louder. There was another sound too. Over to the right, the delf were singing.

Mist engendered mist around the men of the Order. Even as it appeared it rose away from them and went rushing towards the Mage, a sphere of glowing light around him until he disappeared in its brightness and Charlie had to look away.

It flowed down from the delf as well and from their own party, all drawn somehow to the Mage and his own ball of mist. It swirled around him, pulsing with light and power, brighter patches moving within it until the Mage himself was no longer visible.

"I do not fear my fear!" he called out again, each word emphasised.

"Fear be gone! Let the light flow!"

The sphere was a web of shifting light as the lights moved across its surface with ever greater speed. The Mage's voice was a wordless cry of defiance, carried along by the passion welling within him and around him.

The ball became a blur of light, still fed by the streams of mist from delf and human.

"See in this light the hope of ages, you dreamless monsters!" called out a voice from inside it, suddenly clear.

Then the white sphere exploded.

It expanded out from its centre with an arc which scythed across the ground towards the legions of Limbo. Rippling away from where the Mage had stood were coruscating rainbow colours, blending perfectly from one to another as they rushed outwards, throbbing brightly against the dark of the landscape and undimmed as it passed through the shafts of sunlight.

It reached the Limbo host. Where it went, they vanished as if they had dissolved in the air. They did not flee, they simply stood and received their fate. They disappeared in their thousands, the rainbow wiping the land clean until there was nothing on the field but the blades of light which stretched down from the blanket of darkness above.

As the arc reached the valley sides it began to evaporate like steam and drift upwards. It rose towards the darkness, passed through it and vanished. As it did so, the darkness began to fade, come apart and dissolve in the air. Sunshine filtered through more and more strongly, until the valley was a bowl of light cut into the middle of a dark sky.

The army of Limbo had disappeared.

There was no trace of their existence. The only figures left were the sorry, still bodies of Tilley's freebooters and behind them another lone body. The Mage.

Solimo ran out. Esella was not far behind and Raul followed. From the ranks of the delf rode Mondo. Richard pulled Helen onto his horse then urged it on, pausing only to pick up Charlie. Rodon was galloping down from the Order. Most others were frozen in shock and disbelief.

They reached the Mage. He was on his hands and knees, his hair hanging down around his head. He looked utterly spent. He collapsed on the ground and rolled onto his back. He lay panting, covered in sweat and looking at the blue sky above them while they watched him anxiously, none daring to touch him.

"It worked," he said finally, the words coming out as more of a wheeze. "I have never done that before."

Solimo bent down over him. "What did you do?"

"I funnelled the hope. All your hopes. It is old lore. Mage lore. And I am the last Mage..." A faint smile crept at the corners of his eyes and he turned to look at Solimo. "...Of course, you could find the books. My light tower is still there. You have something of the mage about you, Solimo. Given time."

Rodon rode past the group and the bodies of Tilley and his men. The creatures of Limbo were all gone, but the rainbow had not destroyed real flesh as the remains of Tilley showed. Where was the Archbishop? The wide valley floor had been scoured of the nightmare legions, but there was no sign of the man who had once been his master and mentor.

The Mage subsided into more wheezing. Solimo loosened his clothes then sat back on his haunches helplessly.

"I do not know what to do, Mage," he said.

"There is nothing you can do."

He closed his eyes. Esella caught up his hand and looked at Mondo who was standing close by. Mondo simply shook his head.

Then the Mage's eyes flicked open.

"Where is the boy?" he asked.

"Here," said Charlie. "If you mean me."

"I do."

He licked his lips.

"I think I have one final act," he said. "I am going to sleep now. For a very long time. On my way, I will dream. Do you want to go home, you and your mother and father? I can take you. I think. I have time enough."

"You can do it?" asked Charlie.

"Esella, do you have any light left?"

"One," she said.

"I have more," said Mondo.

"Ah, the war captain. A warrior of the light. Good. We have light enough."

"But what happens to all of them? What happens to this world?" asked Richard.

"Stay and find out if you want to. They have much to do, but at least they have started together. Decide quickly. I am not staying long."

"We're going home," said Helen. "All of us."

"Good. Thank you. The women always make the decisions and the men just pretend they do. Nothing changes." He broke into a fit of coughing, spittle in his beard. He licked feebly at his lips as he regained control. His hand moved at his side.

"Lie down here. Solimo, will you be so kind...?"

"I have no bowl," said Solimo.

Charlie looked around. He trotted over to one of the bodies and found himself looking into the face of Tilley. His red hair was matted with blood and sweat. His helmet lay next to him. Charlie picked it up, wondering if he should say something to the corpse. Then he turned and ran back to the watching group.

"Will this do?"

Solimo took it from him and put his hand on Charlie's shoulder.

"Goodbye Charlie," he said.

Charlie looked up at him. It had not occurred to him that going meant leaving his friend.

"Won't I see you again?"

"I do not know. But we can always dream. You came here once. You can do it again."

Charlie hugged him. Richard and Helen watched. Helen had tears in her eyes. Richard looked up at a group of soldiers trotting over. He recognised Lyell and Berwick amongst them.

"You again, Richard of Hadbury," said Lyell.

There was no malice in his voice, only weariness.

"Goodbye Nicholas," Richard said. "We're leaving. Going home."

Berwick reached down and the two men shook hands.

"Good luck," said Richard.

"Same to you," said Berwick.

Then Richard, Helen and Charlie lay down with the Mage, their bodies forming a cross. Helen held out her hands and took one of Richard's and Charlie's in each of hers.

The delf stood back and the men followed, watching curiously.

Above the silent group, the edges of the darkness were fraying. It was streaked with ragged tears of light and wisps of the dark were drifting off and curling into nothing like swiftly evaporating clouds.

Solimo squeezed the sponges and, delf and men looking on, the light poured around the four on the ground. The Denhams were still holding hands as the light rose around them.

The Archbishop looked up from his book and remembered where he was. The books and tapestries were already so familiar, but something was different.

It was as if a background hum he had not noticed before had suddenly stopped or a shadow had fallen across the world.

He stood and went to the window. Outside, the plain was still as empty as it had been after he had sent his dream self to lead the nightmare creatures in battle. But there had been a change. He pondered what it could mean. Perhaps the door was closed. Well he would wait.

He shook his head and rolled his shoulders to stretch them. He would return to the books and then he would sleep. And dream.

Free ebook: *Tales of the Delf*

Being able to build a relationship with my readers is one of the best things about writing. It turns it from being a lonely occupation to a sociable one. Occasionally I send newsletters with details on new releases, special offers and other bits of news relating to the *Light Funnel* series and other books.

If you sign up to the mailing list, I'll send you *Tales of the Delf*. This is a book of short stories from Delf folklore from both before and after the coming of the Order. It provides some extra colour on Delf culture and light lore.

You can get it free by telling me where to send it. Just go to http://eepurl.com/clgE5j.

Enjoy this book? You can make a big difference

As an independent author, reviews are hugely powerful. Honest reviews of my books help bring them to the attention of other readers.

If you've enjoyed this book, I'd be very grateful if you could spend a few minutes leaving a review (it can be as short as you like) at your favourite retailer.

About the author

Find out more about KA Barron at www.kabarron.com. You can also connect with him on Facebook at www.facebook.com/kabarronbooks, He may send the odd tweet from @kabarronauthor, and you could always send him an email at kevin@kabarron.com.

Also by KA Barron

Light Needle

In dreams, something is stirring.

Eight years have passed since the events described in *Light Funnel*. An uneasy peace has existed between the Order and the Delf. Now, rumblings of dissent threaten a return to war.

Inspired by dreams, Jack Silver searches for the descendants of the adventurers who left Outreterre centuries before and never returned. With their help, the Delf could be overthrown forever.

Former adversaries Berwick, Rodon and Raul secretly follow Silver and his protectors across the sea; Solimo, still haunted by his experiences, is about to face his greatest fear, while a footloose Charlie Denham will soon be fleeing for his life from forces he does not understand.

For an old enemy has found a way out of Limbo and will stop at nothing to purge the worlds.

When he returns, a great city will burn and a society will be torn apart. Only a fragile web of alliances, old and new, stands before the terrible new power emerging from Limbo.

In this second book in the Light Funnel series, multiple storylines weave together culminating in a climactic confrontation.

Travel and humour (as Kevin Barron)

Into the blue

Half-planned travels of an amateur vagabond

Kevin Barron feels guilty if he stays at home and does nothing. His solution is to visit other countries and do nothing there instead. An added benefit is that writing about it gives him something to do at home.

Lose your ticket before you've even set off, find out what whalers think of Greenpeace, dodge dive-bombers, meet dangerous truckers, interview a tennis star, witness horror, walk all night, fish for your dinner, watch sunsets in the wilderness, ride legendary highways, stargaze in the Rockies, hitch-hike through the outback, be rescued by an angel, become Robin Hood, escape from Colditz.

This collection of stories covers more than a decade of travel, so throw your backpack over your shoulder and head off...into the blue.

Not there yet

Wandering home with an amateur vagabond

When you leave, at what point do you start going home? And when you leave and don't come back, where is home?

Moving to another country for a while provides an excellent opportunity to travel on the way. Having threatened The Big Trip for years, Kevin Barron finally takes the plunge and, as a result, finds that the idea of home is not as clear as it used to be.

Kayak in the rain, meet an Aboriginal elder, make conversation with a grumpy barber, kill sheep, crash a car, eat entrails, be in the Middle East on 9/11, ride legendary highways, find yourself face to face with an elk, get lost in the African night, have the best view at Shangri-La, fight a fire, be ill on an overnight bus, search for intruders, flirt, haggle, dance, joke, eat, hike, misunderstand, leave home and return.

This collection of stories follows those of Into the blue, so throw your backpack over your shoulder again and set off on the never ending journey home.

Tales of Socks and Splendour

The Grumpete is a disgusting yet warm hearted character who lives alone in a land beyond the Ocean of Spleg. Embarking on an adventure one day, he encounters the Kazza Princess in a distant castle and their lives are never the same again.

Join the foul-bummed Grumpete and the kimmering Kazz as they shine, explode, wander, flatulate, burn, run, reproduce, eat and fight their way through a series of far-fetched adventures in glorious nonsense verse.

Whether read out loud or quietly to yourself where no one will find you, these fast-moving and humorous poems are sure to entertain children of all ages...apart from perhaps those of a delicate disposition.

Business (as Kevin Barron)

How to Run Facilitated Workshops

A pragmatic guide to successful meetings

Are your meetings a waste of time? Get productive.

We've all had those moments when you wonder what the point is of getting together at work. People wander off topic, take over, tune out…

In today's fast moving business environment, you need to make the most of people's time, energy and knowledge.

This book is packed full of advice and techniques to help you prepare for, run and follow up on facilitated workshops. Not only is the process described, but there is advice for dealing with problems along the way, notably managing behaviour that can kill productivity and collaboration. There is a focus on planning the workshop and setting out the agenda. A set of sample agendas covering a wide range of project scenarios is included.

With the advice in this book, gleaned from twenty years of experience in industry and consulting, you can pre-empt problems and be well on the way to saving time and achieving usable outcomes that will accelerate your projects.

Kevin Barron has worked in industry and consulting for more than 25 years. He has led teams, worked on projects and delivered training across many sectors including banking, media, retail, wealth management, telecommunications, transport, IT services, utilities, local and national government, and manufacturing. He has facilitated hundreds of workshops in the UK, Australia, New Zealand, Sweden and Germany. He is also an experienced business analyst and agile practitioner.